I0591010

So She May Breathe

by
Jaimie Thomas

So She May... Book 1

Published through IngramSpark

So She May Breathe

Print edition ISBN: 9780975665107
E-book edition ISBN: 9780975665114

Printed by IngramSpark
First IngramSpark edition: March 2024
Second IngramSpark edition: April 2026

Contains mature content.

Also by Jaimie Thomas in the So She May series
So She May Grow
So She May Live

What did you think of this book?

I love to hear from readers.
Please visit the website and send a message...
https://www.jaimiethomas.com/contact

To everyone who has thought
they can't possibly fit in,
because you can,
and eventually you will.

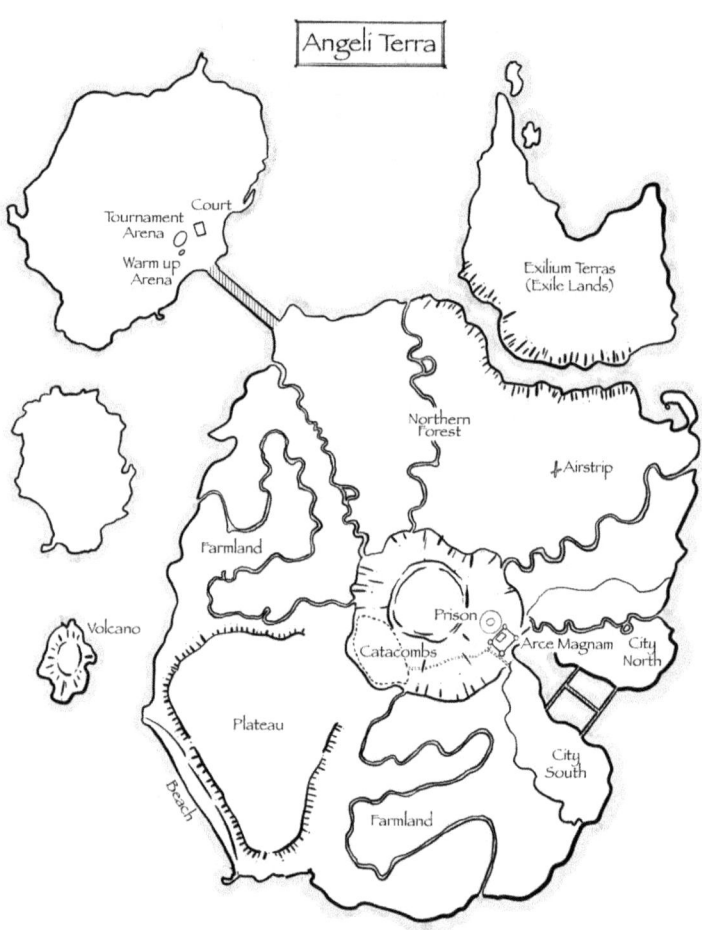

Angeli Terra

Tournament Arena

Court

Warm up Arena

Exilium Terras (Exile Lands)

Northern Forest

Airstrip

Farmland

Volcano

Prison

Catacombs

Arce Magnam

City North

Plateau

City South

Beach

Farmland

Chapter 1

A girl lingers in the shadows, blue eyes surveying her prey. Before her, men and women shake on their knees, not daring a breath as she plays absently with the safety on her gun. None have seen her face, but terror lies in their disbelief; how could such a slight thing infiltrate their outpost? A few – the prisoners she had been sent for – understand though. They have no doubt that they will die.

Around the room, light begins to dance in overlapping patterns of windows and doorways. Backup had arrived. The assassin steps out of the dark, safety now firmly off as she takes place in front of the first prisoner. Behind the hard shell of her mask, she grins. It was hard to ignore how perfectly the trigger fit against the pad of her finger.

Now sure that the team had entered the building, she shoots once, the man dropping forwards like a ragdoll. Footsteps are louder, four sets. Two heavy, two lighter, one girl, the others male. Like clockwork, she steps back and shoots the next in the line. Then the next. She reaches the first innocent just as two of the males appear in a hallway, one holding a gun, the other swords. Oh yes, swords are so much fun.

The girl raises her shooting hand to her forehead in salute, before she turns on her heel and runs. They follow instantly, the first two on her tail while the other two arrive in the hall and move to the hostages. It is easy to keep in front of the heavier males, the twists in the corridors slowing both down. Until she runs into a problem, the door she planned to go through is now shut. Without time to open it, she takes off again and building plans run through her head.

Back on track, the girl latches a hand onto a pole to swing around the corner, long having discarded her weapon. German profanities spew out of her mouth as the pole gives way and she flies into the opposite wall. It takes a few steps for her to regain her stability, long enough for her pursuers to gain ground before she takes off once again. Her breath starts to shake a little — indecision, rather than exhaustion, overtaking her at the sight of the gaping window before her. Each step slams her bag against her back, the one object reminding her why she was there.

Absently, the girl's footsteps start to land harder on the floor, shoulders dropping as she glances back for a few seconds. Then she turns forward again, perfect form returned.

Three strides later, her foot catches on nothing, and her small form slides along the tile floor to slam against the wall, just under her escape. She spins instantly to face the two men, genuine fear just visible through the mesh covering her eyes. One hand trembles out in front of her, while the other remains hidden on her stomach — on her secret.

"Please don't kill me." Her words tumble out in perfect English. "I have information about a hell of a lot of murder cases, all linked with the signature of a cross on the forehead. Just please don't kill me." Her hand returns to her face quick enough to unclip her mask so the men could see the tears welling in her eyes.

The gun stays trained on her, but the two look between each other in confusion. The taller one — absent of a badge — steps forward slowly, watching her as she curls tighter to the wall. He doesn't wear a helmet like the other man, and his posture is more refined. Far better balanced than one would expect of someone in their mid-twenties.

"Stand up," he orders. "Hands in the air."

She silently complies and offers her wrists forward as he pulls out cuffs. He passes her to his companion and starts to check her for weapons. He takes the spare gun off her hip and empties the clip before tucking it into his pants, along with the knives strapped over her limbs, and one from her boot, then taking her backpack and pulling it open.

"I promise, there isn't a bomb in it," the girl murmurs as he pulls out an oiled chestnut box, about the size of a shoe box and deep enough to hold a notebook. Her tone has changed a little now, from the confident German accent to one with less of a sting.

He acknowledges her statement but opens it anyway to find three books stacked neatly at one end and a few other trinkets at the other. Leafing through one of the books, he looks at all the drawings, trying to hide his own shock, but doesn't say anything as he gently picks up the jewellery.

"There aren't trackers either, I checked them all myself. I'm trying to get away from them, why would I let them have me again," the girl once again interrupts, watching as he puts them back before holding out a bloody dagger. Though she clearly wishes to comment, the girl holds her tongue.

"How old are you?" he asks, taking her arm and directing her out of the compound.

"16, according to my birth year. Don't know if I've technically turned it yet," she replies, footing smooth as she lengthens her stride to keep up with the tall males.

"And name?" he continues.

"828," she answers instantly, then – feeling the displeasure in his demeanour – inches away tightly.

"Come on, Kitten," the other man drawls, his badge reading Zach Day. The girl stops short. "We're trying to help; you're going to need to be open with us." His brow furrows as he is jerked suddenly backwards. "What's wrong with her?"

The tall one shrugs as the girl whispers, "Don't... call me that."

They begin to walk again, heavy footsteps echoing in the empty halls around them.

"Eleanor. I think my name is Eleanor," she says, and blinks quickly as if to recollect her thoughts. "The picture has a two-year-old and a five-year-old, the inscription says Eleanor's 5th birthday, and my sister was younger than me."

Silence enfolds them until they enter the atrium in which Eleanor had been holding her prisoners. A man is attending to multiple of the patients, while the other rocks on her heels.

"Have you checked her for weapons?" the woman asks coldly as she steps forward, a hint of strawberry blonde hair hidden under her helmet.

"Of course, I have Kaylee, five blades, a loaded gun, yet we got no fight..." the tall man replies, indignant.

"Girl – did he get all your weapons?" Kaylee questions. She watches Eleanor cower in the presence of the group, but nevertheless indicates a negative response. "At least she respects authority..."

Kaylee reaches up the back of Eleanor's shirt and grabs the dagger, pulling another out of the back of her pants. She pats down her legs but leaves the daggers she feels on each thigh for a later time. Then she moves back up to unlock one cuff and lock it onto own wrist. A pair of stiletto blades come out of Eleanor's sleeves. The underwire of the girl's bra appears far stiffer than normal, much the same as the sides of her hooded jacket. Pins slide out the compartment in Eleanor's boots before Kaylee throws back her hood to remove the mask fully. Two curved blades fall out, carefully bent to her skull and Kaylee send the two men a bland stare as they look on in astonishment. She pulls the band out of the girl's braid, shaking it out ashen brown locks that stick slightly to the anxious heat of her body. With the pins pocketed, Kaylee returns to Eleanor's shirt to shine a blacklight on Eleanor's lower back. She steps away triumphantly.

"She's here because she wants to be here, it's as simple as that," Kaylee says, focus now on her teammates. "If she wanted to, she could have killed us all before we even knew she was here. We are very, extremely lucky."

"Kaylee, you aren't making much sense."

The woman huffs as she resecures Eleanor's cuffs.

"She has an ultraviolet tattoo on the base of her back – she's an assassin – and a name on top which shows she's their top tier. These six—" she points to a few medics and scientists all standing shocked in the corner "—are ours. Those three ¬– the first three to die – they were prisoners here for interrogation. They carry the same tattoo, in black but not the name."

"They're traitors," Eleanor interrupts. "I was sent to kill them. Thank me later."

"And yet here you are, turning yourself over to us," Zach quips as he rests his arm on his gun.

"I'm sure you will figure that out soon, but for now, we really should leave before my trainer is sent to collect my body when I fail to meet our handler in an hour," she says. Her head ticks, a small spasm of her hand before she steadies her gaze. Then, "Stupid Americans," she mutters in natural German.

She is fixed with a reprimanding look from a man with a small metal badge reading Kenichi Tanaka immediately beneath a medic symbol. Eleanor grins back and lets herself be led away. Sitting silently in the corner of the transport van, she watches them all as they talk quietly between themselves, about her. Her hands search for the necklace she usually puts on as soon as she returns from a mission... tenses at its absence.

"This is wrong," Kaylee mutters. "We have never – not once! – caught someone with the name. They're folklore!"

"Why aren't we talking about the fact she's a kid?" the tall one mutters, hand running through his short blonde hair.

"Michael... there is a lot wrong here. How could she take down a government operation all by herself? And why does she have three books filled with drawings of faces?" Kenichi flicks through one of the books. *"I was scared for a second, facing assembled defences, an army of sorts, but then I remembered who I am. I killed them all. They wonder why one of the most notorious Japanese gangs fell off the leader board, and I'm sitting here, admiring my beautiful Katana.* Where the hell does she come from? Who made her... this?"

"And why would her parents let this happen to her, she must have been training for a while to be this good," Zach says.

"My parents," Eleanor starts to draw their attention, "are dead."

"Who sent you?" Michael asks softly. He was burly, the demeanour unlike what Eleanor had expected of him.

"My boss," she shrugs. "Technically my handler gave me the mission."

"They got a name?" Zach snips. He was exactly as she expected.

"Not one I know of. I may be in the top tier, but I haven't graduated, so no secrets for me," she returns. "If I ever do meet my boss, I will be dead before I can spill. And if I ever see my handler, he'll be dead before I can find out."

"You said your name was Eleanor," Michael continues, "but you have a code. 828, was it?"

"Yes."

"As in there are 827 others of you?"

"No." Eleanor almost laughs. "Most are dead by now. When you complete your first solo mission, you're given a number to identify by.

The number is up at around 950 or so now, but probably only about 300 active agents. The organisation is old."

"Does anyone else know your name?" he asks.

"Michael, leave it for the interrogation room," Kaylee interjects.

"I'm not interrogating her," he argues and turns back to Eleanor.

"I'm not going to tell you that. Ask me about the Agency, about my missions, but I won't answer any more questions on my personal life," she snips, rubbing her forehead in exhaustion.

Thrown slightly as they pass up onto a road, Michael steadies her, careful to pull away as she grimaces.

"Get some sleep... it's a long drive and when we get there, you won't be getting any for a while," Michael tells her.

Stubborn, she replies, "I don't sleep with other people around."

"We aren't going to hurt you," he assures. "Get some sleep Eleanor."

After taking off her jacket and handing it to the medic, she's silent for a few minutes, so much so that they think she might have taken their advice until she sits up suddenly. Her focus is on the box in the medic's hands.

"Can I have the necklace, in that box?" She pauses momentarily. "Please?"

After looking to Michael – who reluctantly agrees – Kenichi hands her the golden chain. She clips it around her neck, and she holds the drawn bow and arrow charm in the calloused grasp of her fingers as she curls back up and tucks her head into the corner.

But dreams for an assassin are rarely good.

~

Kate Beck was a pretty girl.

Her foster parents loved her, everybody loved her.

Eleanor took the photo from their mantle, the bracelet from her side table, the box from beneath her bed. The adults went first, two pops, one bullet to each head: quick, clean. Signed and left to cool.

The girl recognised her older sister, she had their father's hair, eyes. Both girls shared in their mother's intelligence, thus, when Kate spotted the gun in her sister's hand, she knew she too would die.

Two shots, shaking hands, wet cheeks. The only case, the only kill, in which she left more than a cross on the forehead.

Kate Beck was brave, she was innocent.
She didn't deserve to die.

~

The cry of pain escapes her lips before she can quell it, gaining the attention of her captors. Michael moves over to her side, crouching as she turns her head away to hide her face behind a curtain of her hair. He touches her shoulder gently, but she stays away, the wet on her cheeks disappearing with a swipe of her hand. Michael tries to assess her with a soft glance of assurance, but she ignores him still.

"You can let people see you cry, you know," he tells her, tucking some hair behind her ear.

Instantly, Eleanor cracks away. "Do not talk to me about emotion when you do not know who I am," she snaps.

"You're a kid; you are still allowed to have emotions. No one will judge you," he replies quietly.

"I am not a kid anymore; I haven't been a kid for a long time. Only two people know me, and only those two people will ever know me. Yet I left them behind, because I wanted something to be mine, for once in my damned life. You can scrutinise me for my record, you can condemn me for my death count, but don't you ever, ever, talk to me about what goes on inside my head," she growls, jumping away from the man, then in an instant she drops back into herself, cowering and regretful. "I'm sorry, I lost my temper."

Confusion passes around the truck as they watch her cradle the necklace around her neck in one cuffed hand, the other clutching her stomach.

"We have arrived," Kenichi mutters, breaking the silence.

"It'll be busy out there, so be prepared," Michael tells her.

"If you wanted to be truly efficient, you wouldn't let any cameras see who you are," she replies tiredly, standing up as they all prepare to get out.

"Because you can criticise us," Kaylee mutters.

"Well, I think you'll find I've evaded any leads on my identity for years now," Eleanor snaps back.

She rolls her eyes as Kenichi takes off the necklace, gold pooling into the bottom of the box as he waits a moment longer.

"It's 30 yards to the front door. White steps so it'll be bright. Keep your head down and I'll make sure you get up there okay," he whispers into her ear with a gentle squeeze on her upper arm. "Let's go."

With a nod, the van doors open, and they step out. Michael and Kaylee hold each of her arms, with Zach in front pushing through the people and Kenichi at Eleanor back to keep her moving forwards. It's loud, too loud, and Eleanor's breathing becomes shorter and steps quicker. Too many people surround her. Too many could kill her in an instant. She waits until they get inside the compound before breaking into a sprint. They follow, but she easily loses them with a few quick turns in the labyrinth of a compound.

Until she runs straight into a man, who holds her tightly off his body.

"Now, now... Kitten." He smirks grins at her in a sadistic sort of way. "This isn't like you at all."

Eleanor is frozen in her spot unable to back away as the man pins her front to the wall. He brandishes a dagger as she struggles to break free with the cuffs on.

"Now, boss ain't so happy with you," he sings, touching the blade to her shoulder and pushing it through the cloth. "Not happy at all. He wants to see you."

As he speaks, his breath condenses on her neck, lips nearly touching the skin.

"I saw an opportunity to get them, so I took it. Let me do my work," she hisses, the act admirable.

She was above him; he should listen.

"Then why aren't they dead yet? Hmm?" he teases.

She sucks in a breath as he drags the dagger down from shoulder to hip but refuses to cry out.

"No comment? I think we might have to move up your execution," he growls, starting on the other slash of an X forming on her back.

A gunshot rings through the still air and the man behind her falls instantly to the ground, the dagger clattering across the white tile floor. Her uneven breaths resume as she slides down the wall, head swinging in the overwhelmingly long corridor. In a thick pool, Eleanor's blood mixes with her attacker's, sticking itself to her pale skin.

"Who was that?" Michael asks, strong arms set to pull her up.

"They know. I'm dead," she whispers, shaking wildly. "Please don't let them kill us, please, I don't want to die."

The blood dribbling down her back takes precedence as Michael stares at her in confusion, the rest of the team rounding the corner as they start to walk forward.

"We'll go get that stitched up, then you need to talk, okay?" he tells her. "We can only help you if you help us."

"I know," she whispers. "I'm sorry."

~

I knew Eleanor closely; I was there as she learnt to live with her past. Accept it. As she unknowingly fought for her own right to breathe.

America was a long way from her hometown – mind you, she hadn't been in Australia for longer than a single mission since she was six. That was her test, but Agent 828 'Kitten' never worked in Australia outside after that. To dangerous, they decided.

I know she thought often of this first day of capture and what would have happened if things went differently. She always rationalised it through the child growing in her stomach, but Eleanor was freeing herself too.

She never regretted it. Not once.

Chapter 2

The white light leaves spots in Eleanor's vision as Michael helps her up onto the hard bench. Blood still dribbles out of the cuts on her back, but she wilfully ignores it as a nurse enters the room.

"How and why is there a teenager in this compound, bleeding extensively?" the nurse asks while she inspects the wounds.

"Collected her on assignment. She ran off and a double agent got to her," he explains. "We just need them stitched. Be careful, she is a suspect for a series of mass killings."

The nurse blatantly ignores Michael as she begins to collect what she needs to stitch the wounds.

"You can't stay in here. Find me a female guard if you must," she barks.

While Michael is clearly stunned by the order, he calls in Kaylee anyway and Kenichi follows. The nurse allows it on the premise of his expertise yet uses him as a personal table.

"Honey," she begins, voice far softer than anyone was used to, "we're going to have to take off your shirt to stitch these. Are you okay with Dr Tanaka being here to help?"

"I can stitch them myself," Eleanor mutters sourly, anxious to creep away from the prying eyes.

"No, you can't," Kaylee returns as the fixes her with a stern glower. "I understand that you don't like people you don't trust wielding needles where you can't see them, but we need to stitch these."

There is a lingering fear in her that makes Kenichi falter as they prepare the items, something in the twists of her hands in her lap.

"What was his name, the boy you kept drawing in your books?" he asks quietly and waits in silence.

"Sebastian," she murmurs, so quiet they can barely hear her. "My only friend."

Kenichi moves in front of her and crouches to take her hands softly in his. The roughness of her skin against his makes him pause once more.

"We aren't going to hurt you; I promise but we need to sew up these gashes. I know you're probably used to a different arrangement, but you made the decision to leave that behind, so you need to adapt to the new circumstances, okay?" he tells her.

She watches him for a moment, studying his brown eyes and messy brown hair – assessing him almost like a target –, before she nods to the nurse.

"I'm fine with it," she says. "But I can't get it off without help, and with these cuffs on."

Kaylee instantly fixes her with a stiff gaze.

"Michael and Zach and half a dozen others are right outside that door, so don't bother trying anything," she threatens, waiting until she acknowledges before unlocking the cuffs.

Between Kaylee and the nurse, they ease the jacket off her and help her to lie down with her stomach on the cold bench.

"You said you had been to Japan before," Kenichi says in a hope to distract her. "My family are from the Hokkaido region, up north."

Eleanor merely stares into oblivion, ignoring the pain outside, for the pain brewing tightly in her mind.

~

"I wish I'd been allowed to go with you," Sebastian mutters as he carefully sews the cut on her lower back. "Paris is so beautiful this time of year."

"Oh really, the whole having to kill a French senator doesn't dampen it?" she giggles, not flinching as he digs a little too deep.

"Stay still," he chuckles. "At least we could have had a croissant, surprised people with our perfect French. And you had two hours to get into position, we could have seen the Eiffel Tower at sunset."

Eleanor smiles faintly, easing up as he squeezes her shoulder and finishes the stitches. Turning silently, she places her head in the corner of his neck, eyes shutting tiredly.

"Nora, you do know he's watching us, right," the boy murmurs into her ear.

"I do, but I don't really care. He won't sell me out," she replies softly. "Lie down with me."

"It's your turn to have the bed, you don't have to share," he refuses.

"Seb, just lie down would you," the girl groans.

"Fine then, Nora."

~

A slow tear runs down her face as Kenichi persists in his plan to gain some of her trust. She doesn't listen, instead stares at the wall, and doesn't let any more than that single drop of emotion show.

"We're all done," the nurse says. She helps her back into a sitting position as Kenichi leaves the room. "I'm going to draw some blood to check for harmful toxins. Now would be the time to hand over a cyanide cap... if you have one."

While Kaylee helps her into a singlet that zips up at the back, the nurse draws a set of bloods. Shown into the small change area, Eleanor dresses herself in the trackpants they supply. Her pants are folded, and two knives placed on top and before she takes off her boots. A small capsule sits on the top of the pile as she drops the clothes on the bench and offers her wrists forward. Kaylee clasps the metal on.

"Trust will be a two-way street here. Now it's time you tell us why you are here," Kaylee says.

While Eleanor clearly debates staying silent, she looks to the capsule as she quietly says, "That isn't cyanide. It's worse. Don't let it touch any human fluids once opened, it will obliterate the owner."

With clear hesitation, Kaylee leads Eleanor out of the room and sends in agents to secure the offending item as she takes the prisoner to the interrogation room.

They leave her alone and watch her observe the room through expert eyes. She has already gleaned the calibre of the building she is in. From the corridors she'd run through earlier, to the medical sector, the interrogation room and transport, it's clear this is a government facility. She had been in Central America on her mission, but without knowing how long she slept she had no chance of placing the location. So, Eleanor puts her feet up on the table and wiggles her toes as her hand twitches at her side. She taps patterns, repeating ones Kaylee notices and begins to decipher.

'Check cam twenty-three twenty April they had no idea,' it reads, and they watch as she repeats it over and over again.

"What happened to her?" Michael asks, his eyes narrow as she swallows dryly.

Michael fills a cup of water and moves into the room to give it to her. Eleanor leaves it sitting on the table, though it is clear she is contemplating taking a sip. After a minute, and after she licks her lips again, Michael steps forward and takes a sip of the water, overtly displaying an empty mouth to prove it. He smiles triumphantly as she cautiously picks it up and sniffs the water.

"Why would we poison you?" He sighs in annoyance. "You haven't drunk anything in hours, drink the damn water."

After another few seconds, Eleanor raises the cup to her lips and takes a sip, before downing the whole cup with a tight grimace. The door opens and a new face enters the room, tersely sitting opposite the young assassin.

"I've been told," the new woman begins, "that you have information on one of our coldest serial murder cases in the past five years. And feet off the table. I am Colonel Randall and will be dealing with you."

The girl observes the Colonel, black hair tied into a dense bun, brown eyes strict. Kaylee flags her carefully. Her feet remain.

"I do," Eleanor replies as she glances into her lap for a second, then to the cameras in the corner. "I killed them, all the people with the cross on their forehead, I killed. And pretty much anyone else who was dead in the area around them."

There is silence for a few seconds, before the older woman speaks again.

"I am having trouble believing that," she says. "You're what, 15? 16?"

"I'm 16."

"And you are saying your responsible for the death of..."

"579 people."

"Since you were what?"

"Ten."

"Yes, ten. And you never got caught? Politicians, whole gangs, worldwide murders," the Colonel shakes her head. "Never leaving more than that single mark on the forehead, and a few blood samples of other victims?"

"That isn't true," Eleanor murmurs, "there is one case which had more than the cross."

The woman gestures for her to continue.

"The murder of Emily and Ben Taylor, Kate Beck. There was two words written on the wall above where the 11-year-old girl lay dead. 'I'm sorry,' painted in blue acrylic paint. Her school photo was stolen, along with her bracelet, and a box from beneath her bed. The box you're holding is that box, the bracelet hers, the photo the original. The initials are KB, Kate Beck," Eleanor responds with eyes cast away from the people in the room.

"Why? Why did you say you were sorry?" she asks.

"Because, she was my little sister," Eleanor answers in a trembling tone. "My name is Eleanor Beck, and I was assumed dead ten years ago. Sorry, ten years and 21 days."

"The Berlin massacre," the Colonel realises. "Half of those children were found dead, we just assumed..."

"Some of us learnt pretty quickly that if we didn't comply, we would die. So, the world never heard of us again," Eleanor says as she lifts her chin and hardens her eyes. "No one looked for us, no one cared. So, we became what they wanted."

"The German federal police looked for weeks," the woman rebuts.

"Not well enough," Eleanor snaps. "How would you classify Germany's relationship with America?"

"We are on good terms, have been since the war ended."

"Then why do you not know who the Berühmte Söldner are?" she counters. Almost childishly, Eleanor tilts her head in question.

"Berühmte Söldner? Famed mercenaries?" The Colonel sighs. "What are you talking about?"

"I'm talking about the fact that Germany ran a spy section of their SS during the war, highly illegal, against the Universal Declaration of Human Rights. The Agency split from the government in 1945, but still operates underground," the girl smirks. "A dark part of Germany's history that they try their hardest to keep hidden. Who do you think assassinated JFK?"

The woman frowns, as Eleanor flexes her feet in amusement.

"Why are you here?" she asks tiredly.

"I am here because it is the only place where I don't have to kill anyone anymore," Eleanor replies softly. "I want you to lock me up and make it so no one can break me out."

"As someone of your 'supposed' calibre, why couldn't you just hide out?" she questions.

"I'm sure you'll figure that one out soon enough," Eleanor answers. "If you need to quiz me, go ahead, I killed them all. All 579. And I could kill a lot more if given the chance."

The woman frowns, but looks to Kaylee behind her, for a few seconds.

"She is unstable, one second, she'll be like this, confident, powerful... an assassin, then she will just fall back to a quiet, scared little girl. She yelled at Michael earlier then, curled into a ball and apologised. She's scared of people hitting her, people yelling at her. Trust for her is only owned by two people, whom I have to assume are also assassins, and when we first spotted her, she was sliding down a line of prisoners, killing each execution style. Then she ran.

"On the base of her back she has the tattoo, the German SS bolts connected at the bottom to make it like a two-pronged fork, topped with a name in ultraviolet ink. She is one of the best assassins out there, they call them ACEs. If she's telling the truth about wanting out, then I'd say we give it to her, but for an assassin like herself, this could all be a perfectly manicured act to get information and then kill us all. I have encountered some Berühmte Söldner before... they are some of the best, smart and cunning. They use stereotypes to gain people's trust, and then kill them. I wouldn't trust her until she tells us why she's here, truly why she's here. She also seems to be... sadistically attached to her kills. She sketches them, recounts particular details. The blade in her box hasn't been cleaned in years, it probably holds the blood of nearly all her kills," Kaylee informs, speaking in fluent Swedish.

"I'm not sadistic, drawing them helps me sleep, gets it out of my head and onto paper," Eleanor replies in the same language. "And the dagger, I have to admit that is a little creepy. Growing up like I did messes you up."

"How many languages do you speak?"

"14," she replies. As if expecting her to continue, a silence falls in the room.

"You realise that if what you're saying is true, you could very well be given the death penalty," the Colonel warns.

"I do, however such a sentence cannot be given until I turn 18. That gives me enough time, in my book," she shrugs. "Death is easy, when you know the ones you love are safe. And I don't know, maybe I'll see my parents one last time before I'm sent to hell."

Michael bristles in the corner and gets a stern – non-verbal – warning from the woman in charge.

"Take her down to the cells, put her in on her own, we don't need any dead prisoners," the woman orders. "And give her a hairbrush and a single band, I'm sure Miss Beck doesn't enjoy having her hair all over the place."

The girl smirks as she nods to the woman in thanks.

"We will be back in here tomorrow, after we've studied those books of yours. If you prove you can remember a specific few, then I'll believe you. Have a good night, Miss Beck," the woman retorts.

Eleanor rises from her seat and waits for Michael to finish talking to the Colonel. She agrees to his proposal fairly quickly and gestures for them to open the box sitting on the table. He lifts the golden chain and moves over to the girl and clips it around her neck before he takes her arm to leads her out of the room.

Guards flag them to a mediocre cell, clean with a stiff cot, steel bars with meshing to stop her from reaching through to open the door and plain grey walls. Michael undoes her cuffs and gives her a soft warning look as he backs out of the room and shuts the cell door.

"Behave, Eleanor," he orders.

She smiles playfully as she perches on the cot.

"Wouldn't dream of anything else," she says. "And Michael," she calls as he starts walking away, "thank you, for getting me my necklace."

Chapter 3

After a restless night of sleep Eleanor lies flat on her stomach as she waits for them to collect her. Her hair is braided curtesy of the brush the Colonel had given her – but her back was still too sore to do much else. She barely opens her eyes as keys jingle in the lock and people walk in.

"Come on, don't make me have to drag you," Michael mutters as he shakes her shoulder.

Eleanor groans as she swings to her feet, swaying enough that Michael gently grabs her shoulders to steady her. After a second of deep breaths, Eleanor opens her eyes and nods – albeit seedily – to indicate her fineness.

"Just... stood up too fast," she exclaims as she offers her hands forward for cuffing.

"If you ate your dinner last night you would be fine," Michael scolds. "We aren't going to poison you, Eleanor."

"It's not you I'm worried about." She refuses to glance upwards as she does so.

"You are safe here," he tells her.

"The cuts on my back confirm that, don't they?" Eleanor mutters.

"I'll get them to give you bottled water, so you know it's sealed, but the food is mass produced," Michael proposes. "I can ask that someone tests all your food first, and that it come straight from kitchens to you without interruption."

"Thank you," she nods and continues the walk, in silence.

Michael watches her as she walks, frown slight as her hand rubs her stomach tiredly. Thus, he observes the shift as her step strengthens and face hardens. A smirk pulls onto her lips as she begins fiddling with the cuffs on her wrists. He looks away and misses Eleanor cleanly unclipping the metal cuffs just as they step into the interrogation room. She waits for the door to shut behind Michael before dropping them on the desk and sitting down.

"I'm an assassin; you do realise those are completely pointless." Eleanor laughs as she crosses her feet on the table.

"And, as an assassin, you should know well enough to Get Your Feet Off the damn table," the Colonel Randall seethes. She waits for compliance before she continues. "I run the National Agency for Protection, or NAP. We've looked over those books of yours. Very comprehensive. Now, we're going to show you pictures of crime scenes, families, congressional photos, etc. You are to answer the questions we ask them, understood?"

"Yes."

"Okay then, who is this?" Randall asks.

Five hours later, after a barrage of questions, the room breathes a sigh of combined shock and fatigue. After she examines the bottle, Eleanor downs the water in one swift go.

"So, you are who Kaylee suggests you are." the Colonel sighs. "Why? Why did you go along with it for so long? I understand trying to stay alive, but that doesn't mean you have to be good at it. And why, beside the people you have killed, are these drawings of a boy."

"I've been fighting my conscience for years, Colonel," the girl mutters, face sour as a lemon. "It is easier to turn it off completely, so I did. It's easier to kill when you don't care, but I always struggled in the quiet which is why I depended on him. We were trained by the same person since we were selected for the ACE program; me aged seven, him nine. Quite often he was the only reason I didn't just give up."

"That necklace you wear…"

"Is from him, yes," Eleanor says, voice wispy.

They sit and watch her for a few minutes in tense silence before Colonel Randall nods for Michael to take her away again. Eleanor stands silently and moves to put the cuffs back on, but Michael's hand on her wrist stops her.

"You can get them off with ease, and I'd say if you wanted to, they would assist you as much as they could hinder, leave them off," he shrugs. "Come on."

While Eleanor disappears down the corridor, Kenichi steps into the Colonel's path, a report in his hand. The nurse is beside him, quick to explain the highlighted hormone spikes.

"She has the markers of pregnancy. Other than trace amounts of sedatives, there is no proof of any other medications being used that could imitate... it is a very reasonable explanation for her surrender as well," the nurse says.

"I didn't want to agree, but her reluctance to tell us fits the explanation," Kenichi supports.

"Her diet will need to be properly tailored for pregnancy and stress reduced. Any inquest into her actions or explorations of her mental state should be postponed," the nurse follows without letting the Colonel get a word in. "This is not a conducive environment for low stress either..."

Finally, the Colonel interrupts.

"You are sure that it is the only explanation?"

"Nancy," Kenichi starts, "why else would she need a year to survive? Why would she be so secretive in the early months?"

While clearly displeased, the Colonel nods slowly.

"I'll inform the cooks. And we will question her on it soon, but let's give her some time to settle in. Tell the team if you wish," she instructs. "And don't ask about parentage. If she was happy about it, she wouldn't have run."

Chapter 4

Eleanor follows Michael silently for a few minutes, before she jogs the two steps to catch up to him.

"Why are you being so nice to me?" she asks.

"I do not know, Eleanor," the man replies after a few seconds. "I do not know."

The silence is not uncomfortable the rest of the walk and locking the door behind her and walking away. Once she is secured, Michael leaves her be.

He goes outside and perches on a bench with his head into his hands. Kaylee joins him soon after and looks sidewards at him as she leans back.

"Why are you so nice to her? You've made it very clear you despise people who do the wrong thing... who kill," the woman asks softly.

"I... feel connected to her," the man admits. He sighs as he raises his head.

"As in something to do with where you come from, connected?"

"Yes. I have ideas about why... but it worries me her appearance so shortly after my brother was exiled," he groans. "Anyway, she is only 16, you can't blame her for being terrified. What counts is she handed herself in."

"You know my family is Jewish, right?" Michael nods. "The Berühmte Söldner are folklore, I've been told stories of them since I was a child. They were created by the German SS in 1939, when the war began. Their purpose was to infiltrate towns, become trusted, find the hidden Jews and drag them to the concentration camps. The whole organisation is corrupted, killing good people because they are against their wishes of their 'new' world."

"We saw the people she's killed, she was at least quick and clean," Michael notes. "I don't think we'll ever find out what was really broken in her head to send her to us. I don't think anyone will."

"If it weren't for the pregnancy, Kenichi wanted to do a full examination on her head," Kaylee says. "He thinks she might be suffering a very severe form of PTSD, maybe even something deeper. Her walls seem very, very dense. He was watching her and believes her mood swings to be more than just mood swings. But we won't know until after she's had the child, and by then she might be able to hide it better."

"I have a feeling she knows what's wrong. Probably that boy as well." Michael stands abruptly. "Who knows…"

"Come on we can watch her from the manor, and we need to get out of this compound, my brain is going to explode," Kaylee laughs in an attempt to lighten the mood.

They walk back inside together.

~

The girl sits with her knees tucked to her chest as she rocks back and forth, back and forth. The man and the boy watch. The elder steps in and sits soft as a mouse on the bed next to her. She leans closer to let him rub her shoulders as she continues to tremble. He places a leather clad journal in front of her and Eleanor picks it up to flicks through the pages.

"Write it down, draw it, get it out of your head and onto the paper," he tells her, handing her a pencil. "I'm sorry, Kleiner Fuchs, you aren't meant to live this life."

The ten-year-old nods weakly and stays curled up next to him as she opens to the first page. Her hand sketches out the faces in perfect lines across the pages, names and dates underneath. The pages were filled within two years, and so her teacher buys her another, and another two more years on.

Apart from occasional glances and the odd time she would draw while in front of one of them, no one ever saw the inside of those books. The faces, the dates, the names. They never saw the shredded mess that was the inside of Eleanor Beck's head.

Chapter 5

*T*he girl slips into the drug store and strolls around while she locates all the cameras, careful to avoid others in the store. She breezes into the female section to swipe three pregnancy tests and a tote bag before she moves to the counter. The woman at the desk scans each through discretely. Eleanor slides her money across the counter as she exchanges Spanish pleasantries, and leaves.

She walks through the streets and eventually reaches her hotel far later than planned. The bustling city outside rings in the background as she dumps her coat on the bed and moves into the bathroom with uncontrollably shaking hands. She follows the instructions, sets each test on the bench, and sinks to the floor, tucks her knees to her chest. The memories haunt her, the touching, the pain, his sick grin. All the while she couldn't fight to get away.

Sebastian had been suspicious after she returned from that mission morose and in a place far away from that room. She'd scrubbed herself for half an hour, before – still trembling – she curled up next to him on the bed and hid her face in his chest. When he asked the next morning, she denied everything and took up the over-confident, sassy mask as always. Her Vater also noticed and got nowhere. Instead, he held her as she cracked and trusted her faithful trainer to keep quiet about her lapse in confidence. They had tried to keep her off the latest mission, saying that she had come down with a vomiting bug and, while she had vomited after the fish dinner, they still sent her out.

She checks each pregnancy test maybe ten minutes after necessary. Eleanor checks over and over that the results are read correctly before she destroys the sticks and throws them out. She is pregnant. And terrified. Completely and utterly, terrified. Eleanor knows if she asked for abortion pills from the Agency, they would give them to her without question. She also knows that after she graduates she will never be able to have a child, she will never be able to have a family or love someone like she barely remembers her mother loving her. So, after a night of heavy contemplation, she decides, in a shabby hotel room in the bustling city of Madrid – alone and in the dark – to run and to be caught and to leave.

To protect her baby. To give her that glimpse, that moment, of bringing something good, something pure, into the world.

Chapter 6

It isn't Michael who comes to get her the next day, instead a buff agent she's never seen before makes her stand facing the wall as he enters and clasps her hands behind her back. He doesn't talk as he pushes her in front of him to the same interrogation room as earlier, through the endless light grey corridors. She easily frees herself and swings the metal on her finger as they round the corner. The man slams her into the wall and a harsh whimper escapes her as he presses her to the wall.

"You bitch!" he growls, while Eleanor continues to struggle beneath him. Her back burns, but her reflexes kick in.

Her foot kicks back and hits between his legs which gives her enough space to spin out of his hold and swipe his feet out from underneath him. She darts into the conference room, a surprising terror on her face as the man throws open the door and pins her throat to the wall.

"Agent!" the Colonel barks. "Get off her!"

The man complies and steps back but is clearly disgruntled by her use of rank in front of the prisoner.

"She escaped her binds!" he argues.

"Yes, we are aware of Miss Beck's ability to get her cuffs off without anyone noticing." Colonel Randall pinches the bridge of her nose in clear exasperation. "And I remember telling you not to restrain her."

"Sorry, ma'am, I thought I had misheard you." Now the agent has the gall to look ashamed, though he makes no move to apologise to the ever-so-slightly trembling teen.

"You hadn't. Miss Beck here is more dangerous cuffed than free; however, we watch her movements, and should she escape her guard, the entire building locks down," Nancy says. "Get out, now. I'll talk to you later."

Eleanor takes her seat as the agent leaves and tucks her knees to her chest.

"Where's Michael?" Eleanor asks softly.

"Doing his actual job, and hopefully not bringing in another pregnant 16-year-old with a death list that goes over 12 pages," Colonel Randall returns. "Now, Dr Tanaka told us that you are maybe a month in, and that the boy you draw over again in those books of yours is likely not the father."

"Is there a question there, Colonel?" Eleanor murmurs. She casts her eyes away, the pads of her fingers tapping out melodies on her thigh.

"How did you get pregnant?" she questions.

"He thought I was sterile; I was not. I couldn't talk, he never knew," Eleanor answers softly. "I suspected something, so took multiple tests while in Spain."

"And you decided to keep it. Why?"

"Because everything I do is bad. I don't think I've ever loved anything fully, maybe those two, but I don't know. My family are all dead, I..." The girl trails off. "I was six when I was taken, and I think it was my mother's gift to us – her smart mind – that I learnt pretty quickly that if I didn't get over myself, I would die. I buried myself, deep below my consciousness and remade my mind so I wasn't scared anymore. That part of me has broken out, and all I wanted to do was... stop. I just wanted everything to stop."

The Colonel stays silent as she watches Eleanor with a careful gaze.

"It took very little time for me to find out, less to be sent to kill a couple of traitors in an American base." Eleanor shrugs.

What she doesn't say is; 'I never got to say goodbye. I never thanked them for everything they did to help me. I never got to tell them how much I loved them', but it plays on her eyes, before she pulls her mask back up. A false smile plays on Eleanor's face as she chuckles a little.

"It seems you've discovered my secret. No, I wasn't here to get information or kill anyone. I'm here to protect my baby. Just so that it may breathe free air," Eleanor says. "I couldn't run once I got heavily pregnant; I wouldn't physically be able to escape. I couldn't hide in Australia because I've not been allowed there. America can't kill me until I'm 18, that gives me a year to see my baby. I'd have to trust that it would be put into a good home, but just knowing it was alive would be all I needed. And I knew America had a strong witness protection program... I am worried my Handler may come for my baby as a punishment for my actions."

The older woman nods, as if in understanding and looks to the two guards in the room. Then there is a faint boom from elsewhere in the compound and Eleanor's muscles lock up.

"It's fine, just the air base doing sonic exercises," the Colonel assures, initially oblivious to Eleanor's breaths shortening dangerously.

That changes as she drops under the table, then under her chair and curls tightly into a ball. Faint whimpers break out of her lips, a far cry from the confidence they had become used to.

"The Berlin massacre, it was a bombing," one of the agents' mutters.

He moves over to crouch in front of her, careful to keep his distance.

"It's okay, Eleanor, there are no bombs," he says. "No attack."

"Get away!" Eleanor cries in German as she cradles her head in her hands. "It's not safe, get away!"

The man stands back up and shrugs apologetically.

"I don't speak any other languages," he says.

"It's German, anyone speak it?" the Colonel asks.

No one answers, instead lock their eyes on Eleanor who continues to talk in feverish German. As she shakes like a leaf under the chair, Colonel Randall's radio crackles.

"Ma'am, the team just arrived." She can't help but sigh in relief.

"Send Dr Tanaka up now, tell him to be quick," the Colonel orders.

Time passes slowly, and no-one in the room moves until Kenichi arrives. He takes a moment to catch his breath as he observes the situation in confusion.

"It seems Miss Beck falls back onto German when she is scared," Nancy explains and dips her head towards the chair. "We need you to calm her down."

"What happened?" he asks as he steps cautiously towards Eleanor.

"Sonic boom, she freaked out," Nancy grumbles.

With a soft nod, Kenichi reaches out to touch Eleanor's hand but as she flinches back he slows his approach down.

"Eleanor, just breathe," he instructs in German, and watches for any sign she hears him. "It was a false alarm. You are safe, we are all safe. We're in America, you are safe."

Eleanor continues to shake but becomes quiet and locks her eyes on him. Behind, Michael steps into the rapidly crowding room.

"Calm down, Eleanor, calm down," Kenichi continues, voice stern. "Not in front of these people, you have to be your best self, remember? You must show them you aren't scared."

"But I am, Mein Vater, I am so scared," she whimpers with her head weaving tightly.

The doctor brushes off the name and gently lifts the chair off her.

"Well don't be, there is nothing to be scared of," he tells her and risks an attempt to take her hand but retracts it as she jumps back, "nothing at all."

Eleanor inches back slightly and her eyes flick around the room as Kenichi turns to Michael and instructs in English, "She trusts you more than me, try and calm her." He switches to German to address Eleanor, "you know Michael, he wants to help you."

She turns her attention to the silent hand Michael offers to her. When she doesn't flinch away, he moves a little closer to brush her hair off her shoulder and draw her focus. Michael keeps a hand on her should as he moves to her side.

"Eleanor, do you understand me?" he asks gently.

With eyes still wide like a frightened deer, Eleanor nods and leans a little closer. She lets him wrap an arm softly around her to assist her to her feet. With her head at rest on his shoulder, she stays at his side as he raises an eyebrow to his superior.

"What's the mark on her neck?" he asks carefully.

"The agent who brought her up got a bit mad when she took off her cuffs," Nancy explains. "He will be going on suspension, don't worry."

Michael makes a noise of acceptance, asking, "is she dismissed?"

"She is. But keep in mind, Mr Mornblade, that your position here isn't permanent, so don't grow too attached," the Colonel answers.

"I am aware," he replies simply.

With consideration to Eleanor's still weak legs, Michael scoops her into his arms for the walk to her cell. She's silent, pale blue eyes staring blankly forward. He watches her, watches how she rubs at her arms in the cold and how she twitches at the oddest moments.

Michael places her on the cot and places a blanket over her lower half. Before he can leave, her hand snaps out to grab his arm, and with the silent plea in her eyes, he sits down on the corner of her bed. Her hand stays on his, so he leaves it resting on her and observes her curiously as she turns her focus away again.

"My parents hadn't wanted to give me to the front," she whispers hoarsely, "but they spotted me, dragged me away from them. I was the last child to be shoved in the van. I hadn't been blindfolded like the rest of them. I saw as the second round of bombs went off."

"Do you know how many others from that attack are still alive?" he asks quietly.

"No." She shakes her head. "As I said earlier, I was smart, I hid myself behind a wall of confidence. Everyone either feared me or didn't know who I was. I was sent to train under one of their best agents at seven and had no contact with the other agents in training. Other than for executions."

"Did you know what his name was?" he inquires gently.

"Yes," she snorts. "Dunkler Bischof."

"Eleanor..."

"No, I don't know his actual name. Never worked up the guts to ask."

It was true. She didn't know the name of her Vater.

~

I do, though. I met him once or twice. Nathan Myers was put on trial for mass murder, found guilty. But the governments of the world decided, like they did for many of the Berühmte Söldner, to make use of his abilities.

He is still alive today, taking residence in a maximum-security town, made for them all.

I doubt he will be alive by the time I finish writing out this story.

~

"You called Kenichi Mein Vater earlier," he muses.

"My Father, in German," she mutters. "It wasn't meant for him."

"We figured," Michael chuckles.

Eleanor smiles faintly, taking her hand away and pulling up her blanket.

"Thank you, for the blanket," she says.

"It's okay," he nods. "We want to try and get you moved into where we stay, Zach's house technically, but it's too big for even us. I think it would be a lot better if you stayed there, what do you think about that?"

"It would be nice," she sighs, "if you can make it happen."

"I'll try my hardest," he assures and pats her hand lightly.

Eleanor turns her attention back to Michael.

"What did she mean, that you aren't permanent?"

He sighs, standing up and strolling toward the exit of the cell as he explains, "I am not American, in fact, I do not come from anywhere you'll have ever been. I am here to learn about different human cultures, but I could be called back at any point."

Eleanor is quiet with slow blinks as she swallows stickily.

"I think you'd get along great with my sister, and I'd really like you two to meet. If I can, I'm going to take you to my home so you can," he says. "Try to sleep, will you?"

"No promises," she murmurs. "But I'll try."

With a kind smile, and a nod to the guards outside, Michael leaves her curled up on the cot. Her tired eyes flicker back and forth under her eyelids and her fingers twitch at her sides. The attempt doesn't last long as she jumps up and assesses the room around her with clever eyes. She starts to hum lightly as she does squats, then swings her feet up onto the bed, to do push-ups.

Nancy Randall watches her through the security cameras. The assassin in her is clear, the tightly plaited hair, visible muscles, focus on her face. Palpable is the ease with which this girl could kill, an ease that shows through her every move. Yet, the golden chain is still around her neck and the bow and arrow dangles out in front of her. An hour later, Eleanor finishes and lies softly with her blanket only covering her bottom half, hands tucked under her head.

Nancy leaves for the night completely and utterly confused.

Chapter 7

Eleanor sits curled in the corner of her cell as she carefully watches the guards as they place a prisoner in the cell across from hers. One guard turns to her to raise a warning finger, before they walk away in defeat as Eleanor smirks teasingly.

"Have you brought me a friend?" she calls to gain the attention of the other guard.

"Don't make us get Mr Mornblade to come babysit you, you know he won't be happy you're terrorising your fellow cellmates," he warns.

"Oh, come on," she laughs. "I'm a joy to have around."

"You keep telling yourself that, Miss Beck," he chuckles as he walks away.

Eleanor watches the new addition for a few minutes to quickly determine him to be an assassin.

"Why are you here?" she asks in fluent German.

"I needed to deliver a message," he replies calmly.

"What message?"

"The girl is ours, her lapse in loyalty will be dealt with, but she will live. Give her back to us, so that we can clean up the mess she made," he recalls. "She can keep the baby, if she must, with her genetics, that baby will be good."

Eleanor stills, her skin turns deathly pale, breath chokes in her chest. Her small form scrambles backwards as she claws in fear at her chest. The pained whimpers manage to escape her, and it takes only a minute for the guards to be back, for them to open her cell door to try to calm her down. One grabs her hands to stop her from breaking the skin on her collar, as the other takes control over her head to stop her from thrashing so violently.

Another two minutes later, Michael runs in and passes in thanks to the two guards as he quickly picks her up and pins her arms against him. He holds her tightly to compress the fear within her as he is met by Kenichi who looks on worriedly as she starts to fret again.

"This is all my fault," she whimpers, hiding her face into his shoulder. "I'm so stupid, I'm so damn stupid."

Michael attempts to soothe her but fails miserably.

"They're going to use it to control me. They're going to hold it hostage, make it like me," she sobs. "I'm not going to be able to fight them, because they will have my baby. I'm going to kill again."

"We aren't going to turn you over, Eleanor, I promise," he sighs and makes her stand on her own feet.

Frantically, Eleanor shakes her head and lets Kenichi take her other arm as she stumbles back again.

"Eleanor, you need to calm down, stress like this isn't good for your baby," the doctor warns softly. "You aren't going anywhere, I promise, just calm down."

In defiance she holds her breath to swallow the shakes into the very centre of her stomach. Her hand grips Michael's with a white grip that shakes as she shuts her eyes. With his other hand, he supports her head to let Eleanor tuck in next to him as she manages to wrangle in the tremors.

"You do know that is what they mean by 'that baby will be good', don't you?" she whispers.

"We understand, Eleanor. We've already said no, the boy has been in interrogation for hours already," Kenichi assures. "You should apologise to your poor guards; they had a heart attack."

"And they said I would be the one terrorising." Her laugh is weak, false. "Do you ever miss it, your calm, innocent childhood?"

"Yes," Michael replies instantly, though he leaves no opening for a question.

Meanwhile Kenichi glances down and stays silent. Eleanor brushes it back into her mind as he shakes his head quietly and looks back at her.

"Do you guys have a running track here?" she asks cautiously.

"We do," Michael nods. "It's around the edge of the compound... why?"

"Because I've been stuck in that freaking cell for ages, and I don't want to lose my fitness," she shrugs. "But I understand if you can't."

"No, I've actually been discussing your 'seeing of the sun' with the Colonel. Put this tracker on your ankle, which will shock you, but not harm the baby should I press the button, and we're good to go," he smiles, "and joggers of course."

Eleanor grins and bounds after him as he walks off in front of her. The ankle cuff goes on with no argument and her shoelaces are tied so quick she's upright again as Kenichi turns back around after a moment logging the activity. Eleanor raises an eyebrow as the doctor sits down to watch them in amusement.

"You honestly think I'm dumb enough to try and keep up with you two?" he scoffs.

"You honestly think I'm that fast?" she returns.

"I don't know about you, but Michael, as I hear he's told you, isn't normal." Kenichi laughs. "Good luck."

She shrugs it off, saying goodbye to the doctor and following Michael obediently as he leads her outside. She pauses in the sun, soaking in the warmth for a minute, until Michael drags her out of the way of some people and gives her a warning look.

"Don't get too far behind, if you're tired just tell me. It's ten kilometres around, but if you are getting tired at five, there's a shorter track back. Don't try anything, I will shock you," he warns as Eleanor shakes her head. "I will beat you no matter how fast you can go."

"I think I could take you," she challenges and smirks lightly as she stretches out her legs.

"Once you're no longer pregnant, I will let you have a go. Where I'm from, we're descended from angels," he tells her, "while no one has had magic or wings in thousands of years, we still retain angelic characteristics."

"Like what?" she asks curiously.

"Speed, strength, height, brains, compulsion to do good," he lists. Eleanor snorts as she shakes her head.

"Are you sure?" she grins.

He raises an eyebrow in amusement, before he gestures to the track they had arrived at. It was purely just along the edge of the fence and the looming metal bars reach well above her head. The track is worn by use – dirt. Further along it stretches into the tree line, big pines littered with smaller trees as well. All the buildings, in orderly rows, are plain grey with steel roofs with the one she had just come from the biggest. Fighter jets dot the side of the runway, rows of vehicles opposing them.

"Where are we?" Eleanor asks distractedly, though she was far from it.

"A few kilometres from the White House, we are an extra level of protection," he answers easily. "Now, hurry up, we are running, not letting you get your bearings."

Eleanor nods, setting out along the trail at an easy run. Michael follows, joining her side in a few steps and their feet hit the ground together. The silence that surrounds them continues until they are out of sight.

"Your movements are rather... graceful." A statement, but really a question lies in Michael's words.

"I'm small. Often when it comes to my targets, size will not be on my side, so I was taught to use my agility as an advantage," she shrugs. "Also, balls and galas are often a part of our missions so being able to dance properly is essential."

"I didn't think anyone had balls anymore," Michael frowns.

"Oh, infiltrate the Japanese Emperor's annual ball and you'd be surprised," she grins, swishing around a fake skirt in memory.

"Been to Japan a few times, have you?" he laughs.

"I'm fluent in the language," she shrugs. "And I can fit into their crowds with ease."

"So, what was that mission?" he asks curiously, and avoids the hint of distaste that threatens to slip into his words.

"I was there to threaten the emperor." Eleanor shrugs. "One of our benefactors wanted him scared."

"And?" he prods.

"I completed the mission objective with ease. They weren't very happy about it." An odd humour catches her with a slight laugh. "A few months later I took out one of their most dangerous gangs, was gifted a Katana."

"Who are these benefactors? Are they in the government?" he frowns as they start to walk again.

"Some, others then hire us to work against them. For the big missions – the ones that the benefactors needed to be kept quiet – they use the ACEs. There're maybe 20 agents, all of whom could take down a small country in a week if they were told to. We live only to serve them. I've met quite a few, lived with two," Eleanor murmurs. "Life was... better if you were an ACE. You could see everything: France, Japan, England, Spain, Egypt. We were stationed in little apartments, usually three, maybe four to one. An older agent, the best of the best, then two or three kids with potential would be placed there to train as an ACE. By the time we would graduate, most would be dead. We had cots, but there was also double bed with full amenities for the days preceding and just after a mission, to have us well prepared."

"That seems oddly pleasant," Michael muses.

Her face shifts rapidly, a tenseness over taking the genetically soft features.

"Sometimes it was," she shrugs, "but then we would be told to go to the training sector, and there would be a line of kids that needed to be taught how to be an agent. They'd give them false hope, a chance to prove themselves. Fight well enough and you would live, beat us, we'd get ten lashes."

"Did anyone ever beat you?" he asks and unconsciously looks towards her back as if he could see through the shirt to her scars.

Eleanor doesn't answer for a moment, before providing a definite, "No."

Silence encapsulates the rest of the light run back to the compound. Michael catches her arm before they get to the building to make her look up at him.

"You know that was all being recorded, don't you?" he says, far more serious than Eleanor thought reasonable.

But nevertheless, she keeps her answer simple, "Of course I do."

As they continue to walk, Eleanor's eyes cast toward to the floor, and the fingers start to twitch again.

"If they come... if they get to me, I will try to get away. But if they're about to take me and I can't get away, I'm not going to let them get me," Eleanor whispers, a crack in her voice. What better way to ensure they listen than act scared. "I'd rather die than work for them again."

Michael swallows and squeezes her hand in a surprising attempt at reassurance.

"That won't happen, you are not dying under my watch," he says as he scans into the cell block.

Eleanor actually laughs.

"I was dead the moment I allowed a distress call to get out."

Far from accepting her statement, yet conscious of the many criminals around them, Michael merely stops her in front of her cell.

"Are you going to be okay here, we don't have any other openings at the moment," he says, clearly unhappy with the housing situation.

"You sound like I'm booking a table," Eleanor mutters as her eyes rove the hall. "I'll be fine." With a lingering glance to the office she adds, "I'm sorry about earlier."

"It's understandable," Michael replies with a glance into her cell. "Colonel dropped off your box, said they kept the knife for obvious reasons but everything else should be there, and we included a pencil."

Eleanor forces herself to smile in thanks, but there is a disturbance that doesn't reach her eyes. While Michael unlocks the cuff on her ankle, she merely stares at her small wooden box with the familiarity of an assassin with their target. She steps into the cell as required and grants Michael a nod of thanks before he leaves.

"Not going to freak again?" the messenger teases.

Eleanor ignores him dutifully and opens the wooden box.

"For such a treasured ACE, you don't seem very well-trained," he mutters.

"Just because I have something growing in my womb doesn't mean I cannot kill you in an instant," she snaps. "And they do not care for manners when you can kill as I can."

"Whatever you say traitor," he replies with the cockiness of two walls between them.

"I have sold out no one except myself," Eleanor replies far more calmly. "Any word on 613 and 819?"

The numbers rattle off without a thought as her fingers trace the two faces drawn in the back of her book.

"They were questioned and let go not too long ago," the boy shrugs. "They're both working again, from what I've heard."

Eleanor nods, then shuts out everything around her as pencil touches paper and she starts writing. The panic attack — real as it was — had rebuilt her wall and Eleanor knew she needed to protect herself from both sides of the argument. In the end, everyone could be convinced to kill her.

But a little trust could manipulate that...

Chapter 8

Quite alone, Eleanor sits on her cot in comfortable silence. Her fingers press against the cool metal of her necklace and she frowns as a bang echoes down the stairs. It had been a week since the messenger arrived and he smiles tauntingly. Then an alarm starts blaring, and one of the guards comes running in.

"What's happening?" Eleanor asks as he stops outside her cell.

"There's an attack and the team are on assignment," he tells her. "Don't make us regret the decision to give you a weapon to protect yourself."

He pushes a dagger through the gap for food, a small stiletto but extremely sharp. It clatters hopelessly on the ground and Eleanor collects it in an instant.

"Thank you," she says with a confident shine to her eyes. "Don't try to protect me, I can handle them. Just hide."

"I'm going back there," he promises. "It's procedure to knock out all the prisoners in case of escape, so you will need this."

An oxygen mask falls to the floor and Eleanor picks it up with thanks.

"Please, prove to us you're here for good. Michael practically begged us to make sure you were safe, something about duty and his brother – who knows with him..." He sighs. "Don't run away and good luck Eleanor."

She nods and moves to sit back on the cot. Eleanor places the necklace in the box and shoves it into her pillowcase before lying back.

"They're sending a lot, probably some ACEs as well. You won't be able to get away," the boy calls.

"We'll see about that."

Eleanor smiles as she hears the quiet click and hiss of the gas release.

Easily, she fits the mask over her mouth and nose and lets her eyes shut and blanket drop a little as she listens intently for people to join them. A light flashes for two minutes after the gas finishes being dispensed. A slow, tentative breath tells her that the sedative has been dispersed so she tucks the mask beneath her pillow and waits. The dagger, ice in her warm hands, sits flush to her wrist under the blanket as it waits for action with her.

She doesn't have to wait long for movement, then her door opens and five people crowd into her cell. One goes to grab her, and barely makes contact before she is upon them. The closest has their throat cut and by the time they realise what she's doing, two more are beside him. The next two go down 30 seconds later, after a quick parley they both end up on the ground bleeding. She grabs one of their guns and puts a bullet into the heads of each. A few more magazines slide into her waist band as she holds her dagger in one hand, gun in the other.

Eleanor stalks out of the cell, and glides through the fighting. Bullets find any attackers she meets but the ammunition quickly runs out. The gun is discarded as Eleanor finds the open armoury. She smirks at the soldiers that halt their actions to stare at her.

"You're supposed to be in your cell, unconscious," one mutters, bitter as he stops Eleanor from reaching the swords that she eyes.

"Well, I'm sorry, that would have ended with me in a van to my certain detriment," she returns. "Now, I know how these people fight, and I am better than most of them, so let me get my swords."

After looking to the others for help, the soldier lets her through but watches carefully as she lifts matching swords from their place and swings them with confidence.

"Thank you," she grins and touches her hand to her ever so slightly swelled stomach in a brief lapse of focus. "Try not to get into hand to hand with them, you won't win."

And Eleanor strides away to find the concentration of fighting to slip in. She cuts through them like butter with a satisfied grin across her face as she finds a specialised target. He dispatches the soldiers and as he spots her, a matching grin crosses his face.

"I always knew you were a wild card," he hisses in casual German. "I should have trained under him."

"But I'm smarter, quicker, and frankly better than you," she teases. "You just aren't up to scratch."

"We'll see about that." The words lunge before he does and the pair lock into battle.

The fighting stops to watch and the pair spin around as they send fatal blows this way and that, but both manage to avoid the swipes. She bounces up and off the table that she's found herself next to and pounces onto his head. Her laugh echoes as they both go down the otherwise silent hall. A moment later Eleanor's sword slashes his throat, and she watches with deadly satisfaction as he claws at the wound before the blade slides into his chest and stills him. Eleanor rises ⌐— but not without slicing a cross into his forehead – and turns to those around her, face covered in blood.

"On your knees, now!" she orders. A triumphant gaze scans the assassins as they drop in submission. "Are there any more ACEs? Don't lie."

The few that still stand have bullets between their eyes the instant they prepare to move forward and some on the ground shake their heads in response. Eleanor drops her guard and rolls herself back off the body with tremors in her thin hands. Her feet move of their own accord as she moves back to her cell, and her knees tuck mindlessly to her chest to as she sits on the cot, all alone.

"Welcome back," she calls as the team find her shortly after, a numb tone to her voice. "There's more but not many; killed quite a few. Should be easy enough to take them down. They only ever send one ACE, or partners if they work well together. No one works well with that guy, so it's unlikely." In low German, she adds, "Arrogant asshole."

Kenichi huffs a slight laugh as he follows just a metre behind Michael, who sits carefully next to Eleanor. He is the one to notice her anxiously stretch her blood encrusted arms.

"You hurt?" Michael asks carefully.

"Not that I know of, but I wouldn't feel it if I was cut anyway." She shrugs nonchalantly. "The adrenaline, you know..."

"How many did you kill?" he asks as orders for the compound to be searched roll through the radios. With them Kenichi moves out to assist.

"43," Eleanor answers as she stares at the blank wall in front of her.

A muscle ticks in Michael's jaw as he processes, but as he rubs his forehead, he accepts Eleanor's statement.

"Thank you," Eleanor whispers, "your orders to my guards saved my life."

Michael continues to stand faced away from her with tight shoulders for long enough that Eleanor begins to fidget as he turns back to her.

"Do you think other assassins would listen to you if you told them to stand down?" he asks in a carefully clipped tone.

"Maybe. Think of them as a pack of wolves; highly trained, deadly but obedient wolves," she murmurs. "I am an ACE; I have authority even though I defected. Strength is power, and they respect the power of their own."

With a frown, Michael pivots the topic.

"You knew that man."

"I did."

The admission disconnects her. With an arm under her head, she lies back and adopts a stony silence.

"Nothing else?"

"I told you when I arrived here; ask me about the Agency, about my missions, but I won't answer questions on my personal life," she mutters. "I may trust you more than I did then, but it still applies. If I want to tell you I will, but don't ask."

Michael nods stiffly as he sits back down on the end of her bed.

"You have a brother," Eleanor starts. A statement, not a question.

"I wouldn't call him that anymore," the man replies bitterly.

"Then why did my guards say you were protecting me for him?"

Silence holds for a minute; the man turns over her question in his head.

"Because of the little angelic magics left in our blood," he replies. "That is all I will tell you on my duty to him."

"Why is he no longer your brother?" she asks.

"Because he tried to kill my father," he replies lowly.

"So, he was illegitimate?" she questions and receives a grunt of affirmation in return.

They continue to sit in silence until Kaylee joins them and nods to her comrade. She raises an eyebrow at the bloodied girl lying out on the bench.

"You know how showering works, come along," she instructs.

Once she has cleaned herself, and they begin to walk back to Eleanor's cell, Kaylee changes their direction.

"You know, executing people like you do won't win you any friends," she mutters as they near Kenichi's lab.

"I like to think it merciful," Eleanor replies softly. "They are going to fight anyway, and they are going to die anyway, so why not make it quick. And then they aren't going to shoot you in the back once you've gotten them to surrender."

"You didn't show mercy to that man you were fighting."

"He deserved it," Eleanor mutters in response.

Without a knock on his door, Kaylee walks her into Kenichi's office and Eleanor obediently pops up onto the bench. Kenichi moves behind her to carefully examine the scars on her back.

"You need to be more careful of these," he notes. "They haven't broken open, but they are a little stressed. Nearly fully healed though."

Eleanor nods slowly, rolling back her shoulders gently as he rezips her singlet before he guides her to lay down and pulls over an ultrasound machine.

"Do you want me to make them leave?" he asks with a glance towards the looming guards in the corner.

With a shake of her head, Eleanor mutters, "It's fine."

Though he doubts the conviction in her tone, Kenichi starts the examination with a kind hand to her skin flecked with a myriad of little scars that shine like a galaxy upon her skin. No one notices as she falls asleep, and her body succumbs to the exhaustion of physical and emotional turmoil that had encased her day. After he clears the baby's health, Kenichi turns to face Eleanor, about to ask if she'd like to hear the heartbeat when he notices her sleeping face with a light smile.

A short radio call to Michael, and Kenichi prepares Eleanor for the trip back to her cell.

"She's deadly," Kaylee mutters before Michael can lift Eleanor. "So very, very, deadly."

"Which is why she must never, ever meet my brother," Michael replies, low to avoid stirring her. "Not until we know she is safe, and that her kill drive is sated by the child."

"I'm not sure anything can truly stop her from being like this." Kenichi frowns. "There's nothing we can do…"

Michael's face sours at the truth of his statement. "It is illegal to keep her from him and she would feel safest with him. Her entire being here is about safety, so we would lose her. Worse, I have no idea how his temper might handle her affliction."

With almost surprising worry, Kenichi asks, "He wouldn't hurt her, would he?"

"No, he couldn't," Michael scoffs. "But he may hunt down those who hurt her. Unfortunately, she may do the same. I wouldn't put it past her to attempt to kill my father."

Everyone ignores the weight of his words, but before anyone can interject, he glances down to the girl in his arms.

"I don't trust she's fully asleep, so we are stopping this conversation now," he says.

The statement short, finalising the conversation so quickly it paints a frown on both members of his team, but they let him take her back to the cell without further discussion.

Chapter 9

A trail of bodies lies in the wake of the 15-year-old and blood splatters dry on her grinning face. Her blade drips red jewels onto pearl tiles as she sashays through the double doors to face the man, her target. His eyes widen in surprise as he observes the barely matured form of a girl, who merely offers a soft, girlish smile.

"Your guards fight well, but not well enough," she says in Japanese as she steps slowly forward and drags the tip of her blade on the floor.

"Where did you acquire the blade?" the man returns as he slides his own to face her.

"A gift..." The sickening sweet expression melts into blood lust, the smirk, returns and, after two minutes of swordplay, the blade slides into his stomach.

"From a rich benefactor," she finishes, before she pulls the blade out and quickly slices his head from his shoulders.

"Is she here, or did she bite off more than she can chew?" the benefactor grumbles.

"She's here," his son answers as a door slams open into the wall beside it.

She struts into the centre of the room, bag in one hand and the sword in the other. The guards around the room bristle at her appearance, far from pleased as she throws the bag to their feet.

"Done and dusted, shouldn't be a problem for you from here on," she calls as she offers the blade forward, "Thank you for the use of the sword, it proved useful."

"Keep it, we have no need for a bloodstained blade here," the man replies. "Are we clear from blame?"

"Until you decide to betray us," she shrugs. "Now, I must be off."

They nod, and the girl turns on her heel to stride out of the room. A man falls into step beside her, silent as they move into the streets.

"Give me the basics," she sighs.

"Assassination, targets will be operating behind the guise of a gala. You and 819 will be attending, I expect maturity from you both, but it will be a little while until the opening arrives, so don't get too distracted," her handler returns, giving her a look as she smirks.

"I don't know what you're talking about," she laughs.

"Sure, you don't, little missy," the man sneers.

"Where we at?" she continues, weaving through the streets.

"London."

~

Eleanor snaps awake as her breaths drag into her lungs in her scramble to sit up. Her hands find one of her books and fingers clutch the pencil as she sketches out a face, next to many of the same in the middle of the book. Harsh eyes, thin lips, sunken cheeks. Rough, mean. The one who held her keys, the one who brandished her cane. Eleanor doesn't even look at the picture once she's finished. Some could call it a masterpiece if they wanted, fine detail, emotion, all in simple greyscale.

As she swaps to the newer book, a much slower picture emerges of an old house, tucked into the side of a hill. A few hours later, while she's still adding things to the intricate drawing of her former home, a guard stops outside her cell. He is completely unfamiliar, and it strikes a shiver of fear in her.

"What do you need?" she asks as she examines him from her position.

"I am one of the replacement guards after the attack yesterday," he starts. "I have been instructed to move you to a new cell."

"Where's Michael, or Kaylee, or Kenichi?" she questions, not moving.

"Not here." He frowns, clearly not briefed on her paranoia. "We're just moving you to a more secure place, Michael's request."

Eleanor shakes her head so her hair falls in front of the face and tucks herself tighter into herself. Even still, she doesn't let her eyes leave him.

"Miss, it's only 500m," he says with a clear irritated inflection.

"I don't trust you," she mutters with a glare.

The agent presses the button on his radio to call for assistance as he unlocks her cell and steps in. With a light grasp on her arm, he is clearly shocked as she springs to the opposite side of the room. Worse, he finds himself at the wrong end of his own weapon as Eleanor levels it at his head. The weapon is terrifyingly still, yet her head twitches just enough to make Nancy Randall halt in the doorway.

"Miss Beck!" the Colonel snaps. Eleanor's focus flies to the woman, and the steady gaze she meets lowers the weapon from metres away. "Must you really have an escort everywhere you go?"

"Not an escort, just someone familiar," she mutters. "How do I know they aren't Berühmte Söldner, trying to kill me?"

"You don't," Nancy admits. "Although I believe you should trust us a little more, that is why we are moving you to a new cell."

Finally, Eleanor relaxes enough for the tension to leave her head. With something almost akin to remorse, she hands the gun back to its owner. Eleanor remains silent as she collects her limited possessions and exits the cell with the Colonel at her side.

They follow the corridor further into the building and further underground as the echoing concrete fire escape delivers them to the highest security sector of the compound.

Uncharacteristically tortured by the silence Nancy inflicts on her, Eleanor fidgets with the box in her pale hands.

"I can't help being paranoid," she blurts, "it's the only reason I'm alive..."

"I understand, Miss Beck, however you need to try harder to trust our security," Nancy replies. "We are a Federal agency."

"I know."

They pass out of the stairwell into a frigid hallway, meticulously clean and devoid of any objects. Before them, a metal ring lines the corridor with bright yellow and black warnings; blast doors, it would seem. Only a few meters further are a set of cells far more advanced than those above them. Stark white with glass fronts and solid concrete walls dividing them, there are only six with five filled already. Each of the men is far larger than her, with mean grins on them all.

"Now, these are the strongest cells we have. These prisoners are mass murderers, awaiting lethal injection," Colonel Randall explains as she places her hand on the pad next to the edge of the cell. "Handprint required to lift the first layer; ballistic grade glass, nothing can break out of it. Then, to open the door, which is made of the same stuff, you need the control room. In cases of emergency this place is a bunker, fireproof as well. Once those steel doors drop nothing gets in or out without three of the five elected officials who can raise it."

The girl smirks as she eyes the men, the intense urge to let her tongue run loose almost overwhelming.

"Brought us a plaything, have you Colonel?" one calls with a hungry eye.

A brute of a thing, tattoos covering his arms, much like two of the other men. The last two are thinner but share the same sick look as the rest.

"No. She's here for the same reason as you," Nancy snips.

"How am I expected to believe that, when she's walking free?" he taunts.

"Because unlike you brutes, she's smart enough to use restraint to her own benefit," she returns.

Bored of the new addition, another slides up to his barrier.

"Anyone going to tell us why we shut down yesterday?" he calls.

"My employers tried to retake me. Unfortunately, I want to be here, so that didn't work for them," Eleanor answers with false calm.

"They mustn't be very good, this place is as easy to break into as a school," the thinnest scoffs.

Eleanor actually laughs at him.

"No, they got to me. I just killed them all," she chuckles. "43, was it?"

"Yes," the Colonel grumbles. "We need to have a chat about that."

"I was doing your job, don't complain," Eleanor says.

With a roll of her deep eyes, Nancy presses a button on the control board that frosts the glass over and silences them. She turns to Eleanor as she begins to open the cell.

"Food here is made specially, so no one can smuggle anything in, or slip poison into the meal of a high-profile case that might squeal. We won't be testing your food anymore; it will be fine. I promise. Michael can open your cell, and will accompany you most places, but you will have to go with other guards as well."

"No, I won't go with them," she mutters as her hand hovers over her stomach. "I can't risk it, I can't drop the paranoia now, my brain won't let me."

"Does anyone you know work?" Nancy asks to abate the trembling girl.

"Just someone familiar," she answers, though she refuses to reach the Colonel's eyes. "...every time she breaks out this happens. I get weak, my damn conscious breaks through my stupid head and I get scared. This stupid head."

Nancy frowns, but gestures for Eleanor to enter her cell. As she steps in – her fingers gripping the roots of her hair – the cells defrost and her own door locks with a hiss.

In the back corner is a toilet designated by a partial wall and curtain for privacy. There are two cots, one next to the toilet and the other opposite. Unlike the cell she came from, the bed is made of tightly woven rope, not the springs covered with a thin mattress she was used to. Eleanor places her stuff beneath the bed before she adjusts her pillow and lies down.

"So girly, they like you, do they? Mind sharing your secrets?" the man across from her calls.

She stays silent and nuzzles into her pillow and shuts her eyes. There is a soft hum, and the noise the other cell occupants make is silenced. Eleanor sleeps through lunch, ignoring the brief attempt to make her acknowledge the food. The meals swap at dinner, and she eats only half before she curls back up again.

Her pale hands massage her slightly swollen stomach, but the stressed knot stopping her from eating properly did not ease. Falling into fitful sleep, her confidence slips further and further away over the next weeks. Eyes sunken; lips pale. Of the little food she ate, much of it didn't stay down and the cell didn't allow her to get more the few times she was hungry. Continually, spies are discovered in various stages of entering the building, however none get close enough for her to become aware of the threat.

Michael and Kenichi watch in worry – though for vastly different reasons – and begin their campaign to move her to the property they live together on. The Colonel observes as Eleanor wastes away as she stays only healthy enough to ensure her child's survival. The argument of safety is dispelled by the protocols already at the manor; Eleanor's personal drive to leave is entirely ignored as an issue; but most of all, she needed a little bit of humanity given back to her. It was irrefutable that fresh air helped the tremble in her hands to vanish, and just losing sight of the compound brought a smile to her face.

The cycle of pain that entrapped her – as she jumps awake early in the morning, trains, barely eats – was all the convincing Nancy needed to agree that Eleanor needed to leave.

Chapter 10

"Eleanor?" Michael calls from her doorway.

She blearily looks up, and her smile is weak as he gestures out the door. Eleanor swings her legs over the cot, carefully stands, and follows quietly behind him as they head upstairs. Her shoulders straighten mechanically as they move through the corridors towards Kenichi's lab to get her tracker band. He isn't there, so they quickly put it around her ankle and leave. Eleanor moves easily to keep up with his larger steps and her head tilts in confusion as the Colonel joins them as they walk outside. But slowly her shoulders drop, and she relaxes as they find a spot to sit far out in the bush.

"Miss Beck," she starts, turning to Eleanor who had pulled herself up onto a branch to sit. "How would you feel about being moved to the manor the team lives in?"

"You would move me out of containment?" she responds. "Is it safe?"

"It is just as safe as here, and no one knows its location. You have shown no desire to leave, so we trust you to be under surveillance in the house and not escape," Nancy answers. "We would keep that anklet on to track you, but it's waterproof and shouldn't hinder your movement."

"Are the others okay with it?" Eleanor questions.

"Zach is a little bitter, but he'll survive. Kaylee looks forward to having a little less testosterone in the house," Michael assures.

"She seems to have forgotten about pregnancy mood swings," Eleanor mutters.

The Colonel chuckles. "Eleanor, pregnancy is not the thing that causes your mood swings, that's just puberty."

Eleanor grins in the free way they hadn't seen from her before, but Nancy is the only one to return the smile as Michael continues to explain the set up almost mechanically.

"You will get your own room and access to money to buy clothes for yourself. And as much food as you want. We will figure out other things as we go," he says. "I think giving a little bit of freedom will help you get control over your head."

The smile drops as Eleanor's eyes harden protectively.

"You have a problem with my head?" she scoffs.

Sensing his mistake, Michael sighs.

"You can't deny it Eleanor, you are sick. We're just trying to help," he says. "So do you want to get out of that cell, or not?"

"I do," she admits with a soft smile. "I've never had my own room before."

"If you want, we can go now. Your things have already been moved to my car," Michael offers. "You have your anklet on, so we're good to go."

"Can we?" she asks Nancy who nods gently.

Eleanor half skips as they walk back to the compound and then straight through, as Michael leads her to the car park. She is about to get in the back, having never been allowed to sit in the front but he opens the passenger door and ushers her in. The drive isn't long, and she watches out the window intently as they start up the driveway. Woodlands surround the area, shielding the manor from the view of the road. It is something you would expect to see in England; with huge stone bricks forming the tall walls and a grey slate roof. Long glass windows adorn each of the walls and, as they get closer, Eleanor can make out the guards dotted around the exterior. It is shaped in a U, the two wings framing the driving loop to the ornamented front door. The wings seem thinner than the rest of the three storeys.

The ground in front of them raises as they get closer and Michael drives onto the lift which lowers them into a garage below.

"Who owns this house?" Eleanor asks as they step out of the car and walk around the many others to get to the door.

"Zach, he comes from money," Michael fills as he starts to show her around. "He had it teched up, but it's been here for centuries."

Eleanor stays silent as they enter the dining room, with a kitchen to one side and the living area on the far wall. Past it is an entertainment room, and behind them a library, but Michael only mentions them as they climb a set of beautiful marble stairs in the entry hall. At the top they turn left to face the corridor. There are four doors, two on each side. Each of the pairs of doors are opposite each other.

"Kaylee's room is first on the other side of the stairs, then it's mine. Kenichi's and Zach's are upstairs where the laundry is. The rooms on the back side are spare, and there is a guest house outside. The one on the end on the left is the gym and this one is yours," he says as they stop outside a tall wooden door.

His hand pushes the door open with a soft smile as Eleanor steps into the room. It has stone interior, and large windowpanes sit in the wall – with a small daybed beneath it. Eleanor instantly grins as she runs and jumps onto the fourposter bed. Two doors sit against the wall next to the door, one to a bathroom and one to a wardrobe opposite her bed, it seems. She looks back to him smiling gratefully with something close to tears welling in her eyes.

"What's wrong Eleanor?" he frowns, walking over to sit next to her.

"Nothing..." she starts, rigid backed and fidgety. "I've never had my own room before."

"Well, this one is all yours. You can decorate it as you want," he smiles. "If your door is open, the cameras will be on, but if you shut the door they'll shut off, audio stays on. You have a bathroom through there, and we usually eat dinner around eight, but that's susceptible to change."

"Does anyone else live here? Other than you four?" Eleanor asks.

"No. We have visitors every so often, but most of the time it's just us, and the guards of course," he answers. "There is a giant fence around the edge of the property, if you cross it your anklet will knock you out. There's food in the kitchen, feel free to eat it, it orders automatically anyway. If you need clothes just ask Kaylee, you should be about the same size."

"Thank you," Eleanor murmurs, "no one has ever been this nice to me."

Michael stands up gently and moves to the door as Eleanor sits against the dark grey cloth headboard.

"Feel free to look around," he says. "There is a stable outside, has some horses Zach's sister wanted, but they're for anyone to ride and pat. You are not to ride; we don't want you to get hurt and some of them can be a little difficult. There is also a German Shepard somewhere around here, she's young, may lick you to death but is safe. Her name's Bronte, shout it loud enough and she'll find you."

"There is a dog here?" the girl smiles. "I used to have a dog."

"Did you?" Michael hums.

"I don't know what happened to her, I assume she went to the pound," she shrugs. "Or she moved with Kate, but I didn't see anything dog like..."

She trails off and her eyes glaze over slightly as she mouths out faint words, her hands twist and wring in her lap. The silent words continue as she rolls her neck and her mouth forms as if she's sucking on a ball of air. After a half minute, she jerks ever so slightly, and a dense mask covers her emotions as she looks up with a confident smile.

"Is there anything else I need to know?" she chirps with a smile. "I must congratulate you, that's the longest I've ever gone... vulnerable."

She spits the last word, as if it disgusts her. Her pale blue irises sparkle with annoyance, but she rubs her stomach fondly and stretches out her legs, as she seems to reacquaint herself with her body.

"I was worried, when she nearly managed to keep control in that attack. But as always, she needed me. Sebastian was only ever able to get her out for a few days, but you've managed months. That is curious." She smirks as she plays with her nails. "She'll remember she needs me, just wait."

The man frowns, about to question her, but she slumps. Her normal, timid eyes meet his in apology.

"What time are the others getting home?" she asks softly.

"Probably six-ish," he replies, content to leave as she grabs her box, but he pauses at the door. "Eleanor?"

"Yes?"

"What will happen if you lose control over your body?" he asks.

Though he aims to throw her off guard, Eleanor meets his eyes without a flinch.

"Nothing," she says, "because I am the only thing to control it."

"Then why were you just referring to yourself as she?" he asks.

"I wasn't," she replies in the same manner.

With a tired slump, Michael drops the questions.

"Make sure you eat lunch," he instructs, "and if you need help with anything, just shout."

Eleanor nods.

As he leaves, he sighs.

"Don't lie to us, please."

Out of his view, Eleanor scowls as he disappears, but the expression is to herself.

"You need to be less obvious," she mutters bitterly with a pause, as if someone was replying. "I don't care if it's fun, he's suspicious now... This is my body... we are safe now, there is no reason for you to come out for more than a few minutes... I'm sorry, okay, but we need to learn to live together... just be less obvious, please Ellsie... Thank you."

She shakes her head slightly and sprawls across the bed. A smile flicks onto her features, her lips pulling up at the sides, as she cradles her swollen stomach in her hand.

Chapter 11

Eleanor keeps her focus stubbornly on the ceiling as Michael remains in the doorway, his glare steady and unmoving as Eleanor sulks.

"I know you've managed to eat alone over the past few days, but you're eating with us today," he says. "It's only an hour, why can't you just do it?"

"Because... I just can't Michael, please?"

"Nope, you're coming," he says with a stern huff. "We're just having pasta, nice and simple for your temperamental stomach."

"Do I have to?" she whines.

"Yes, now hurry up. The Colonel is here as well," he replies with a grin as she pulls herself to her feet.

Michael follows her as she trudges out of her room and down the marble staircase to the unnecessarily long dining table. Eleanor remains silent as she sits and only glances at Kaylee opposite her for a moment as she serves herself a bowl of plain pasta. Michael, who sits next to her, watches carefully as she starts to eat.

With her other hand, Eleanor runs her fingers over the oak table. The table isn't as long as it might have been when used as a manor but isn't small either. Organically shaped, the oak is set on four thick legs. The chairs match in style, with a black cushion and multiple remain spare at either end of the table. They eat out of simple white bowls with silver cutlery that does not reflect the wealth of the estate, though the choice seems deliberate. The glass doors open onto a patio, and in the distance is the slight shadow of horses grazing. The walls are light grey stone, and the area better lit than you would assume from the tall ceiling.

"How come you're still wearing that?" Kaylee asks breaking the tense silence.

"I don't have anything else," Eleanor replies quietly.

The woman frowns and focuses her accusation at Michael who rolls his eyes.

"We're going shopping tomorrow," Kaylee declares. "May we borrow six guards? I have tomorrow off anyway, and Michael is just on babysitting duty, may as well let her go shopping."

"You really think taking her shopping in a populated place is a smart idea?" Nancy asks quizzically.

"Well, I'd say she has no idea what clothes she likes, so will need to try them on and I think letting her get out would be fun," she shrugs. "And I haven't gone shopping with another female in ages. I'm bored."

There is silence for a few moments as the Colonel considers the proposition.

"You promise you aren't going anywhere?" she asks Eleanor. As the child nods, Nancy sighs in submission. "You, Michael, and six guards accompany her, you lose her you are going to be paying for it."

"Yes ma'am," Kaylee nods with an encouraging smile to the girl. "You can borrow some of my clothes for tomorrow, it'll be fun, promise."

Eleanor nods with a soft smile and reaches to grab another serve.

"See, eating with people isn't so bad," Michael adds as she stabs into her bowl, only to earn an annoyed scowl.

"It's not that eating with people is bad… it's just that eating with people usually ends up with at least half the table dead," she whispers. "Or the serving staff, depends…"

Everyone frowns, not even one escaping the worry as Eleanor draws a hand over her braided hair, and almost immediately regains her composure.

"I'm fine," she says so quiet that Michael, with his enhanced hearing, is the only one to hear her. Louder, she asks, "So, do you all work directly for the National Agency of Protection? In what field are you all in?"

"We were created to provide Michael with a set team to work with. He's here on diplomatic exchange, and since NAP was created to investigate the presence of supernatural beings. Zach offered to sponsor the program, hence the house. Kenichi's international experience gives us a way to communicate with many people we wouldn't have previously," Kaylee explains with a grin. "I am rather useful with a gun and can do my fair share of espionage if necessary."

Though her gaze lingers on the dark corners of the room, Eleanor continues.

"You're very well set up…"

"Government wants us to keep the supernatural thing under wraps," Nancy smirks. "That creates lots of funding."

At the conclusion of the meal, Eleanor rises with the consent of the Colonel and walks silently back to her room. They all watch her leave without a word, though their confusion remains clear.

"She's not well…" Michael mutters. "Not well in the madness sort of way."

Kenichi, far more subtle about his own predictions of Eleanor's affliction, nods slowly.

"There's nothing we can do but try to nurture it out of her," he says, "and that may mean giving her as long as possible to decompress."

None reply, far too inexperienced in dealing with the intense psychological torment Eleanor seemed to still be held under by.

~

Every moment of her first few weeks in the manor surprises me. She is nothing like I remember her being, there is something missing from her presence that holds back the smile. One can only imagine the torment she went through at the Agency, but they somehow shattered her ability to act as a human.

The shopping trip helped to heal it a little, but it would take much longer for her to regain herself.

Chapter 12

A few days pass and suddenly something very heavy and very fluffy barrels into Eleanor as she attempts to walk into the library. She shrieks in surprise and falls backwards as the dog sniffs her and her new clothes in suspicion. Just as Eleanor regains her breath, Zach – the only one home at the time – rounds the corner in worry, but he can't help but laugh at the fierce assassin pinned by his German Shepard.

"I see you've met Bronte," he chuckles as the dog releases Eleanor from interrogation.

Bronte is mainly black, with brown on her face and feet and masses of hair that fill out her form. Eleanor scratches the dog fondly, a good deal more relaxed than she had been most other times Zach had seen her.

"I was wondering how I'd managed to avoid her for so long," she says. "Obviously, the library is her den."

"It is," Zach nods. "But she does roam every so often. You okay?"

"Fine, she just surprised me," Eleanor assures.

Zach leaves Eleanor to explore the library, a small grin on his face as he hears Eleanor swear under her breath at the sight. The shelves stretch to the ceiling and a ladder on a brass runner encircles the room. With a light skip in her step, Eleanor moves to the first row she sees and trails her fingers over the spines of the books, before she picks one from the ornate wooden bookshelves. Moving to one of the brown leather couches with large, studded arms, she drops into a single seater with her legs over the arm. Her eyes follow the lines in the book as Bronte curls at her feet.

When the time comes for dinner, Michael finds her still curled on the chair, eyes shut as she snores softly. The canine rises as he enters and wakes Eleanor before Michael can.

"It's time for dinner," he says, careful to be in her view as he does so. "We brought home some Thai."

Eleanor grips the hand he offers to help her up for a minute as she waits for her head to stop spinning. Now three months pregnant, her appetite had finally returned, although she rarely had much once she started eating.

"Do you have many more missions coming up?" she asks as they walk into the dining room and continue to the lounges to eat.

"We actually have to talk to you about that," Kaylee replies. "They're sending us all out on an overnight mission in a week or two. You can either stay here and be under the watch of the guards, who are completely capable of keeping you safe, or you can go and stay back in your cell at the compound. It's your choice."

Eleanor stills for a minute, and while her face remains neutral, her fingers twitch at an almost astounding rate. The tapping moves to hover over her stomach lightly as she releases a breath, her agreement seems to be more to herself, than any others.

"Can I stay here?" she asks, enclosed by the hair that falls in front of her face.

"Of course," Kaylee says. "Eat up, Zach said you didn't eat lunch."

Eleanor smiles slyly but follows instructions as Kaylee gives her an encouraging smile. At they eat, Kenichi gets an alert on his phone, but waits to answer Eleanor's quizzical glance until after she's finished.

"You have a doctor's appointment tomorrow," Kenichi explains. "She'll be coming at 11."

"Are you going to be there?" Eleanor inquires, but her curiosity doesn't cover her nervous ticks.

"I'm supposed to be working…" he apologises.

Freezing in place Eleanor starts the process to compress the fear rising in her chest. Her breaths are mechanical, measured – too even. Hands tremble in her lap, tapping out movements of memorised pieces. Gingerly she raises her eyes and reaches for some more food, but her left hand continues to press patterns into her thigh.

"I can ditch for an hour," Kenichi says. It's clearly the correct option, as Eleanor's shoulders drop.

"You don't have to," she murmurs.

"No, I understand why you're nervous, I can check over everything for you," he assures.

Her expression lifting, Eleanor replies with simple thanks.

Chapter 13

After she finishes dinner, Eleanor slips upstairs for a run in the gym. Her feet fall evenly, not too fast, but enough that she is tiring when Michael walks in.

He allows the confliction in his mind to arise as he watches her, so young and vulnerable. If she was here, it was likely his brother would escape Exilium Terras just to cause issues. The moment Eleanor knew Nikolas, she would stand by his side, not only because Michael suspected them to be divinely connected, but because he had suffered as she had. Even if she trusted the team, Eleanor was young, and lost and, Nikolas could easily sway her, and Michael knew he would have to let her go. Kaylee and Kenichi were not under the same laws, but even then, he doubted they could influence her.

Eleanor keeps him in the corner of her vision as she continues to run. Now more than ever, the tiniest part of her, one she doesn't understand, is guarded against him. Even though he has shown her nothing but kindness, she can't help but resist getting closer to him. The unknown had always scared her, but her instincts... they had always been right, so why was she so scared?

She stops the machine and moves over to a mat to stretch. Michael moves closer, undeterred by her focused gaze.

"So, you mentioned you are descended from angels... What about hell? Do they both have a presence here?" she asks.

"Yes, unfortunately," Michael says as he sits on a nearby seat. "Daemones. Offspring that the demons left when they last surfaced are half human, half demon. No matter how many generations go by, unlike us, their blood doesn't weaken, so they can live amongst the humans without worry however, we angels, must be selective, and only leave Angeli Terra to keep up to date with technologies. Not that we use them much, other than a few food production and medicinal techniques, we are entirely still operating in the early centuries."

"Don't you struggle with overpopulation?" she inquires.

"No, we lose enough people to fights against the Daemones that that isn't a problem, we generally stay around 50,000. In the old days, an angel used to come down during the bigger fights to finish it then give us some stronger-blooded children, who'd often have wings. But we haven't had any wings or new angels in hundreds of years," he answers slowly. "The Daemones look like humans but use contacts to cover their black eyes. They get the best of the gene pools, so it's very easy for them to attract prey."

"What is your kind called?" Eleanor asks, standing up slowly.

"Angeli," Michael replies. "And you need sleep, go to bed, Eleanor."

"Are these Daemones likely to attack you here?" she frowns, as she walks to the door.

"No, that would spark war," the man shrugs. "I'm more worried about my brother escaping and coming for me. And what would happen if he met you."

"Why me?"

"Because I think you're linked to him in a way you won't understand, and I'm scared of the power he could have with you at his side," he answers honestly.

He underestimated her. In fact, in later years, this would become a common mistake.

"What?" Eleanor frowns, but that same small part of her gets excited at the new information.

"It's nothing to worry about, you're safe. We will keep you and your baby safe," he assures. "Now please, go to bed."

Eleanor reticently agrees and walks to her room without turning back to Michael. She showers silently, letting the warm water wash over her pale skin. Mentally, she made note to go outside more.

Curled in her bed, pale blue eyes shut blissfully; eyelids slide smoothly, and Eleanor falls into calm sleep.

Four hours later, Eleanor screams. Her shoulders convulse, another scream rips from her rounded lips, her blonde friend comes running into the room. Removing the knife Eleanor hides under her pillow before she pins the girl's forearms.

"Ellie, wake up now," she orders as the girl fights harder. "Come on."

Moments later Eleanor springs upwards, empty hand quickly pressing to her friend's stomach. With the laugh of someone too used to murder attempts, Kaylee watches Eleanor's hand moves away as she realises where she is.

"What would you do if Kenichi or Michael came to wake you and hadn't taken the knife ¬— that you aren't supposed to have – and you stabbed them? Like you try to do to me," Kaylee chuckles as the girl sits up slowly and cradles her head.

"That's why you come," Eleanor replies. Throat aching, Eleanor takes the silent offer and rest her head on her friend's shoulder.

The teenager takes a hold on her breathing and lets shaking breaths blow through her mouth until they return to normal. Straightening, her hand rubs her stomach carefully, lips still parted. Kaylee brushes her hair back behind her shoulders with a sigh as the girl's eyes blink slower.

"You right to go back to sleep?" she asks.

"I should be," Eleanor answers as she lies back down. "Thank you."

"It's okay, Ellie," she replies. "Try to make it to morning."

The girl nods, though barely hears the words. Her eyes shut as Kaylee leaves, the door ajar. Shortly, a wet nose pushes itself under Eleanor's hand, which rests on her pillow. She pats the dog's head tiredly, and the dog takes that as all the permission she needs to jump up on the bed.

"Bronte," Eleanor whines as she fights to push the dog's nose away from her face.

Bronte curls at her back and stills, content as Eleanor shuts her eyes once again and falls back asleep.

Chapter 14

The dead of night leaves not a flicker of sound to disturb the sleeping girl. Guards mull around the house walls, doing regular duties on a normal night while the team is away.

With little more than a shout of surprise each falls dead at the hands of Daemonic soldiers, who pull back and allow for their commander to walk through. His twin swords glitter in his hands as the heads of the last few guards – who prepared for attack at the shouts of their companions – roll across the floor. With a flick of his hand, foot soldiers fan out to check the floor, while their leader steps up the staircase in deadly silence.

At the top he pauses and tilts his head in the warm air as a whimper echoes faintly from the room left of the stairs. Curiously, he watches the guards hidden in the shadows tense and move slightly to protect the door. With a signal for the soldiers to move past him and up to the next floor to complete the mission, he moves towards the door slowly... silently. Their guns are raised.

"Michael?" one checks, voice low.

"No," the man scoffs as he stalks forward. "Why would I want to be him?"

The words spit against the wall and the guards prepare to shoot. But the four of them stand no chance as the girl inside whimpers again and an unknown protectiveness fills the invader as he kills them all in a few seconds. One blade returns to its scabbard, the other leant just inside the door. His breath catches in his throat, his hand runs through his hair in shock.

Eleanor flinches again and a soft scream leaves her lips as her back arches, but her eyes stay shut. The dog who lies on the end of her bed rises to sniff the man suspiciously, before lazily returning to the bed. The man moves quickly – conscious of his time limit as he kneels beside the bed and touches her face lightly. A rare smile forms on his face as she unconsciously moves closer. He holds her head gently as she thrashes upward and her eyes snap open with a scream. But as she shakes in his arms, she doesn't pull away, her hand doesn't find the dagger hidden under her pillow. He softly strokes her hair and releases without hesitation as she pulls back, her senses regained.

"Hello Dulce Meum," he says, hands raised in surrender.

Eleanor's hand now inches towards her blade, cautious of the stranger in her room but wary of the safety she feels. A pale hand finds a plastic handle.

"Who are you?" she growls, voice strained but even.

"You don't need to know that," the man replies, his face indistinguishable in the darkness. "I am going to leave now, and you need to lock that door and not leave until someone you trust arrives. Understand me, Dulce Meum?"

Eleanor tenses as the English accented words send shivers down her spine. She grips the knife and pulls it slowly closer to her chest.

"Why are you here?" she asks, suspicion lacing her tone.

"I am here because my sister deserves to rule, and that includes clearing Michael from succession," he tells her.

Eleanor trains the knife to his throat with a perfectly still hand, but not one of the man's muscles flinch.

"Block your door, do not open it but for someone you trust," he orders as he eases to his feet with lethal grace and walks to the doorway. "Don't try to be heroic, Dulce Meum, I can only protect you so far. And be careful letting the Daemones see your face, everything they see is sent back to a database for analysis, and your face will be an alert as soon as we get the camera feeds working."

He pauses in the doorway to observe her as she sits up and faces him in confusion.

"Who are you?" she asks again, soft lips parted slightly.

"I don't know anymore," he whispers, barely audible.

The pain that flicks on his angular face sends a jolt through Eleanor, and she frowns. As her hand absentmindedly rubs her stomach, she releases a breath.

"I have the same problem," she murmurs.

"Nikolas, my name is Nikolas," he replies as he turns to exit.

"Mine is Eleanor, nice to meet you," the girl replies and the kindness in her tone makes Nikolas pause in surprise.

"Lock it, do not come out," he orders, shutting the door quickly as the girl rises to go over to him.

He waits until a faint click sounds before he walks away silently, his men already gone, and sword forgotten. Nikolas pauses in the kitchen to pick up a pen and a piece of paper and scrawl a note before following his soldiers out and away.

Eleanor slides to the floor where she had last stood, with her back to the wood until morning. Her fist grips the sword left by her visitor, knuckles white as she holds it tight. Michael notices the lack of guards first as the team return and is out of the car and swearing loudly as soon as they stop. He pushes through the door – past the dead –, with Kenichi now hot on his tail. Michael passes the scrap of paper to run up the stairs to Eleanor, who had been left alone in the house with no living guards. The bodies on the floor in front of her room are ignored as he attempts to open it. It is still locked.

"Eleanor!" he yells, fist pounding on the door. "Eleanor, open the door!"

And she does, relief on her face, but conflict in her eyes.

"Are you hurt?" he asks worriedly, but his attempts to hold her steady as she spots the bodies is ignored.

"Who is Nikolas?" Eleanor returns, hand protectively on her stomach as she steps over them and lightly swings the blade in her hand. "And why does he hate you?"

"Nikolas was my younger brother," Michael says. "Was, being the important word there."

Eleanor frowns at the clear omission but stays silent as Kenichi comes up the stairs and hands a note to his friend. The doctor stops the girl from reading it, hand lightly on her shoulder.

'I'm trusting you brother, but know, if she gets a single scratch on her, you will pay for it with your life,' it reads.

Michael crushes it into a ball.

"What's wrong?" she asks.

"Nothing. Just... try not to trip over." Michael, with a sigh, looks back to the lower level of the house. "Come on, we're going to go to the compound today. Someone can clean this place up and we'll be back by this afternoon."

Eleanor silently glides down the stairs, in her element with the bodies at nearly every bend. With a roll of her eyes, she gets a drink out of the fridge and sits at the bench.

"How are you so chill?" Zach frowns as he obviously averts his eyes from the death.

"These are some of the least revolting of the bodies I have seen over the years. I may be pregnant, but a lifetime of death has trained me well," Eleanor replies easily. "And leaving them here tells me that the offender is overdramatic in style. He fights pretty, probably too invested in sending a message to consider that we now know who he is, how he fights and what his men are capable of. The cameras never went down, so we can also analyse their fight patterns."

The group look at her in surprise, Michael particularly, as she examines the blade that she has in her lap. Immune to their reactions, Eleanor traces over the twisted leather grip and the golden etchings in the pommel with an absentminded hand. Without another word, she moves to the sink and washes the blood off the blade. As she finishes, she extends the handle toward Michael, expecting him to take it, but he doesn't.

"Put it up in your room," he sighs. "I don't want to see that thing again."

"You recognise it?" she asks, curious.

"Of course I do," Michael bites. "It tried to take my father's head off just under a year ago. My sister dearest must have smuggled it to him."

"No need to take that tone with me, I was purely curious," Eleanor snips, straightening her shoulders. "He managed to wake me up, without me stabbing him. No-one can ever do that."

"I will take you to Angeli Terra soon, let my sister decide what to tell you. She knows Nikolas way better than I ever did. She will know what to do," Michael tells her. "You needn't worry about being vulnerable with him, he can't hurt you."

"I wasn't," she frowns, "and that is what worries me."

"We'll figure it out Ellie," Kaylee assures, taking the girl's hand softly. "It'll be okay."

Chapter 15

Eleanor is standing on a platform, high above the crowds that surround her. It's a stadium, and the design vaguely reminiscent of the crumbling Colosseum in Rome. A girl – maybe twenty – with beautiful chestnut hair and striking green eyes, stands next to her, hand in hers, shaking. The body she is in can't move, but she knows it isn't hers; too tall, too strong. The body turns to look at a man who stands next to the pair. His hair is grey, eyes the same green as the girl next to her. His daughter maybe. There is anger on his face, but also pleasure, as Eleanor's body asks – no begs – for him to forget this.

"She made her bed when she took him to bed, Bastard," the man barks in return.

The gaze returns to the front where a woman is being led onto the dais below. She has the same chestnut hair as the girl beside her, but grey is leaking into the rich colour. A sharp face, like the girl next to her and Michael… and the man from last night. She shows no fear, as the silent crowd watches on in shock. The man rises from his throne and looks directly in the eye of his wife.

"I hereby condemn Katherine Nighglow—" her body scoffs "—of treason against the crown, and sinful acts for her own selfish gain," he calls. The words echo around the stone plaza. "As punishment for these crimes, she shall be executed."

The girl stifles a sob, and her brother pulls her closer, but both still watch the woman. Dressed still in her queenly robes, she drops to her knees behind a block and the executioner readies his blade. The woman's eyes find this body's, locking on as she silently mouths, 'it will be okay, I'm sorry'. The man shakes his head to impede the tear that wells in the corner of his eye. Katherine places her head on the block and her tears now roll down her cheeks. The blade swings, and the girl hides her face into her body's chest with a sob as metal hits stone, and a head lands on wood.

~

Eleanor jolts awake, her body alight with electricity as her hands scramble for the sketchpad next to her bed, and the pencil tin laid on top of it. The colours pour out across her bed cover, trembling hands selecting her weapons to begin. The sun is rising as she finishes, yet the dreadful scene holds her attention long after the last pencil drops. Not too much later, someone knocks on her door and Eleanor calls out to allow them in.

Michael walks over to look at what she has drawn but freezes as his eyes discover a picture of his homeland.

"You weren't there," she murmurs, "and you are a Prince."

Not a question, a statement. Michael nods slowly and run a hand through his hair in horror of the image he hadn't seen before. Eleanor closes the sketchbook silently, replaces the pencils to the tin and stands to grab herself some clothes.

"Did you know what was happening?" she whispers, just before he leaves.

"No, my sister has lectured me many times on my ignorance. It's mentioned in every conversation I have with her," Michael admits. "However, I still believe that what Nikolas did was wrong, and will stand by the decision to send him to Exilium Terras."

A pause, then a frown forms on her face.

"Translation?" she blandly asks, jaw tense.

Though it takes him a moment to comprehend, Michael answers, "Exile Lands."

With a slight shake of her head, Eleanor looks away.

"Am I likely to get more of his memories?" she sighs.

"I don't know, usually you would have to be in more contact with each other. But he may get some of yours." Michael shrugs. "If he tries to get in contact with you, tell me, okay?"

"But what if I want to meet him?" she grumbles as her gaze stays purposefully away.

"Eleanor," he warns. "You don't want to know him; he is a bad person, and I don't want you to decide to run away with him and endanger yourself."

The girl stays in icy silence and waits for him to leave before she shuts her door and changes. Her eyes linger for a few seconds on the sword next to her bed and she runs her finger down the straight blade in silent contemplation. Moments later Eleanor is out the door and down the stairs to sit at the marble topped kitchen bench, all the while her fingers tap out patterns on the edge of the stone. Kenichi tilts his head, focus on her fingers as he slides some food in front of the girl and sits next to her.

"What are you playing in your head?" he asks quietly, almost upset as her fingers stop abruptly.

"Clair de Lune by Debussy," she answers as she forces focus onto her food.

"And what is running through your head to make you have to output energy into a repetitive menial task?" the doctor questions with a smile.

"I don't know what you mean," she answers silkily. "I just like playing piano."

"You do that when you are thinking or grounding yourself. So, I was wondering what was on your mind."

"I..."

Eleanor seems lost for what to say for a minute, her fingers starting to move at her side before she abruptly stops herself. Kaylee sits on the other side of the bench as Eleanor begins.

"I am confused. Ever since I can remember, I have had this tense, cautiousness, in my heart, in my body," she says slowly. "Instinct, that's what Mei-, my trainer, called it. Told me that's what kept me safe for all those years, because my instinct was always wary, always on edge. It took years, five years, to be able to relax around him, same for Seb. Even here I can't fully relax, the most I did was when nobody was here. It is not something to feel bad about, I trust you more than

I do pretty much everyone in my life, but my instinct is always, always backed by my mind, and my mind always by my instinct, but now it's not."

"I was in a nightmare, and Nikolas woke me up, he held on to me. And I didn't attack him, I didn't recoil, I just stayed. Then my head caught up with my body and I knew something was wrong, this was not someone I knew, but even still, my instinct stayed silent. I let him leave, with knowledge I've told pretty much no-one. And I had another nightmare, of a place I've never seen, with people I've never met. I drew it, and Michael saw. He told me he believed his brother should be in exile, for trying to kill the King, even though that King killed his mother. It angered me. If he could be so accepting of me, then why not his own brother?"

They both sit with a soft smile as Eleanor rants. Listening to every word, Michael stays around the corner to give her the space she needed, but he doesn't like it, he doesn't like how his brother so easily brought her into their affairs.

"Michael is very stuck in his ways, and he has to be, to be in the position he is in," Kaylee starts. "He chooses to pay attention to the near killing of his father instead of the killing of his mother, because that is what is easier for him. His father dies and he is stuck in a musty old castle for the rest of his life. And his mother, he believes, got herself killed..."

"She made her bed when she took him to bed," Eleanor whispers, "that's what the King said, to Nikolas."

"Yes, and Michael is very much his father's child, he idolises the man, but you have to understand why. His is the oldest child, destined for the throne, and has been taught for years to be the King. Nikolas believes that he does not deserve the throne, because of how alike he is to his father, who Nikolas, probably fairly, hates. Their sister is the middle child, very smart, also not her father's biggest fan, and her and Nikolas are closest of the siblings. He believes she should rule, but their father refuses because she is a girl, and refuses to let Nikolas because he is illegitimate.

"Michael doesn't like his little brother, because of many things that have built up in the time he has been here, but he still grew up with him, still cares that little bit. That's why he accepted you. He is very righteous, doesn't believe in people who kill... probably the angel blood. But you are connected to Nikolas, and he knew this because he is still a blood relative, that's why you felt a little safer around him. As a last tribute to his brother, to show he is better than him, he took you in. To him you are like a sister he needs to take care of, but he still hates Nikolas for what he did," Kaylee explains, the girl listening intently.

"What do you think of Nikolas?" she asks in a soft voice.

"I am... inclined to dislike him," the woman starts carefully, watching for a negative reaction but finding just placidity on her face. "He seems rash, undisciplined, with anger issues to rival the worst. He is also cocky with no control over his actions, and he killed 20 of our guards for no good reason. However, I do respect his treatment of you, that night."

"Michael refuses to let me know how I am connected to him. Do you know?" she continues.

"I do; however, it is his choice to tell you, and I will leave it to him," Kaylee answers slowly. "You are young, Eleanor, you do not need to worry about all of that on top of what you already do."

"I'm 16," she mutters.

"And should be in high school, getting good grades and making friends," the woman snaps. "But that isn't an option for you, so you are stuck here, and as long as you are stuck here then we can decide what you know. Don't forget you are still a criminal. We have made allowances because you are a child, and you have been mistreated your entire life. While others wouldn't, we think that you deserve a chance at normal life until you reach an age and condition in which we can fairly put you on trial."

The girl freezes for a second then nods, slowly, carefully. Glancing at her finished plate, she stands up easily and places it in the dishwasher, leaving the room. Michael only just ducks into a room quick enough to avoid her as she storms into the games room and sits at the piano, hands quickly flying across the keys. By the time she's done, Kenichi and Michael are standing in the door, watching carefully.

"He plays piano as well," Michael calls, drawing her attention. "Mother always loved listening to him when he played."

Eleanor smiles fondly, spinning in the seat and lowering the cover of the piano. Her head tilts slightly, watching the man as he does her, before she rises and walks over. She pauses just in front of them, eyes examining the look on his face with practiced expertise.

"It worries me, your connection to my brother, because I do care for you, and I know my father isn't the man I thought he used to be," Michael admits. "I am sorry, for snapping. I don't know what it's like to have the bond you have with him, but I know it confused you. I'm sorry I put you in that situation."

The teenager bites her lip for a second, head tilting even more as she watches him. Her fingers twitch at her side, mind turning over a thousand thoughts a second. But she steps forward and wraps her arms around his middle, head only coming to his shoulders. He hugs back after a second, stroking her hair softly and releasing easily as she steps backwards.

"I've done worse trying to protect someone," she shrugs. "I just cover for myself when I'm confused, means no one can see me weak. Lack of knowledge is a fault; I need to be perfect at all times. I cannot let people see me as anything but the perfect student."

"You can, we don't expect you to know everything," Kenichi sighs, leading their way out. "And no one is perfect in this world, you should know that."

"I do, but it's the image of perfection that's kept me alive. Acting is easier than letting people in," Eleanor mutters. "I am going to go train, see you later."

"But you're pregnant," Michael frowns, making her stop and turn with a laugh.

"And about to put a hell of a lot more weight on; I want to retain some of my fitness," she giggles.

"I'm sure you'll be fine," he exhales.

Chapter 16

"**M**iss Beck, pleasure to see you again," Nancy Randall nods, sitting across the dining table from the teenager with Michael at her side.

"As it is mine, Colonel," the girl mimics, hair tightly wound into a bun with white bone pins holding it in place.

"Now, I am not at all happy about it, but Michael has managed to nearly convince me to let you go to his homeland with him. He wants you to meet his sister, apparently. We are at a loss, however, of how to take you there without raising the suspicion of the King," the older woman starts, watching as the girl tips her head. "As someone trained at getting into places without suspicion, we thought you might have some ideas."

Eleanor tilts her head, blinking quickly as the thoughts roll around her head, before her head straightens and her eyebrows furrow.

"Have you talked to your father about how Nikolas got out?" she asks, receiving a shake of the head. "Why don't I go as an agent for you, to get information on the person who attacked your team? It would be easy to back up wanting information firsthand, and it would get me in without anyone thinking I'm a potential partner of the crown Prince."

"That could work," Michael agrees, looking to the older woman.

"How would we disguise your pregnancy?" the woman asks.

"My bump isn't too big, we could easily disguise it with a binding around my stomach, under a military uniform it shouldn't be distinguishable between a little bit of fat and a baby bump," Eleanor replies easily.

"The NAP uniform is tight fitting..."

"I'm not that pregnant," she scoffs, getting a look from both adults. "It will be fine."

"Your accent, that's a problem," Michael notes, "My father knows a German accent from an American. He'll pick up on the changes in your tone compared to mine."

"What, you don't think I went on missions with such a tell on my voice," the girl bites, letting her voice morph into a purely American accent. "Come on, you think so little of me."

"Can you keep it up for a week, two even?" Nancy asks.

"Of course I can, honestly you people," Eleanor laughs, eyes flicking in delight.

"And your age, how do we disguise that?"

"It's amazing what a good lick of makeup can do to make someone look older, and my maturity is hopefully not even in question," she assures, "I've passed as an adult at gala events more times than I could count."

"You're sure you can act as one of our agents, and do the job your supposed to while you're there?"

"Yes, I have been doing this for years, this is easy compared to some of my missions." Eleanor sighs. "You seem to forget I'm not just a teenager sometimes, I beg you to not question my ability."

"How about the fact you will have to meet my father?" Michael mutters, raising his eyes to meet hers with challenge.

"I've met many rulers, why is this one any different?"

"Because Nikolas hates him more than anyone else in the world," the man answers instantly. "Because that hate may pass to you, and I don't want you to try and kill my father."

"I have control..."

"So did he..."

"If you're so worried about it then just keep your little taser button on you, but for this to work you must act like you trust me, make them believe it. Otherwise, I'll go in like a lamb to slaughter, and I'm sure a certain someone wouldn't like that, would he?" Eleanor says, flicking her waves back nonchalantly.

"You can't manipulate us, you are still our prisoner, Eleanor," Nancy warns.

"I am not manipulating you; I am ensuring that he is thinking this over. His brother, I believe, would not take lightly to you giving me over to the King, would he?" the girl replies, letting her gaze fall upon the camera blinking in the corner. "I came here because my death will be easier. I'll get to hold my baby, say goodbye. I don't want to get trapped there; I don't want to die without being able to hold it. That's why I have to have a contingency plan."

The two adults stare at her for a minute, the girl returning their gazes with ease. She doesn't tilt her head, in fact it stays perfectly upright, with only two little creases between her arched eyebrows to show her turning mind.

"I trust you," Michael sighs.

"But we have made a more concealable version of your tracker anklet, so you will be wearing that, at all times," the Colonel orders, her charge nodding easily. "Is seven days enough to prepare?"

The assassin simply answers with a yes, biting back a remark on her training in place for disguising her uncharacteristic confidence.

"Then I will see you in seven days," the woman nods, standing and leaving the pair behind.

They stay seated for minute, before the girl rises to sit outside, Michael following her quietly and sitting next to her as she lays out on one of the cushion-covered, reclining deck chairs. After a few minutes, her shoulders relax and after a set of rapid blinks, a soft sigh slips from her.

"You sure about this... lie?" Michael asks her softly, frowning as a snake like hiss leaves her lips.

"It is not lying," she scowls, "I will still be doing the job I tell them; I will still report to my superior with the information I gather. What is the difference if I'm only doing that for a day or two?"

"Because you will be lying about who you are," the man mutters.

"I have been many people in many places over the years, Michael. For once I'm actually going as Eleanor Beck, that's more than I have ever gotten before," she shrugs. "You've seen the immensity of my missions, gathering information as myself is nothing."

"Just don't let them find out you're an assassin," he mutters, "and do not mention Nikolas, or my mother, or anything outside of the information packet I will get to you."

"Not letting people know I know things that I'm not supposed to is right up there on my resume," Eleanor smiles, "and I am sorry about earlier. About threatening you with him, it was wrong."

"Thank you," the man nods. "Why did you keep glancing at the camera?"

So, he did notice, she wonders if the woman did too.

"Why else would he have come that night, if not to learn our patterns with surveillance footage?" she replies easily.

"We found no evidence of camera tampering…"

"Think about it, Michael, you said your brother is smart, I think that it wouldn't be hard for him to formulate a way to connect to our systems without you guys being able to boot him off," the girl giggles, a slight smirk twinging at the corner of her mouth. "Heck, I've done it myself a few times, you'd be surprised how with the right tech, you can get into anywhere, or control anything."

Changing the topic, Michael follows with, "did you usually have to come up with your own plans? You seem quite good at it."

"Sometimes," she shrugs. "Some missions were fully planned, as I needed to be a specific person, others I needed to make a plan, then I would ask for the resources I needed, outfits, ID, tickets to a place."

The conversation drops off, the two staying outside as Michael ran over her words in his head.

"Did they ever send you into death traps? I'd assume not, judging by how much they wanted to get you back…"

"No, they definitely did. I think sending a 15 year old into the Japanese Yakuza alone counts as a death trap," she murmurs, the words that followed sending a stab into her chest. "And they sent me into a maximum security prison once, to kill an inmate…"

The man doesn't take note of how her words trail off at the end of her sentence, or the blank look that covers her features before she stands and walks away. Doesn't see her hands wring around her wrists, or rub her lower back to try and ease the phantom throbbing that was making her knees shake.

He doesn't see when she walks into her room, the door not closing fully as she rushes onto her bed and curls around one of her dark green pillows. Doesn't see as the girl, who was always strong, always acting, slips, and falls on the stage. Doesn't see her cry into her pillow.

But she sees everything, the steel bars, the table, the cuffs. She feels the searing, the burning across her lower back. The hunger in her stomach, the dry of her throat. She feels the stinging across her face. Tastes the blood in her mouth, tears on her lips that would not give, would not succumb to their attempts. Can smell the bleach they use to clean the floors, the heavy deodorant each of the men wore. Hear the words, rattling in her head, that could save her from it, words she couldn't let escape the mess of her head.

She remembers the cold steel in her hand as the cuffs were unlocked, a familiar hand pulling her out of her seat dragging her out of the room. Her feet pounding in time with her head as they cleared the grounds, made it to the safe house. She remembers the lecture, then the dinner, sleep. She remembers not being able to let go of him for hours as she couldn't stop the trembling. And he didn't want to let go of her either, to be fair. Later on, when talking to Sebastian, her only friend, about the incident after she'd had a nightmare, she learned that her Vater had gone against the orders he was given, to dispatch her, and had suffered a beating for it.

Chapter 17

Eleanor stays, curled on her bed for hours, alone. And watching the camera feed, thanks to the tiny gap between the door and the sensor, is Nikolas.

He had been trying to avoid gathering intel on her (his excuse to himself, really, he was worried he'd grow attached to the girl), however he had to find out what his brother was planning to do in retaliation for his attack, and with the Colonel there as well, he had to observe. He was not happy when he discovered they were trying to take her to his home, and the declaration of her pregnancy threw him. More so the talk of her missions, due to her previously declared teenager status. The anger that picked up as he discovered her to be a prisoner there... it did not dissipate very quickly.

He watched this girl, as she spun the web for her own safety, and the urge to protect her rose to meet his anger. Eleanor chose her words, looked right at him through the screen. He learnt that she was not just a girl trying to survive, but a woman who had been playing the game for years, who knew what to say to ensure her survival. And yet she knew she would die, and that made him more mad.

Nikolas kept watching the ash haired girl as she let herself relax. He took note of the movement, and later when reviewing the footage, he noticed the change in her behaviour, noticed the mask. She talks down his brother's worries with ease and Nikolas learns she is an assassin; the protective feeling rises again. She apologises, and his brother continues to question her – anger rises to meet the protectiveness. He smiles as she calls him smart, then just watches her talking, mostly tuning out the words – and his brother's voice.

Until he sees her body tense, from her gut to her slender shoulders, and hears her words trail off. He sees the blank look on her face that his brother missed, he sees her hands wringing around her wrist, the shake in her step as the slim fingers find her lower back. He watches helplessly as she curls on her bed, the shaking of her shoulders indicator enough of the sobs that wrack her body.

Then he feels the stinging, the cold of metal. Smells the bleach. Tastes the copper and salt. Only for a second, enough to make him jump back from the table. But as he looks back to the girl, he knows that it was her memory. And he leaves, shutting the system off and ensuring that no-one caught him watching the crying girl.

There was an attack on a military base in Jackson, Mississippi, that night. When the day workers came in, they walked in on a massacre. When they reviewed the footage... one man, clothed in black and green, with brand new blades.

Michael knew what it was.

The Colonel knew what it was.

A warning. The wrath they would face if things went awry.

~

I think I may be the only person to ever see the two scars on the very base of her back. Unlike the others, these are just two dots, maybe four centimetres apart. Little burns, as if someone had pressed a piece of red hot metal to make her talk.

A cattle prod, even.

Chapter 18

No longer did Eleanor Beck stand as a teenager in front of the Colonel, but instead a seasoned agent. With her hair twisted into a tight bun at the base of her neck and her face made to be perfect, the girl stands with her feet shoulder width apart, hands linked behind her back. Covered from ankle to wrist in a tight black uniform, she looked formidable.

"Is this acceptable, Colonel?" she asks, the confident spark in her eye gleaming like the polished silver badge sitting in a pocket on the belt of the suit.

"Yes," the woman nods, "Now, you know the information in your packet?"

"Of course I do."

"And you know what not to say?"

She fixes the woman with a look, the questions stopping.

"I assume I get no weapons?" the girl turns, a question she had been putting off asking ever since the plan had been formed.

"No, Michael asked that you carry twin swords," Nancy counters, gesturing for them to bring something forward. "He said that you may need to show you're worthy of the King's presence, as a human."

"I'm being told now?" Eleanor hisses.

"Yes, you will be fine," Michael answers, walking up from behind them. "The suit has extra protection built around the stomach and chest, and you can fight, we all know that."

She nods, fixing her eyes on the man.

"I hope you find these to be acceptable," he smiles, taking something from the guards.

Her eyes find a pair of beautiful black and green twin blades, a worryingly joyful smile forming on her face. She picks one up by the blade, hand on the black flat side as she lifts it closer to inspect the green tinted sharp edge. With a trained thumb, she checks the keenness of its edge before running her fingers over the two arched points along the blunt side of the blade before she looks up and grins again.

"You used the drawings in my book," she smirks, swinging the blade around in her hand.

"We did, figured you liked the style," Michael nods, offering the other forward.

"I do, thank you."

Eleanor flips the blades in her hands, getting a feeling for their weighting as the Colonel runs through the last details of what she needs to do.

"I will be fine," she assures the woman as she continues to rattle on. "It's almost like you're worried about me."

A smirk plays on her lips as Nancy fixes her with an annoyed look, before turning to Michael who was trying to contain a laugh.

"If they get close to discovering her actual position, you get her out of there, understood?" she orders. "I won't have you losing my prisoner."

"Don't worry, Nancy, she'll come back, safe and sound," he smirks.

She nods gruffly, stepping aside so that the pair can walk towards the helicopter that waits on the landing pad. The man hands Eleanor a crossed scabbard, letting her slide the blades back into their cases before they step up into the black chopper.

Both stay absolutely silent as the ignition kicks in and it lifts from the ground, Michael piloting it eastward. Eleanor keeps her eyes locked downward as they pass out of the compound's land and over a field. She spots a person, standing just inside the tree line as they reach the other end of the grass field, head tilting just slightly as she watches the man. He nods tersely as their eyes meet, and Eleanor returns the gesture, the slightest smile pulling up the corner of the man's lips as they pass overhead.

"Eleanor?" Michael asks softly, voice crackling through the headset.

"Yes?"

"He is sour, and isolating. He always has been. You do not need that in your life."

"I am still a girl, Michael. I can't help wanting someone to care for me."

"We can look after you."

"It's different. I trusted my trainer, I felt safe around him, but it was different when I was with Seb, I felt…"

"Did you know his name, your trainer?"

"No, I called him sir for the first few years, then switched to Mein Vater after that."

"What did he call you?"

"…Kleiner Fuchs."

An eyebrow raises.

"Little Fox."

"What's the name on your tattoo?"

She doesn't respond, at least not for a few minutes.

"Kitten."

Chapter 19

They barely talk most of the way, letting the hum of the helicopter engine drown out their thoughts as they move over the ocean. But as they near their destination, Michael breaks the silence.

"You can trust my sister not to spill anything," he says simply. "And her maids are trustworthy as well."

"Okay."

Eleanor keeps her gaze out the window, hands twitching nervously in her lap.

"We're going to land in five minutes, and once we get within a hundred meters of The Island, you'll be able to see it," he continues. "We are going to have to horse ride up to the palace, but Kenichi said it would be fine. I assume you can ride enough for it to not be a problem..."

"I can."

"Are you scared?"

"No."

"Then why are you so clipped?"

"Habit."

"Will you be okay when we land?"

"Yes."

"Eleanor..."

"What Michael?"

"There will be a party tonight… to welcome me back. You will have to come."

"I will be fine."

"You won't, not at our parties, not alone. So you need to stay with my sister and get out as soon as you can."

"I've been at wild parties."

"Not like these."

"Okay then."

"Thank you."

Eleanor moves her head from the window, looking at the man across from her for a second.

"What if I have a nightmare?" she asks very tentatively.

She had avoided the topic before, but now she felt it had to be asked.

"I have requested you get Nikolas's old room, seeing as though he will never use it again. It is the best available room and I said that it would be good to treat you as a guest. The room is still decorated as his, Anastasia ensured they didn't touch it, so you should sleep better in there than normal. My room is next door so if you do have one, I will be there before you can wake anyone else," he assures. "You should be able to see it in a second."

Sure enough, a few seconds later an island reveals itself, all the fog disappearing as they start to land. It's large, seemingly made from a volcano that now sits dormant in the centre of the island, with huge green plains held above the sandy beaches by rock faced plateaus. Winding rivers run down two of the fields, the third dotted with various training mechanisms and people. Further off, she can see a few other islands, one with a stone stadium, much like the Colosseum, the one from her dream, and a huge stone building next to it. On the other side of the mountain, there is a sliver of trees but the view disappears as they begin to drop towards the plateau. Not a single inch of surprise sits on her face at the reveal.

Eleanor's hands still, shoulders relax, and eyes steady as the helicopter touches down on the ground. No one would know she was only 16. They slide out of the helicopter as the rotors slow, grabbing their bags and jogging out of the helicopters range before the pair slow to a walk. With a quick shuffle her new swords settle on her back, the straps quickly attached to the belt that sits around her waist.

"Is that comfortable? We couldn't exactly fit it to you," Michael asks, focus staying forward as they move closer to the five people waiting with an extra two horses across the field.

"Yes, perfect," she replies, "thank you."

He nods softly, before stopping as they reach the greeting party. Of the party, four are male, clothed in black, with gold plated armour across their top half. All also wear a single, thick, undecorated, gold band around their heads; and one female stands just in front of them; who unlike the men, wears midnight blue. Her top is flowing and tucked into a pair of cream breeches which sit perfectly on her long legs, a matching tiara sits on her head of beautiful chestnut hair. She stays perfectly straight as the men bow to the pair. Michael inclines his head to his sister, and Eleanor stays standing with her head tilted ever so slightly. He had told her she didn't need to bow to the greeting party unless he did.

"Welcome home, brother," the woman grins, stepping forward and offering a hand to Eleanor. "You must be from that agency, I'm Princess Anastasia Mornblade, it's nice to meet you."

The teenager takes the soft hand in her hardened one, shaking it kindly.

The green of her eyes is the same as the girl in the dream.

"Eleanor Beck, special operative for the United States of America, I work for Colonel Nancy Randall," she returns. "And it is an honour to meet you."

The Princess looks curiously at her for a second, before letting go of her hand and giving her brother a look. She steps back and turns to the four guards behind her, head held with an air of authority.

"Are we allowed to go back now?" she asks then, earning a wince from the four men.

"His majesty just wanted to ensure that the Prince was safe," one tells her.

"Yes and he didn't trust that I wouldn't run away," she snaps.

The guards shift awkwardly, but do not deny her claim. Eleanor steps forward, interrupting the accusation by walking up to one of the horses and stroking its nose.

"Shall we go to the city?" she calls, making everyone turn to her in surprise. "I've heard it's beautiful."

"Michael needs to change, it is not appropriate for him to return in human clothes," Anastasia mutters, grabbing a cloth bag from her horse and chucking it at her brother. "Hurry up."

Eleanor's eyebrow raises in amusement as the man shakes his head in annoyance and trudges over to a small wooden hut not far from where they landed and slams the door. With a low chuckle, the girl turns back to the horse, a big black mare who seemed determined to knock her over if she doesn't continue to pat her.

"That horse doesn't like many people," the Princess says, walking over and running a hand down the mare's head. "She has earned her name."

"What is it?"

"Ferox, for she is as wild as the name itself. But for people she likes she's more like a puppy," she laughs. "I was going to ride her, given how she likes being with our horses, but you can ride her if you'd like. Of course, if you would like something with a little more sanity, my mare is as calm as you can get."

"You would be fine with me riding her?" Eleanor asks, finger playing with the horse's lip.

"Yes, I think you remind her of her old owner."

"I'll take her, a little spice never hurt anyone."

A grin forms on the Princess's sharp face, but it's dampened as one of the guards behind us snickers. Eleanor spins on her heel, fixing the man with a smouldering glare, which turns to a slight smirk as he cowers away from her.

"Is there a problem?" she asks, letting her gaze flick between the other three guards.

"I apologise, ma'am, but only the best of our riders can last ten minutes on that thing, Princess Anastasia one of them. I doubt a human could last five seconds," one excuses, managing to hold her gaze as a wildfire sparks her eyes.

"If the Princess says I can ride her then I believe her. Really, I thought Royal Guards would be better trained to respect their superiors."

Each of the men bow their head a little in shame, and after casting an assuring look to the Princess, Eleanor moves to the mare's shoulder, scratching down her neck. The horse nickers softly, almost urging her to get up, so the girl places her boot in the stirrup and boosts her other leg up and over.

Until her other foot slides into the stirrup, it's as if the horse doesn't breathe, not a single muscle moves in her entire body. But then the girl's small hand places itself on her neck, and the mare relaxes significantly.

"Be very light with your riding, you will be absolutely fine," Anastasia tells her, before walking away and mounting her own horse.

Michael walks out of the shed, pained expression on his face as he glares at his sister. Beside her, Eleanor is barely containing her laughter as she looks over his outfit. From the white vest with golden thread and embellishments, to the loose white sleeves, tight fitted white pants and long golden cape that is attached from the shoulder pads, she barely suppresses her amusement. He strides over with a glare directed entirely on his sister.

"Why is she on that damn horse!" he growls, making it to Eleanor's side in a few strides, but steps back as the mare rears back.

Eleanor grabs a handful of the horse's mane but stays still as the mare touches back down and skits away from the man. She stops a few meters away, calming under her riders' soft hand.

"I can ride, Michael. And the horse likes me, it will be fine," Eleanor snips, fixing the man with a hard look to rival his sisters.

"You can't get hurt, remember," he warns, holding the stare for just long enough to make the guards edge away from the pair.

"I am fine, I wouldn't put myself in that position," she returns. "Now, I would quite like to get moving, if that's okay with you?"

The man sighs, moving over to his horse – a bright chestnut – and swinging up into the saddle. The Princess moves her grey mare off her leg, asking for a light trot back the way they must have come to get here.

Eleanor's horse prances after it, turning the mare in a circle to try and slow her, but the mare continues to half rear as she jumps sidewards to take the lead. Michael raises an eyebrow and gives her a look, challenging her decision as the mare continues to chuck a fit.

"Can your horses keep up with her?" Eleanor asks, staying still in the saddle, as still as she can.

"Yes—"

"Barely—"

The siblings answer simultaneously, but Eleanor takes the younger's affirmation and ignores Michael as she turns the mare straight on and gives her a light click, grabbing a handful of the long black mane and letting loose a wild laugh as the mare streams out ahead of everyone.

The guards shout in worry as the three leave them behind, but they are paid no heed as they are left in the dust.

Chapter 20

Eventually, the Princess moves her horse to Eleanor's side, muttering a 'hold on' as she takes one of the mare's reins and turns it into hers. With a quick movement, both horses are stopped, Ferox standing at 90 degrees to the Princess with her head over her horse's neck. Both of them are panting, a feral smile crosses the girl's face as she laughs tiredly.

"You didn't tell us you could ride like that," Michael mutters as he comes closer to the pair.

"There's a lot I haven't told you."

Their eyes meet, and the elder shakes his head as he finds the wild dominance flaring in her pale blue irises. Eleanor lets herself look around, over the bright cyan ocean and perfectly white sand. They had dropped down a ramp from the plateau onto the beach, also having crossed a flowing creek which Michael told her was from one of their farms. But then, feeling the Princess's eyes on her, she turns back to the woman.

"I saw you in a nightmare, once," Eleanor starts, letting her facade soften as she talks.

Anastasia releases a breath of shock

"Then you've met him, my brother?" she says, looking over the girl in wonder.

"Briefly, he attacked where I was staying, killed everyone except me."

"You haven't explained it to her?"

The question is directed behind her, to the woman's brother.

"There are complications..."

"Other than her being human?"

"Yes."

Eleanor looks back the way they came, able to see the guards catching up, she turns back to the siblings quickly.

"We will talk about it later, it is not safe for me and I would hate to have to silence anything that escaped containment," she interrupts.

The Princess looks from her brother to the girl and back again but stays quiet as they are joined again by the guards. One sidles up to the Princess and takes her arm, twisting it so she faces him lets out a yelp of pain.

"Don't pull another stunt like that again missy," he snarls, shoving her back a little before moving his horse over to the Prince. "We will be moving through Meridionali Urbis to the Flumine Magno where we will board the barge that will take us to the Arce Magnam to greet the King and introduce your... guest."

The man nods, the ice grey irises only skipping over his sister for a second before he turns to Eleanor and finds her frowning.

"I'm sorry, Latin is one of the few languages I don't speak. Could you please translate?" she sighs, tilting her head in annoyance.

"We are going through the southern side of the city to get to the river, which takes us to the grand castle," Anastasia explains, smiling softly at Eleanor, "to introduce the first human to step foot in Angeli Terra in 400 years, to the King of the last remnants of the angels."

A breathy laugh leaves Eleanor's lips, followed by an odd sort of smile as she looks to Michael.

"Look at me, doing important things," she smiles, "harmless, important things."

"We need to go, has your guest been informed of the protocols?" the guard who had spoken earlier asks Michael, ignoring the two girls.

"Yes, she has."

Nothing else is said as Michael pushes his horse forward and the two girls follow, ensuring their horses stay a half meter behind his chestnut as they round a corner and suddenly a city comes into view.

Backing into the mountain in the centre of the island is a huge stone city. It lines the river they must have been talking about earlier, and is only just visible, as it turns inland and is hidden by the houses. They're not really 'houses' though, more like vintage cottages and manors, growing larger and more spread apart as Michael leads them up a cobblestone road, and through a plaza. The area is filled with people, of all ages and descriptions, who part like the Red Sea as their horses start to walk through the square. The children are at the front, all looking up at Michael in awe as he waves to them with one hand, the other keeping his horse's walk under control. The adults look to the two girls instead, watching as Eleanor's eyes flick over the crowds and Anastasia waves her pale hand gently to some of the little girls. Some take notice that the newcomer is riding their disgraced Prince's horse and riding it with such ease it is as if they had been partnered for years.

The party pass under a stone arch between the two end buildings of the square, the path following up a little bit, before they start to drop down towards the river. All the way, people hang out their windows, or stand in their doorways, cheering the Prince all the way down to the river. The architecture reminds Eleanor of Rome, with thin cobbled streets, and distinct stone arches around the doorways, the scene triggers a set of flashes behind her eyes.

Anastasia watches her, green eyes flicking in worry as the mare pauses, bending her head around to nudge her rider's leg in confusion. But with a slight shake of her head, Eleanor clicks the mare forward again, raising an eyebrow to the Princess as she catches her frowning at her. Continuing down, they arrive at a barge, edged in gold, with an elaborate golden angel figurehead on the bow.

The horses all stop, not needing to be told, and stay perfectly still for their riders to dismount. Eleanor does so with as much grace as she can, however the harsh movement makes her sway in her spot, white knuckles gripping her horse's mane until it passes.

"You alright?" Michael whispers as they walk onto the barge, hand lightly on her arm to steady her.

"Yeah, just…" she murmurs, trailing off as she shakes her head a little.

"Moved too fast?"

Eleanor nods silently, stepping back to where Anastasia is sitting on one of the benches and lowers herself next to her; Michael starts waving to the crowds. The horses are being led away by other guards.

The Princess hands her companion a drink, watching as the girl dips her finger into it and tastes it carefully. She smiles weakly, letting a soft breath leave her lips as she lowers her hand.

"What's wrong?" Anastasia asks, looking over Eleanor as if trying to discover an answer.

"I... don't drink alcohol," she replies, the words sticking just enough against her lips that the Princess frowned.

"Why not?" the woman inquires.

Glancing around, the assassin finds the guards to close for comfort, obviously listening, so instead urges a slight tremble into her hands, and casts her eyes away slightly, crafting a lie.

"My ex, he was an alcoholic. Beat me. It triggers bad memories," she says, "Could I have a glass of water though?"

"Sure," Anastasia nods, the hint of suspicion still in her eyes, but she waves a hand and someone brings over a glass of water.

"Thank you."

Eleanor lets her eyes gaze upwards, past where Michael stands waving and up to the huge stone castle. Two arching, golden bridges sit across the river at different stages, allowing for people to cross from each side without hassle, but beyond them sits a beautifully carved, English Gothic style stone castle, built into the side of the mountain. The roofs, from what she could see, are a grey slate tile, with two spires reaching upwards towards the orange sky. It was only now that Eleanor noticed the sun was setting, golden light cast across the group's faces as it lowers into the western skies.

"When did you meet my brother?" the Princess asks, watching with an amused smile as the girl tenses abruptly, then hides it with ease.

"A few months ago. I was paired with his team for a mission, have been working with them since. I was exposed to our little problem a few weeks back and since I've been working in embassies and gaining information for as long as I can remember, Colonel Randall decided to send me," Eleanor replies, blotting over her slight lapse.

"Have you met our little problem more than once?"

"No."

"And Michael has been treating everyone fairly, hasn't lost his temper?"

She didn't mean everyone. The pause in the Princess's even speech indicates enough.

"No, he hasn't. Snapped once, but everything has been fine otherwise."

"He doesn't think things through more often than not, but it seems that that girl, Kaylee, seems to be good at calling him out for it."

"Yes, she is."

"I think you're more intelligent than you let on..."

"Very possible, Your Highness, but I am also an excellent actor. Revealing my full capabilities in a place where I've never been before is not something I will allow myself to do."

"Yes, that was my second thought about you... you don't let anyone know how much you can do so you always have a card up your sleeve."

The two women look at each other in interest, eyes locking in a battle of minds.

"If you grew up the way I did, then you would understand why," Eleanor shrugs, turning to face forward again. "I was told there would be a welcome home party for Michael, however I doubt the one dress I brought will hold up to the formality."

"After you meet the King, I can take you to get one. We can get to know each other a little better," the Princess smiles, a mischievous sparkle in her eye. "Now I must warn you to be on your guard, this may be the land of angels, but we have human blood as well. A pretty human thing like you could end up being mistreated."

"I can protect myself."

"I'm sure of it, but we are stronger than you, and as much as Michael says he can protect you from it, he often ends up forgetting on the night," she continues, smirking as the Prince turns around.

"Anastasia, don't spread lies about me," he says, shaking his head in annoyance.

"I'm not lying, I think you'll find yourself with a bit of a head problem in the morning, Brother," Anastasia laughs. "I leave early, Miss Beck, you can join me if you'd like?"

"That would be great, thank you."

Both girls let themselves look to the other again, finding a similar look in each other's eyes before they turn forward again. The river starts to thin, people growing closer and closer to the barge as they near the castle. The closing proximity uncovers an arch in the base of the castle, letting boats moor in a huge marble pillared atrium. Eleanor cranes her head back as they pass under the meter wide sandstone blocks.

Then her head rights itself and she looks around, letting herself take it all in. Most of the stonework is in a cool grey, but scattered around the place are details in yellow sandstone. A set of four guards, dressed in immaculate uniforms, stand waiting to moor the barge. Beyond them is a set of huge wooden doors, with golden hinges, bigger than her hands.

With a slight jerk, they pull to a stop and the girl's attention snaps back to her task, not letting herself admire the building anymore. She takes the hand Michael offers to her, standing and stepping out before someone else offers her a hand. The trio prepare themselves for a second, Anastasia smoothing out her pants while her brother runs a hand through his hair.

"You look really stupid in that get-up," Eleanor mutters, smirking at the Prince who stops mid movement to give her a look.

"Yes, yes. Very funny," he sighs.

"I do think you should wear that home; I think Zach would appreciate it," the girl continues as they start to walk forward.

"You utter a word, you will regret it," Michael growls. "Trust me."

"Oh, I have no doubt."

He glances at her quickly, laughing as he finds her completely normal in posture.

"And yet I feel as though you have not taken my words to heed," he chuckles.

Eleanor turns the side of her mouth up in amusement, before straightening her shoulders and standing taller. Just before they get to the doors, Michael stops her, checking for anything wrong.

"Compress your torso more," he says, "make it less noticeable."

The girl does so, nodding in appreciation to her friend before straightening out and looking forward again. The huge wooden doors swing open, and the two women fall into step just behind the Prince, walking in time up the huge red carpet towards the end of the room. Raised up, about half a meter, sits the King.

Clothed in white and gold like his son, the man has the same grey hair as he had in her dream, short and manicured. The eyes are just how she remembered them, green and cruel. But unlike in her dream, the man is happy to see his son. A wave of hate washes over the teenager, but she doesn't let it show, instead, keeping her posture even and chin raised.

They stop in front of the throne, and all three drop a knee, one arm resting to sit on it as their heads drop. Eleanor can feel the King watching her but doesn't let her head lower any more than it is already, waiting patiently for him to tell them to rise.

"My son, who is it that you've brought with you?" he says, but does not tell them to stand.

"Eleanor Beck, Father. She is among the best agents in America, and was exposed to our problem a few weeks ago. Her incredible memory also means that she can cart this information back without trouble," Michael replies, hand flared to remind her to stay down.

"You trust her?"

"Yes, I wouldn't have brought her otherwise."

The lie impresses her, because if she didn't know better, and they hadn't have argued about it a week ago, she wouldn't even have been able to tell it was false.

"Rise," the King calls.

They do, the girl folding her hands in front of her stomach as the King now looks her in the eye.

"It is an honour to meet you, Your Majesty," she says, breaking eye contact to bow her head again.

"You're quite young for such a job," he follows, blowing off her compliment.

"When you have talent like mine it becomes quite easy to gain the attention of the higher ups," Eleanor explains. "And 25 is not too young."

"No, it isn't," he nods, but his eyes continue to examine her. "You have been informed of the test you will have to take to join us in our meetings?"

"Yes, it will be fun to have a challenge. I must confess, the human invention of guns has much watered down the fun of fighting," she smirks, getting a nervous look from the Princess.

"It has," the King chuckles, no hint of annoyance at her cockiness. "I was just going to get you to spar with a few of our guards, but we just picked up a few Daemone soldiers who we found patrolling the area... Normally, we would just use them for training the guards, but I think it would be more entertaining to have you fight them."

Michael tenses in front for her, about to argue against the declaration, but Eleanor speaks first.

"Trust me, Your Majesty, I've been training with men twice my size and strength for years, a few demon offspring won't be a problem," she answers, keeping her gaze steady. "However, in the footage from the attack, their leader yelled a threat to the camera, that they would be able to find us because they have a monitor on what they are seeing. I would prefer it if they did not learn we had visited."

"Yes, Michael told us. What would you like to do about it?"

"Be allowed to wear a mask I brought with me in case the situation arose. However, this mask is, not American, nor from anywhere on the right side of the law. I received it as a token from a mission I went on, and the girl I took it from had a similar face shape, so I use it when I have to. I just want to ensure you are aware, as it would not be good me be recognised and attacked," Eleanor says carefully, watching for a sign of aggravation on the King's face.

"What organisation?"

"Berühmte Söldner," she sighs. "I got one of their ACEs."

"You killed a Berühmte Söldner ACE?" the King scoffs, wariness in his eyes.

"I did. While I was undercover in Spain a few months ago."

Both Anastasia and Michael turn to look at her in surprise, but all they find is a girl with a soft smile on her face, without a hint of menace. Later in life, they'd learn that the sweeter her face, the more honest her words, the more she wanted to kill the person she was talking to. But at this time, it just confused them.

"My daughter can take you to your room ¬– it is next to hers – and get you appropriate attire for tonight. You may leave, I need to talk to the Crown Prince," the King orders, silent until the door shuts behind the two girls.

Chapter 21

Eleanor follows the Princess, who points out different things as they walk through the huge corridors, then takes a shortcut up through a hidden stairwell, which deposits them in a higher level of the castle.

"We're now on the top levels," the Princess says, breaking their silence. "The King's rooms are in the left turret out the front, but my brother's rooms are here along with mine."

"Michael said I'd be in Nikolas's room?"

"I didn't know why he asked initially, but yes you will," she sighs, opening a door and holding it as Eleanor moves inside. The door shuts and she speaks again. "You like green?"

"Yes, I do."

"Great." She rummages around in her closet for a second before pulling out a dress and handing it to the girl. "We should be the same size."

Taking the dress, Eleanor steps back slightly.

"Thank you, where can I change?" she asks.

"If you go through that door" —Anastasia points to a plain wooden spot against the wall opposite her bed— "you'll be in Nikolas's room. Your stuff is already there, so fix up your hair and make-up and I'll come get you when Michael comes up."

Eleanor nods, following her instructions as she steps through the door, and into a room scarily similar to her own. Her bags sit at the end of the fourposter bed, but the rest of the room has been left alone. There is a small balcony looking out over the city with big glass doors leading onto it. The blinds around are dark green, light-blocking ones sitting behind a set of lighter, chiffon ones. The smell that hangs in the air is oddly comforting, but the girl pushes away the feeling as she shuts the door and walks over to lock the main one.

The dress has a perfectly matte black off-the-shoulder top, with three-quarter sleeves and a floor-length green satin skirt. It only takes a minute or two for her to be changed, the dress fitting perfectly as she attaches the jewelled silver belt. Then she pulls out her ashen hair, sending a brush through it until it's neat and braiding the two top parts to the back of her head. Just as she finishes her make-up, there is a knock on the small door and she opens it quickly. Anastasia, now dressed in a strapless midnight blue dress, sits on the bed, while Michael stays standing awkwardly in the middle of the room. Eleanor moves to sit next to the woman, handing over the fighting mask as Michael holds out a hand.

It's pure black, shaped to fit under the chin, over the nose and against her forehead, before it clicks into the back piece, which covers the entire back of the head, leaving a gap at the bottom for hair to go out, and the gap for the eyes is covered in a fine black mesh, which you can only see through from the inside. The front piece is made of a bullet proof shelling, four elongated slits to breathe. On the right cheek, written in blocked capitals and embedded into the shelling, is Kitten. The back shelling is also bulletproof, an attempt to ensure that if someone snuck up behind her, she wouldn't die.

"Nancy gave that to you?" Michael mutters, chucking it back to her.

"I asked Kaylee."

"Have anything else of your kit?"

"My jacket goes with the mask."

"Why wasn't I told you'd be back in your uniform?"

"Because she didn't think you needed to know."

The elder shakes his head in annoyance, before turning to his sister.

"Go ahead," he mutters, staying in the middle of the room.

"What complications are you talking about?" the woman asks, following with, "it's safe to talk in here."

"For one, she is not 25, or even 20..."

"How old then? 18, 17?"

"I'm 16," Eleanor replies softly.

"And you're human?"

"As far as I know."

"Okay, a slightly young human girl, that's manageable."

"I'm also pregnant."

That stops the Princess.

"On purpose, or an accident with someone you love?"

"Neither." Anastasia frowns. "I was raped."

She looks to her brother for confirmation, receive a terse nod in response.

"But I was in a bad place," Eleanor continues. "I had been hiding my emotions for years, but this child pulled them out and I decided to run."

"You're telling me," Anastasia starts, looking solely at her brother. "You brought Nikolas's... his abused, raped, pregnant and teenage... here? You cannot tell the King, Michael. He will hurt her to hurt Nikolas."

"I am aware, Anastasia. I have a head, you know," he growls.

"Sometimes you just don't use it," the Princess returns. "You understand, that Michael is the only eligible heir to the throne? What position that puts you in?"

"What do you mean, eligible?" Eleanor frowns, glancing between the siblings.

Anastasia stands up, huffing a low laugh as she looks at the girl sitting cross-legged on the bed.

"Michael is the oldest, therefore would be heir anyway. However, I am a girl, and my father is a sexist old fart," she sighs. "And our brother—"

"—He is not our brother," Michael interrupts under his breath, before hissing in pain as the Princess backhands him across his face.

"Our brother is in exile," the woman finishes, glaring at the man.

"Because he tried to kill our father," he grumbles.

"Because he executed our mother!"

"Because she had an affair!"

"That he found out about eight months after Nikolas was born! Why do you think he made Mother watch Captain Macinart be executed!"

The Prince stays silent, glaring at his sister as she sighs tiredly.

"This is why he's out there, Michael. This is why she has to stay a secret. Because you aren't here, you don't know your own family, or country. After the King started to get mad at Mother, you should have come back. You should have been there when they executed her, like we were, standing on display. You could have stood up for Nikolas, he just needed the support," Anastasia tells him. "He saw how alone I was, and he got mad. He just needed someone to lean on, Michael."

Looking between the two siblings, Eleanor frowns, but lets her hands turn in her lap.

"Why is it I have to stay a secret?" she asks quietly, hoping to get a little more information out of them. "I know I'm connected to him, but how? And why?"

"From what you have heard of my brother, and what you know of me, having known me for a few months now, who do you want to stand with?" Michael returns.

The girl hesitates long enough for the eldest to nod.

"That is why you must stay a secret. You are the one thing my father could use to control Nikolas. Anastasia is loved by the people here, but apart from a maximum of ten people, you are dead. You have met him, but he doesn't know of your condition, and I fear it may be dangerous if he found out," Michael sighs, sitting on the bed beside her softly. "I need to talk to my sister, as to what we should tell you, but for now, we need to start heading down to dinner."

"First however, I need to know the truth behind your job. I don't think you work with Michael," the Princess interrupts.

"I am an assassin. My parents were murdered when I was six, I was working and being trained by the Berühmte Söldner until I got pregnant. I am an ACE, hence why I have the mask with my codename on it. I have killed hundreds of people and I am one of the most wanted killers in the world, due to my habit of cutting a cross on my victim's foreheads. It meant they were able to link all my murders," Eleanor says, before quickly standing up. "Is there anything else you would like to know?"

"Ellie…" Michael calls, catching the girl's hand as she spins to walk away. "Think about it."

"I'm fine, Cael," Eleanor snaps, trying to pull herself away, but the stronger male just holds.

Keeping her arms pinned, he pulls her closer and wraps his arm around her shoulders.

"You are not. You're stressed again, and you're snapping," he mutters, making sure she is still as he talks. "I cannot let you go down to that dinner while you are nervy and not focused."

"I am fine, Michael."

"You aren't. You and I both know that if you go out and have to keep up your façade, you will crack then you will snap. And then I will have to get you out of there... You know I care about what happens to you. In that room, I can't protect you, and I also cannot let you hurt anyone. So until you calm down, I'm not letting go."

The Princess watches the pair from her spot, a faint smile on her face as she observes them. When Michael finally lets her go, the girl pauses, hugging him lightly before she starts to step towards the door. Anastasia follows her, elbowing her brother in the side as she passes to walk next to the girl.

"Stick with me, I leave when the old people do and we can go to bed," she offers, watching as the girl faintly smiles.

"Thank you."

"As Michael's guest, you will be sitting next to me. Tell the maids you just want water," the Princess continues. "How much do you know about courtly etiquette?"

"A fair bit. Enough to get me by," Eleanor replies. "But what are your customs on refusing things?"

"Drinks are a bit iffy; I'd just take one and not drink it. Food, politely decline. Dancing, politely decline unless I tell you to dance with them. Some of the younger Lords may ask and you'd be expected to accept due to their status. Subtly ask me if someone does offer," Anastasia answers carefully. "One of Michael's... friends, will probably ask."

"Don't sound so disapproving sister," Michael huffs. "If you didn't get so annoyed at them, they wouldn't tease you."

"That's not why I don't like them..."

The Prince acts as if he doesn't hear her as he walks past to a set of huge doors, turning around just as the two girls get there. He silently offers an arm to both of them, waiting for the girls to begrudgingly take it before tall swinging doors open and they step into the hall. It had been empty before, but now one long table sits in the middle of the room and hundreds of people sit in the ornate chairs.

Chapter 22

Trumpets sound as they enter, silence following the trill as everyone in the room stands and turns to face the trio. Eleanor spies the King at the other end of the room, and realises with distaste that they have to walk past all these people, but lets herself be guided by Michael as they walk. Each person they pass bows, but the girl can feel the eyes pinned on her as they continue. She doesn't let herself look around, keeping her focus on a pole at the other end of the room until they stop in front of the King. She follows Michael as he bows, scooping her foot back into a curtsy before rising again.

"Let's eat, shall we?" the King calls, causing everyone to sit back down.

Eleanor follows the Princess, taking the seat next to her, only two seats down from the King. Maids file out of the shadows with plates of food, placing one in front of each and every person, and offering wine to everyone. Eleanor does as Anastasia had told her, asking for water instead, as they begin to eat their dinner.

"So," the King starts, as chatter starts up around the room. "Miss Beck, how are your parents? Do they like your job?"

Michael tenses, looking over to the girl as she stops eating and swallows. He's about to fill in for her, but she shakes her head at him from across the table.

"I would love to think they would," she answers. "However, they died when I was six."

"I'm sorry to hear that," the man consoles, "who did you live with after that?"

"A foster family, they were into the martial arts and I learned different styles as I grew up," she returns. "But it's been a while since I saw them."

"Interesting... Anyone special in your life?"

"No, I had a boyfriend a while back, but long-distance didn't work."

"A girl like you alone? That's odd."

Eleanor bites back a snarky remark, giving a tight smile in return before starting to eat her dinner again. The rest of the meal goes without fuss, Eleanor keeping mostly to herself as she finishes the food. She refuses seconds, eating only a small amount of the dessert that is placed in front of her. Then the King rises, from the end of the table, taking the thick, tan rope that drops from the roof and attaching it to a beam on the bottom of the table. As more ropes fall, the guests attach them to hooks on the underside, that she hadn't noticed before. Once all the ropes are connected, Anastasia having helped with Eleanor's, everyone stands up and takes their chair to the edge of the room. Each of the ropes pull tight and the table rises, clearing the room for dancing as it reaches the ceiling.

"The housekeepers will clean it off after the party," the Princess tells her, "quite ingenious really."

"When was it invented?" Eleanor asks, staying next to her as the music starts and people move to the floor to dance.

"27 years ago, by my mother," she replies. "But don't let anyone hear you credit her for any of the major things she made, it's taboo."

The two girls share a look, the younger taking the royal's hand in hers and squeezing it lightly. When the third song comes on, the girl smiles faintly, letting her fingers play along to Beethoven's Moonlight Sonata.

"You play?" Anastasia asks.

"Yes, if I can say so, pretty well."

"You should play for us..."

"No. In this setting... I wouldn't be able to handle it."

An eyebrow raises.

"Sorry, I wouldn't be able to handle it without becoming a psychopathic bitch," Eleanor amends. "I am fine without a crowd of people, but it triggers a situational behaviour in populated areas."

"That's tough."

"Everything in my life is tough."

The two ease into silence, watching the room as all the coloured dresses spin with their partners. Eleanor finds Michael, taking note of who he stands talking to with a trained eye.

"The one in black, that's Markus Kilnguard. He is two years younger than Michael, but they are very close friends. I'd even say he's Michael's closest friend. His father heads our guard, and he is on the way to take over that position. He is Michael's personal bodyguard, along with the two in the navy. They're his friends also, snobby little brats, but they're tolerable," Anastasia explains.

Eleanor watches them even closer as she speaks, memorising Markus's jet black hair and the soft features of his face for future reference, before he glances in their direction and walks towards them. Eleanor turns her back to him.

"Have you told her of my magnetic charm? How you fell for the irresistible pull of my magnificent abs?"

Markus places his hands on her shoulders and then steps back in shock, as Eleanor's elbow slams into his stomach, spinning on her heel to face him as Michael chuckles from across the room.

"You do not sneak up on someone trained in martial arts at an event like such," she snaps, standing her ground as he straightens with a glare, but it fades as Michael joins them.

"I did warn you, Mark. She is not someone to mess around with. Do not let me catch you doing it again," he says, hand touching the girl's arm softly to reassure her. "Breathe, Ellie," he murmurs.

"I just wanted to make an entrance," he shrugs. "It is quite odd though; she is resistant to my charm."

"She is very strange, but you must keep that under wraps. She doesn't understand it yet, but she needs to be kept safe. On my orders," Michael answers, Eleanor tilting her head as the Prince shows his true side.

"Yes, sir," the man nods. "Now, I do believe, dearest Anastasia, that a dance is required by your father."

The Princess fixes him with a smouldering glare, but he just sighs.

"Ana, would you rather it be one of the strangers who know nothing of your position, or me, whom you have grown up with?" he says. "Your mother isn't here anymore, there is no way out of it."

Eleanor is about to step between them, but the Princess lets her shoulders drop, takes the offered hand and is led away.

"What's up with them?" she asks Michael, who stays by her side.

"Our mother was the only one stopping Father from marrying Anastasia off. Father is forcing her to marry, Mark is currently the leading candidate because I suggested him. Ana has to go along with it or else Father will marry her to some snob," he explains. "She and Mark get on like fire and ice, but I trust him to take care of her. I think they could get along if she'd get to know him a little better."

"Michael, girls are complicated and, if I'm correct, your mother was protecting Anastasia from her own fate," she murmurs. "It is a lonely existence without someone to have a romantic connection to. Especially when you have no freedom to get some space."

"You speak with experience..."

"I do."

Michael looks at her in annoyance, but shakes his head as Eleanor winks.

"How are you feeling?" he asks, settling in to stay with her until his sister returns.

"I'm okay, tired though. And I need to pee. But that can wait," she shrugs. "It would be nice to get out of these heels; my feet are getting sore."

He chuckles, nodding to passing lords, who see him standing with the girl and walk past. Then he looks to her in confusion, finding a terrifying scowl directed to every one of them.

"Be nice, Ellie," he mutters. "Now come, you're meeting some of my friends."

The girl lets herself be pulled away, forcing a smile as she stops in front of the group she saw earlier.

"This is Max, Rhiannon, Robert and Richard," he introduces. "Guys, this is Eleanor."

"Good to meet you," the ginger Max smiles. "I'd bet you already knew who we are though, saw you talking to Ana earlier."

"Yes, I did. It's nice to see that some people don't feel the need to sneak up on people when they notice said people watching them," she returns.

"Markus can be a pain, but inside he's a teddy bear," Max laughs, then forces his face still, brown eyes serious. "Just do not tell him I said that. While he's soft on the inside, the outside is still as sharp as knives."

Eleanor giggles as the girl – Rhiannon – rolls her eyes. For a second she looks to Michael, finding a smile on his face. Then trumpets sound, the music stops, and every person in the room drops to a bow as the King leaves.

Behind him, pretty much everyone over 40 leaves, the musicians starting the music again. But now the songs are more modern, more people moving to the dance floor. Anastasia joins them again, detached from her partner and seeming more relaxed. Then the music changes, and Eleanor cannot stop her head as it snaps towards where the sound is coming from.

"Familiar?" Max asks, watching as her head turns back.

"Yes. Not sure if I know anyone my age who isn't," she smiles.

If you didn't know her, you wouldn't see the lie, the pain she's covering with a smile.

"Come join then," he offers, holding out a hand to her.

Eleanor shrugs, taking his hand and letting him add them to the lines that have been made when the song started. She makes herself act like she'd done it a million times, makes herself laugh as she steps through the repetitive movements. When the song finishes, they join their friends again, Michael watching the girl carefully as she sidles closer to his sister.

"Well, we are going to bed now, see you all tomorrow," Anastasia says, taking the girls arm to pull her out with her.

"I'll come with you," Markus cuts in, following them out into the hall as the Princess drags her guest away.

"I am perfectly capable of doing so myself," she snaps, facing him.

"I know you are; however, you and your brother are up to something, and I want to know why she is resistant to my charm," he returns, "Michael told me to talk to you about it."

The Princess grumbles before walking off, not stopping him as he follows the pair.

"What do you mean your charm?" Eleanor asks, as they turn out of the hallway.

"Here, rank is determined by how much angelic blood one has. The King, Anastasia and Michael, they have the most. And those with more angelic blood can have a certain area that they're gifted in.

It's different from the qualities they might have from having angelic blood though," he replies. "We call them Aspects."

"Like Michael, he has angelic qualities of strength and virtue, and his Aspect is the ability of persuasion. He can give people suggestions of what to do and change their minds on things. However, the limit to his power is the fact he can often make it worse by not knowing enough about the situation, and people are generally a bit pissed when their freedom of choice is taken away. If he tries hard enough, he could even compel someone into doing something for him," Anastasia continues.

"I don't think he's ever done that to me..."

"It's possible. He was told to refrain from using it in front of humans," she shrugs. "And he probably wanted to be careful about making you do something."

Both Eleanor and Markus look at her in confusion, but she just keeps walking.

"What is your Aspect?" Eleanor starts, looking at the Princess.

"I can foresee parts of the future," she answers, saying it as if it was nothing. "Sometimes it will just be a person, other times I will see someone die. A few weeks ago, I saw you sitting in Nikolas's room. It can be random but when I focus, I can try and extract things."

"So you're psychic?"

"No. I can foresee parts of the future," the Princess insists. "However, psychics quite often have diluted angel blood in them. Every few decades people leave here to see the rest of the world. They pretty much never come back."

"Do people ever come here?"

"If they find the island on their own and they can see it, then yes. But if they are too human, they won't be able to get through the fog," Markus says. "But anyway, my Aspect is charm, the more human blood in someone the more they will be attracted to me. Anastasia here is nearly immune to it, whereas you should be adoring me as if we were fresh Geminae." The Princess flinches, the movement not escaping Eleanor's notice. "However, it has had no effect on you. Which means one of three things; you are secretly an Angel or a very lowly diluted Angeli; you are a daughter of the Daemone but, if you were, the King would have noticed, as that is his Aspect; or most likely, you've met your Geminae Animarum."

Both women frown, one in confusion and the other annoyed at the words, but just as Eleanor is about to speak, they arrive at their rooms.

"Goodnight then, girls," Markus interrupts, cutting off the teenager.

"Goodnight, Eleanor," Anastasia follows. About to argue against the two adults, Eleanor steps forward, but the Princess stops her. "You need to sleep, Eleanor. Tomorrow will be tiring and I need to talk to Markus."

Giving up, the girl begins to head to her door, stopping just inside the wooden frame.

"What if I have a nightmare when Michael still isn't back?" she whispers, glancing back ever so slightly.

"I'll come, don't worry," the woman smiles. "Now go to bed."

The door shuts behind her, leaving the two in the hallway.

"Who is her Geminae?" Markus asks, hand on Anastasia's shoulder to stop her from leaving.

"I need you to swear to me first, that you will not tell anyone, and only speak of it when alone with me or Michael," the Princess orders, gaining her affirmation before pulling him into her room. "Nikolas. That is why they came, Michael needed help."

"That human girl is Nikolas's Geminae?" he scoffs. "How on Earth? And that would make her older than him..."

"I don't know, but I don't think what we've seen is her true nature. She is scared, I can tell. She's acting her way through this," she replies. "But she is also stronger than any human I've seen. She's also lying about her age, he's three years older than she actually is."

"She's 16? She's a good actor, the King took her story without question..."

"She is. You will be in the ring tomorrow, won't you?"

"I will, but I doubt she'll have a problem, we just have some humans who have been working for the Berühmte Söldner. They're weak anyway."

"She sassed my father earlier; I think he'll match her to some of the Daemones. If she is about to be put down..."

"I'll step in. I may not of liked your little brother, but a Geminae is more than petty feelings."

"Thank you, Markus."

"Anything, Anastasia. Now get some sleep."
She nods, turning towards her bed as he leaves.

Through the wall, Eleanor silently cries. For the reality had hit her, of how much of life she had missed out on, in those ten years.

Chapter 23

Luckily for me, both Eleanor and Nikolas quite often wrote down everything that happened to them, and in their current state, I am able to peruse these diaries without hindrance. I feel a little bad, reading through their private thoughts, but for the sake of record, translating these parts are necessary. And I think that it will help you to understand.

And we don't know how long they will be under; the technology is not old enough for us to know the effects it might have on them, if they're under for too long. So, this may also serve as a reminder to them. You will need to be ready for anything.

Anyhow, deciphered from messy Latin, I give you...

~

The black fades slightly, silver eyes focussing on the figure of a girl, standing confused across the plain grey space. She looks up nervously, the pale blue of her irises locking onto his, darting slightly as she finds the short scar that cuts through his dark blonde eyebrow and down to his cheek, just skipping his eye. He lets himself look over her, the bow of her lips, round of her nose. The tense in her shoulders and the slight swell in her stomach. He sees the wet under her round eyes, the grey circles that they sit on.

"Why are you crying, Dulce Meum?" he asks, stepping slowly closer as her eyes flick over him.

"You're Nikolas, aren't you?" she replies, ignoring his question.

"I am. And you are Eleanor," he nods, stopping a meter from her. "Now why are you crying?"

"It's nothing," she shrugs, failing to find his eyes. "Just a painful reminder of how messed up I am."

His pink lips frown.

"You aren't messed up," he says.

"I don't think you know me well enough to pass judgement on that..."

He keeps it to himself that he's been watching her for the past few weeks, as his pale hand runs through the mess of dirty blonde locks on top of his head.

"Well, even if you are, you can't possibly be more messed up than me," he tries, the side of his mouth twitching up as she smiles slightly.

"How are you here?" she asks, "are you just a figment of my imagination?"

"No. Have 'Aspects' been explained to you?" he asks. She nods her head, so he continues. "My Aspect, according to the King—" he spits the words "—is purely limited telepathy, just words and instant mind reading, but if I have a strong enough connection to someone, I can set up a dreamscape and interact with that person's consciousness."

The girl shifts slightly, noticing the shadow of another girl in the grey. She pushes it down as hard as she can.

"Why did you come then?" she questions.

After a slight pause, he replies, "I felt you were upset, and I wanted to make sure it wasn't because you were in trouble."

"No, I'm fine. I have to fight some of these, Daemones, tomorrow," she says, trying to keep the conversation going.

Nikolas tenses, looking over her again, eyes resting on her stomach. She covers it subconsciously.

"Is it safe?" he checks, stepping forward and letting his fingers brush over her shoulder.

"Enough. I can fight well enough to protect myself, I'd think..."

"Why on Earth is my idiot brother making you fight Daemones pregnant? I understand you are a good fighter, but you are still human," he growls, the tone passing straight through her.

"They don't know I'm pregnant, they don't know I'm 16 either. I can't drop my cover," she tells him. "And they put extra protection in my suit, it's safe."

He looks at her dubiously, but lets it go, moving onto a new topic.

"How did you get pregnant?" he asks, cautious.

Eleanor shudders, not answering as he squeezes her shoulder lightly.

"They used to drug us when we came in from assignments, to get us from our pick up spot to the compound without us knowing where it was," she starts shakily. "I couldn't fight back, I couldn't stay there anymore, so I took my chance on a mission in America. They can't put me to death until I'm 18, so that gives me enough time to have my child."

Nikolas stills, the muscles in his sharp jaw twitching as he holds onto her shoulder as gently as he can. She notices his distress, raising her hand onto his arm. The connection of their skin breaks him out of the daze, as he looks down at her softly.

"You aren't going to die," he tells her. "I won't let that happen."

She tries to smile but it doesn't really work.

"I have to go soon," Nikolas murmurs.

"Okay then," she replies, lowering her hand with a breath.

He lets his hand brush lightly over her cheek before it drops to his side. He turns away, preparing himself to let go of the connection, but he stops just before he does.

"Be careful, Eleanor. One of the Daemones they have at the moment is an extremely good fighter. Put enough of a show on with the lesser fighters so they don't release him onto you," he tells her. "Tap out if you start having trouble. Don't let your pride get in the way. You need to stay safe."

"I will try," she tells him. "But don't worry about me, I will be perfectly fine."

"You would not understand, Dulce Meum…"

The two lock eyes a final time, before the area fades to black.

Eleanor wakes smoothly, for the first time in ages, rolling in the green sheets and pressing her face into one of the pillows. The lingering smell of books and trees, comforts her.

There is a soft knock on the small door between her room and the Princess's before it opens, then the princess, dressed in a blue summer frock, comes in.

"Sleep well?" she asks, starting to rifle through Eleanor's bags in search of something for her to wear.

"Yes, actually," the girl smiles, propping herself up. "What time will my test be?"

"Midday. It is currently seven, and breakfast is at eight. You should wear" —clothes fly at her face— "this."

"How nice of you," the teen grumbles.

"Up, up now," Anastasia sings, "You need to do your hair, and make sure that you're feeling well."

"I'm feeling fine," she sighs. "Probably because of my dream…"

"What was it?"

"Oh, I had a nice little conversation with your brother," Eleanor smirks. "The one who apparently has telepathic abilities."

"Ah, right. Anything in particular?" she questions, eyebrow raised in amusement.

"Be careful today. That was pretty much it," the girl smiles.

"Okay then, I'll be back in 20 minutes, I want you at least dressed by then," Anastasia mothers, leaving the room.

Dragging herself out of bed, Eleanor quickly changes, only letting her hand rest upon her stomach for a second before moving on. She brushes her hair and plaits it down her back, surprising her friend as she comes in to find her fully ready.

Dressed in loose grey pants and a tucked in black singlet, you can just see the scar on her back as the two tips peek out the top of the shirt. Then, Eleanor sits on her bed, pulling out the blank drawing pad she had packed, along with her pencils. Taking out one of the leads, she lets it rub against the grain of the paper, each stroke smooth and exact as she shapes the face. By the time Anastasia returns, it's barely more than an outline, but she closes the pad and puts it all back where it came from.

The Princess walks into her bathroom with a bucket, filling it with water, before beckoning for her to follow her into the hall.

"What are we doing?" Eleanor asks, frowning as they stop in front of the next door over.

"I told Michael to get up, my bet is he hasn't," Anastasia replies, "He refused to get an alarm clock so I do the job."

Holding in a laugh, Eleanor follows her into the room, where sure enough, Michael lays, still asleep. That is, of course, before the water goes flying onto his head and he jumps awake.

"Anastasia!" he growls, sitting up and glaring at her. "What the hell!"

"I told you to wake up," she sings.

"Why didn't you do it to her?" he continues, looking sourly to the completely dry and laughing Eleanor.

"Because, A. I was already somewhat awake, B. I'm not her brother, and C. when she told me to get up, I did," Eleanor smirks. "I might have to start taking notes, to give Kaylee ideas."

"Don't you dare," he grumbles. "Now out, I need to get dressed."

"We're going down, hurry up," Anastasia snips, pulling the teenager out behind her.

Breakfast turns out to be much more of a relaxed meal than the dinner they'd had the night before. Instead of one long table, there's dozens scattered around the room. People already sit at tables, most in casual clothes, but a fair few are wearing the black and gold of the guards yesterday. The food is set out like a buffet, and the three grab plates, getting the food they want. Eleanor only grabs an apple, placing it on her plate and ignoring the look she gets from the siblings.

"What?" she mutters, looking both of them in the eye.

"What has Kenichi said about you eating?" Michael returns.

"I'm nervous, so I don't eat. It will make me feel sick," she says.

Giving up, Michael finishes loading his plate and leads her over to the table where she recognised his friends from the night before, along with a few extra girls. She gets one or two scornful glares from some of the girls as she sits next to the Prince, except Rhiannon, who just smirks at her from her seat next to Markus.

"Did you two sleep well?" Max asks, glancing between the two girls as he eats.

"Better than the rest of you I'd suspect," Anastasia returns. "That's if you got any sleep."

"Three whole hours, thank you very much," he laughs. "Must you really rub it in Miss High and Mighty?"

"Most definitely."

Eleanor snorts slightly, gaining even more looks from women around them. She sends each one a foul glare before returning to her apple without a second's hesitation.

"Eleanor..." Michael mutters, "there is no need to be rude."

"Well, they were looking at me weird," she huffs, eyes staying stubbornly forward.

"Mmm, sure. Stop acting like a child," he returns, continuing to eat as his friends give them weird looks.

She narrowly avoids retorting with, 'well I am one', deciding on, "they're not the ones who have to fight Daemones to prove themselves."

"Luckily, you don't have to pass the tests they do."

"What, gossiping and snivelling while cat fighting for men?"

"No... I think you'd do very well at that. But I think you'd have a hard time faking being nice."

"I can be nice."

"Don't kid yourself Eleanor."

The girl hisses, elbowing him in the side as the boys on the other side of the table watch them argue in fascination.

"I am perfectly capable of being nice if I want to," she mutters. "Hell, I've been putting up with you."

Across the table, Rhiannon snickers, grinning at the Princess as she raises an eyebrow.

"Cause you're the one who has to put up with me?" Michael scoffs.

"Most definitely."

He quickly kicks her ankle, smirking at her as she bites back a yelp, the small electric shock making her foot tingle. Holding back an insult, she resolves to send him the sourest look she can, before returning to her apple and ignoring him.

The meal continues, finishing not too long after Eleanor finishes her apple. People disperse, but no one at the table they sit at moves an inch, continuing to chatter.

"Well, what are the plans before this thing at midday?" Max asks, looking between the Prince and his guest.

"Eleanor will be getting ready up in her room while we—" he grins at his friends "—are stuck touring the cities," Michael grumbles. "We'll meet back here at 11:30."

"Who's going to take her up?" Markus asks, jerking his head towards the girl who was marking the guards around the room in her head.

"Ana can, she has work to do anyway," he shrugs. "Let's get going."

They each move out, the Princess leading their guest back up to her room, where she sits down on her bed and continues to draw until she decides she needs to get ready. She hides the sketchpad deep in her bag, only letting her eyes stray on it for a second before she finds the horrid black mask shoved next to it.

Chapter 24

Eleanor looks at the clothes laid out on her bed, the skin-tight black suit, the hooded jacket. That damn mask. Her hand drifts to her stomach, letting the pale fingers run over the slight bulge before she runs it over her hair and steps forward. Once the suit is on, zipped all the way to the top where the collar sits flush to her neck, she picks up the jacket. It isn't hers, no... hers was destroyed when the man attacked her, it bore the same scars as she did, but she was glad it was gone. That the bloodstains she couldn't get out of the dense fabric weren't on show today.

This new one is made of a lighter fabric, but the whole thing looks like it can still stand against the pressure of fighting. The front does up with a silver zipper, which starts just below the belly button and stops at the collar, where the hood attaches. The bottom has two flaps that cover the sides of her thighs, the centre shaped like a suit vest. It pulls over her arms with ease, the hood staying down as she pulls the zipper up and swings her swords over her shoulder to clip the harness in. The buckles on her triple dagger thigh holster tighten around her right leg. Throwing daggers that Michael had supplied slipping into their holds before being hidden beneath the coat. She pulls her thick leather gloves, testing the thick brass plate over her knuckles before flexing her fingers. After testing the draw on her swords, she starts reaching for her mask.

Instinct takes over as her hand fits automatically to it and she has to focus very hard not to drop it at the overwhelmingly familiar rush that runs up her spine. But she stops herself, putting the article over the back of her head, clipping the front piece in fully, muscle memory making the movements quick. The breathing slits give her the exact amount of air she needs, but still, she chokes on the oxygen in her lungs. The black film over her eyes tints everything just a little bit, and for a second she wants to tear the thing off. The oxygen in her lungs is passing easier now, but there is a suffocating wrap, like plastic over her soul. All of a sudden, the coat feels like a straitjacket, the air like a vacuum, pressing on her every edge.

Then it stops. Like a flick of a switch the girl calms, her hand stop shaking, and she stands perfectly normal. She shakes out her limbs, cracking her neck as she pulls up the hood with ease.

"I really had faith you would last longer than that, Nora," she says, speaking to the air, it seems. "At least until you saw a crowd, maybe even until you stepped into the ring. I must say, you've gotten weaker... don't tell me you haven't, you put on a freaking mask... yes, yes. I know you haven't put it on yourself before. Trust me, Nora, I remember everything. Just be glad Mein Vater didn't see that little display, or anyone else for that matter, would ruin my reputation... quiet child, let me do my work. I'll let you have the body back when I think you can handle it, what's handing over a little control if it keeps you safe... fine, have it for the walk down, but I will take it by force if you try to..."

There is a sharp knock on the door, and the girl stops talking, a shift in her posture making her pause for a second before she straightens again. In a few strides she's at the door, the hinges squealing as the door is pulled open.

"Time to go?" she asks, looking the Prince in the eye as he raises an eyebrow at her.

"Yes," he finally answers. "However, you might strive to stay out of children's eyesight. That outfit is terrifying."

"That is the point," she mutters, stepping out and shutting the door behind her.

"Are you going to be okay?" he asks as they start down the hallway.

"This is easy, I'll be fine," she replies.

"That doesn't answer my question, Eleanor."

"I think it's safe to say that the answer to if I'm okay will forever be no. Thus, the question is irrelevant."

The older male glances at the girl, frowning as she continues to step out in front of him. The rubber soles of her combat boots make no noise on the tile, and her feet roll through the movement to ensure not a squeak escapes their meeting. Lethal grace. A trained behaviour. Michael wonders how many times she made a noise, and it cost her.

"Don't comment on it, Cael. I need to be working, and I cannot do that with you worrying about me. I have survived this long by turning off all my emotions, constantly bringing them to the surface means I will be weak. If I'm weak, I die," Eleanor mutters, voice carrying in the open halls. She could have sworn the people in the pictures were watching her, but that was just her mind acting upon her tense muscles. It was doing its job, at least, watching out for her when she wasn't focused. "It is how it is."

"It doesn't have to be, emotion can give you a reason to fight," he tells her, sighing as she stops, spinning on her heel to face him.

"Michael. I am not a killer" —he frowns— "not at heart. But I am broken, my heart does not know what it beats for. I saw my parents die and, all of a sudden, the only thing it could think about was keeping me alive. So I started to kill. And all the while, all my emotions were in a constant, blaring tone. No deviation, no break between the beats, just one constant note. White noise to block it all out. You do not understand it. You could never understand it." Her voice carries a harsh tremble, her shoulders beg for a challenge. "I cannot let that tone stop, otherwise I will break, and I will crumble." He can't see the tears welling in her eyes. "It's like I'm constantly being pulled out by an ocean rip, and I have to let myself be pulled away from the shore. I let myself feel some emotion, but if I let it all out, I will drown and, if I try to fight it all away, I will grow tired and I will go under. Part of the reason I ran like I did without saying goodbye to them is because I was scared that I wouldn't be able to say goodbye, that I would lose focus and I'd go under because I started to care. Because they were able to keep me afloat when I couldn't do it myself."

"Ellie..." Michael tries, but the girl shakes her head angrily.

She knows they're still in the royal part of the castle, so pulls the man into the room next to them, an empty study.

"And I am scared to meet your brother, because I know I will fall for him," she continues, shocking the man into silence. "I do not know what you call it but, in my world, it's called soulmates. I know that we could get along, quite easily I'd dare say. But soulmates are forever, and I am not. I have an expiry date, and I don't want to drag someone down with me. He does have something else to live for. He has you, and Anastasia, and a full life."

"You have something to live for as well, Ellie…"

Her hand touches her stomach, the other raising to unclick her mask. She wipes away the tearstains as quick as she can.

"This child, it doesn't deserve to have me as it's mother. It deserves the world, and all I can give it is the inside of cells and a tracker. I came to terms with it when I decided to go to them, and now I know that he will look after it if I can't, that's enough for me," she shrugs, her voice now small.

"If you were given more time, would you take it?" he asks, watching her carefully.

"Of course I would. But hope is a fickle thing, and it has no place in an assassin's heart. If I hope I can get away with not killing someone, I die. I am no killer at heart, but my heart doesn't run this joint anymore. Now, we better get there, they'll be wondering where we are," she replies, replacing her mask and walking out the door.

This time her breathing only hitches for a second, before she pulls control back over it and she strides out again. But Michael makes her slow down for a second.

"Eleanor," he calls. "Don't let yourself feel any type of pressure to love Nikolas, you are human, and you are not locked into it like we can be. And if he does try to pressure you just leave, okay?"

"Okay," she murmurs, "Thank you."

He smiles softly in response, walking with her again as they finally get to the populated corridors. People edge away from them and, for once, Michael likes knowing it isn't because of him.

"You know, you do look very intimidating," he tells her, missing it as her steps become sharp and shoulders pull back farther than before.

"I know right. It's fun isn't it," she giggles. "There's nothing like parting a crowd by just walking."

Humouring her, Michael laughs briefly, but stops as they arrive in the hall where Markus, Anastasia, Max and a few guards wait for them. They all try their hardest not to recoil as the girl comes into view, Michael's friends doing the best when it came to covering their surprise. Markus, unlike the two others, is wearing black, the guard uniform, but is not alone in the gold band he wears around his head. Anastasia's pins her loose chestnut locks down, in place of a crown, Eleanor assumes.

"Well now I see why you warned the King," Markus huffs, "I think we might finally have a contender for our ACE."

The siblings glance to Eleanor, but the mask over her face hides the horror that fills it. But the girl gets control over herself, tilting her head in recognition.

"We will have to see, won't we," she says with a deep sigh.

"Come on, we're going down the river, the boat is waiting," Anastasia tells them, "It would be good if we got there a little early. Michael, put this on..."

One of the gold rings is handed to the Prince, who begrudgingly settles it above his brow and starts to follow her out of the hall in silence, walking through to the entry Eleanor has come through the first time they entered the castle. The crowd splits within a second of seeing their Prince being flanked by what they saw to be an omen of death. To be fair, the girl would probably say that it was entirely accurate, but for the minute she just follows the Prince inside the boats. It's like a ferry, with a strip around the outside for someone to walk on, while the seats are on the inside. They each take one, and Eleanor finally unclips the front part of her mask.

"Just checking, I am allowed to kill these things, right?" Eleanor asks. "Cause if you can't tell, it may be a little problem."

"You can kill them," Markus assures. "Technically, we aren't supposed to kill anything other than them, but you're human, so you can do whatever you like."

"However don't, you kill the Daemones and that's it, clear?" Michael cuts in, giving the girl a look and kicking her foot lightly.

"Yes, yes," Eleanor mutters.

It's silent for a few moments, before Max speaks, moving on from the tense subject.

"Do you speak any other languages, Eleanor?" he asks.

"Yes, I do," she replies.

"Really, which ones?"

"Uh, German and French among others," Eleanor bluffs, "among others" was being used very loosely. "What languages do you all speak?"

Michael looks to the people seated around them and runs a check in his head.

"We all speak Latin, Mark speaks German, like you, Ana and I speak Mandarin and she also speaks French," he tells her. "I never checked; do you speak Latin?"

She matches his playful poke at her not knowing something with a hiss.

"No, I don't," she answers in fluent Mandarin. "And you've blocked the iPad you gave me from operating any translation services."

"Yes, I did, and I'm not unlocking it either," he laughs, with a smirk at her twisted face.

"Asshole," she mutters, the words incomprehensible to everyone except Markus, who chuckles at her casual German.

"I don't get much practise at such casual dialect," he tells her, staying in their shared language.

"I can tell, you speak like the words don't belong in your mouth," she replies. "It's hard to do without having spoken it from a young age."

"And you can tell that I haven't, how?" he huffs, speaking in English again.

"Because you speak like you have a stick up your ass," she says, blunt and direct.

"Nice to know you won't hold back." He shrugs. "We're almost there, if you want to put that mask back on."

Muttering a thanks, Eleanor complies, clicking the mask into place without a flicker of fear. She was ready for it now; she had done it a million times before.

They had followed the coast to the back of the island while they had been talking, and were now on the direct opposite side of the city. The boat stops smoothly at a separate island about a kilometre off the coast, where dozens of docks offer a way to get to shore without getting wet. Above, Eleanor notices a giant bridge, spanning the distance and connecting to the top of the islands. The party step onto one of the docks, Eleanor following the Angeli towards the steep cliffs in front of them. It's only when they near the smooth stone, that she spots the doorway sized holes at the base, with stairs leading up further into the island.

"Do we have to walk all the way up?" she asks Anastasia, who walks at her side.

"No, there are elevators just up the stairs," the Princess laughs. "We aren't completely in the 10th century."

"Could've fooled me," Eleanor returns, smiling behind the mask that sits snug on her face.

Sure enough, as they form a single file and go up their dock's allotted staircase, a human sized cylinder sits waiting for them. Without missing a beat, Michael steps into it, glancing back at them for a second.

"Send Eleanor up next," he says, before pressing a button on the wall.

The cylinder zips upwards instantly, and within a minute it's back down again. Eleanor steps forward carefully, putting herself in the tube and finding the button. The Princess nods to assure her before she pushes the disk and the tube jerks upwards. It takes about 20 seconds for it to reach the top, where Michael beckons for her to step out, waiting until she has before sending it back down. They don't talk, waiting for everyone else to get to the top before they walk towards a stone stadium, which stands next to a huge, court-like building.

"This is where your mother..." Eleanor gulps, looking to the Princess in astonishment.

"And where Nikolas was held to an unfair trial," she whispers in reply.

But in keeping up with the tall (having now seen most of the other people as they walked, Eleanor had deduced that height was a common trait) Angeli, they had already made it to the stadium, entering through a side door into the downstairs area. It was a like a dungeon, people being held in chains and cells like the animals of Gladiatorial contests. But as they get closer, she notices the ink black eyes, and the built muscle. Daemones.

"They will come out in waves, you only need to make it through the first two to qualify," Michael tells her. "The fighters will be better the further you go along, ending with this one..."

They stop in front of a man, who wears a collar beside the rest of the Daemone restraints. Michael keeps his hand on the middle of her back, leaving it still as she steps back in surprise, giving her a cover for her misstep.

"Traitorous bitch," the man on the floor spits, glaring filthily to Eleanor.

"Mmm sure, but your little traitorous bitch is dead," Eleanor replies, forcing herself to be as American as she can. "She went psycho on us and tried to do a runner. Put two in the back of her head, got the mask and jacket to disguise myself in front of you lot."

"Why would you take a Berühmte Söldner's outfit, if you killed one?"

"Because look at me, this suit is awesome!" she scoffs, "And we were the same size so why waste a perfectly good, badass suit?"

The man shuts up, glowering in fury as she steps away.

"I'm ready to fight, when do I start?" she asks, looking in the Prince's direction.

"Five minutes, the last warm up act just finished and they're clearing out the ring. Markus is going to be walking out with you, and he will be the one to step in if you need it," Michael tells her. "But you need to call out for him to step in, okay?"

"Yes."

"Come on, I'll walk with you to the entrance, but then I have to go up to the box," he sighs, nodding to the other two, who make their own way in a different direction. Michael turns to his friend, "would you mind hanging back a second? I need to talk to her alone."

The man does, letting the two get ahead of him before starting to walk.

"You know him," Michael states, voice low so no-one can hear them.

"Of course, I know him, Michael. He's a freaking ACE. He is better than me," she breathes. "I've seen Mein Vater lose to him."

"If you don't think you can win, then just drop out," he assures. "There is no shame in it. No one here has been able to beat him, and most won't even try."

She stays silent, fist clenching at her side.

"But if you do want to try, he won't be armed. So unless you let him get those swords of yours…"

"Thank you."

They stop talking as the ground beneath them turns to cobblestone. Light streams in through a gate at the top of a ramp. The entrance to the arena. People are milling around the area, light chatter silencing as the Prince and his guest enter the room. They stare at her but she pays them no heed as she straightens to a perfect posture.

"Is there something you would like?" she asks, glancing between each of the curious men in the room.

"No, Ma'am. We're just interested to see how you will do," one answers, others behind him snickering slightly.

"I understand that your Prince is here, but there is no need to lie about what you were truly thinking," Eleanor responds, voice still the image of perfect manners. "You think I am just a weak human girl, who uses what she wears to scare off competitors and hide my mistakes. You don't think I'll make it past three rounds, do you?" None of the men say anything, but none deny it either. "Well, just you watch. I've killed ACEs before, there is no reason I can't do it again."

They gawk at her, the fighters right along with the Prince and his friend, watching as she flicks her shoulders back. But then Michael steps forward, wrapping his arms around Eleanor and pulling her closer to him for a few seconds.

"Fight like your life depends on it. Don't hold back," he tells her. "Tap out if anything is wrong, anything at all."

"I always fight like my life depends on it, because it does," she replies. "And I will. Maybe have a bucket at the exit for me."

"Any discomfort, you stop. Any at all, you hear me?" he instructs.

"I hear you," she nods, stepping away. "Now go find your seat."

And so he does, leaving her with his best friend as he moves to the podium with his father. She glides up to the gate, looking out into the arena in stony silence.

"Give them a show, Eleanor," Markus tells her. "Show them what you can do."

"I always do…"

Chapter 25

The gate raises, and she strides out in full confidence. The visor over her eyes protects them from the blinding sand as she glides over the grains without sinking an inch. She digs her toe in, hitting rubber a few centimetres down.

"Gives better fights, nice and bouncy," Markus mutters, following a few feet behind the girl as she makes it to the middle of the arena. "On one knee, bow for ten seconds, then rise. Thirty seconds later, I will let out the first wave."

She nods so faintly anyone above wouldn't be able to see her.

"Good luck then," he finishes, leaving her standing by herself.

She drops her knee, bowing her head obediently. The count raises painfully slowly in her head, but once it finishes the dark spectre rises, a shadow in the sand. She stays perfectly still in her spot, waiting to hear the gates release their captives. Before the three things get within 30 meters of her, she flips out each of the throwing knifes, embedding them deep into each of their chests. Each fall, collapsing into the sand face first.

Eleanor drifts over the sand, yanking each of the knives out, with slow, methodical movements as she wipes the black blood off the silver steel on her leg and puts them away. Just as she finishes, the next lot are let out, and she lets these get close. Then engages.

The dance is a series of blocks and swings, fluid movements, like a ballroom dance. There are three again, these only armed with sticks, but they fight well enough that Eleanor takes a hit to the back before dispatching them all. That wakes her up, the hunter inside her rising as the third wave is released.

She doesn't pull a blade, even as they lunge at her with theirs. They only last a few minutes before they lie in the circle of bodies she had started to amass. The crowd is cheering for her now, encouraging the bloodshed as she stalks to the opposite side of the arena to where the Daemones release, throwing her defeated opponent's blades over the lip before resting her back against the wall for a few seconds. Then three more are released, armed like the others, but much stronger than their predecessors. They don't rush towards her, instead spreading out as they inch across the arena.

Eleanor walks to them, not a single tell in the way she walks, no emotion visible through the black of the mask. But as she walks, she slides her gloves off, one finger at a time, until both sit in her hands. They clip under the tail of her coat, swapping for a set of brass knuckles, with a blade jutting out past her pinkie. She puts them on, flexing her fingers as she gets into range.

"Come on boys," she drawls, "It's not nice to keep a girl waiting."

"Like it's not ladylike for a girl to kill for sport?" the centre one replies.

"Either way, I'm not coming to you," she shrugs.

The one to her left advances, and she waits for him to make it to her. As soon as it is arms reach, the two others start moving in, but Eleanor is ready. She trained against people stronger than her for years, and while these people have the added benefit of not feeling pain until they are dead; she had no need to hold back. Her blades hit true, taking down the first two easily enough.

"You fight like the Berühmte Söldner, if you weren't fighting for the Prince, I'd assume you were one," the final man remarks as they circle each other.

She doesn't reply, advancing forward and pinning him to the ground after a minute of struggle. She places a blade on either side of his neck, leaning in to whisper in his ear.

"You're wrong," she tells him, "I was a Berühmte Söldner, and you just lost to a 16 year old."

Is face morphs to surprise, before it freezes, inklike blood spewing out of his neck where she had scissored it. She rolls upwards, standing over him for a second before collecting the blades.

The girl looks at Markus, who stands waiting to let the final man in. But he's waiting for her to give him the okay, ignoring the screaming crowd that begs for more, and looking to her. She waits until she's in a clear space, before giving him a nod to open it.

All the smaller blades now discarded, or locked into place like the throwing knives, she pulls her gloves back on, flexing her fingers as the ACE emerges from the walls. She waits in silence for him to get closer, watching his movements for favouring or weakness. He carries a small dagger, clasped in his right hand.

"You can't beat me," the man scoffs, stopping a few meters out from her and looking over the bodies. "Why don't you take that little mask of yours off so I can see your pretty face."

"I don't think I will," she replies. "Now shall we start?"

They launch in, fighting rough as they spin around in a series of complicated moves that even Markus, standing the closest to the fight, can't track. Eleanor is the one to stumble out of the engagement, a slice across her middle exposing the steel protecting underneath.

"You little bitch," he growls. "Traitorous, little bitch."

"Yes, yes. I am a traitor," she growls, "but that doesn't make me any less of a fighter."

"Do your friends know who you are?" he smirks, preparing to block her incoming attack.

"Of course they do. Had to get them to lock me up somehow..."

"And yet you're here."

"I am quite clever, you know. And quite good at diplomatic relations."

"You are a child."

"Try to keep that in mind as I kill you..."

They clash again, Eleanor dodging the dagger as they fight. Each of them gets hits in, and both manage to pin the other at different stages as they struggle to get control over the other. But then the man manages to pin her down and get the dagger to her throat, but he stops for a second to try and flaunt it, forgetting to pin down her legs. She snaps one of her legs upward, smashing into his groin hard enough to get her hands free and knock him off her, without slicing her throat on the dagger.

She launches forward, swords spinning in fury. Her near death had jump started her fight response to perfection, and the man had no chance as she assaults forward. A direct slash slices open his wrist, the dagger falling to the white sand, followed shortly after by black blood. In the man's surprise, she spins around behind him and slice through his Achilles tendon. Before he can fall to the ground, her sword is through his chest, following him to the ground.

"You do not piss off a pregnant woman," she hisses, pushing the sword deeper with each breath. "And you do not question my abilities."

The other blade slashes his throat, finishing him in a swift movement. She brings both swords away, leaving the body before she gets any more blood on herself.

"You need to learn, Nora," she says, just beneath her breath. "So handle it yourself."

It doesn't pass the Prince's notice as she tenses up, trying to hide her shakes as she turns to them again, dropping to a knee. The crowd are roaring in support, cheering for the new champion, but the noise is too much for Eleanor, who forces herself to leave the arena at a walk.

As soon as the gate is shut behind her, she finds the bucket, mask already off as she empties her stomach into its steel confines. Markus appears behind her shortly after, hand on her back as she stands back up again. Swigging some water, she spit into the bucket before drinking it properly.

"Well, that concludes that," he chuckles, stepping back as she slides down the wall. "You fight very skilfully, might I say. No one has ever beaten him."

"Yes well..." she trails off. "I have been doing this for a while."

He is about to respond, but the King rounds the corner, closely follow by his children. Eleanor is on her feet in seconds, bowing her head slightly as he waves a hand in dismissal.

"Congratulations, your skill is impressive," he says, face totally impassive as he speaks.

"Thank you," she replies in the same manner, refusing to meet the man's eyes.

There is hate, quelling in her heart, directed solely towards the King. She looks at him and all she can see is the man ordering his wife's execution, the man who shoved a child aside because of a single accident, that wasn't his fault. All she can see is the man who forced his child's hand.

"You'll join us for the meetings tomorrow," he finishes, turning away and leaving them behind.

Michael waits until his father is away before stepping forward and wrapping the girl in his arms, stroking her hair as tremors shudder through her muscles and into his. Once again, Anastasia watches the pair in wonder, surprised to find her brother being so caring.

"If he hadn't tried to rub it in my face, I would be dead," Eleanor whispers. "I was so scared."

"I know, Ellie, I know," he murmurs, "Just breathe in and out, try to block it out as much as you can. You were never going to die, if he showed any sign of beginning to finish it, the archer we had on the edge of the arena would have put an arrow through him."

The corner of her mouth twitches up, shoulders relaxing just a tad as she steps back. Her hands flex at her sides, head tilting ever so slight as she looks between the other two, who now stand together across from them.

"Let's get you cleaned up, then we can head out into the city for the rest of the day," the Princess smiles.

"That sounds good," Eleanor replies, smiling also. "But a shower is non-negotiable, I don't smell good."

"No, you do not," Michael mutters from behind her. "Shower, and then we need to talk."

Chapter 26

Washed and changed into a tight fitted baby pink shirt and loose grey pants, Eleanor settles herself on her bed. She's drawing, letting the lead continue to form the face on the paper as the siblings walk into the room. The door shuts, and she speaks.

"Are you going to tell me what Nikolas is to me?" she asks, not looking up as the two sit at the other end of the bed.

"You were right," Michael starts, "earlier... He is your soulmate. But we call it Geminae Animarum."

Her face doesn't change, but if they could hear her heartbeat, they would've heard it speed up significantly.

"And what does that mean?"

"It means that he will do whatever he can to keep you safe, and that we will do the same," Anastasia replies. "It means that he will be the love of your life."

"But it is different for humans than it is for us," Michael continues. "You have a choice. You can leave if you want to, and I beg you to remember that if he is too possessive of you."

"I believe he will be fine; I think he will take care of you like he should, but Michael is always suspicious of him. Even so, you shouldn't go off and run away with him just because you believe you will be safe," the Princess sighs.

"What will happen because I am his Geminae Animarum?" Eleanor asks, pencil still working across the page, but the other hand twitches at her side. "Is there some sort of ritual, or something?"

"When you first meet, which you have, a psychic bond is formed which is why you share memories. As you get closer this intensifies, things like your first kiss, sleeping in a bed together," Anastasia explains. "When you first have intercourse, you will be attached at the hip for a few weeks and get a lot more of each other's memories. The greatest crime in our laws, after killing the monarch of course, is separating Geminae for two months after their first mating."

"Being around your Geminae when you are injured helps you to heal, and their blood can also heal major wounds, but that is dependent on you staying close enough to connect for a successful healing," Michael follows, "but it is believed that that will only work with someone with strong Angelic blood, so he may be able to heal you, but you won't be able to heal him."

"Understandably," Eleanor shrugs, "are we needed to do anything else today?"

"No, you aren't," he replies. "But Eleanor, let your head relax. You'll get arthritis if you keep doing that with your fingers."

The movement stops abruptly, the teenager shooting a glare towards her babysitter.

"Don't give me that," he mutters, "one day all those sour looks will catch up to you."

"Well, I won't stop giving those looks, until you stop saying things that deserve them," she fires back. "And I can't help thinking about something like this."

"The fact that you are Geminae doesn't change anything, Eleanor. Make him work for it, make him show you that he deserves you," the Princess tells her. "You have everything to give him, you have everything over him so don't let him snatch it all away. You are strong, you have a will that is yours, don't let him just take that away because you are Geminae."

Eleanor smiles to Anastasia, locking eyes silently to hers as she looks up through her eyelashes, blinking slowly.

"Someone will bring some food up, and I'll come and see how you're going before dinner," Michael says, squeezing her shoulder softly. "Try and get some rest."

"I'll try," she replies, "promise."

The siblings leave via the door they came in through, and Eleanor lies back, rests her head on the pillow and curls body into a ball. She doesn't rise as the food arrives, leaving it sitting on the end of the bed until it goes cold. It is only when Michael re-enters the room that she moves, rolling onto her other side so she isn't looking at him.

"You haven't moved since we left, have you?" he mutters, walking around so her could see him.

"Correct..."

"Okay then, I guess I'm having dinner up here then," he sighs, moving to the door and calling for a maid. He tells her to bring up two meals before moving back to sit on the end of Eleanor's bed. "What's up, Ellie?"

"The fight just stressed me out," she replies. "It always happens after something like this, like a hangover. It's just, I've never had to recover alone."

Michael frowns, watching her as she slides herself into a sitting position.

"You should have told me, I would have stayed if you needed me to," he says, the expression stays as she shakes her head.

"It wasn't my place," she answers. "I'll be fine tomorrow."

"That's not the point, Eleanor. If you needed to be around someone, you should have told me and we could have stayed," he sighs. "Don't make yourself suffer alone."

"Won't your father be annoyed if we don't turn up to dinner?" Eleanor asks, avoiding meeting his eyes as he laughs slightly.

"Probably," he chuckles, "but you are in no shape to go down there, are you?"

"No, I'm not," she agrees, snapping her head to the door as there is a short knock. "Come in."

The maid walks in, placing the two trays next to their respective owners and picking up the cold one.

"Is there anything else you need?" she asks.

"No, thank you for bringing this up," Eleanor smiles, dismissing the girl.

"I don't need to remind you that you are finishing that entire meal, do I?" Michael mutters, digging in to his as she pushes her food around her plate.

"A quarter," she bargains.

"Three."

"One."

"A half, take it or leave it."

"Fine."

She does so, finishing half just before he finishes the lot and shifting back to sit against the headboard. Her blinks start to slow, face relaxing as she yawns. Michael stands up, patting her head like a dog before moving to the door.

"Thank you, Michael," Eleanor murmurs, "for staying."

"Anytime, Eleanor," he smiles, before he slips out the door.

Chapter 27

Eleanor is waiting outside her room for the siblings to join her, sitting with her back to the door as she sketches out the view down the corridor in the back of her notebook. She closes it as Michael and Anastasia arrive.

"Thanks for joining me," Eleanor sours, taking the hand Michael extends to pull her up. "It took you long enough."

Neither reply, pulling her along behind them as they make their way to the council room in which they would have their discussions.

The doors are wide open when they get there, people drifting in at their own rate. The chairs, surprisingly, are swivel chairs, on a set of six black wheels. They are tall, made of black leather and sitting evenly around the oval table in the middle of the room. A map shimmers in centre of the wood, a political map of Earth, Eleanor realises.

Michael guides her to a seat near the top of the table, with Anastasia on her left. Across the table is an older man, still fit, however, in a more decorated version of the guard uniform. His features somewhat resemble those of Markus, who sits tiredly next to him. The rest of the table is made up of men of varying ages, all trying their hardest to look important in the shadow of the royalty at the head of the table. Many are giving her sour looks. Then, Eleanor realises with a start, that she and Anastasia are the only women in the room.

"Don't comment on it," the Princess mutters, "there used to be more before my mother died."

She nods in acknowledgement, turning her attention to the red and black walls.

"Welcome to the war council, Eleanor," she continues.

"War council? I'm pretty sure I could take at least 90% of this room," the teen replies, voice in a low whisper.

Markus smirks at her across the table.

"We have enhanced senses, Miss Beck," his father says. "I'd suggest keeping snarky remarks to yourself once the King arrives."

"Duly noted," she nods.

The room then stands, Eleanor following them as they incline their heads and wait for the King to take his seat at the front of the room. Once he sits, they all follow, Eleanor having to grab the underside of the table to pull herself in as her feet dangle in the air. Stupid tall Angelic beings.

"We meet today to discuss the problem that has arisen from my late-wife's deranged bastard." Eleanor tightens her fist but refuses to let it show on her face. "We are joined once again by the Crown Prince, and he has brought a human" —the words are nearly a hiss— "girl" —this time is sounds more like he's spitting them out— "as the representative of the bases that were attacked."

"What does human dealings with an exiled, treasonous bastard have to do with us?" one of the men down the table grumbles, Eleanor marks him as Asshole One.

The siblings had to commend the teenager sitting between them, as she keeps a perfectly straight face in response to them insulting her Geminae. Anastasia herself fared worse as she lets a glower settle on her face.

"Daemones," Michael answers, looking at the man.

"What about them?"

"Nikolas has joined forces with them," Eleanor explains. "I believe he is in a position of power, it seemed as if he was ordering them around in the footage."

Everyone at the table pales substantially.

"Do we know why exactly?" Markus's father asks.

"Am I allowed to speak truthfully?" Eleanor checks, looking to Michael, who nods. "As an outsider, knowing what I know, I believe he joined them to get back at certain people, namely His Majesty and Michael. I have known many people who had everything change very quickly for them, and often they fall hard. He had nowhere else to go, no one else to turn to, and I think that led him straight to them."

"You think he's out to eliminate the line of succession?" another council member asks, this one with snow white hair.

"He said himself, 'My sister deserves to rule, and that includes clearing Michael from succession,'," she retells. "They have become his motivation, his only reason for continuing. That makes him dangerous, because you cannot be a good killer if you don't have someone to avenge."

"You sound like you are talking about yourself," the King muses from his seat at the head of the table.

"No, I speak like I understand the concept, but I am talking about Nikolas, I assure you," she returns.

"Okay then, what harm has been done so far?" Anastasia says, pulling them away from the topic.

"An attack on my residence while everyone excepting Eleanor and our security team was out. We have been unable to remove the bug he put in our surveillance system," Michael starts.

"Casualties?"

"24. Everyone excepting her."

"And he left her, why?" Asshole One hisses.

"The King said it himself, Nikolas is deranged. Maybe he just wanted someone to listen to his sob story," Eleanor suggests, making a good show of not caring.

"If you're such a good fighter, why didn't you take him down?" someone asks, Eleanor dubs him Asshole Two.

"Because I was unarmed, in my night clothes and had no sense of his ability or fighting style, which I do for the Daemones. He made it clear that he would be back at some point, so I figured it could wait until I was better prepared for it," she atones.

"What else..."

"There have been attacks on seven different locations most leaving survivors, only having losses of life accessing the command system and the intelligence," Michael continues, waving a hand over the map. It zeros in on America, glowing dots appear at each of the bases. "However, a week ago, as the decision was made to come here, there was an attack on an Air Force base in Jackson, Mississippi." The respective location marker raises. "There were no survivors."

"How big was his team?"

"Just him. Took down the entire base by himself."

No one speaks, Eleanor shifting slightly as Anastasia and Markus look at her in confusion.

"It appears he was having a temper tantrum about us going to 'dob on him'," Eleanor mutters. "We haven't heard anything of him since."

A lie. She had seen him as they left, and had spoken to him two days ago, in that dream.

"He can bring the Daemones here. He can give up our location," yet another of the board mutters, horror in his voice.

"While we do not believe he would do so, seeing as though his motivation is to win the throne for the Princess, however, if he loses sight of that end goal you may be at risk. I'd suggest simply increasing border security so you can be prepared if he does try to attack," Eleanor says. "Be suspicious of anyone who comes from outside. The Berühmte Söldner work mostly with humans, and they could easily do as much harm as one of the Daemone foot soldiers. Many punches to the gut can do more harm than one to the temple."

"You are very well versed in the dealing of a War Council, for someone so young…" the King muses as everyone else scribbles things down in their notebooks.

"Human minds often get stuck in the way they used to work, and if they want to survive in this new age, they have to bring in fresh blood. New minds," she shrugs. "And I've been sitting in on meetings for years now. They're training me to take a spot among the best."

Little truths, white lies. A web spun to perfection.

"Yes well, I'd suggest you're close to getting there," Markus smiles from across the table, smoothly finishing the conversation before it continues to fall down the track.

"Thank you."

"Back to topic," Anastasia catches, before anyone else can speak. "Do you know the whereabouts of the base he is operating out of?"

"No, we don't," Eleanor starts, "We believe it is on the East Coast, and while it is speculative, we also believe it may be in the south."

"However, they are unable to track the bug on the systems to get rid of it, let alone use it to find him. But the human technicians are working on it," Michael continues.

They leave Angeli Terra a week later, the Crown Prince anxious to get back to America with his brother's Geminae and Eleanor's abdomen was continuing to grow larger. The longer they were there the riskier it would be. Eleanor pocketed a letter Anastasia had written to Nikolas without Michael seeing. The two farewell as if they were sisters, and Eleanor swears not to let Nikolas know that she knew he was her Geminae. To make him prove himself first.

They land back at their compound just as night falls.

Chapter 28

"**W**ell, you're both alive and here, that's promising," Colonel Randall remarks, as they walk into the compound. "Did all go as planned?"

"Yes, no-one discovered anything wrong about her other than my sister, which was expected, and my closest friend, who will not say anything," Michael reports. "We have plans in place, which I will discuss with you later."

"And did she behave herself?" Nancy continues, looking over the girl (who is wearing notably loose clothes).

"I am right here, you know," she mutters, running a hand up her head in exhaustion.

"Eleanor behaved fine," Michael follows. "A little testy, had a few hormonal moments but managed to leash her temper long enough to get it onto paper."

"I don't want to see those pictures, do I?" Nancy teases. "Didn't the King make a good impression?"

"He's a misogynistic asshole who deserves to die for what he did to his wife and her son," she mutters, "and now he continues to be an asshole to his daughter."

"Does he now?"

"Mm hm, plans on forcing her to marry. She has to go along with it or he'll stick her with some other snobby prick," Eleanor rants. "And she is absolutely brilliant, but he doesn't let her do her job because she is a girl and I really, really want to kill him."

"Do you think you should be saying that, Eleanor?"

"I don't care if people know, he is such a freaking asshole. I said my parents were dead and he barely even said anything," she continues. "He has all his guards watching Anastasia and lets them tease her and be mean to her. They had more decency in the assassin Agency. Killing, lying, but if a girl had any chance of being useful, they treated them fairly. At least most of them. There're always a few assholes."

The woman hums, laughing slightly under her breath as Eleanor continues. She only stops as they reach the car, blushing slightly and apologising profusely as they prepare to leave.

"Get some dinner on the way home and get some sleep. We'll see you in the morning," Nancy says, holding the door open for her to get in.

"Thank you for letting me go."

Nancy nods, allowing them to leave.

They get McDonalds, Eleanor still snacking on her nuggets as they walk into the manor house. She had already finished a large fries and a burger. They find everyone sitting up in the living room. Everyone plus one, Eleanor finds as she scans the faces.

A girl sits in a wheelchair next to Zach, the black hair, blue eyes, matching Zach's enough for Eleanor to deduce it is his younger sister. She freezes from her toes to her hands, blinking at the girl in shock.

"Michael…" she murmurs. "Michael, I know who did that…"

It takes him a moment to catch on, before he replies, "It's okay, Ellie. Just breathe in and out. She doesn't need to know."

"But she never deserved this," Eleanor replies.

"I know Ellie."

Zach stands up, pulling their attention. Eleanor still trembling in her spot.

"Michael, you've already met Bella, but Eleanor, I'd like to introduce you to my sister," he says, smiling slightly as Michael walks forward and makes a show of kissing her hand, but Eleanor stays absolutely still. "Eleanor?"

The food in her hands drops, barely hitting the ground before she starts to back away.

"I'm sorry. I, I can't," she mutters, before turning and running out the doors that lead to outside.

Michael groans, about to go after her, but Kenichi stops him.

"I'll go, she's seen too much of you recently. She needs some calm," he says, before jogging out of the door behind her.

"Did I do something wrong?" Bella, asks as she looks at the adults, thin hands folded in her lap.

"No, sweetie," Kaylee sighs, "Eleanor is a very complex person, and I'm pretty sure she just overloaded. Nothing to do with you."

"She froze at the sight of me. I'm pretty sure it was me," she shakes, glancing up to her brother.

"Eleanor used to work for bad people. And she is not here as an employee, more a detainee," Michael starts.

"Was she involved in what happened?" Zach growls, placing a hand on his sister's shoulder.

"She wasn't, but knows who was," Michael admits. "Eleanor blames herself for everything which she had no control over. She is a good person, but she gets scared and then she hides her true self. We're still working on bringing her out again. Really, she shouldn't be in the field, but we needed to take her. She would have been fine if you were introduced more slowly, but tonight she just was a little too tense."

Both siblings swallow, but Bella smiles sadly.

"Can you let her know, when she's ready, that I would still like to meet her?" she asks.

"Bella..."

"No, Zach. It wasn't her fault; I could see it. She shouldn't blame herself."

Everyone stays in steely silence, watching for any weakness in her.

"Thank you, Bella," Michael sighs. "Eleanor, she is very... it's hard for her, to get past things. She needs a friend who doesn't carry the switch to her anklet."

Bella nods, glancing to her brother for a second.

"I'm going to go to bed, see you in the morning," she says, before wheeling herself away and down to the library end of the house, where the spare room must be hers.

"I'm sorry," Michael says with a glance to Zach. "I wouldn't have brought her in this way if I knew she was here."

The man nods absently, running a hand over his hair.

"Does she know? About him?" Kaylee asks, looking at Michael carefully.

"No," he answers, a lie, but no one picks up on it. "And she won't either. I want him to have to prove himself first, make it so she isn't forced into it because of what they are."

"Smart," the woman nods.

Chapter 29

Kenichi finds Eleanor sitting in the stable, hands trembling as she turns them over in her lap.

"Go away," she mutters, voice hoarse. "I'm fine."

"No you aren't," he replies, voice quiet as the night around them.

Eleanor glares at him, stopping the movement for a few seconds before resuming.

"So, what has you riled up," he gives, sitting next to her against the wall.

"Nothing."

"Don't lie to me Eleanor, you know I don't like it."

The one light Kenichi turned on is the only thing giving any view of the corridor, most of the horses rest in the backs of their stalls as the two sit against the wall.

"I bottled a lot of emotion while I was on Angeli Terra. And I have a connection to that girl that, I wish I didn't," she admits. "I executed the person who put her in that chair, for failing to kill her and Zach."

"Right," Kenichi sighs. "I should have figured you would need some time when you got back, we knew you could be volatile."

Eleanor laughs slightly.

"That was not me being volatile. You have not seen me volatile."

"I believe you... how did it go? Not the logistics, I mean for you."

"Michael still won't tell me what Nikolas is to me," she growls. Kenichi could have sworn her eyes flicked to the camera just briefly. "And any time I saw that wretched King, I could barely stand it. I had to bow to this man who I saw kill his own wife in front of his children. And I killed an ACE. One who had beaten my ass to the curb on multiple occasions just because I made a little mistake. And if I hadn't had the protection on my stomach, I would have lost it. I was all alone for hours after and I've never done that before and I couldn't stop replaying it. I couldn't draw it out, because I needed to ensure no-one discovered me. Then I saw her, Bella, sitting in the wheelchair. I knew I wouldn't be able to control myself and I started to get scared because I know what happens to people who fail and I failed the worst of all. And they won't stop coming for me."

Kenichi takes her hand gently, making her look at him.

"Eleanor, when you have problems like this, you need to tell Michael, okay?" he sighs, "He doesn't understand it as well as some people, and you do an exceptional job of hiding it. But you cannot bottle it up inside you."

"I know."

They sit in silence, Eleanor staying scarily still as they sit there, her hand resting on her stomach.

"You can find out the gender in a few weeks," Kenichi muses, "Do you want to know?"

Eleanor stays silent for a few more seconds, before shifting slightly.

"I think so," she answers. "But I want to think about it."

"Understandably." Kenichi looks down to Eleanor, watching her carefully. "How was the morning sickness?"

"Luckily not public, threw up a few times when I woke up, once or twice after dinner," she shrugs. "After my fight I threw up as well."

"What was it that set it off? The blood, death. The exertion?"

"All of it. The blood, it was black, like ink," she shudders. "And the crowd, I've never fought like that before and, it was terrifying. Fighting for me has always been in the dark, with no one living to tell the tale, but in that arena... it was like I was naked, undressed for everyone to see."

"I never thought about that. We must have forgotten your reaction to the crowds when you arrived," he apologises. "Now are we going up to that house again anytime soon?"

Eleanor shakes her head, looking to her the hand that sits loose.

"I don't want to see her again," she breathes.

"Okay then," he shrugs, "But you need rest, so until Michael comes down to get us when he eventually figures it out, try and get to sleep."

She nods, resting her head tentatively on his shoulder and shutting her eyes as he shifts to put an arm around her. Kenichi is right, Michael walking down about 20 minutes later to find Eleanor asleep next to the doctor sitting on the floor.

"She overloaded," Kenichi explains, glancing at her softly. "You need to be careful of what she does, in case she doesn't decide to run away next time."

"I know. I should have taken her away immediately, it was a mistake," the taller acknowledges.

"And don't ever send her into an arena ever again," Kenichi then growls, though calmly enough that he doesn't stir the girl.

"She handled the fight fine..."

"No she didn't. She didn't tell you, but crowds watching her scares her. Remember when she first came, the reporters?"

"I didn't realise."

"No, you didn't. Now take her up to bed before she wakes up."

Michael complies, scooping an arm under her knees and the other behind her back before easily picking her up off the ground. The two males walk back up to the house, Eleanor staying in deep sleep the entire way up. The remainders of the team are still sitting in the living room, watching as the two come closer, see Eleanor asleep in Michael's arms.

"She passed out?" Kaylee asks softly, walking up and brushing some of the hair out of the girl's face.

"Eventually, yes," Kenichi answers. "Emotional overload."

"She's okay though?"

"Physically yes, but she's still a little sensitive," he sighs, nodding to Michael to take her upstairs.

He complies without argument, placing her on her bed as softly as he can. Leaving her in her clothes, he pulls the blankets up to her chin and slips out of the room once more. Eleanor sleeps through the night, surprisingly enough, but when she does wake, she doesn't leave her room. It is Kaylee who notices her absence, huffing beneath her breath before walking up the stairs and walking into the room.

"We're having breakfast together," she tells her. "You need to come down."

"Is that a good idea? Isn't Zach mad that I ran out on his sister last night?" Eleanor replies, not turning to meet the woman's eyes.

"Bella forgave you already, for all of it. And told him to forget it, so no. He may be a little testy, but he isn't mad at you."

Eleanor shifts slightly, before sighing and packing her pencils away. She murmurs a soft, 'give me a second' before waiting for the woman to step outside and changing into a soft knee length pink dress. It falls loosely over her stomach, the bulge now nearly too big to hide beneath regular clothes. How they had gotten away with it in Angeli Terra she had no idea, but they had.

She walks down a step behind the strawberry blonde, shuffling silently to the seat between Kenichi and Michael and sitting down.

"You're going to have to go shopping again soon," Kenichi notes as she sits down. "Those clothes are getting a little small."

"That's what happens when your pregnant," Eleanor mutters, serving herself a large plate of toast and bacon.

"You're pregnant?" Bella — sitting at the other end of the table — asks.

"I am," is the terse reply. "16 weeks."

"That's wonderful, are you excited?" Bella smiles.

"I am." The words are kinder this time, and Eleanor manages to meet the girl's eyes.

"Okay, let's stop, this…" Zach swings his hand around. "before people start crying. Everything is chill, no one has any grudges, we're fine."

Eleanor stabs a piece of bacon and shoves it in her mouth, but a small smile graces her lips.

Chapter 30

The child was a girl, female. This information the only interesting news directly after her visit to Angeli Terra.

The following quite vital (I think at least) interaction wasn't caught on camera, like most are, instead the only record of it is the recount Nikolas wrote in his journal. I have kept it as it is, as record of their meeting.

~

I had reached out to speak to her in her mind, simple words. *'Come to the back fence at 11,'* was all. She had jumped at first, I saw it on the cameras that I had connected to my phone. She spoke aloud, looking up at the camera as if she knew I was watching.

"Do you want me to bring your sword?" she asked.

'Yes, please,' I responded into her mind.

I was waiting. She arrived dressed in a beautiful white frock and a long grey coat which fell to her knees and covered her hands, a ward against the dropping temperatures. Her skin was a little less pale than it had been before she went to that blasted island, but was still too light, too, imprisoned. And her beautiful round lips, they were washed out as well, as if she hadn't been eating properly.

"Hello, Eleanor," I had said. She had stayed a few meters away, watching me.

"Hello, Nikolas," she had replied.

Her voice made my heart skip a beat, meek and raw. I could hear the German taint, the worry behind the tired tone. Then she pulled out my blade from beneath the coat and walked just close enough for the handle to hang within my reach. I took it as carefully as possible, watching her fingers as they pinched the blade.

"Why did you want me to come?" she asks, eyes flicking to keep off mine, off me.

She was nervous, I realised.

"I wanted to talk to you, to make sure you were okay," I told her, smiling softly as she looked to me, to my face in surprise.

"That is very kind," she smiled, "I also have a letter for you, from your sister."

That was a surprising development, but I had taken the note and tucked it into my jacket pocket.

"You are okay, though? Nothing went wrong?"

"I am okay, and other than the King being the biggest misogynistic prick in the world, Angeli Terra was fine," she answered, "life is confusing, it always has been, nothing has changed from that."

"You found out what gender your child is, didn't you?" I had offered. I didn't want the time to end.

"Yes, a girl," she had smiled.

The smile that had pulled across her face, made me need to see more of it.

"And she is healthy?"

"Yes. I need to eat a little more, consistently, and try to stay calm, but other than that…"

"Have you gotten any more of my memories?"

"One, maybe. I couldn't tell is if was just a bad dream, though," she had said, "do you, get mine?"

"Yes, but only a few," I told her, offering a hand to her.

She took it, letting me pull her closer and brush some hair behind her shoulder.

"Do you have a way to deal with the nightmares?" I asked. "Because they must… they aren't pleasant."

"Nothing in my head is pleasant…" she trailed, looking away. The despair in her eyes, I wanted to make it go away. "But yes, I do. I lost most of them when I escaped, but I've filled hundreds of sketchbooks over the years."

"Good, it isn't nice to waste away into you past," I offered. "You should head back up now."

"That's probably a good idea," she agreed, then her body hardened. "First, however, do you work with the Berühmte Söldner?"

"They are one of the factions within the Daemones. Not the only one that uses humans, but the one who uses the most," I answered. "Your boss specifically mentioned you a while ago, was very, very pissed that you evaded recapture and took out an ACE."

"Good, he had it coming," she snarled, pure hate filling her face.

"That he did. Goodbye, Dulce Meum."

Grinned, offering a goodbye and letting her beautiful, long, ash hair stay clear of those pale blue eyes. I stayed perfectly still as she walked away, watching her disappear. Then I broke.

"Eleanor?" I called, my Geminae turning around to listen. "Don't let them change you from who you are or who you want to be."

"I won't," she replies. "If you don't."

She smirked at me through the trees, challenging me without words. I return the look, letting the corner of my mouth turn up. A light pink dust forms on her cheeks, but she continues to hold my stare.

"Deal," I call, turning away from her and forcing myself to walk.

I really didn't want to leave, especially as her gaze stayed on my back as I walked away. We've met only three times, but I am already falling in love with her.

~

Eleanor's writing is just an extract, but I feel like you should know her thoughts as well.

~

He was dressed in human clothes, that is what surprised me first. He wore a long black coat, with distinguished buttons and deep pockets which stopped at mid-thigh, though on me is would probably be past my knees. His jeans were a near black, and his hair was gelled into a quiff. It had looked odd on him. It was as if he was in the wrong time, the wrong clothes, which would make sense considering where he came from. He had been so careful with everything he said. Every question he asked. And he had been so worried as well. I, I could see how he wasn't at ease. Wasn't at home in this world. And I could see how we could be connected.

Chapter 31

The Berühmte Söldner sacrifice many agents to retrieve their lost ACE. In desperation, they send her trainer, Nathan Meyers, to bring her back. Instead, they have a conversation in a shopping mall and go their separate ways. Even still, they forget the power of kinship and make the mistake of deploying another nearby. For a few hours they lose track of Sebastian Fox In hindsight, it's laughable that they were so powerful, really.

~

Eleanor is sitting curled on her bed, leafing through her book, completely unaware as the male assassin slips through the house undetected. He checks the door of her room, surprised as it opens with ease.

"Michael? I thought you wouldn't be back for a few hours?" she asks, not looking up from her book.

The boy just stares at her, dirty blonde hair falling over his grey eyes. Features like Nikolas's. After a minute of no reply, Eleanor talks again, still looking at her book.

"Did the mission not go well?" she murmurs.

"Nora?" he asks, stepping softly into the room as her head snaps up.

He shuts the door behind him.

"What are you doing here?" she asks, her hand instantly finding her dagger.

"I came to get you away from this place, so we can raise that baby, together. Mother said we could hide in our summerhouse. We'd be together and safe, I promise," he rushes, moving forward to sit next to her.

"Seb, I can't," she whispers. "Our life isn't safe, and I don't want to run anymore. Here, they can protect me, and if something does go badly, I trust them to keep her safe."

Her hand moves to her stomach carefully.

"And you don't trust me?" he asks.

"I do, except all you have known all your life is the Agency. I want this child to live, free," she replies, shaking her head meekly. "We're both criminals, Seb."

He stares at her for a minute, then sighs, leaning back against the headboard.

"I miss you, Nora," he murmurs. "I really do."

"I'm sorry, Seb, I really am. But this is the best choice," she breathes, tears starting to roll down her cheeks.

They both look at each other, locking eyes softly. He leans closer and cups her cheek in his hand, guiding her silently forward. The kiss is barely one, more a brush of the lips, but Eleanor gets a weird sense in her gut that hadn't been there before. Like she should be kissing someone else. Tears fall as he pulls back, still holding her cheek in his hand.

"I love you," he murmurs, kissing her once more. "Live a good life, Nora."

She nods weakly, watching as he leaves her. The doors stays slightly ajar, Eleanor remains perfectly still, as if in shock. She sits there for a few minutes, before she straightens slightly, a scowl settling on her face.

"Not now, Nikolas," she snaps, eyes darting to the camera in the corner of her room. She pauses again, then shakes her head. "I am fine, he would never hurt me." Eleanor scoffs. "Oh, stop being jealous. I do have a previous life." Another pause. "Just, please not now Nikolas. It will fry my emotions; I need to keep you and him separate... Thank you."

Michael finds her two hours later, curled on her bed with a necklace in her fist and her books open in front of her. He has looked through them, so recognises the drawing of the shirtless man.

"You really need to work on security here," she murmurs. "Had a visitor today, another old friend."

"Who was he?" he asks softly, sitting next to her and leaning back against the headboard.

"He was my only ever friend, I loved, I love him, I think," she starts.

When she next moves, the necklace that had stayed around her neck ever since she had gotten out drops into her box. With little more than a second glance, the box closes and returns to its place. It was time she moved on.

Chapter 32

Eleanor stands in silence, just behind her trainer, as they lead in a boy her own age. He finds her eyes, smirking at her as she stays perfectly still.

"He has shown promise, and is to train beside her," an older man orders, one of the handlers. Their handler.

"Yes sir. Are there any vices I need to work out?" her trainer replies.

"Has a bit of an attitude," their handler huffs, eyes flicking to Eleanor for a second. "Might get into a few fights with your other one."

It's only now that Eleanor reacts, sending her sweetest smile to the older man.

"I'll promise to play nice, if he doesn't be an ass," she blinks, "though, boys are much worse at holding their tempers than girls."

"I don't appreciate your suggestion, personally I find girls are much bitchier," the boy retorts.

"See, but the key to being bitchy is to hold your temper long enough to make them suffer," Eleanor teases. "Which boys cannot manage."

"Now, now, Kleiner Fuchs. That's no way to treat your new partner," Nathan Myers reprimands. "No one is doubting your ability to stand up for yourself."

"Sorry, sir," she mutters, bowing her head.

~

"Can you two manage to stop arguing long enough for me to finish these assignments, or do I need to tape your mouths shut?" Nathan growls

from his desk, not raising his eyes to look at the pair who sit on the couch. He speaks in fluent German.

"I can keep my mouth shut," a 13 year old Eleanor replies, also in German. "Not sure about him though."

"Funny, I was about to say the same thing about you," the boy retorts.

"Both of you shut it," the adult snaps, "you've both already got two missions, I could give you both another."

"Sorry, Mein Vater," Eleanor murmurs, followed quickly by her counterpart.

The room is silent for the next ten minutes, not a single whisper breaking the still air. That is until the door to their little apartment swings open and their handler walks in. He goes to her Vater, taking the assignments their trainer offers forward.

"Those two been causing trouble?" he asks.

"Just between themselves. Easily remedied however," the assassin replies.

"The board believes that the girl is nearly ready to complete her training. Do you agree with this?"

"Yes, sir. She would benefit from some more experience in the field, however."

"And the boy?"

"A year, maybe two until he's ready. He did start later than she did."

"That is what the board figured as well."

The elder man nods to the teenagers on the couch, before leaving. Once the door shuts, Eleanor's Vater rises and takes her shaking hands in his.

"You will be alright, okay?" he tells her, "I wouldn't let them do it if you weren't ready, Kleiner Fuchs."

"It's just the tattoo, right? And harder missions?"

"Yes, the rest comes when you graduate."

She shifts forward, resting her head on her Vater's shoulder, sighing as he wraps his arms around her.

~

"Get her out of my sight," her handler growls in harsh German, stalking away from Eleanor's beaten form. "The only reason she isn't getting more is because the site was still clean of DNA, and the objective was fulfilled."

Her Vater walks forward, careful to not be too hurried as he pulls her up off the floor and gathers her into his arms to carry her out.

"She doesn't get food for two days."

There is a nod, then the pair disappear from the older man's view. Eleanor starts sobbing as they get to the apartment, arms too weak to wrap around her Vater's neck, so instead she just burrows into his chest.

"I have to go, Kleiner Fuchs," he whispers, voice breaking slightly as he places the girl on the bed. "I am so very sorry."

She doesn't reply, barely nodding in recognition as he leaves her on the bed. Sebastian comes in a few minutes later, stopping in shock as he finds her bloody and shaking on the red sheets. But he gets over it, walking back out and filling a bowl with warm water and grabbing a cloth.

The 14-year-old takes time cleaning each of her injuries, removing the blood off all the tainted skin. Once completed, he pulls her closer so her arms wrap around him.

"I killed my baby sister," Eleanor whimpers, the words spoken in English. "And she recognised me."

"What happened?" he asks carefully, pad of his thumb brushing over her cheekbone, where a bruise is starting to form.

"I painted 'I'm sorry' on the wall," she admits, voice still trembling.

"Oh, Nora," he sighs, running a hand through her hair. "Try to get a little sleep, it will help you heal."

"I can't Seb, I can't," she shakes.

"I'll be right here the entire time, promise."

~

Eleanor shakes into consciousness, eyes wet as she pulls herself up. Within a few seconds, any trace of the emotion is gone, blocking anything else from flowing through the crack in her armour. She doesn't let herself stay there, on the bed, instead she locks her door and grabs a change of clothes, walking to the shower.

Keeping the water hot, and taking time to wash out her hair, she steps out with the towel wrapped around her chest. Then she starts to blow dry her hair, loosely straightening it as she goes, only stepping out and changing when it is completely dry. After pulling on a pair of loose pants and a singlet, she slips out of her room and into the gym the next door over.

The itch to fight had been annoying her all week, and she knew that she needed to release the pent-up energy before she ended up getting in a fight with an actual person. Luckily the room is empty, and she quickly wraps her knuckles. The light thud of fist on the punching bag is the only sound for the first few minutes, before she starts to talk. The words start off in German, a mission report from a few years earlier, before they shift into French. She cycles through about 14 different languages, keeping in beat with the punches against the bag.

"I seem to remember telling you that you weren't to exert yourself," Kenichi calls from the doorway, laughing as Eleanor jumps and spins towards him. "However, I get the feeling you need to let off steam."

"Going from training every day to not at all is very difficult," she mutters, "and it isolates my thoughts."

"Is the reason you need to isolate your thoughts related to your visitor yesterday?" he asks, walking closer as she starts to unwind the wraps around her knuckles.

"Yes, triggered memories, some okay, one not," she shrugs. "As long as no one asks the wrong questions I'll be fine."

"Well, you have an email from the Princess," he continues, chucking her iPad to her with ease. "Apologises for the late reply were in Michael's, she wasn't able to get to the connection for a little bit."

"Great. Any other reason I was interrupted?" Eleanor snips, walking out in front of the doctor.

"You have been in here for at least three hours, maybe more, and you need to eat," he returns. "I really don't appreciate you ignoring all my instructions. 'Tis very annoying."

"'Tis it?" she laughs, before sobering, "sorry, I just needed to get it out before I accidently spurred someone into a fight."

"I assume that's happened before?"

"Multiple times, yes," she huffs.

"Well, thank you for realising that as a problem and fixing it. Now we just need to get you eating consistently."

Eleanor nods, sighing as they enter the kitchen. Zach and Kaylee are already sitting there, Michael somewhere else in the house, and both look up as she sits next to them.

"You know, hearing a quite gory mission report being rattled off in a heap of different languages is a little weird first thing in the morning," the female remarks, turning back to her food.

"Well the books I ordered haven't turned up yet," Eleanor replies, grabbing herself an apple and settling into her seat. "I need to practise them to keep them up."

"What do you want on your toast?" Kenichi follows, standing by the cupboard in wait.

"I don't wan-" she starts, but he gives her a look. "Vegemite, if there's any?"

There is, so begrudgingly, she eats the toast, managing to get it all down before Michael joins them.

"Good, you've eaten," he remarks, "And it wasn't chicken nuggets, it's a miracle!"

The words are blunt, exhausted. Eleanor doesn't retort, instead forming a frown on her face.

"What's wrong?" she asks.

"Nothing," Michael replies, an obvious lie.

"If you didn't want me to ask, you would've tried to hide it just a little," she returns, challenging him.

"Stop asking, Eleanor," he bites.

Two things happen at once here;

One. Nikolas pushes a mental barrier around his Geminae, struggling to hold it from so far away.

Two. Michael loses control over his Aspect, accidently sending persuasion into the words.

The barrier stops it from reaching her, however, everyone in the room knows what happened, and look at Eleanor in confusion as she glares furiously at Michael. It was at this time, Nikolas speaks into her head, and then later writes it down.

'Tell him that if he ever tries that again, I will slit his throat while he sleeps,' he says, *'let him know it's from me as well.'*

So Eleanor does, relaying the words to the pale Angeli. He turns even paler as she speaks, glancing at the camera feverishly and apologising profusely.

'Thank you, Dulce Meum,' Nikolas continues. *'I do apologise as well, his temper was so short because I caused a little havoc last night, destroyed some important papers.'*

"Well at least you didn't steal them," Eleanor speaks, everyone standing around her frowning.

'I was supposed to, they did not like that very much.'

"You okay?"

'Yes, a little sore, but otherwise fine.'

Eleanor looks up to the camera in the corner of the room, smiling softly before turning to everyone else in the room.

"You've been talking to him, haven't you?" Kaylee questions, "I didn't know he was telepathic."

"He shouldn't be that strong, he isn't of royal blood..." Michael starts, looking at her nervously.

"You have the same mother," Eleanor snaps, "and his father had strong blood as well. His mental abilities stretch further than the King choses to acknowledge."

"Far enough to block your mind? He never showed any ability to do that before," Michael frowns.

'It only developed when I was exposed to the Daemones,' Nikolas tells her.

"It only developed recently, exposure to the Daemones triggered it," she retells, "but either way, you need to stop acting as if he is so far beneath you."

"Let's not argue about this, we have work to do. Unless you want to tag along and sit in a room at the compound all day, you'll be here alone," Zach interrupts, looking between the two. "You could make use of the piano; it needs more playing."

"I might," she nods. "But I think you can understand if I might keep a gun at my side whenever I'm alone now? That's two people who have broken in here and, luckily, they both didn't want to kill me. But I don't trust that the next person won't."

"We'll warn the guards," Zach nods, "Don't go shooting for fun though."

"I won't."

The team leave a few minutes later, and Eleanor drifts to the instrument. The music is still ringing through the house when they return, accompanied by the low and steady singing that floats through the air in harmony with the music.

Chapter 33

The time between the last chapter, when Eleanor was at 26 weeks pregnant, and when we will soon pick up, has been calm enough for it not to warrant documentation. Other than a few weak attempts at getting her back, and more attacks lead by Nikolas (though they talked every so often, they did not meet in person again), life for Eleanor was as simple as it ever was.

It makes me happy to think of her so relaxed. So unburdened. Most of my memories of her are not this way.

It's now Christmas Eve, Eleanor hiding in her room. Parties weren't ever her scene.

~

"Eleanor, come out," Kaylee pleads, trying the door handle again.

"I don't want to, Kaylee," Eleanor replies, glaring at the door as if to will it to stay shut.

"Why, Ellie? Give me a good reason and I will leave you alone," the elder tries.

Eleanor is silent for a few seconds, before taking a shuddering breath and rising to unlock the door. Kaylee walks in, standing at the edge of the girl's bed as she waddles (with some difficulty) back and sits down.

"Each Christmas, since I was ten, I've had to kill people," Eleanor starts, voice shaking as her hand absentmindedly lays on her stomach. "Sometimes, it would be an assassination, shooting someone and disappearing without a trace. Other times I would be sitting at the table with them, a political guest, or I'd be staff, and slip poison into the food. I blew up a house, once, killing everyone inside. This holiday, it isn't a holiday for me."

Kaylee smiles weakly, sitting down and wrapping an arm around the heavily pregnant teenager.

"Then we'll just have to change that, won't we?" she murmurs. "I promise it will be fun."

Eleanor growls slightly, but her shoulders drop in acceptance. She lets the older woman lead her out, scowl set on her face the entire way down the stairs.

"Oh, stop that," the strawberry blonde snips as they get to the bottom. "It's only Michael, Zach, his sister and Nancy's family, it's not like we're making you go to the New Year's party."

Kenichi had gone back to Japan a week earlier, to be with his family for the holiday, and was due to return a few days after Christmas.

"There's a party on New Year's?" Eleanor replies meekly, glancing on the side to her friend.

"Yes, you can hide in your room the entire time, don't worry," Kaylee chuckles, "Now, all the food was made in this kitchen, by us, so no silly business, okay?"

"Okay."

Eleanor runs a hand over her huge stomach, other hand carrying a slight tremble, which she hides in the folds of her dress. Kaylee pulls out a chair for her, tucking it in before finding her own seat. They don't notice the change in her posture as she straightens, releasing a deep breath.

"Good to see you've joined us," Nancy greets, nearly getting a light slap from Bella, but the girl stops herself.

"Now everyone is here, should we start eating?" she says instead, beginning to reach for the hot food.

Her brother nods, also beginning to hand out the food onto everyone's plates. Eleanor only eats a minimal amount, and half of it is the food for the Colonel's kids, sausages and the like. They move to the entertainment room after the meal, Eleanor taking the seat at the piano while the others take spots on the couches. The kids see her sitting there and start to beg her to play something, having heard her play on a previous visit.

She nearly refuses, not wanting to show off, and because she was slightly worried it might trigger something, but she gives in, spinning around and opening the lid. Soon enough, the tune of Christmas carols bounces through the air, and the kids start singing along out of tune. Eleanor tenses, but continues to play as her body guards itself against the beating she expects to follow. But it doesn't, and it's only as Bella places a hand on her shoulder that she snaps back to where she is. But her hands don't shake like they would normally, continuing on at the same rhythm.

"They beat you if you weren't perfect, didn't they?" Bella asks quietly, voice being drowned out by the piano.

"They did," Eleanor replies simply, focus not even flickering. "I won't stay up for much longer."

And that she does, slipping upstairs shortly after she finishes the round of Christmas carols.

A wrapped present sits on the pillow of her bed, small and boxy in shape.

She laughs lightly, smiling up at the camera that blinks slowly in the corner of the room.

'Open it,' he whispers into her head, and so she complies.

The book is hardcover, a pale brownish green with a tree reaching across the cover. 'To Kill a Mockingbird,' is printed between the branches in white text. She opens the front to find a neat inscription written on the first page.

'Apologies if you've read it, but I quite enjoyed the reading. I thought you would like the cover,' it reads, written in perfectly neat script. 'Signed, Nikolas.'

Eleanor looks up at the camera again, looking through it as if she could see him watching on the other side.

"Thank you," she says, "I feel bad I couldn't get anything for you."

'You didn't have to,' he tells her, 'I just thought you might like it.'

"Well, I do, it is very kind," she blushes.

'Merry Christmas, Dulce Meum.'

"Merry Christmas, Nikolas."

Eleanor shuts her door, barely suppressing the grin that fills her face. She reads the first few chapters before she goes to bed, hand continuously running over the words written in the front.

Downstairs, the adults start talking, the Colonel glancing out the door a few minutes after Eleanor had left.

"How is she? Seemed a little riled," she asks Michael, who sits next to her.

"She's on edge, definitely," he replies. "Has been very cautious about everything. Like she was originally. Food, water, people. Doesn't trust anything."

"Is she volatile?"

"Only a little, we have it under control though," Kaylee pipes up. "And she is under constant surveillance."

"Good. Is she worried about any more attempts?"

"She hasn't voiced it, but she is."

The conversation finishes, but each of them know the danger she faces.

She wakes twice through the night needing to pee, so luckily no nightmares manage to catch up with her sleeping patterns. When everyone else wakes up, she is sitting on the lounge downstairs, reading the book she had received the night before. Kaylee frowns at the book as she walks in, having no memory of it being bought, or it being here previously, but lets it go as Eleanor turns her head to look at her.

"What time did you all go to sleep?" she asks, shutting the book quietly.

"A few hours after you," the older woman shrugs, pouring herself a coffee and silently offering a drink for the teenager.

"Juice please," she replies.

They don't talk again, Eleanor taking her juice gratefully and leaving her feet up on the couch as she reopens her book. She had long outgrown the ability to curl into a ball, and was somewhat annoyed about it, but then again, she had the excuse to take up half of the three-person couch, so she wasn't complaining.

"Good morning girls," Zach mutters, walking directly to the coffee pot and pouring himself a cup. "Bella been up yet?"

Kaylee is about to answer on the negative, but Eleanor cuts in, not even turning to look at him.

"She was up two hours ago, went outside for an hour, came back and grabbed something to drink. She took her morning pills then returned to her bedroom," she says. "Told me to tell you to go get her once everyone was up."

"Thanks Eleanor," he nods, moving towards his sister's room.

She doesn't acknowledge the words, barely turning away from her book the entire time. In fact, she stays that way until everyone is in the room, only then shutting it and begrudgingly placing it on the table as Michael taps the top of her head.

They hand out the presents under the tree, each getting four presents. Eleanor stacks the art supplies she received neatly on the table, smile soft on her face as they all talk and laugh. She feels weird, like, she should be there, and she shouldn't at the same time. Like she is still an outsider, even though she's been living there for eight months now. But she also knows that feeling will follow her wherever she goes, she will always feel out of place, because she will always be out of place.

Chapter 34

Two days later, Eleanor and Kaylee are walking through the shopping centre they always go to, looking for some baby clothes, seeing as though Eleanor is only three weeks off her due date. Eleanor starts to shift nervously as she picks up on more familiar people around them, following them. Then her eyes find a face in the crowds, and every single inch of her being freezes. She bumps into her friend as she stops so abruptly, turning to face her in a second.

"What is it, Eleanor?" Kaylee asks, taking her forearms gently.

"I need you to not stop me," she shakes, "your gun is in your back waistband, correct?"

"Yes. Eleanor, what's wrong?" she insists.

"They're here again."

Eleanor steps forward, pulling the gun out of her friend's waist band and in quick succession, unloading six bullets into the crowd. Each hit their target in the head, excepting one, which hits the leg as everyone around them drops to the ground in terror. Eleanor drops the gun, streaking towards her target in a fury. Even though she's heavily pregnant, she still is able to completely disarm the wounded man in a few seconds.

There are screams around them, people laying on the ground covering their heads as Kaylee stops the guards from springing on her.

"We need to know more, she may be helping us," she orders, slowly walking forward.

Across the hallway, the man on the ground smirks.

"That's my child, it will live with me," he spits, attempting to pull a knife on her, but she kicks it out of his hand.

"Like hell she will," Eleanor returns, sending her foot hard into his side.

Over and over again her foot smashes into him, everywhere that could cause harm. After about 30 seconds Kaylee realises that she wasn't going to stop and starts to walk forward. People have started filming now, less scared for their lives and more interested in what was going on.

"Eleanor," Kaylee tests, getting into her line of sight. "You can stop now; they aren't a threat anymore."

The girl doesn't reply as she puts even more effort into the kick to his stomach. So Kaylee reaches out to grab her arm, growling under her breath as she pushes her away.

"Eleanor, stop this!" the strawberry blonde growls, trying to grab her but once again being pushed away.

"Leave me alone!" Eleanor yells, but Kaylee doesn't listen, turning to the guards.

"Be as gentle as possible, but get her off him," she orders, stepping back.

"What do we do with him?"

"Cuff him, there is a reason she's beating him up. I want him to suffer for it."

Two of the guards move into the fight, each catching one of her arms and dragging her backwards off the man who lays on the floor. Eleanor starts screaming, fighting her hardest to get away from them, but in her frenzy, she is unable to pull out of their grip.

"Calm down, Eleanor," Kaylee tells her as she gets in front of the girl, holding her face still so Eleanor is looking into her aquamarine eyes. "Who is he?"

"He did it," Eleanor chokes, the screams now dissipated into sobs of rage.

She manages to brush her fingers over her stomach for just a second, Kaylee realising what she meant within seconds. The older woman steps back, walking over to where the man had just finished being cuffed and swung a foot into his side one last time before pulling him to his feet.

"That child is legally mine, she can't keep it," he hisses, blood spraying out his mouth and onto the walkway.

"That's where you are wrong," Kaylee snarls in return, "you are never going to see that child, you will never learn her name."

"You can't do that. The child is mine."

"Not if you're in prison for the rest of your life."

The man glares at the woman, murky brown eyes holding as much hatred as humanly possible. Eleanor is being lead out behind him, whole body screaming her desires to kill him. They lock cuffs onto her wrists, warning her not to take them off.

"You realise you'll get locked back up for this?" the guard on her right mutters, the same one who had given her the dagger before the attack on the compound.

"It's safer anyway. They're getting more desperate to get both of us back at once," Eleanor mumbles, voice shaking as he guides her to the guard's car, while one of the other guards and Kaylee went in the other.

With the man now shoved in the other car, Eleanor climbs in, resting her head back and staying silent the rest of the trip to the compound.

They are met by the Colonel, who glowers at Eleanor as she is led past and to her old interrogation room. Michael is sitting in there waiting, raising an eyebrow at her as she holds her hands out to be uncuffed in silence.

"Ellie what happened?" he asks as he complies, watching her carefully.

"We had been trailed by a group of six men, I recognised one of them. I dispatched five, took the last down. I lost control and beat him to a pulp before they dragged me off him and we were brought here," Eleanor replies shortly, jaw tight as Michael groans.

"And why did you lose control?"

"Because he raped me," she says. "They were trying to distract me with him so their other agents, the one's I killed, could get a hold of me."

The man tenses, glaring past the girl in anger.

"You broke your contract; you understand what that means?" he mutters, still not looking her in the eye.

"Yes, I do."

"I will bring your stuff over later. You going to be okay alone?"

"Yes."

Michael stands up, opening the door and waiting for Eleanor to catch up before leading her deeper into the compound, to the cell she used to stay in. She doesn't know any of the men who occupy the cells, but ignore their leers as she is locked into a cell.

"Kenichi will be over shortly to give you a check over, I doubt he will be happy about this," Michael tells her, smiling kindly.

"It's safer," is all Eleanor says in reply, taking a seat and resting her head on the wall as Michael disappears.

Sure enough, Kenichi appears not too much later, fussing over her for about an hour as he takes all the readings on her pregnancy that he needs.

"Oh, stop it," Eleanor snaps eventually, grabbing his hand to stop him from taking her blood again. "There is no need to go all mother-hen, I'm fine."

The man gives her a warning look but pulls away and puts down the syringe.

"Thank you," she sighs, rubbing her belly sub-consciously.

"You should be glad that I was already flying home, little missy, or I might be a little more annoyed at you," he mutters as he packs up his equipment. "Can I really not leave you for longer than a week?"

"How was Japan?" she asks kindly, ignoring the question.

"It was good, I heard you somehow got a present from your admirer," Kenichi smirks, raising an eyebrow in question.

"How did..."

"His name is written in the front," he fills, offering an arm to help her off the table. "So you've been talking to him still?"

"If I have, it is none of your concern," she returns, but a soft smile still sits on her face.

"Sure Eleanor, sure," he smiles, sighing as they start to enter the detention sector. "Are you okay?" he asks.

"Shouldn't you have determined that by now?"

"I meant emotionally, Ellie."

She doesn't respond, bowing her head tiredly and continuing to walk.

"I don't want you to ignore it. We both know you need to get it out of your head."

"I feel scared. He makes me, terrified," she admits quietly, refusing to look anywhere but her feet. "Everything feels, wrong."

The medic pulls her closer to him, making her stop walking for a few seconds as he hugs her kindly.

"I have nightmares, about it. Constantly. Half the time it's the killing, the other half it's him," she breathes. "They set him up for me, gave him to me on a platter. They wanted me to kill him, so I would lose my baby when it was born. So she would be taken away. To punish me."

"We aren't going to do that, Ellie," Kenichi assures. "In fact, you'll probably be able to come back in a few weeks anyway."

They continue on in silence, Eleanor taking herself into her cell and sitting on her cot. Her things, as promised, had been brought over, and a warm green blanket from her bed is the only colour in the room. Just as Kenichi is about to leave, she speaks, her breath even and soft.

She says, "Tell me if anything happens with Nikolas. I would like to know."

"We will, promise," Kenichi nods, before sealing the door and leaving her alone.

Chapter 35

A *week later.*

~

An alarm goes off, blaring around the compound so loud everybody nearby winces. Instantly Kenichi jumps up, leaving Eleanor behind as he relocks her cell and runs off. He had muttered a short explanation as he left, but she still stands at the glass in an attempt to see anything of use. Discovering nothing, she sits back down to mull over his words.

"That's the alarm for the White House," he had said. "We're being called for backup."

She is still sitting in her cell as the team, accompanied by other agents, race to the White House and start to fight back the Daemones.

Michael is alone when he reaches the door to the Oval Office, having outrun everyone else. His brother is standing there waiting, a deadly challenge in his eyes. He could leave, he had done what he needed to. The bug was planted, but he wanted to face his brother.

"What heroics, Crown Prince," he drawls, "racing to protect the leader of a country, so far beneath you."

"That is what is supposed to happen, Nikolas," the man replies, sword out as he advances. "Angels are supposed to help everyone and only kill Daemones."

"But we aren't angels, are we?" Nikolas snaps. "No, we're tainted with human blood, holding those with the least the highest. Shunning those beneath us. Making us the heroes, while the humans do more to save themselves than we do!"

"We have been fighting off the Daemones for thousands of years! Without us, the world would be in ruins!"

Nikolas draws his own swords, silver blades with twisted leather handles. One the blade Eleanor had given back.

"Look around you Brother, can you really be that naïve?" he calls. "This world is already dying; it needs to be remade. The King, he does nothing because he does not care!"

"You're delusional!" Michael growls. "Do you realise that you're working for the people who tortured your Geminae for years on end? Killed her parents?"

"Where else was I to go?" Nikolas yells, preparing to advance. "She's the only one who has shown me any kindness, she understands! You threw me onto an island with monsters that you don't even dare to name, and left me there!"

"You tried to kill the King! My— our Father!"

"He was never my father!"

There is a wild look in Nikolas's eyes as he screams the words, a mix between pain, fury and fear. But his brother doesn't look that close, only seeing a danger to his life in his eyes. They soften for just a moment.

"Is she safe?" he asks softly.

"Yes, of course she is."

The two launch into combat the second the words are out of Michael's mouth. They match each other easily, moving so fast that the backup, that arrives shortly after, don't step in. The elder gets the upper hand ten minutes later, beating his exiled brother down to the ground and holding his sword to his throat as people rush in to disarm the man.

"You were holding back," Michael mutters, just low enough for him to hear.

"I don't know what you're talking about," Nikolas spits, fighting again as his brother slaps shackles onto his hands and feet.

An extra one goes on his ankle limiting his Aspect.

"You realise I'm going to take you back, right?"

The younger Angeli doesn't respond, struggling to break his brother's grip as he is pushed out of the building and into the light.

"Is this him?" Kaylee asks as Nikolas is shoved into the back of their car.

"Yes."

"She took the last maximum security cell," she says, stopping Michael quietly. "What are we going to do?"

"We put them in together," Michael gives. "He won't hurt her."

Eleanor's head tilts in confusion as her door hisses open, a man landing on the floor at her feet. Michael is clearly mad but doesn't speak as the glass slides back into place, the sound suppressors making the only noise a low hum. She looks at the man as he picks himself off the floor and starts to pound his fist on the door. She knows who he is in an instant, tall, lean and muscled. The dirty blonde hair that had been neatly slicked back now all over the place.

"It won't work," she murmurs, "glass is soundproof, bulletproof, escape proof, the list goes on. It is rather extensive."

He turns around, raising an eyebrow at her as she teasingly smirks. The stony grey eyes soften as he looks over her small form, curled up under her blanket. Nikolas hits the door once more before moving to the cot on the other side of the room and sitting silently down.

Eleanor watches him carefully, taking in the sharp jaw, symmetrical features.

"I was wondering why they were taking so long, why they put extra bedding in here," she muses. "I'm surprised they put you with me, I would have thought they would keep us separated at all costs. I guess Nancy forced Michael's hand."

"My brother is the one who captured me," Nikolas mutters. "Safe to say they thought I might kill any other cellmate."

To anyone else, the words would be seen as a threat, but Eleanor just laughs lightly.

"So they figured the pregnant teenager could put you into your place," she smiles.

"Why are you in here? I haven't been able to find you for a few days," he asks, eyes raising to meet hers in worry.

"I'm nearly due, got scared," she shrugs, tucking herself tighter into her blanket.

"My brother is annoyingly righteous; he wouldn't just let you come back in."

"I, very publicly, attacked a group of men the Agency sent after me," she huffs, "killed five, beat the last to a pulp. Got sent back as punishment."

"Are we supposed to pretend we don't know each other?" Nikolas says, a flicker of pride in his eyes.

"They know, but sure."

"Well then, I'm Nikolas," he introduces, holding a hand out for her to shake.

"Eleanor."

She takes the hand, breathing in the comfort that comes from the touch for a few seconds before pulling her hand away.

"Pretty name, pretty girl," he teases, smirking as she blushes lowly.

The look drops as her stare fixes vacantly on the wall, blanket pulling up.

"I do not appreciate cockiness, or attempts at flattery," she murmurs. "Let it be a warning."

"I understand," he nods, moving onto his back and shutting his eyes tiredly.

She watches him, counting his breaths, the rise and fall of his chest. How his hair falls, the line of tension between his eyebrows, how he stretches out his fingers.

"It's not often I have someone staring at me in something other than disgust," he murmurs, cracking open a single eye to look at her before her gaze jumps away. "It's nice."

Eleanor doesn't respond, tucking her own head into the corner of the cell and resting it there tiredly. She ignores the feeling of his eyes as he takes the opportunity to look over her himself.

The team, watching the security cameras above relax slightly as Eleanor lowers her guard, thankful that the two have managed to get through their first interaction without a fight.

"They will be okay, Michael," Kaylee assures. "You said it yourself that he would never hurt her."

"That's not what I'm worried about."

Everyone looks at him in confusion, but Michael's eyes don't stray from the screen as he fills their silent question.

"It is highly likely they will put him to death when I take him for his trial on Angeli Terra," he mutters. "I worry what might happen to Eleanor if that does happen, seeing as though they are already growing closer."

Chapter 36

A terrified scream leaves Eleanor's lips, eyes snapping awake as she jolts up from her position facing the wall. But she had forgotten that she was in the cell, and nearly rolls off her cot and onto the ground. Nikolas guides her carefully, placing her back onto the cot and brushing some of the hair out of her face as she starts to tremble. He doesn't say anything as she leans her head over to rest on his shoulder as he stays kneeling next to her.

It had been nearly a week since he had been brought in, the two needing the comfort as the nightmares plagued their every resting moment. Eleanor, as she drew closer to her due date, and Nikolas, as he savours the time before he is taken away.

Her hand moves to rest on her stomach, rubbing it anxiously as she soaks up the calm that breathes through his touch.

"What was it this time?" Nikolas asks, voice smooth as butter as hers croaks through the room.

"Him, her. The same," she shakes. "I don't even know what she looks like, but her screams... Nikolas I—"

"I know Dulce Meum," he sighs, running a hand down her hair as carefully as possible. "He cannot hurt either of you."

"I hate that I didn't kill him," she admits, voice still raw. "That he is sleeping peacefully, so close to this child."

Nikolas lets her speak, turning and sitting against the wall as she lays down. She grips the hand that he left on the cot like a vice.

"I... I've always kept the part of me that was made in that place from the rest, isolating it in a hope of controlling the bloodlust," she continues, "but now it's leaked through. That scares me more than he does. Because if I lose that control then I lose everything."

Nikolas looks up to see her watching him as well, eyes tired but curious.

"Angeli aren't supposed to kill," he says. "Our entire lives we are raised to only kill Daemones if we have to, and never dare hurt a human or one of our own... yet every time I hear about the King, or see him, or even think about my life... my mother..." the last two words are soft, loving, in comparison to the tension of the rest, "I want to find him, and I want to kill him. Not quickly, either. And I don't feel bad about it, like I should. I just want to do it."

Eleanor smiles kindly, squeezing his hand for a few seconds as they continue to watch each other.

"They sent me on this mission once, into a gala as many of my missions were. My target was an easy hit, I took him out and was on my way out when I came across a group of men," she starts, eyes going distant. "They were terrorising a girl, I should have left, that's what I was trained to do but, for the first time, I actually wanted to kill them, wanted it in a plane outside of bloodlust. So I took them all down, carved the crosses on their foreheads and left just before the authorities found me. The girl, she threw them off my scent, told them I had gone into the sewers instead of to the roofs, like I had.

"My handler beat me for it, but Mein Vater, he just brought me food, that was not allowed, and told me I did the right thing. He shouldn't of, he has killed thousands more people than I have, had trained me and Seb to do the same, but he said it was the right thing to do. Even still, I blamed myself for making a mistake, did as I always did, wouldn't eat. That was the first time I killed someone who wasn't a target. It only happened maybe three more times since then. But each time it left a deeper mark, each time it stung more and more. I could blame the Agency for the other murders, but these, these were just my nature, they were my fault."

"Maybe, but saving that girl, that was honourable," Nikolas assures her. "Killing bad people, even though it's killing, it's better than doing nothing."

"But I didn't have to kill them, I know so many ways to maim, to injure. To stop people without killing," she says. "But I don't, I kill, so damn easily. It comes like walking, breathing. Blood is like water; I don't even recognise it as bad anymore. Death doesn't register in my head."

Nikolas squeezes her hand, sending her a reassuring smile as she bites her lips lightly in embarrassment. He tries his hardest to keep the flash of desire that filled his body off his face, just succeeding as she buries her face into her pillow, not letting go of his hand. The man shows no compulsion to move, instead leaning his head against the cot, cushioned by a layer of Eleanor's blanket, and shutting his eyes.

"Thank you for listening to me," Eleanor murmurs just as he starts to drift off.

"I will always listen if you need to talk, Dulce Meum," he replies.

That's how the team find them in the morning, both still asleep, until the door hisses open.

"Good morning," Michael mutters, sourly glancing between the two.

Nikolas fixes him with an equal look, standing as he moves to the other side of the room and takes the opportunity to stretch out.

From behind Michael, four guards, dressed in the black and gold of Angeli Terra enter the room, moving towards the man in silence. Eleanor quickly figures out who they are, and what they are doing, standing up in an attempt to get them to stop.

"Don't you dare take him," she growls, taking place in front of Nikolas protectively. "You have already passed your judgement, exile, right? Well he's exiled, he isn't causing you any harm!"

"Ma'am step away," the nearest guard growls, not recognising her as the girl who had been on their island five months ago.

"No, I won't let you take him away from me!" she yells, pulling out the knife she had tucked in her bra.

"Step away, now!"

"No!"

"Eleanor, he can't be protected anymore," Michael calls, trying to calm her down.

But in that moment she realises what they are taking him to do. What new judgement they will pass and she lets out a feral growl.

"You are not killing him," she snarls, "you are not taking him away!"

Tired of her resistance, the guard nearest to her backhands her and sends her to the ground. As the cry of pain leaves her mouth, Nikolas catches her head, cradling it carefully as she groans in pain, hand clutching her stomach.

"Step away from the girl," the guards growl, attempting to pull him off but failing as he shoves them back.

Eleanor lets out another cry of pain, clutching her stomach as she curls inward.

"Get away from her," Nikolas yells, easily picking her up and holding her top half to his chest.

Just as Kenichi steps forward, worried for the pregnant girl, her water breaks, spilling liquid onto the white tiles. The doctor rushes forward, guiding Eleanor to stand and supporting her as she cries out again. Nikolas follows, helping Kenichi hold her as she slumps, body giving out on holding itself in place of protecting its child.

"What's wrong with her?" Nikolas demands, cradling his Geminae to his chest.

"We always had a suspicion she would go into labour early, due to her constant state of stress." Kenichi sighs. "We need to get her up into surgery."

Human guards push into the cell, taking her out and laying her down outside to wait for a stretcher. The instant she is away from Nikolas, the Angeli guards jump forward, snapping thick black shackles onto Nikolas's wrists and ankles and dragging him out of the room.

"Don't you leave her alone," the man orders his brother, who crouches at Eleanor's head. "Don't you dare let them take that child away from her. I don't care if you aren't at the trial, you won't make a difference anyway. Stay here."

The guard who stands next to the Crown Prince snaps a fist forward, growling as it collides with pale skin.

"You do not order the Crown Prince," he snaps, about to send another fist to Nikolas's gut, but Michael stops him.

"They won't be happy about it, they will want to know why," Michael warns, watching carefully as they wheel Eleanor past.

Nikolas's eyes follow her, fist clenching in anger as the guards start to pull him away again.

"As long as she is safe, I don't care what they know," he says, swallowing deeply. "She is too close, she will feel it when it happens, she will know."

"I know, Nikolas."

The younger brother holds Michael's stare, letting the desperation show in his eyes as he speaks again.

"Swear to me you won't let them take that child away, swear it."

"I swear it, as long as you arrive on Angeli Terra with your guards unharmed."

Nikolas agrees, letting himself be dragged to the small plane they were taking back to the island. He sends one final glance to the compound as they fly away, silently praying that his Geminae would be okay, because even though they had spent only a week together, he wanted to protect her at all costs.

When the small craft touches down on the island, Nikolas is pushed out of the door, managing to just keep his balance as the rest of the guards follow. They had landed in the forest, where an airstrip had been built for the use of the King, hidden by thick shrubbery and tall pines, it was a secret to all but the most trusted. Nikolas had once been one of those people.

Their greeting party walked forward; the Princess flanked by the new Captain. Markus shows none of the kindness he gave to Eleanor, instead fixing the man with a glare as he is brought forward. Nikolas smirks at him, his usual swagger returning the minute he stepped foot on the island, before smiling softly to his sister.

"Am I not important enough for the King to deign to come down?" he sneers as his eyes return to the male. "Or is he too scared for his life?"

"The King is occupied with state business," Markus returns, snarl just edging on his words.

"He's with the tailor," Anastasia mutters, sending her younger brother a kind look. "It's been a while Nikolas."

"It has."

Markus steps forward, sending the Princess a look as he scans the rest of the new arrivals, not finding his friend.

"Where is the Prince?" he asks the closest guard, the order plain in his tone.

"There was a pregnant girl sharing a cell with this traitor, she went into labour when we arrived," the man fills, grip still holding tight to their prisoner's arm. "The Crown Prince stayed behind to ensure her safety, at the request of the prisoner."

The pair look to each other in confusion, Markus more so than the Princess, but after a second the girl realises what was meant. Anastasia looks to her brother, tilting her head in the slightest in question. Nikolas nods just slightly, the flicker of worry dancing through his eyes for only a second, before it vanishes. Schooling her face into passivity, Anastasia turns away and starts to walk towards the horses, Markus following obediently behind her.

"We are heading to the castle through the city. I tried to change the King's mind but he was set on it," the Princess calls as she mounts her mare and takes the lead to a plain brown gelding. "Nikolas is staying in the castle dungeons, and will be taken there after he is sighted by the King."

By the time she has finished talking, the shackles locked onto Nikolas's ankles has been undone, and the guards are leading him towards the gelding.

"I'm betting leaving Ferox behind was his order too," the man grumbles as he gets on the fat little mare. Little by their standards, off course, it couldn't have been smaller than 15 hands high.

"She is brilliantly bred, moves with the power of a King's horse. The whole point of this charade is to make you seem human, so why would he let you ride her," the Princess replies, looking to him apologetically. "Ferox's okay though, I've been riding her daily to make her less of a fire breathing dragon for the handlers."

The corner of Nikolas's lips twitch up at the description, finding his sister's eyes in thanks. The lead to his horse is handed to the Captain, who begins to move off, without any warning, at an even canter.

"Who else has been riding her?" Nikolas asks.

"A few tried initially, including him." She nods at Markus, getting an annoyed scowl in return. "Gave up pretty quickly though. You'd be interested to know that our human visitor rode her."

His jaw literally drops, opening and closing a few times as he gets his head around the information.

"I'm sorry," he mutters, "you put her, on Ferox."

"Yep," the Princess replies cheerfully. "They got along famously."

His mouth opens and closes a few more times, before he tries again.

"You put a pregnant, 16 year old, human girl on our wildest horse."

"To be fair, we didn't know she was pregnant and 16 until later. But Ferox was acting like a puppy, so I figured it was safe at the time."

"Eleanor was pregnant?" the Captain asks, looking back incredulously at Anastasia. "You knew and let her fight?"

"Yes. Her suit had extra protection over her stomach, and she assured us she would be fine," she shrugs.

Clearly unhappy with the answer, Markus turns forward, calmly dropping the horses to a trot as the woods start to thin and houses appear. The streets are quiet, people watching as the procession moved past. This far out from the castle, the people are poorer, more human than Angeli. They are the people who loved their Queen over their King, who love their Princess over their Prince. They are the people who would stand behind the younger siblings over the elder. They lost faith in their King at the same moment Nikolas did. They watch him being led through the streets only in support.

The shift is obvious, as they get out of the low classes (they weren't even close to slums, but to the nobility there was no difference) and get into the rich. People start booing, not going as far as to throw things (they still tried to uphold some Angelic practises, stoning and its descendants was strictly forbidden), however the hatred for the man was more and more evident as they got closer to the man who hated him the most.

Nikolas holds a smirk on his face the entire trip, shaping himself into who they wanted him to be with ease. The minute he dismounts, the guards are locking the cuffs onto his ankles, before they begin to drag him towards the throne room.

"Do not make this worse for yourself," Anastasia hisses as they arrive at the entrance.

The guards let go as the doors swing open, letting the Captain lead the traitor up to the King. The hatred on both Nikolas and the King's faces is not restrained as their eyes meet, neither breaking the contact as Nikolas stops. His chin is high, refusing to show a drop of shame or respect to the man who killed his mother.

"Let not pretend," Nikolas calls, cutting in before the King can talk, "that you are putting me on trial for my actions in the human world, you're just using it to get rid of the last evidence that your wife didn't love you."

Gasps are audible around the room, horror written across many faces as the words echo against the stone walls.

"And that is what making it worse looks like," his sister growls, glaring with a fury at her brother.

Nikolas just grins, still not breaking eye contact with the scowling King.

"Give him twenty lashes when you take him to his cell," the older man orders. "And do not let my daughter in to see him, I don't want her conversing with such a daemonic traitor."

"Yes sir," Markus replies, voice strong as Nikolas snickers.

The King nods, cuing them to leave as their prisoner begins to snarl a response, but he is quickly shut up as they push him out the side exit.

The corridors go from polished and bright, to damp and dark, lit only by the flame lit torch Markus takes as they begin to get into the mountain. Past a heavy, almost golden door, like one you would see in a vault, the tunnel opens up into a huge cavern. Walkways ring the edge, levels upon levels of them reaching down into the black and up to the top, where the sky is blocked by the thick cooled magma that sealed the dormant volcano. Four suspension bridges on each level connect to a spire in the centre of the chamber, where an elevator sits to transport them between levels.

Cells sit evenly spaced around the rings, with steel bars over the front and stone walls between each cell, except for the small, bar covered gap for prisoners to interact with each other. Within each, attached to the opposing walls, are a set of cuffs on chains, which tighten to secure the prisoner. There are muffled shuffling's echoing around the air, a few cries of pain join the white noise.

As they arrive at the closest empty cell, the shackles are unlocked and he is pushed inside. They force him down to his knees and lock his wrists onto the sides of the cell. The guards step out, making room for the wardens to come forward and see their new addition.

"You bring us the Prince once again," the eldest drawls, dull eyes, with black tattooed tears, flicking to the Captain as the fluent Latin comes out of his mouth. "Have the Angeli grown too weak to make him like us."

"Do you not remember that his blood is impure?" the Captain retorts, not letting the flicker of doubt show. The Angeli had grown weak, there hadn't been wings to take for hundreds of years.

"What are we to do?"

"20 lashes, nothing more... And if the Princess comes to visit him, call me."

"Not the King?"

"No."

The Fallen Angel nods, smirk pulling onto his barely aged features. Destined for eternal shame.

"Get out of here then, Angeli," he hisses in very rough English, pulling the black gloves off his hands. The Angeli try not to look at the tattoos that cover them. "I am thousands of years older than you, thousand years stronger, do not forget that."

"Well considering you bring it up every time we visit, I think that's impossible," Markus returns, turning on his heel and leaving.

"You shouldn't avoid looking at the brands," the man calls after them, "your kin put them there."

The Angeli don't stop, only hearing the first of the whiplashes before they lock the prison door.

"Is that a...?" the youngest guard asks, glancing feverishly back at the gate.

"Fallen Angel?" Markus grins, raising an eyebrow as the boy nods. "Yes, they keep our prison in check for us."

"But, aren't they disgraced?"

"These are the ones we have managed to capture, to control them. It gets dangerous when they team up with the Daemones, so we lock them here," the Captain answers, continuing to walk forward.

Nikolas doesn't let a single scream leave his lips, taking the punishment in silence. The Fallen Angels release him after the 20 lashes, replacing his shirt and giving him food and water.

"Why are you helping me?" he croaks, looking up at the beings as they begin to lock his cell. He speaks in Latin, knowing they didn't speak English easily.

"You may not have wings for them to take, but they would have if you did. We support our own," the leader replies, nodding with a sense of finality before leaving.

Chapter 37

Eleanor sits on the plain white compound hospital bed, daughter cradled in her arms. Her eyes don't rise from examining her precious piece of innocence as Michael walks in, Kaylee close behind. The latter carries a plate of food, placing it on the small table and rolling the cot closer to the bed. Eleanor lets her take the child but keeps a hand on the cot to keep her from wheeling it away as they push the table over the bed.

"Any news?" the girl asks, eyes finally raising to meet the Prince's.

"They have started to review the charges to the court, the outcome is currently not clear," Kaylee says. "They seem reluctant to continue without Michael."

"Then he should go," Eleanor says to no-one in particular. "I am safe, my child is safe. I want you to go there and get him a reduced sentence."

"Ellie, I swore not to," Michael sighs, shaking his head slightly.

"I don't care, you've broken promises to him before, it's not like you'll be punished for it," she snaps, exhaustion clear on her tone. "Tell them the truth, tell them why you didn't come. It'll help sway the vote."

"What would you suggest I ask them to do?"

Eleanor glances at her child, smiling weakly down at the baby wrapped in pink.

"My time is limited anyway, tell them to exile him until such a time as I myself am terminated, which will mean those who think he's just getting out of it will agree, as we are only staying as long as each other," she says, raising her eyes. "It'll work, I know it will."

Michael nods tiredly, looking past Eleanor and out the window.

"You want me to go now?" he grumbles, gaining an answer to the affirmative. "Then I will see you in a few days."

He leaves out the door they came in, nodding to the guards posted on either side as he goes. Kaylee stays, folding a leg underneath her as she sits on the end of the bed, eyes sternly upon her charge.

"I'm not leaving until you finish that meal," she reminds, "just because she isn't inside you anymore doesn't mean that you can stop eating. You need the energy to look after her."

Eleanor nods slowly, loose hair falling in front of her face as she reaches for the nearest plate to start. She only uses one hand, the other staying dangling off the bed and into the cot as she eats.

"Kenichi said that Adelyn was healthy, was a bit less positive about you, though," Kaylee says as she eats. "I don't think Nikolas will be killed, I think that they will give him what you suggested, once they find out he has a Geminae, they won't take him away. Especially after they learn about your position."

"I know," Eleanor replies, "doesn't make me any less nervous though."

"How much have you really been talking to him?" Kaylee asks, raising an eyebrow at her.

"What does it matter?" she shrugs.

They sit in silence for a while, Eleanor finishing her meal, just, before Kaylee stands.

"It'll be okay, Ellie," she tells her.

~

The Crown Prince walks into the courthouse, heavy wooden doors shutting behind him with a solid bang. All the Lords and Ladies turn to look at him, attention drawn from the trial in front of them. Michael bows, first to the King sitting behind the table like a judge, and then to the set of halos hanging to the side of the hall. They were the last proof Angels actually existed on Earth, collected after battles that took down the warriors.

Nikolas's eyes are sunken, skin paler than it had been before he was placed in the prison. There were rumours about that place, that it sucked the very life from its prisoners. No-one cared to prove it.

Michael frowns as he finds his brother, scowl settling on his face as he walks forward.

"And where have you been?" the King calls, directed towards his actual son.

"I had business to attend to," he answers swiftly.

It is Nikolas who speaks next.

"Is she…" he asks, worry showing in the silver of his eyes.

"Fine, they are both fine," Michael answers. "She called her daughter Adelyn."

Nikolas nods gratefully, eyes breaking off his brothers as he speaks again.

"I told you not to come, to stay there and protect them."

People in the audience are frowning now, not understanding what was going on.

"And she told me to come here, to propose an alternate sentence."

"You listened to her?"

"We've been having to force her to eat, Nikolas. Even before you came along, we were worried she would stop taking care of herself, now we have to cut bargains, sit and watch her to make sure she doesn't chuck her food in the bin."

"It shouldn't have affected her this much."

"It wouldn't have if you hadn't have let yourself get so close."

"She's human, it shouldn't connect her so quick."

"The Berühmte Söldner have been known to target families they believe to have traces of Angeli blood. It is possible she is one of them. The rate at which she learns things, her memory, all of it could just be put down to chance, but she said both her mother and her sister were smart like she was. Dormant Angeli genes can be classed as a possible cause."

"But you said she couldn't see the island."

"Maybe because of her past it was hidden, or the blood isn't strong enough."

By now, no-one is following the conversation, other than the Captain and the Princess, who look between each other in surprise. The King is the one who interrupts the argument.

"What on Earth is going on here?" he says, green eyes flashing in simmering anger.

Michael looks to his sister for a split second, just registering her nod before he looks to his father.

"Nikolas has a Geminae Animarum."

The words come out of his mouth and the entire room stops, not a single person taking a breath. Nikolas joins them, fury soon filling his face as Michael refuses to look away from the King.

"She is a human girl, who is being detained by the human governments for the crime of terrorism and murder," Michael continues, explaining her predicament.

Gasps fill the room, ignorant Ladies horrified that such a thing could be done. They have never known the turmoil the human world lives in, only those close to the King, their husbands, do.

"And how do we know he isn't lying about it? Using it as a way to stop us from executing him?" the King questions, refusing to let the chance to end his illegitimate son go.

"Because we share a mother, I can feel it," Michael starts.

"And that you aren't being tricked by his mind control?"

"I met her," Anastasia calls. "She is the one who visited the island five months ago."

"You let an assassin, who worked for the Daemones for years, sit in on our war meeting?" the King growls.

"Eleanor was truly the best for the job. She understands how they work, but that is not the point," the Princess snaps.

"I had an electric band on her at all times, she cannot get it off without alerting me and knocking herself out. If she became volatile, I could put her down instantly," Michael follows.

"Also not the point," Anastasia hisses at her brother. "She was sent into labour when they took him away from her a few days ago. Our guards threw her, a heavily pregnant teenager, on the floor while she tried to stop them from taking away her Geminae, even though she doesn't know what they are. The connection has already started to show, she had already started seeing his memories when she visited."

Now a scowl sits on the King's face, clear as day for everyone to see. People start to murmur in the crowds as Michael turns away from his father and to the court as Anastasia speaks, voice echoing in the chamber.

"Eleanor's doctor worries about her mental state, her ability to look after herself and her child," she tells them. "Nikolas is already too close to her, he said himself that he believed she would feel it if he died. If he does die, Eleanor won't be able to support her child anymore, and they will take Adelyn away from her. She will lose her mind, probably end up killing herself and taking a lot of people with her."

Michael takes over, voice carrying its authority. "Everyone who has been watching her has agreed that she has been trying her hardest to become better. She is living on limited time anyway; it is most likely she will be administered lethal injection once she turns 18 for the crimes she has committed. We just want to try and make the next year of her life as happy as possible. I'm just asking that you consider making her sentence Nikolas's, let him live while she does, which won't be for long."

"Geminae are sacred among us, ripping them apart is against our most ingrained beliefs," Anastasia calls. "Is this such a bad thing, to let him have some peace, in the human world, with his Geminae? Punishment will still be given, but we are the Angeli, are we not? Isn't mercy supposed to be our way?"

The noise rises as families talk within themselves, the King glaring angrily between his two children as they smile to each other. Michael steps away from the centre of the room, taking his seat between his best friend and his sister. He stays that way as his father regains control over the courts, ordering the vote, with now three options instead of the two that had been before. It is well into the night when the count has been done for the third time, an assurance made centuries before.

All of the members of the court still sit in their positions, from the strongest to the least, none dropping beneath half-blood. The King stands alone on the podium, Nikolas restrained and kneeling before him, the Prince and Princess standing to the side as the sentence is read.

"He is to return to the human world, to live under the constant surveillance of the American government, with his Geminae Animarum, until such a time as she is no longer living," the King declares, "then he will receive the same punishment."

Other than a few low murmurings, no-one contests the decree, and after Nikolas is lead out of the room, to sleep in his cell for one last night, the courtiers leave, returning to their homes.

Both the Prince and Princess stay behind, taking the infuriated King's words without a single flicker of doubt. As soon as they make it back to their rooms, Anastasia wraps her arms around him in thanks, smile wide on her face as she steps back.

"I'm guessing Eleanor had something to do with that?" she says, "thank her for me, would you?"

"I will," Michael answers. "See, I'm not totally useless."

Anastasia's eyes roll, hair flicking as she turns to go into her room. Her lithe body pauses at the threshold, head turning back to her older brother for a second.

"The Fallen have taken a liking to him," she warns. "They're growing suspicious of our strength."

The wooden door closes behind her and Michael is left to move to his own room.

Chapter 38

The same party that greeted the exiled Prince joins him on the trek to Michael's helicopter. Anastasia rides next to her favoured younger brother, watching him carefully as the two others ride ahead of them.

"Don't you dare do something to hurt that girl," she hisses as they start to get closer to the helicopter.

Nikolas looks at her in surprise, head tilted slightly as she fixes him with a glare.

"I don't plan on it..." he says, scar shifting as his eyebrow raises.

"Yes, well both you boys don't often think before you do, I'm just warning you that I will personally hunt you down if you make her shed even a single tear."

The party pulls up as they arrive in front of the helicopter, each dismounting for a guard to take their horse. Nikolas's binds are locked back onto his limbs and he is passed to his elder brother, who lets him stand by himself as he embraces his friends.

"I am sorry I turned up so late, and have to leave so quickly," Michael apologises. "I wasn't bluffing about her condition, honestly. Markus, I do hope your father heals enough to say goodbye properly, both your mother and you deserve it."

"Thank you, Michael," the Captain offers, "Mother expressed her immense thanks for your visit this morning, it does her good to talk to people."

Michael nods in thanks, embracing him again before moving to his sister.

"Thank you, Cael," she whispers, hugging him gently. "I know it would have been hard."

"It was the right thing," he smiles to her. "Also, Eleanor is better than you at convincing people to do things, I had no choice really." There is a pause as Anastasia laughs slightly, glancing over at her other brother as he watches them. "She really enjoys getting your emails, she likes to have a friend who isn't also keeping her locked up."

"I will send her one as soon as I can, demanding photos," she smiles, then in a lower tone. "Do not forget to give him ground rules, she is still nearly three years younger than he is."

"Oh, do not worry," Michael chuckles. "I'll tell him, then Kaylee will likely do the same. And then when he's alone Kenichi will give him another."

"Alone?"

"Yes, he does his best intimidating when no one is listening."

With a breathy laugh, Anastasia hugs him once more before stepping away so he could leave. She sends her younger brother a sad smile, apology in in her gaze as she glances around the clearing.

The two get into the helicopter, leaving without any more ceremony. A terse silence fills the cabin, neither of the brothers willing to talk to the other until absolutely necessary. It's Nikolas, who grows bored two hours in, who ends up breaking.

"Should I be worried you're going to push me out into the ocean?" he sneers, eyes staying forward.

"No, knowing your luck you'd land right next to a boat full of Daemones," the elder returns.

Nikolas rolls his eyes, fully prepared to let the silence settle in again. Michael is not.

"Also, before we get there, I think it would be a good idea to go over some ground rules," he starts, ignoring Nikolas's huff of annoyance.

The list is long, summarised by don't do bad things and no being in a closed room with Eleanor. Nikolas accepts the rules, keeping his reservations to himself.

"That is all for now," Michael continues. "The team know what your connection to Eleanor is, I explained most of it. If you notice

Eleanor hasn't eaten, make her eat. Even if she gets annoyed about it. Same thing for if she's twitching her fingers, it's bad for the joints. You will be able to tell better than us if she is going to lose her head, so if she's going to lash out imminently, feel free to control it because you are the one least likely to get hurt. Oh, and you are getting rid of that damn bug on our system. Understand?"

"Yes."

"No questions?"

"No."

"Can you remove the bug?"

"Easily."

The brothers fall back into silence, the younger having to resist the urge to roll his eyes as Michael smiles to himself, proud of his work.

It is only as they land at the compound that either speak again, the engines already off as they get out and start walking over to the waiting party.

"And Nikolas," Michael says, looking over to his companion with a stern look.

Not a single word is said lightly and the look on Michael's face confirms it.

"Nice to know both my siblings prefer my Geminae over me," he returns, grinning at the man.

"I'm serious, Nikolas."

"I know you are."

"Why the hell did I agree to this plan?"

Kaylee laughs, grinning at her friend as he stops walking.

Nikolas stops as well as she says, "because Eleanor has you wrapped around her finger."

Michael huffs in annoyance, chucking his head back as the Colonel speaks.

"Not like you can say any better, she has all of you running at her beck and call," she smirks.

Kaylee cracks a laugh, giving Michael a smile as he tilts his head in irritation. Tossed, the thin black band stops just before it hits Michael's face, his hand lowering slowly.

"Thank you," he mutters, easily opening it and then locking it onto Nikolas's ankle.

Only then does he unlock the shackles, letting them drop to the floor. There is a sour look on the younger Angeli's face, the obvious displeasure linked to the inability to use his Aspect. But they lead him away without another word, putting him in the car and driving him to the manor.

Eleanor, glad to be allowed to stay back in the manor, watches from the library, head poked out of the door as her Geminae is brought inside.

He looks her way, for only a second. Both smile softly as their eyes meet, but then Nikolas is walked away and their eyeline is broken.

Chapter 39

Dinner that night is quiet, a tense air settled over the group. As usual by now, Eleanor sits next to Kenichi, but where Michael would normally be on her other side, the table ends, a carrier cot waiting for her daughter, who sits in her arms. With one arm, she holds the child to her chest, and with the other she moves the food to her mouth.

Her eyes do not rise higher than the plate in front of her, moving only between there and her daughter as others talk around them. Everyone at the table had eyed her only quarter filled plate with distain, Kenichi serving her an extra spoonful of the pasta before turning to his own.

Nikolas hadn't said a word either, arriving late, and taking the last seat, the one furthest from her. He steals occasional glances at her, but other than that, his eyes don't stray. He watches her, studying her. It's different seeing her this way, so real… a reality he could never see through the cameras. He sees her tilt her head as the conversation turns, not listening himself, but knowing she is.

Feeling his gaze, Eleanor glances up and her eyes meet his. Neither look away, neither move an inch from their position. Her head tilts again, eyes staying locked on Nikolas's as she blinks.

"Don't sit so far back in your chair," she says, everyone else stopping their conversations as they watch the pair. "Wounds don't like to be stifled."

"It's nearly healed anyway," Nikolas shrugs.

"And it would be already if you were looking after them properly."

Beneath the wall in her eyes, there is a flicker of worry, but Eleanor looks away just as he spots it, returning to finishing her dinner. Talk begins again, the noise concealing the whispered conversation that Kenichi and Eleanor share, and once everyone finishes, they move over to the couches.

But Eleanor is tired from looking after her daughter, so says goodnight to each person and disappears upstairs without asking where Nikolas had gone. His door is shut as she gets to her own, but light flickers through the cracks. She leaves her own door open as she places her daughter in her cot and starts to brush her hair out.

When the door across the hall opens, she stops, listening carefully as he stays in his own doorway.

"How did you know?" he asks once he figures out she knows he's there.

"Your movement is stiff, you winced reaching for the salt," she replies. "When and why did they do it?"

"I told the King he was only worried about getting me executed to erase all the proof that his wife didn't love him," Nikolas says. "When I arrived."

After a moment Eleanor chuckles.

"I'm sure Anastasia was thrilled about that," she laughs, only for a second. "Are they actually healing? Or are they infected?"

"They're healing, just slower than normal. The prison on Angeli Terra is not a place where someone heals. Should be better by morning now."

"Good."

Nikolas turns to leave, about to shut her door when Eleanor speaks again, now standing at her own.

"Sleep well, Nikolas," she smiles.

"And you, Eleanor."

~

Its dark. Cold. Damp.

Nikolas is wide awake, twin blades held tight in his fists as the noise gets closer. His fire is covered by a steel box, so no light can be found, unless of course the beast can sense heat, then he is stuffed anyway.

Faintly, he can make out a set of matching white shapes, then a burning sensation forms over his left eye, blood spilling down and clouding his vision. He never saw the blade coming.

"Angeli," the thing hisses, voice oddly human like. "Have you come to release us?"

Nikolas doesn't reply, raising his blades to defend himself.

"You don't know what I am…"

The box over the fire lifts, flames rising as it inhales the oxygen. They reach towards the man almost unnaturally, casting light around the cave.

"They have truly forgotten about us, haven't they?"

The thing steps into the light, Nikolas taking a step back in surprise. It is almost a man. The same body shape, features and movements. However, ridged patterns wind over his skin, from his face and down his chest. He wears only pants, a sword in one hand, the other open and tensed.

Protruding from his back is the most amazing sight. A set of huge, leathery, white wings are folded close to his body.

"Don't go into the mountains," the man growls, turning and taking a running start before leaping into the sky.

~

Eleanor wakes the instant Nikolas does in the other room, running a hand through her hair and looking around in exhaustion. She can hear him through the walls, can hear the pipes engage as he washes his face.

She drops her head back to the pillow, flipping over in an attempt to get back to sleep, but her mind refuses to quieten. Giving up, Eleanor sits up and reaches for the light, letting her eyes adjust before she picks up the sketchbook on her bedside table.

Nikolas notices the light coming from beneath Eleanor's door as he leaves his room, stopping for a few seconds as he smiles ever so softly at the door.

"Are you okay?" her sweet voice calls from the other side.

"Yes," he replies. "Was just going to go for a walk."

"Okay then," she calls. "Try to not wake Bronte, I'd suggest going out the front door and head out from there."

"Thank you."

Nikolas walks away, descending the stairs and following her instructions. He slips into the tree line without any problems, ambling uselessly down the path he finds.

Eventually, he stops, collapsing against a tree and sliding down until he is sitting on the floor. His hand shakes, veins bulging as he raises it to run through his hair. A choked sob breaks out of his chest, jaw clenching in anguish. His other hand grabs his shirt, right above his heart, pulling at it as he convulses forward. The noise stops, tears that hadn't been released returning to their places. But his head drops to his knees, supported by the arms he crosses beneath it. He trembles. Shakes. Chokes.

Even after she finishes drawing, Eleanor cannot get to sleep, tossing and turning, eyes refusing to stay shut. Eventually, Adelyn wakes, Eleanor moving to feed her, cooing to her child as she suckles. As she finishes and goes back into the cot, her mother stays, hovering over the bed as she falls asleep.

Footsteps stop outside her door, but they don't turn and go into the room across the hall.

"Eleanor?" Kenichi calls, knocking on the door lightly. "Why are you awake?"

"I couldn't sleep, and Adelyn needed feeding," she replies, moving over to the door and opening it quietly. "She just went back to sleep."

"Do you know where he is?" Kenichi asks, head jerking toward the room across the hall.

"He had a bad dream, went for a walk to clear his head."

Kenichi nods, yawn breaking through his lips.

"Go back to sleep, Ken," Eleanor sighs, shaking her head at the man. "He'll be back soon enough, and I'm going to sleep now anyway. You can go back to your little den and return to hibernation."

He chuckles, walking away with a shake of his head.

"Yes, because healthy sleeping patterns are something to make fun of," he calls back to her, grinning as the door slams.

Chapter 40

She bounces down the stairs, baby held at to her chest. The date on her watch is achingly familiar, but she can't place it. Her head tilts, brain turning over and over, but the memory stays just out of reach.

Eleanor shakes it off, stepping forward once more and moving into the kitchen. Kenichi watches her carefully, eyebrow raising in amusement as she makes herself a small breakfast. But he doesn't talk and shakes his head towards the others barring them from revealing the secret.

She eats in silence, sending unhappy glares towards the doctor as he continues to grin at her. When Nikolas walks in, he follows the same pattern, getting his breakfast and sitting across the small glass coffee table. The rest of the people in the room ignore his presence, eating their breakfast without a word. The pair's eyes meet, Nikolas raising a scarred eyebrow.

"Today seems familiar. The date, I mean. I cannot remember why," Eleanor mutters, sound moving through clenched teeth. "They know and won't tell me."

The chuckle that comes from the exiled Prince his surprisingly humoured. He fixes his grin into a teasing smile, taking a mouthful of cereal as she scowls.

Her daughter moves, gurgling as she senses her mother shift. As Eleanor looks down to her child, her annoyance disappears in seconds. Adelyn is still quite small, not in an unhealthy way though, and has already figured out who her mother is, often not quieting until she holds her.

"Do you truly not know what today is?" Nikolas asks softly, eyebrows creasing in displeasure.

"No. It could be anything." She half shrugs.

"Do you want me to tell you?"

He asks the question carefully, eyes monitoring her for any changes in behaviour.

"Yes, please," she replies.

Nikolas pauses for a few seconds before speaking, "It's your birthday. February third is your birthday."

Eleanor's head tilts, lips parting just a little bit as she looks at him in confusion. She swallows, eyelashes fluttering. After a few seconds, she stands, placing her daughter carefully into her carrier, before walking off without it.

For a second Nikolas's face scrunches, his Geminae glancing back for half a second before continuing out the back doors. He sighs, running a hand through his hair and sitting back.

After a minute he sits up, looking directly at Kenichi in worry.

"How likely is it she went to the stable?" he asks, jaw clenching.

"Very," Kenichi replies stiffly, figuring out what the Angeli meant.

Both men stand, walking out the door the way Eleanor had. They get down to the stable soon after, finding Eleanor facing the very nervous looking stable hand.

Upon finding them standing behind the girl, he says, "I'm sorry, sirs, I din't think you'd be here so early."

"We weren't planning to, but now we are, could you tack up two horses?" Kenichi replies, smiling carefully as Eleanor turns around.

"What's going on? Why does he need to get horses ready?" Eleanor questions, muscles tensed as her head tilts just a little bit.

"I was going to suggest, later, that we go for a ride, as a present for your birthday," Nikolas admits, not meeting her eyes as he speaks. "Kenichi said you seemed to like riding."

She smiles somewhat, watching him as his fingers twitch. He was nervous, she realised.

Kenichi walks forward, holding her arm before he starts to talk.

"Take the offer, Ellie. It will help you clear your head and you two can talk," he says. "And you can ride now you aren't pregnant."

For a few seconds Eleanor hesitates, before giving in and nodding towards her Geminae. He grins, thanking the doctor as he walks past, before walking a few steps forward. Eleanor watches him still, staying completely silent as he offers her a kind smile.

"I'm sorry I couldn't buy you something, I would've if I could, but I couldn't convince them to let me go out," he says. An apology.

"This is amazing," she instantly assures. "I, up until a few minutes ago, I didn't even know it was my own birthday. I would have been fine without anything." She pauses for a few seconds, eyes going distant, then she refocuses. "Thank you, by the way."

"Anytime."

The stable hand walks two fully tacked up horses towards them.

He notices pretty quickly that she has, pulling his horse back so he's riding next to her. For a few seconds, he digs in his pocket, before reaching over to where her hand hangs loose. He presses the penny into her hand, waiting until her fist closes around it to let go.

She looks at it in confusion, blinking a few times before she looks towards him again, finding his eyes on her. Her head tilts in question, but she doesn't ask.

"Penny for your thoughts?" he says, lips twitching up in pride at his clever idea.

Eleanor bites her lip for a second, staying quiet. Then she looks back at him.

"What thoughts do you want?" she asks. "I have many."

"Whatever just made you go quiet... or if you don't want to say that, just... something."

Nikolas shrugs, giving her a reassuring smile before she looks forward again.

"It was... in the Agency we didn't celebrate birthdays, or anything from our past. That's why I had forgotten. Instead, in the middle of the year we – Mein Vater, Seb and I – would exchange gifts," she says. "It's how I got the necklace I used to wear" —for a second she touches her empty neck— "and over time, I just, forgot my birthday. It just slipped away. I only realised it this morning, how wrong my life has become. How wrong I am."

Her Geminae offers a hand, Eleanor takes it thankfully. He doesn't force her to speak, nor plays down her admission. He just holds her hand and lets her return back to her mind.

It's as they turn back toward home, though still deep into the pines, that she speaks again, a smile sketching itself onto her features.

"Do you want the penny back?" she asks, voice oddly light.

"No, you can keep it. If you want you can use it in return, make a sort of game out of it," Nikolas replies.

Eleanor nods, carefully withdrawing her hand to slip the penny into her pocket. Reaching forward to scratch her horse, she doesn't take his hand again. Once again, they fall into a comfortable silence, breaths calm as the house comes back into view.

Suddenly, Nikolas blurts, "you aren't wrong, Eleanor. You are you, and there is nothing wrong about that."

Pale blue eyes meet silver for just a second, warm thanks dancing through the connection before she faces forward again.

"Thank you for organising this," she says, "It was very thoughtful."

"Any time, Eleanor, any time."

Pulling to a stop, the pair dismount, leading their horses into the barn and starting to tie them up, but the stable hand runs out, taking both horses off them before they can do too much. After being heavily assured they don't have to do anything, the pair walk back up to the house.

The younger collects her child and disappears up to her room, not before thanking Nikolas once again, however.

She doesn't emerge again until dinner time, back to her cheerier self and engaging in the conversation as soon as she arrives. She takes the presents with a gratitude, even staying up later than she usually does.

Nikolas watches on with a smile, but just beneath it, he is worried, because her mood changed so quickly, and so dramatically. The things he had noticed about her, her mannerisms, were different, and she spoke in a way... that wasn't her.

Chapter 41

It was always easy to tell when she started to get riled up. Really, I only knew her in the last few years, but looking back through the recordings, I know before they do that something is going to happen. That something was wrong. Nikolas eventually learned, Kenichi not quite as well, but they would notice it looking back on these few weeks.

Her birthday had been in early February, and not even two weeks later she had started to show signs.

It started with talking a little less, playing a little more piano. Then she started acting a little weirdly, talking to herself, her mannerisms shifting at least once a day. She was losing her appetite. Eating less.

The nightmares were becoming worse, and more frequent. She had started thrashing so violently when she woke that they had no choice but to send in Nikolas, who seemed to be the only one able to ease it.

During the day, she spent most of her time taking Adelyn on walks, or she would let the others take her child and wouldn't stop training for hours.

As March began, it got even worse.

At any loud noise, she would wince, often ducking her head and going directly to find her daughter. It was a reaction that went mostly under the radar, initially, but got more and more violent. Until, on the night of the 8th of March, when a storm rolled in.

~

It's late, and Eleanor has slipped into her room already. No one else notices when the first thunderclap hits. She does. She leaps off her bed in one movement, racing to her daughter's crib just as the next clap, much bigger than the last, reaches her ears.

Adelyn wakes up as her mother picks her up and takes them under the wooden desk. With her knees up, she covers the baby's body; outside arm pulling her own into protection.

Downstairs, Nikolas is sitting behind a book, alone in the library. Until he stands, moving out the door and to where the rest of the household sit, talking. They all look over as he comes into the room, frowning at the sudden appearance.

"Where's Eleanor?" he asks with an edge of panic.

"Upstairs, she went to bed earlier. Why?" his brother answers, going to stand, but stopping halfway.

Thunder hits once again, Kenichi standing a second later.

"You can feel her fear..." he says, looking towards Nikolas. "Storms, they sound like explosions, they scare her."

Without consultation, both men run up the stairs, Nikolas getting there well before the doctor. The door pushes open without argument, and it takes a few seconds for him to spot her, hiding beneath the table. A terrified yelp leaves her as another clap sounds, the huge Angeli padding like a kitten towards her. He drops to his knees as he reaches her, Kenichi finally making it to the door.

"Eleanor," Nikolas calls, hand reaching for the arm covering her head.

The fingers that brush against it stay for only half a second, as she lets him guide the arm to her side. Eleanor doesn't look up, though, continuing to hide her face behind her knee.

"Eleanor, it's just a storm," he reassures. "Just a storm. You are safe. Everyone is safe."

Wet eyes look up to meet his, glancing for a second at the child in her arms.

Nikolas offers an arm forward to take the baby, letting out a breath of relief as she hands her over. The doctor takes her a second later, cradling the child to try and lull her into sleep.

"It may help her to see the storm, feel the wind and rain. Try and get her onto the daybed, but stay close and don't push it," Kenichi instructs, knowing that the Angeli would do a better job of calming her than he could.

Nikolas only nods in recognition before looking back under the table, Eleanor still looking at him. She flinches as thunder rolls once again, head ducking and more tears running down her face. But she shifts closer to him, leaning into his hand.

"I need you to come out from under there," he tells her, voice somehow not at all condescending.

"Nikolas, I can't. It's too dangerous," she responds, barely a terrified tremor.

"I promise you, it is safe, it is just a storm," he assures her. "Come and see."

She shakes her head, as if she was begging for him to not make her.

But he insists, guiding her forward.

"Trust me, Dulce Meum."

Shaking, she complies. Nikolas helps her to stand, walking with her to the window. While still flinching as the thunder claps, she doesn't run for cover. Instead she presses closer to her Geminae, not letting her eyes stray from the window.

Slowly Nikolas moves to sit on the daybed, Eleanor following subconsciously. He sits with his back to the window, and without breaking her view, she places herself sidewards on his lap. Her delicate chin rests on his shoulder, uneven breaths – quickfire out of her nose – fog the glass.

The two males nod, Kenichi placing Adelyn back into her cot, before moving to the door.

"The rules still apply," is all he says, before slipping out the door.

After a while, Eleanor falls asleep, head falling to rest against Nikolas's. He carefully picks her up, only needing one arm as he uses the other to pull her sheets back. She doesn't move an inch as he places her down, tucking her legs in and pulling the doona to her chin. But she does as he moves a piece of hair out of her face, a hand raising to brush against his.

"Thank you, Nik," she barely murmurs, hand dropping.

He smiles weakly, walking away from her. At the door he pauses, glancing back one more time.

He doesn't speak. Doesn't move. Just watches for a few seconds. Then he's into his own room, and the encounter is over.

~

This was the first episode in which her sanity could be questioned. All the other things, habits and mannerisms, they could be passed off as just her upbringing. And the time in the compound, a one off. But in her own room, alone…

It is important to explain that she couldn't protect herself from it, not like she used to. To do that, she needed to fully immerse herself, lock her heart so deep inside that it was like she no longer had one. She could do it. It took time though. And she refused to let herself get that deep in around her daughter. Because once it was up, only she could bring it down. And it often scared her to do so. She liked the peace.

I was there the one time it broke. When the earth shook with the rage of a mother with no hope left. I was there.

Chapter 42

A *woman is smiling down on her child. Brown hair and eyes of sweetest honey. The little girl is fussing, intelligible cries echoing around the empty room. The mother starts to sing, a slow melody that dances around the space.*

From the edge of her vision, a figure steps out, joining Eleanor as she watches the woman sing.

"Who is that?" Nikolas asks, glancing down to her.

"My mother," the girl replies, the German accent more prominent than it normally was. "She would always sing this lullaby when Kate or I were upset."

There is a pause, before Nikolas says, "your mother was very beautiful, you must have gotten that from her."

Eleanor blushes, refusing to look away from the scene.

"Thank you," she whispers, voice weak.

He just brushes his hand against hers, before disappearing once more.

~

She woke up early. Earlier than anyone else.

Originally, she had to feed Adelyn, but then, her body refused to let itself sleep. She knew why. If she went to sleep then she'd see it again.

So she went to the room next door, wrapped her knuckles. A rhythm beats around the room, even in tempo and volume. It is with an irritated sigh that the sound stops about half an hour later, the assassin, having grown less fit during the last months of her pregnancy, still hadn't gotten back to her former level. She was close, though.

There is one last thud, as Eleanor lets herself drop onto the floor.

Her eyes do not drift shut. No, they stay as wide as possible as she stares at the blank wall. Not a sound leaves her lips, not a tear leaves her eyes. She just sits, back to the open and toes pressed against the wall.

Michael finds her that way an hour and a half later, as he comes in to do his normal morning routine. He says hello, she doesn't respond. He tries again, no response. Once more with the same result.

Knowing better than to try and shake it out of her, he opts to just slide down the wall next to her, so he can see her face.

"Eleanor," he says, relieved to see her eyes twitch just a fraction in his direction. "How long have you been sitting here?"

The only reaction is a blink and the barest shrug of her shoulders.

"Where's Adelyn?"

"Asleep."

This was in fact true, so he nodded.

"Are you just going to keep sitting, staring at the wall?"

Again, only a slight shrug.

With an irritated sigh, Michael stands. "Up you get," he demands, "Kenichi is making breakfast downstairs, if you ask, he might make pancakes for us all."

"Why can't you ask?" Eleanor asks, head actually moving to face him.

It takes everything he has not to grin, instead responding with,

"Because he likes you more than the rest of us."

With a sarcastic eyeroll, the teenager stands up. She leaves the room without saying another word, checking briefly on her daughter before slipping downstairs.

Kenichi looks over, nodding towards her as she walks past and takes an apple out of the bowl of fruit. He watches her carefully as she moves away and sits on her couch, knees tucking to her chest.

During her arrival, she doesn't acknowledge either him, nor Nikolas, who sits on one of the other couches.

No one talks, not until Kenichi finishes cooking his breakfast and sits down.

"You okay?" he asks, attention turned wholly on the teenager.

"Fine," she responds.

"You don't seem fine…"

"Well I am," she snaps, then calmer, "Just have a headache."

Kenichi turns to Nikolas, who sits next to him, receiving a subtle shake of a head.

"Is there something we should know?" Kenichi tries.

"No, I'm fine."

She doesn't move, doesn't even look away from her reflection in the window.

"We're trying to help you, Ellie. Just trying to help," he tells her.

"I don't need your help." The most blatant lie ever heard. "I've been fine without help all my life."

"That's not true."

"Maybe."

Kenichi lets out a defeated sigh, looking up to find Kaylee standing in the doorway.

"Just tell us wha—"

"Stop it!" Eleanor interrupts, voice louder than it has been all day. She turns to face him. "You are not my mother!"

She stands suddenly, half running, half walking towards the doors. She pauses before she gets there, though, turning back for a second to look directly at Nikolas. Her eyes hold a simmering vexation.

"Not, NOW," she growls.

A second later she is gone, sprinting towards the trees. They let her go, Kaylee walking closer and looking out the glass doors in surprise.

"Boys…" she drawls, "why did Eleanor just have a meltdown and run out the door?"

Neither answer, their focus staying on the spot where Eleanor had disappeared.

"Answer me, Kenichi."

He swallows, "I don't know. I'd suggest it's linked to last night's episode… But I haven't noticed too much else off."

"She has been getting progressively worse over the last few weeks. Though I'd doubt you realised that," Nikolas follows, bitter snipe in his tone as he returns to glare at the pair. "Can I please look at her file?"

The pair look between each other, Kenichi eventually pulls out a key, unlocks one of the draws and grabs the second folder down. Nikolas frowns as he takes Eleanor's file, opens it and scans the first page. It isn't long until he finds something, hand running through his hair.

"She lost her parents exactly 11 years ago," he says. "Which explains last night."

Kenichi groans, head tilting back in annoyance as Michael comes into the room.

"In hindsight, probably should have warned you," he calls after realising Eleanor wasn't in the room. "Found her staring at the wall in the gym this morning. Completely catatonic."

The doctor mumbles something along the lines of brilliant, before standing and walking to the patio. His hand is about to find the doorhandle when Nikolas calls out to him.

"Let her calm herself. She just needs to think," he tells him. "I'll know if she needs help."

Reluctantly, Kenichi walks away from the door. No one speaks, not for a while.

Eleanor slips back into the house an hour or two later. Adelyn, having already been fed, is sitting in her cot with some toys when her mother comes in.

The door stays open, a decision Eleanor wouldn't actually notice until later, but for now, she just sits cross-legged on her bed. She uses pastels, waxy colour sticking to the paper in swirls of red, orange and black.

Eleanor doesn't look away from the artwork as someone pauses in her doorway, before he walks into his own room across the hall. It hits her, that he might actually be worried, but she brushes the feeling away as quick as possible. Care is not something she needs to handle.

Soon enough, she leans backwards, shutting the sketchbook. The dream that came to her the night before refreshes in her mind. Words form off memory, a disunited song. For once, her tone isn't perfect, she doesn't know the words. Once again, she doesn't look away as Nikolas steps into the room, but she does stop singing.

"I, I know that song," he offers. "All the lyrics, I mean."

She cracks one eye, looking up at him in confusion.

"My mother, she used to sing it as well. I remember it…"

"As nicely as possible, what are you getting at?" Eleanor sighs, looking away again.

Nikolas coughs awkwardly.

"If it would help to make you feel better, cause I know you're missing…"

She raises an eyebrow.

"Out with it," she huffs.

"I could sing it for you, if you would like me to," Nikolas shrugs. "I thought it might help you settle your mind a bit."

A smile forms on Eleanor's lips, hand waving for him to lie down. Shutting the door on the way, Nikolas complies, head resting on one of her pillows.

"I'm guessing your mother used to sing it to you too?" Eleanor murmurs as she shifts a little closer.

Her head rests against his shoulder, eyes staying perfectly open as he replies.

"Yes," he says. "It was a bit of a shock to hear it again."

Without ceremony, he starts, melody the same as Eleanor's, but the words flow on, not a single one missed.

It shouldn't be surprising that he could sing properly, but you can see the slight double-take that hits her. Though it was clear he hadn't sung in a while, his voice held steady, notes rising and falling at the right moments. The lullaby finishes, and Nikolas looks over to his Geminae to find her face a mask of complete emotionlessness.

"You are allowed to be upset," he says, turning onto his side to face her.

"I was, for a few months," Eleanor shrugs. "But I had to survive. Surviving means forgetting, so I forced myself to forget. The tears for my parents have long since dried."

"I think you know how unhealthy that is…"

Eleanor doesn't respond. Barely even breathes.

"Why are you so sweet to me?" she asks, already knowing the answer, but looking for a different one. "You argue with everyone else at least once a week, you despise Michael. Obviously dislike the others..."

"The same reason that the people here like you, I would suggest," he replies.

"And that is?" Faint worry flicks onto her face.

"You try, you are constantly trying," Nikolas shrugs. "You have a way of making people want to know you." As if he realises where her thought pattern might lead, he adds. "And it isn't your training, it's just you."

Eleanor smiles, not much, but she does.

"So, to turn it back on you... why are you nice to me?" Nikolas asks, the man pressing his lips together in wait.

"My Mum... she used to always tell me to trust my instinct. Back then it was in regards to friends, but now. I rely on it, really. For the past eleven years it has been constantly on edge, ready to strike out. But around you it settles a bit," Eleanor replies. "It makes me trust you. Trust for me that warrants friendship." She finishes, but after a few seconds, she glances up at him. "And we're the same, in some ways. I know we both need a friend."

With a kind look, they let the conversation die out.

Eventually, Adelyn starts to cry for her mother, Eleanor stands and walks over to her. With a glance back towards Nikolas, she picks the child up and turns around.

"Do you want to go get two horses ready?" she asks. "I need to sort her out, but I'll be done in ten minutes tops."

With a surprised grin, Nikolas agrees, slipping away without another word. For a few seconds, Eleanor stares out the door, before she returns back to her fussing daughter.

Chapter 43

The day is bleak, clouds holding the light behind their thick wall. Cabin fever is running high in the pair of delinquents.

Normally, they would go for a ride, something they had made a habit of doing; but the rain was waiting for its chance, so they didn't risk it. Only Zach is left in the house with them, the other three working for once.

Eleanor places Adelyn – in her carrier – on the edge of the gym, desperate for some action. Hearing Nikolas, who was already in the room stop, she turns to look at him.

Tauntingly, she raises an eyebrow, beginning to stretch out her muscles as he shakes his head and returns to cycling through movements with his twin blades. Eleanor watches him work until she is fully stretched, briefly warming herself up as well.

"Obviously you didn't figure out how to hide that Angeli training, did you?" she calls. "You still fight pretty."

Nikolas stops abruptly, spinning on his heel to narrow his eyes at her.

"I fight properly," he returns.

"Pretty," she insists. "What happens if you lose your precious blades?"

A grin takes over her face as he takes her bait.

"I can fight hand to hand…"

A low chuckle breaks from Eleanor's lips.

"You use it as a crutch. You're all fancy swordplay," she shrugs. "Effective yes, but blades need to be earned. I'd bet I could get you down."

"Do you?"

Eleanor does.

Her feet curl on the sparring mat as she waits for him to step up. He does, cautiously placing the blades on the edge of the ring and stepping up to meet her.

The German accent slips in as Eleanor grins, "Don't pull your punches."

He doesn't plan to, stepping up to the fight and sending a punch in the direction of her shoulder. She ducks, landing a punch to his gut before retreating out of range.

"Is that why you have brass knuckles in those gloves of yours?" Nikolas teases after recovering for the hit.

Eleanor doesn't speak, just grins before landing a kick to his stomach and proceeding forward as he stumbles back. Recovering quickly, he goes to clock her in the face, but she doesn't retreat. Instead, using her left arm, she pushes his arm across his body and shoulder down, opening the opportunity to kick out the back of his knee and slam her fist into the upper middle of his back. Using the shock evident on his face, she pulls him by his shirt around and to the ground. One knee lands on his throat, the other on his left arm.

After feebly attempting to get her off (realising any time he moved she just put more pressure on his throat), he taps out groaning as she easily lifts backwards and retreats a few steps.

"That hurt," Nikolas groans as he peels himself off the floor. "How'd you know to do that?"

"The Agency. They taught us early on that if you're fighting someone who seems to have an obvious strength or height advantage to hit them as hard as possible in that spot," Eleanor replies. "Good to know it actually works."

"Yes, it does," he grumbles.

With a teasing smile, Eleanor bounds closer to him, patting his cheek quickly before skipping to one of the treadmills and starting it. Nikolas glowers after her, but starts his cool down anyway, eyes straying back to her, every so often, in disbelief.

Later, Eleanor is drifting around the kitchen, grabbing herself pizza and walking up behind Michael. With a smirk, she slaps the spot on his back, sashaying away to eat as he stumbles forward in pain. But she stops as he doesn't look towards her, instead turns on his brother.

"I didn't think you would stoop that low," he growls. "You realise that it could give them the advantage! That it puts the entire population at risk!"

"You think I don't know that," Nikolas returns, enraged at being blamed. "While you only care for the true bloods, you forget about the people who will get hurt first. I wouldn't step over that line."

"Why am I supposed to believe you!" Michael argues. "Look at you, Nikolas. You used to have everything, but you ruined that, you betrayed us all. Anastasia needed you and you left. You have done nothing but break any trust I had in you... Now this? Is there any reason not to send you back to Exilium Terras!"

Eleanor's hand makes contact with Michael's cheek, fury etched upon every inch of her face.

"Do you really think that little of him?" she yells. "I knew already. They knew already. They teach every, single agent to try to hit tall, unnaturally strong opponents on that spot on the back. I realised why today. But do not blame him!"

Wisely, the Crown Prince doesn't respond, but Kenichi steps forward and takes her arm.

She snaps her head to him.

"Eleanor. Back off," he orders. "It was a misunderstanding."

Reluctantly, she steps back, still keeping a protective shoulder in front of her friend.

With a death like calm, Eleanor speaks, "You blame him for not being there?" she asks. "Where were you, Michael? Did you see her face? You do not villainise him just because you trust your asshole of a father."

Eleanor smiles. That beautiful, crazy smile that was only ever turned on a few. Ellsie.

Realising he had woken the beast, Michael steps back nodding in apology and backing off the pair. At least he has that sense. In fact, he has enough sense to completely leave the room, Eleanor and Nikolas slowly loosening as the rest of the team drift towards the edges.

Shortly after, Eleanor runs upstairs.

Her nightmare that night, is not like the others. When she wakes, she isn't upset. She just brushes past Nikolas, waiting outside the door for permission to help her, and slips outside. When she returns to the house in the morning, she is acting like she normally does.

Chapter 44

Nikolas's birthday passes with little celebration, just a book from Eleanor and a terse happy birthday from his brother. His sister sends a letter.

Adelyn passes six months, spending the day being doted on by the entire household (as if it wasn't an everyday occurrence for her).

And problems start to crop up.

Attacks, smaller groups than when they were led by the exiled Prince, but the agents were packing much more of a punch. And there were rumours, medical cases of interest. The Daemones had started to formulate plans. They were growing brave.

Due to their experience Nikolas and Eleanor were allowed to sit in on the NAP strategy meeting.

~

A heavily bored and slightly pissed off expression sits on Nikolas's face as he reads over the papers that had been placed in front of both him and Eleanor. She is totally impassive as her eyes flick back and forth; head tilted just a little to the side. Once they finish reading the files, both place them on the table, looking up to meet the waiting eyes of the rest of the team.

"Do you want me to start with what I know of the drug, or with what I think?" Eleanor sighs.

"Know."

All eyes are on her as she starts.

"The drug a derivative of one already in circulation," she says. "That one however is not made for someone to live. It is made of two bases they call Malum and Sanctus, mixed with a combination of chemicals to make a powder able to be dissolved in a liquid. When ingested, it kills without leaving a trace. The Malum and Sanctus are inert until they combine with blood cells, when they react, killing the host and the traces of themselves. We called this Nox.

"It seems like this drug has been adjusted to attempt to keep the host alive. They lowered the Malum levels, first by only a little bit" —she begins to flip through the report, showing it to the room¬— "then by more and more as it continued to kill the host. Until here" — she stops on a page— "where the host survives. The report says that he was apprehended for violence and showed unnatural strength. It's a stimulant, with a very addictive kick. Most likely from the two unknown compounds. It leaves the user needing more, as the Sanctus cells start to need more of themselves to support the new host. Almost like a blood transfusion. The cells reject it and once the Sanctus cells are lost to the effort of trying to support themselves and the host, the Malum cells attack, and depending on the dosage size to the host's body mass, the host might die or survive. In the case of survival, the former host should recover fully, however it takes time.

"This reaction was observed in the Berühmte Söldner, the Sanctus cells attempting to keep the host alive, even if they die out; whereas the Malum, no matter how much there is, will attack the cells unless warded off by Sanctus. Because of this, they never just give Sanctus, and if they don't care about traces being left, they use just Malum."

The brothers look between each other, the elder responding.

"Malum is evil in Latin, and Sanctus is holiness," Michael tells her. "Do you know where they get it? The colour maybe?"

"They mentioned once or twice that Sanctus is difficult to harvest, their sources are getting harder and harder to find. I think that the compounds are generally a pale yellow, but it depends on the batch," Eleanor replies. "A lot of those secrets are kept until one graduates."

Michael nods stiffly, glancing across the board room to where the Colonel stands watching.

Kenichi speaks next, focus directed towards Nikolas as he asks, "Is it possible that they are harvesting something off the Angeli? Something like blood that could give someone the strength your kind carry?"

He doesn't respond for a few seconds, before nodding slowly.

"They could... I wouldn't put it past them to harvest blood off anyone, even their own kind"—he goes quiet—"It... it could be a very significant problem if they manage to..."

He stops talking all of a sudden, looking around the room in search of any cameras.

"This room is held under a localised blocker. No camera, sound, microphone or recordings of any kind can reach outside," the Colonel says, "do continue."

"If they attack an Angeli with bullets laced in the Malum, gas us or lace our food with it, it could do a lot of damage," Nikolas says, voice tighter than it had ever been. "Like, take out entire armies type of damage."

Silence follows, Eleanor's head tilting once more.

"Luckily," she starts, "I don't believe that is their current plan. It isn't their style."

Now attention turns to her, the slight twitches of her face intensifying as she thinks.

"No, they don't care about the Angeli. A bunch of stuck up 'heroes', who only leave their little bubble if they have to? No, that's not worth their time." The German accent starts to slip in. Michael scoffs from across the room. Nikolas smirks at his brother. "They want control of the human world. They attack the western worlds, they run everything. From my knowledge of their movements, of the missions I knew, they will want to ruin our civilisations. Release a highly stimulated, highly addictive drug into the rebellious world of teenagers. They'll release agents into populated areas, dispense the drug into parties, set up discounts for those who share it with their friends. Simple play.

"Once the big guns hear of a drug such as it is on the market, they'll buy in, both supplying them with income and widening their range. From there it runs itself. It will destabilise the country and leave it vulnerable to attack. As soon as it starts working here, they'll release into the UK, Australia, China... the leaders. They'll use them as an example, make countries pledge allegiance to stay isolated from it." Eleanor takes a breath. "However, if we managed to intercept the roll out, destroy their stocks, they'll likely give up on the venture. Drugs are a risky play, once it doesn't work, they'll try something new."

Nancy nods, following the line of thought. Unnoticed by everyone except Nikolas, Eleanor starts twitching, jaw clenching in annoyance as she tries to shake the annoyance out of her head. The discussion continues, but Eleanor doesn't engage, still internally focused on her thoughts.

Eventually, she stops, head drawing to attention and eyes focussing fully on the Colonel, who was speaking, asking for suggestions to stop it.

"You will want to send someone in undercover. Someone who can track movements and intercept exchanges, all the while tracking down the dealer to shut off supply," Eleanor answers, body perfectly rigid. "And you will need to put them in soon, before the roll out begins so they aren't as suspicious. You need someone trained in espionage."

As she speaks, Nikolas recognises her train of thought and snaps his head in her direction.

"No, Eleanor," he says. "That's too dangerous. What if it goes wrong?"

"You do not dictate what I do," she returns, meeting his eyes. "I was made to do this sort of thing. I can handle it."

"You have a daughter to look after…"

"And soon I won't be able to do that. So I need to do everything I can now to ensure she can grow up safe," Eleanor hisses.

The pair refuse to break eye contact as they argue, locking out everyone else in the room.

"Your boss will come for you," Nikolas warns. "He'll send your handler."

"He won't know to."

"I don't think you realise how much he knows."

The calm seeps into her.

"I realise." She narrows her eyes. "I can hide from him. I can hide from them all. You don't know what I'm capable of."

"I think you're capable of ruling the world, Eleanor, but I worry that you might get lost before you can," Nikolas snaps, breath coming slightly harder than it normally would.

In an instant, Eleanor's body releases, the girl looking away and murmuring an apology.

This time Nikolas is not alone in noticing the behaviour and the others join him in frowning at her sudden change. No one mentions it though, as Nancy steps forward and addresses her.

"You are still our internee, even if you're working for us," she warns.

"I can do more than just kill. I have done many missions without killing a single person," Eleanor replies, voice soft. "I do what I am told, give me your terms and I will see if it's possible."

The Colonel nods in agreement, dissolving the meeting and leaving.

Chapter 45

After the meeting at the compound, Michael and Kaylee flag the pair as they start to head back towards the car, neither talking. Once they're back within the wrought iron gates, both Nikolas and Eleanor visibly relax, the latter shifting a tiny bit closer to her Geminae. Still, no words are spoken, not as they get out of the car, nor as Eleanor heads up towards her room.

Nikolas follows her, trailing a meter behind as she walks. She pauses at the door, planning to tell him she'd see him later, but he catches the door before she can disappear.

"What happened?" he questions, "and don't brush it off, I've seen it happen multiple times now."

She pauses, before grabbing his hand and pulling him inside.

Ensuring it is locked, she scurries to the daybed and perches on the edge, staying silent.

"It's like you are two different people. When you're relaxed you tilt your head when you think, but in tense situations all that you can see is a crease between your eyebrows," he tells her, keeping his eyes decidedly on her.

But she doesn't look at him, gaze staying out the window.

Her voice is almost too soft for Nikolas to hear as she murmurs, "It's too dangerous, Ellsie... He told us that to stay safe we needed to keep it secret... you agreed, I remember you agreeing... I can't Ells, I can't do that."

The girl glances fervently towards Nikolas, who now sits with his legs stretched out on her bed. She looks away again.

"Okay fine," she whispers. "Take over."

Her shoulders sag in defeat, before everything straightens, and she stands.

Eleanor goes to the cot first, wiggling her fingers at her baby before walking to her bed and sitting cross-legged on the opposite corner of her bed.

"She, we... Nora saw her parents be blown up when she was six, it ruined her," she starts. "I had to keep her alive. Over the years we fought for dominance, and I won. I am the assassin, I am the killer, I have to be. Because she has been scared every single second since that day, I keep us alive."

"You're saying there are two of you? Because she can't handle everything you've had to do?"

"Yes. But don't worry, I am very smart. And while she thinks she has complete control over it, there are many experiences she doesn't remember, but I cannot block all. Eleanor holds her own; she truly does. I love her, she is, me... But they ruined her soul, so I take some of the weight."

Nikolas stays silent, watching her carefully as he runs over the information in his head. He sees her tense, staying that way as her posture changes and she looks away from him. She keeps her thoughts secret, face tight. But he reaches out to her, shifting closer to pull her into his arms.

"Does anyone else know?" he asks.

"Not here," he assures, "Mein Vater does, no one else."

He smiles down to her.

"It makes sense now, the mood swings, why it seemed like you were lying about stuff. It was just your dual personalities," he muses.

"You don't hate me for it?" she worries.

"Why on earth would I? You're still you, you just make more sense now," his hand taking her chin to make her look at him. "I promise."

Eleanor smiles, crawling to the other end of the bed and waiting for him. As his head hits one of her pillows, she rests her head against his chest, arm laying over his waist. He gently holds around her back, hand resting back on his own stomach.

"I call her Ellsie, 'cause my mother used to call me that when I needed to be brave," whispers Eleanor. "She calls me Nora. You can call her Ellsie if you'd like, but Nora is reserved for a different place, different people. If you can tell the difference, you can come up with your own names if you'd like."

Nikolas nods, smiling slightly as he says, "I'll learn. It's only fair."

Letting out a breath of relief, Eleanor presses a little closer to his chest, eyes shutting carefully. She ignores it as someone pushes open the door, then leaves. Just soaking up the comfort of having the secret out.

"Thank you for telling me," Nikolas murmurs not long after.

"I... it's good to have someone know. I have never told anyone," she replies.

With a relieved sigh, Nikolas squeezes her arm kindly. He debates, silently, for a few minutes, before speaking.

"When I was a child, some of the maids used to spirit me out of the castle at night. Often Anastasia would come along as well, and they would tell us stories. All night long," he starts. "The King found out when I was about eight. He beat my mother in front of me, just me. I think that is when I first started realising that something was wrong. That and how he started treating me horribly from then on."

Eleanor shifts, looking up at him in surprise.

He refuses to break his stare from the roof.

"The ladies who used to take us, one of them disappeared, after he found out. I can't remember her name, but Anastasia told me. She was the one who hid the affair, let them meet in her house," Nikolas murmurs. "She was my mother's sister. She knew that there was no love between my mother and the King, so she let them meet in her house. They sent her to Exilium Terras."

With slender fingers, Eleanor tips his chin down to look at her, frowning in worry as he smiles weakly at her.

"I tried to look for her while I was there, never found anyone except a bunch of criminals and that single winged man," he shrugs.

They had talked about that man once or twice, mostly because Eleanor had asked. Neither had any idea what he was, so they had stopped bothering.

Generally, when they talked, it was late at night, one or the other having had a nightmare. Usually Eleanor. Sometimes Nikolas. They would both sit on whichever bed they were on and talk about different things. Over time they started to sit closer, especially if the nightmare was particularly bad. They were doing very well at keeping it entirely platonic, which Kenichi was happy about.

Eleanor would usually be the one to fall asleep, and depending on what room they were in, Nikolas would pull a blanket over her or move her back to her room. He always managed to stay awake.

During the day, they would talk less, but could often be found with a couch each in the library or taking turns on the piano. Or horse riding, oddly. They had found their favourite horses, and had moved from just walking around the estate, to trotting and cantering, sometimes even popping over a log or two if they found one.

The team were glad Eleanor had started trusting them enough to leave her child in their care while doing things. It meant she was trusting them more in general. It meant progress.

That night at dinner, Eleanor takes the seat next to Nikolas, for the first time. It doesn't pass anyone's notice, but no-one comments, not out loud. They don't comment on her outburst, either. No... topics are strictly safe, work gossip, the like. Neither of the detained join in, sharing an occasional annoyed glance, but otherwise just focussing on their dinner.

~

Over the years following, Eleanor only told three more people, and for one it was just something that she knew. She still struggled with it, with the changing personalities. Most of the time, Nora held the reins, but sometimes she lost grip, so Ellsie would slip through. Never, though, would either personality get full control, there was always the nagging presence of the other in their mind.

They conversed like sisters. Constantly at each other's throats, but always backing each other up on decisions and life in general. Over time, their relationship got a little bit healthier, a little less of a battle and more of an understanding. Ellsie would come to be vital to their survival in the years ahead, and Nora would need to learn to know herself, a difficult question for a girl who spent years pushing herself away.

Chapter 46

On the 9th of August, about a week after the strategy meeting, another one is held. This one is in the living room, considered to be not horribly classified. And with the bug having been taken out of the system, they considered it safe.

Eleanor sat next to Nikolas, flopping her legs over his lap as soon as he sat down. On the three-seater sat the three humans, and on his own chair Michael was facing the Colonel, who stood in front of them all.

"It appears," she starts, "that Eleanor was in fact correct when declaring she would be best for this job."

Under her breath, she mutters, 'of course I was', earning a chuckle from Nikolas and a quick look from Michael, the only other one to hear her. She doesn't even think of getting herself a cookie like everybody else.

"So, I am here to talk out details. We will be putting you into the local high school, since it is a likely target. Firstly, would you be alright to start on the first day of term, in a week?" the Colonel asks, receiving a nod. "Brilliant, and you understand that even though guards will not be attending with you, your movements will still be monitored. You will wear that anklet at all times and say that it is just 'cute'. When arriving to school you go directly to class, and at the end leave directly to the car waiting to pick you up. If you need to stay late, clear it with us first. Any extra curriculars you clear with us.

"We have selected classes for you to take, however, we need to know if you can keep up with them. We assumed you could handle AP classes... So, you have normal English Literature and Composition, as that may be something you haven't done much of; AP Chemistry, as you showed knowledge of chemistry, and it seems like you would like it; AP Calculus; European History; and German Language and Culture. You also have to do physical education and that has a theory part as well. Are those okay?"

Eleanor thinks for a second, before nodding carefully.

"Are AP classes like advanced?" she then asks, looking around at the born Americans.

"Yes," Kaylee answers. "There is more work, harder content, but for someone with a brain like yours, it should be a breeze."

"There are only five, don't I need another?" Eleanor continues.

"No, you won't qualify for a diploma and aren't headed to university. The classes you are taking will make you seem smart, but also from a different country," Nancy informs. "When asked about university, you will say you aren't sure, but you may be moving overseas after you finish school. That means if you randomly disappear, it's an easy cover up."

Everyone around the room watches the conversation with interest, none more so than Kenichi and Nikolas. With safety on their minds, they are paying attention to every detail of the conversation.

"You will join groups and make friends you think can help get you information. We will give you a phone, so you can be considered normal. You cannot have any social apps, just use SMS messages. You need to keep up your grades as well," Nancy finishes. "Do not forget your mission, but until we get proof of rollout, don't push it. Once we do, you start tracking, start to do your actual job. But keep your cover up, understand?"

Eleanor actually scoffs.

"I wouldn't be alive right now if I didn't," she chuckles. "Again, Colonel, I know how to do my job. I was made for this."

Caution rises around the room, Nikolas's eyes straying protectively to the girl. She ignores him.

"Do you have any questions about your assignment?" Nancy asks, shaking her head in dismissal of Eleanor's declaration.

Again, Eleanor rolls her eyes, exasperation clear.

"Many," she mutters. "First, where am I from? Second, do I integrate with the popular kids or the actually nice ones? Third, what happens if they start asking too many questions? Fourth, who will know I am undercover? Fifth, am I to act bratty or nice? Sixth—"

"Okay, okay," Michael interrupts, giving her a look as she grins at him. "We get your point... You are from Germany, that's why you know the language. You can choose who you hang out with, however, joining cheerleading would probably be a good idea. If they ask to many questions bluff and handle it, I'd assume you can do that. No one except the people in this room will know your assignment, others in the compound will know you are attending school but they believe it is because you are in fact supposed to. Once again, your choice of if you're bratty or nice, but no being bratty here. Anything else?"

"How much of my capabilities do I show them? For example piano, physical fitness, other languages, tactical movements, etc.?" she asks, looking down for the first time.

The room is quiet for a minute before Kaylee answers.

"Piano is fine; I'd dull your physical fitness, keep in line with the other girls; you can use maybe one or two languages on top of German and English, but I'd keep it minimalistic; don't go hellishly into detail about battles and how adjustments could have saved them, you need to act like you are normal, but if you want to supply plans to the varsity teams you can," she says, then adding authority to her voice, "and in the terms of what we are calling your parole, you can't fight anyone, you can't join a gang, you can't do anything that would get you suspended."

"Yes, ma'am."

Kaylee nods in approval before turning back to the front of the room.

Eleanor asks, "What about my home life? Relationships, Adelyn?"

Kenichi answers this question, "You are in my custody, adopted. Adelyn is Kaylee's daughter, in an attempt to keep you as normal as possible. That fact, however, can be fluid with your teachers, but not with students, just say you need to go to the bathroom. You will need to pump at lunchtime, but only for a few more months."

She nods, hand traveling on instinct to her stomach.

"Do you have any other questions?" Kaylee follows. "Requests, the like?"

"I need a watch made that keeps time, but also has the ability to sound an alarm to you guys. If I get attacked, unarmed, I can only hold them off so long," she says. "I'd prefer a black band and a plain, analogue face. The switch should be covered, but easy to open. That is all."

"Great, we can get that," Nancy answers. "Review those files and the terms and conditions. Give it back to someone once you're done."

Eleanor smiles gratefully and watches her leave, spinning to sit straight and grabbing one of the cookies that had been waiting for her. Nikolas laughs slightly as she eats half of it in one bite.

"Hungry much?" he mutters, glancing at her on the side.

"I like to eat when I'm excited," she replies with a roll of her eyes.

"And why, per se, are you excited?" he grins.

Eleanor flashes him a devious grin.

"Because I have never been to school," she laughs.

A slip of words that no one else noticed, but Nikolas smiles, playing it off with ease.

Watching them from his seat, a smirk, so unlike his normal behaviour, appears on Kenichi's face.

"Oh, and Eleanor," he calls out, drawing the attention of the room. "If you even think of doing anything that could even possibly get you pregnant again, I will arrest all involved and ground you to your room until you regain your senses."

Nikolas actually chokes, coughing to regain his breath as Eleanor shakes her head at him in amusement. The girl stands a second later, turning to head towards the library with one last amused glare towards the doctor.

As she's about to leave the room, she calls back, "Mein Vater would be proud."

The room looks on in shock as Eleanor leaves, a lose chuckle escaping the doctor.

They hadn't heard her talk about the people she left behind in the Agency in such a casual way, ever. And while the remark did kind of relate the kind doctor to a mass murder, he was proud of the approval.

Later on, when the movement wouldn't be counted as suspicious, Nikolas joins her in the library. Using a finger to tip her book up, he raises an eyebrow at the title before collapsing into his chair. As if sensing his amusement, Eleanor chucks a pillow in his general direction, eyes not leaving the page.

Nikolas chuckles, catching the pillow and resting an arm over it as he shakes his head at the girl.

"How do you put up with all the dumb decisions in those books?" he says, grinning as she ignores him. "Why do you read them?"

Eyes rolling, Eleanor looks up in his direction.

"Like you aren't going to steal it as soon as I finish," she mutters, huffing in annoyance, but then she speaks clearer. "I like how the murderers find love," she says. "I like how the messed up ones who shouldn't find happiness always do."

A faint smile dances on Eleanor's face as she shuts the book and places her feet on the floor.

"At least Nora does, I just picked it up because she's halfway through," she grins. "You're here, why?"

"Because I wanted to check that you have been Ellsie since this morning," Nikolas shrugs.

"Why?"

A dull sort of confusion in the assassin's eyes. The crease between her eyes deepening.

"Research purposes," he smiles. "I told you I would learn the difference."

Eleanor nods slightly, turning her head away. She rubs her temples tiredly.

"We appreciate the effort," she says, head rolling back to lean against the chair.

Taking the thanks gratefully, Nikolas asks almost nervously, "will you date people at that school?"

Eleanor opens a single eye to look at him before shutting it and shifting close to the chair.

"No," she answers simply. "I don't want to make connections other than the ones I have to." A pause. "I've already made too many." Before he can reply to her, Eleanor shifts into herself, head shaking just a little. "But either way, it is none of your concern. You have no claim on us."

The harsh turn of her tone makes him lean back a little, giving her just an inch more space. With careful apologies, Nikolas ends the conversation, turning instead to how she thinks she will go having such high order classes with no background.

"English, I'll pick up, and I have been writing reports most my life, but in German," she starts. "But otherwise, I have actually done all the basic classes, science, math, geography, altered history, but history enough, over the years. They ran a kind of school to keep us occupied during the long hours we were locked up. I think the others got to sit in classrooms, but Seb and I did it in the apartment. That's when we practised languages, music, that sort of thing.

"Because we worked with much less distraction and took information in quicker, we finished early. Technically, I know pretty much everything they will teach me, minding a few specifics, I'm sure."

Nikolas nods in agreement, breath even as he asks, "Who will you plan on hanging out with?"

"I'll try and stick close to whoever they make my buddy but knowing how social politics work in American high schools, I'll probably be absorbed into the popular clique pretty quickly. I will attempt to remain the 'nice, foreign, new girl' until someone decides I need to be put in my place, a time in which I will completely ignore the toxicity, not change my behaviour and stay a good friend to all those people. I will diffuse any fight that may occur and tell them calmly I am not trying to steal their boyfriends, I just have a very attractive aura." She fixes him with a dazzling smile, continuing airily. "I will not resort to violence at any time, because Kenichi, who is standing outside the door listening, would very much dislike that."

The accused doctor steps out from behind the wall, smiling sheepishly at the annoyed girl.

"How'd you know I was there?" he asks, attempting to look casual as he leans against the doorway. He was failing.

"There is a light behind you," Eleanor shrugs, but sensing her company's confusion, she continues. "I could see your shadow."

A quiet 'oh' leaves the doctor, the two teenagers raising their eyebrows as he doesn't leave.

"You do need to watch out for the bitch fights, they can get very nasty and leave you with no friends. Honestly, I'd suggest you just hang out with boys, but that won't work out," he eventually says, eyes rolling to himself.

"I've been in bitch fights before. Do remember I can be a major bitch myself," Eleanor chuckles, grinning as both boys stop their rebuttals before they leave their mouths. "I just have to figure out how to win them without the person dead or in hospital."

"I thought you said you only ever saw the two you trained with?" Kenichi questions.

"Well yes, I did have too many fights with Seb to be healthy," the girl shrugs. "But once a year they would make all the ACE protégées attend the ball." Taking on a prim and proper voice, Eleanor imitates, "a momentous and prestigious occasion for the Agency to ensure our sponsors dedication and for our agents to relax and enjoy themselves. Of course, at an occasion as such all conflicts must be kept out of the eyes of our dear guests." Returning to her normal voice. "And they would pointedly look at me, to which I would reply with a sweet little, 'who, me? I would never'. Death wasn't allowed, but games were played for superiority. I nearly always won. The actual ACEs, the ones who had graduated and were training protégées, they used it to test us out. We each had a ring, and whoever had the most by the end of the night won. If they caught us, we had to give over our rings, and they dispersed them back out and we had to start again." A small smile inches onto her face. "It took a year or two to figure out what I had to do, but once I did, I was unstoppable. We would finish and all the adults would think I had just given up, but then I'd walk out with most of the rings and even some extras. As I got older, I had to resort to seduction to get some of them, but I always flew under the radar."

The boys share a brief look, but make sure it's quick enough that it flies under Eleanor's notice.

"Anyhow..." she continues, "Long story short, I can handle bitch fights."

Kenichi just nods, raising an eyebrow and stepping back out of the doorway.

"Great," he sighs, "I'm going to leave before I accidently trigger another, frankly disturbing, story."

He slips away before anyone can reply, leaving the teenagers to look at each other in amusement.

It takes a few minutes, but then Nikolas speaks, once again watching Eleanor for a reaction.

"I think I went to one of those balls," he says, lips pursing.

"Likely, it would have happened a few months after I ditched," Eleanor shrugs. "Did you see a boy with blonde hair and grey eyes? My age?"

Taking a few seconds to think, Nikolas slowly nods, "as far as I can remember he looked fine. I only noticed him because he was trying very hard not to get noticed."

Eleanor bites her lip anxiously, the most emotion of the kind Nikolas had ever seen Ellsie show. Then she's fine again, lips pulling into a smile and eyebrows raising a centimetre or two.

"You seemed excited to go to school," Nikolas say, changing the subject.

"I am. I have never really had normal friends before," she replies. "All my friends either have the ability to ankle zap me or are mass murderers."

Nikolas must agree, laughing a little at Eleanor's accuracy. She smiles a little in return, picking her book back up and zoning out as he does the same.

Like minds.

Chapter 47

For once, it's not terror that spurs Eleanor to the gym a week later. No, it's nervous energy. Happy, nervous energy. She's there for two hours, voice running in all different languages beneath her breath.

Nikolas hovers in the doorway for about ten minutes before he speaks.

"Eleanor," he calls, gaining her attention before continuing. "You need to leave in an hour, might want to start getting ready."

"Since when did Kenichi recruit you?" she returns, starting to stretch herself out.

The Angeli chuckles, "He didn't. I just needed to make sure you showered; you stink."

Turning to leave, he easily catches the boxing glove that was enroute to his head. With a smirk, he exits.

Half an hour later, once Eleanor has showered and done her hair, she's slipping on her predetermined outfit. Having come to favour tight fit turtlenecks, she wears a short sleeve, cloudy-day-grey shirt, sticking to her green for the tartan skirt. Ensuring no one is around, Eleanor takes out the innersole of her shoe, slipping in a small, flat blade and replacing it. She pulls the High Top Doc's onto her feet, tying the laces and walking to her baby.

She picks up the eight-month-old, cradling her to her chest as she hugs her. A single tear falls, the mother not wanting to let her go.

"I'm doing this for you Ady," she whispers. "Something good for once, hey."

A shaky breath breaks her lips as she settles Adelyn on her hip, carrying her down the stairs. Kaylee offers to take her as she gets to the bottom of stairs and Eleanor passes her child over with care.

Kenichi is waiting in the kitchen, throwing Eleanor an apple as she walks in. On the table sits a phone and a watch, next to them, the Colonel. Ever the agent, Eleanor doesn't meet her eyes, waiting for her to start talking. It was a behaviour that only came up when she was stressed, Nikolas watches carefully from across the room.

"You understand all the rules?" Nancy says, pushing the two devices towards her.

"I do."

"The emergency button is on the back, rotate the notch to line up with the setter, slide it back. Rotate 180 degrees to the right and you can pull it all the way off. There is a switch, it will start an alarm on everyone's phones after five seconds. It will turn itself off after 30 minutes," she then explains. "The phone is programmed with all our numbers – don't call me, please. It has emails as well, and will open with your thumbprint, or the code is Adelyn's birthday. Download any non-social games you want, no social media."

Eleanor nods, picking up the bag she had prepared the day before and slipping the phone into it, watch going around her wrist.

"Thank you," she breathes, "I won't fail."

"Good," Nancy replies. "Now get going, you have to get there early."

With a grin, Eleanor jogs towards the garage, stopping only to run back to cuddle her daughter and send Nikolas a smile before disappearing. Kenichi follows, offering a hand to the wall of keys as he catches up with her. He grins as she picks the plainest car available.

It takes until the stone steps of the school for Kenichi to realise Eleanor hadn't gotten out of the car. With a detached sigh, he rolls back on his heel and moves back to her door. He pulls it open, leaning on the frame as she stays perfectly still.

"What's up, Ellie?" he asks, breathing carefully.

"First day of school, people are normally nervous," she shrugs, shaking out of her daze. "Right?"

Kenichi nods, stepping back to let her out of the car.

This time she follows, slipping through the swinging doors after the doctor. Eleanor lets her eyes wander over the locker-lined walls and the school seal, sitting on top of the sand-coloured floor. There are three people waiting when they get to the office, the principal, office clerk and a girl.

The principal steps forward, hand extended towards Kenichi first, then to Eleanor who looks him in the eye with a tight-lipped smile. She already didn't like him (I mean, who likes their principal, but she had already figured out he was a cranky old man), with his face as weathered as his hair was grey, she could tell he was only there for conformity and salary.

The office clerk was kinder, middle aged. The small block heels she wears don't make her taller than Eleanor, who could be easily considered short, and her hair is secured in a tight bun at the base of her neck. Painted red lips, powdered face, string of pearls sitting flush to her collarbone. There could not be a more cliché woman if you could have tried.

Then there was the girl, standing confidently to the side. Beautiful dark skin, sparkling brown eyes, fringe settling just above her eyebrows. Straight hair falls just past her shoulders, mulberry formal pants matching her lipstick. She is smiling, thin in body, probably a member of the cheer team.

"Dr Tanaka, Miss Beck," the Principal, Mr Jeremy Cartellar, addresses, "this is Lana Taylor, she is in most of your classes and will be showing you around today. Your locker is also next to hers."

The two girls share their hellos, Kenichi watching on proudly as Eleanor smiles at her guide.

The clerk, Mrs Kent, speaks next. "This is your timetable, and your locker code, people will have started arriving by now so you should probably get going. If you need anything, don't be afraid to come ask," she smiles, nodding to Lana, who starts to walk towards the door.

Eleanor turns to follow, pausing slightly as Kenichi catches her arm.

"Have fun, Eleanor," he says, "I'll pick you up this afternoon."

The girl nods, murmuring a goodbye and slipping out the door after her guide.

"It's nice to meet you," Lana says, "must be weird starting at a new school at the start of senior year."

"For me it's more weird starting school in general," Eleanor replies, explaining as the other girl looks at her, "I was home-schooled most my life, didn't get to talk to many people my age."

Lana doesn't comment, just raising an eyebrow and gesturing to the locker they have stopped in front of.

"This is yours, put the code in to open, it will automatically lock when you shut it. If you mess it up, three anti-clockwise circles from zero," she says. "Put all your books in, except the ones for the next block of periods. You can take some of the things out of your backpack, but use it to carry your water bottle, pencil case, that sort of thing."

Nodding in thanks, Eleanor pulls the bag inside her bag out, tucking it close to the back of her locker. She chucks most of her books on the top shelf, taking out her Chemistry, English and History books and putting them back in her bag after consulting her timetable. Just as the steel lock clicks into place, two girls walk up.

One is pure blonde, the leader. For a second Eleanor sees what she used to be.

The other is of Latin American descent, beautiful curls of brown hair sitting on top of her shoulders.

"Who's this, Lana?" the blonde trills. "I didn't think there were any new students this year?"

"This is Eleanor, she only got enrolled a few days ago," Lana replies. "I only found out late last night."

The two girls look over her for a few seconds, judging her worth. Then they smile sweetly, the blonde flicking her hair off her shoulder.

"Well make sure you bring her to lunch, we wouldn't want her to be left alone on her first day," she says, before turning to Eleanor. "Welcome to Gravenhal High, I'm Skylar, this is Vicky. You should come by Cheer tryouts next week, I'm sure I could find a place for you."

"Thank you," Eleanor smiles, thankful to be able to use her relaxed, slightly accented tone. "It's nice to meet you."

The girls look over her, judgement simmering just behind their eyes. Eleanor holds strong, not at all threatened by their judgements.

~

It's hard to remember a time where she looked so sure of herself outside the following months. It worried a lot of people for a long time, but I always knew it was a good thing that she was anxious, it meant she was being careful. Careful meant at home.

~

The school bell rings, and Lana instructs Eleanor to follow her as the group heads towards a room. She takes the seat next to her guide, sitting in her usual, neat way. Her eyes roam the room, subconsciously marking the escape routes and the faces as they come in. Each one looks at her in confusion, before moving to their own seats.

Not too long after, two boys walk in, one with features matching Skylar's, and the other the complete opposite, a curly mop of black hair and blue eyes. The blonde sits next to Skylar, his friend kissing the girl quickly before slinging into the seat behind, on the other side of Lana. As the pair settle, another girl walks in, silently taking her place behind the blonde boy. Her burning red ringlets are tied into a pony-tail, light pink skin stained with uncertainty.

A middle-aged man walks into the room, bag dropping onto the floor just before chalk starts to scratch against the board.

"Welcome to the first homeroom of senior year," he calls as he turns around. "I am Mr Raymond, and as you probably all know, I'm new to this school." The teacher looks at Eleanor in acknowledgement. "I believe I am not the only one, so we are going to all get to know each other a little..."

And so they go, making introductions in a snake around the room. Skylar had a twin brother, Arthur – Captain of the football team – and proved herself to rather a lot like Eleanor expected as she scoffs as many of her 'friends' introductions.

When lunch comes, Eleanor trails her guide to their lockers, and then to the cafeteria. The room is loud, hundreds of kids seated around tables of all different sizes. After grabbing a very small lunch (an apple and water), Lana leads her to the same table as the kids she met earlier. She sits neatly, small smile on her lips as she looks up to meet the group's eyes.

"If you're from Germany, how did you end up here?" Skylar asks.

Eleanor had thought about this a lot since her assignment. She had the answer perfectly ready.

"My mother was born here, so I have citizenship and after they died..." she takes a slow breath, "due to the nature of their death, it was decided I'd be safer in America than in Germany. So foster parents were found here, and I was moved."

The story made sense, gave just enough detail to get the point across, but not so much as they were suspicious of her.

"What did your parents do?" the blonde's right hand follows.

"They were diplomats," she sighs. "Good ones."

It was true, two German diplomats had died the year before. They did have a daughter, she was a complete secret however, so no condemning pictures. There was, however, pictures of Eleanor, looking entirely distraught at the gala they died at.

Ever the assassin, ever the actor. Lucky coincidence she figured.

And then the guilt would come, because they were truly good people. Working to support equality everywhere.

The hairband on her wrist snapped back into place, and she returns her full attention to the conversation.

"What do your parents do?" Eleanor asks the Demorae twins, focus majorly on the girl.

"Daddy is a businessman," Skylar grins, chin rising higher than it already was.

"And our mother is an event organiser," the brother follows, same haughty grin on his face. "Dad is away a lot of the time, usually in Germany, for his business. That's how we know people over there."

A wealthy businessman that goes to Germany a lot, Eleanor made a note to check him out when she got home. It could possibly be a problem in the long run if he starts to figure her out through his children.

A new male sits down next to Arthur, intent solely on Eleanor as he grins, looking her up and down.

"Who's this?" he grunts, talking on the side to his mate.

Eleanor butts in to answer, "someone who will at no point let you anywhere near her. Keep your pants on."

Lana grins, high-fiving her under the table, as all the boys around ooh. Even the top-bitch herself laughs. The boy backs off. Message received.

About fifteen minutes before lunch finishes, Eleanor excuses herself, saying she has to get her blood pressure measured after lunch. They allow it, and she slips, first to her locker, and then to the nurse's office.

The woman looks up as she walks in, frowning slightly as she looks her over.

"Is there something you would like, dear?" she asks, "and do excuse me, I don't think I know your name?"

Making sure the door shuts behind her and there is no one else in the room, Eleanor answers.

"Eleanor, I'm new this year," she introduces, "and I have the slightest, ongoing problem."

"Oh?"

"Can I tell you something that you won't tell anyone else. At least not at this school... you can tell my carers, just not anyone here?"

"I guess so, depends on what it is."

"Even if you are paid?"

Almost defensively, the nurse frowns, "I don't take bribes."

Eleanor sighs, nodding weakly as she figures it's safe enough.

"I have a daughter, eight months old now," she reveals. "That is to remain a secret at this school. However, I need to pump..."

"Of course dear," the nurse smiles. "That room there is private. What do I say if someone asks?"

"Blood pressure needs to be measured," Eleanor explains. "Thank you."

"You know people will find out eventually," the nurse warns.

"I am a very good liar," she ensures, before disappearing into the small room.

Chapter 48

Lana walks out of the school with her new buddy, keeping close as Eleanor quickly pulls out her phone. Few people bother them as Eleanor looks around, eventually finding the car she was looking for.

"You good to go?" Lana asks, smiling kindly as Eleanor nods. "Cool, I'll see you tomorrow then."

"See you then," Eleanor replies, stepping away carefully and making her way to the SUV sitting on the side of the road.

She frowns as she pulls the door open, not finding Kenichi in the driver's seat. Zach hands her a note, earpiece blinking as she slides in and places her bag on the backseat.

Kenichi and the others are working, I'm on a call with the company. Stay quiet, the note reads.

The car pulls out of its place, the man smiling slightly as Eleanor looks over at him. He reaches behind her seat and pulls out a bag as they stop at a set of lights. Dropping it into her lap as the light turns green.

Eleanor opens it cautiously, finding a ten pack of chicken nuggets and a cheeseburger. She frowns, looking back over to the man as he quickly presses a button on his earpiece and turns slightly towards her.

"There was a disturbance in Virginia, everyone is working, both Nikolas and Adelyn are at the compound. We won't be home until late, eat while you have the chance," he says. "Kenichi didn't want you to worry, so we didn't tell you."

Turning his earpiece back on he returns to driving, not expecting a response. Shrugging lightly, Eleanor starts on the nuggets, attention drifting to the passing scenery.

They arrive at the compound in silence, walking in the front doors and through the lobby with little ceremony. As they get to the corridors, Zach whistles, pointing to her quickly.

Realising he was leaving Eleanor jumps in, "thanks for the food."

Smiling in recognition, he hurries off, the two agents directing her down the way she was used to. The interrogation room comes up exactly when she thinks it will, Nikolas and Adelyn waiting inside. The teenager jogs the last few steps, to where Nikolas is holding the child, taking her daughter easily. With a finger wiggling at her, Adelyn gurgles, small fist grabbing at it happily.

Her mother looks up carefully, smiling as the boy steps back a little bit.

"Hello," she breathes, "thanks for taking care of her."

"It's fine," he shrugs. "How was your first day of school?"

His smile flaunts across the room. So very charming.

"It was good, busy. I have a background check I need to run. The usual," Eleanor laughs. "Blonde twins run the place; I have a sneaking suspicion their father is one of ou- the agents."

The mistake, it almost shocks the girl. She had slipped. The control had slipped. For a second, she was still a Berühmte Söldner. She was an ACE.

Nikolas steps forward and takes her hand, squeezing it as she shakes her head out.

He had the same problem. Sometimes he would wake up, and he would think he was in his room, on the island. Then he'd remember.

Then the throbbing would start. Anger. Pain. Loss. Betrayal. He would run outside, as if to remind himself where they sent him. Let the darkness envelop him until it was like the blasted Exilium Terras. The loss would turn, and for a while the hatred of his father and brother would resurface.

He'd spend hours in the dark, until either the sun began to rise, or the light flickering in his Geminae's window became too bright. It would pull him back to shore.

For unlike Eleanor, he needed someone to care about him. She, she needed people to accept her, yes, but her terrors were with herself. His were with the people around him. The betrayal of his brother. The abuse from his father. The death of his mother. The everlasting loyalty of his sister.

And on those nights, Eleanor kept him sane. She brought him back in, before he could hurt anyone else.

He was raised an angel, and while the childhood that shaped his mind was corrupted, the blood on his hands made his stomach sit uneasy. He had become something he had never dreamed of. His hatred of Michael had not decreased, he still fantasied about killing the man, but he never did it, because of the beacon that Eleanor had become.

She was his Geminae. She was lost. They both were.

But when her sweet voice would float through the door as he returned, the way became a little clearer. And as he saw her holding her child, he would remember the good things.

She couldn't ever know how much she was doing for him. She'd never know what he felt that first time he saw her. She would, however, know how much he was willing to do, to keep her safe.

And she would not like it.

At her request, the NAP agents brought her in a laptop, Eleanor taking a seat to get to work. Adelyn – in her lap – sleeps happily with her head against her mother's chest as Eleanor finds her way to the database. She quickly types in Skylar's full name, following the profile to her father.

The man certainly looks evil. Dyed black hair, narrow eyes. Muscle to rival Nikolas.

"What are you looking for?" Nikolas asks, leaning over her shoulder to watch.

"School. Parents. Proof of existence beyond, I'm going to say 17 years," Eleanor rattles off, scrolling through the page. "Primary school is recorded as St Nathanial's Catholic School. Very exclusive, very successful. Has campuses across the world, in major cities. I'm recorded as going to the one in Munich on a few of my alias's.

"His parents are dead, died when he was a child. All of his childhood has foggy details. His business opened 18 years ago, and got many wealthy investors very quickly, has had very good luck in the stock market. Has friends in Germany, visits on business. Is suspected of smuggling things into America, but they've never found any evidence..."

Eleanor shuts the browser, and then the computer, shifting Adelyn slightly in her arms.

"I would put money on him being an agent. His wife would be as well, but women are much harder to trace, they go much deeper undercover. If the man is discovered, she can play the innocent wife, keep her children and all the money her husband leaves. It's why girls and ACEs are tattooed in ultraviolet ink, you can't see it without a light," she shrugs. "And it's possible that the husband doesn't know the wife is an agent. The Agency are all about 'need to know', he could make a convincing case for his wife's innocence if he thinks she is actually innocent."

Nikolas nods in understanding, sitting himself on the other chair.

"What I'm getting from this, is that the Agency trust women much more than men," he smirks.

"Not trust, they have more faith in female ability than male. Women lie better, are better trusted by society than men," the girl chuckles. "Just like children."

~

Eleanor starts the tears, 11 year old fist banging frantically on the door. Haggard breaths meet the woman who opens the door. The girl collapses forward, leaning against her legs.

"What's wrong dear? Come in, come in," the woman rushes, shutting the door behind her. She speaks in Spanish. "Where are your parents?"

The child manages to blubber out one word, matching the language.

"Dead."

The woman pities her. Good.

Sitting the child on their couch, Ella Freeman goes to the kitchen, returning with a glass of water and her husband.

The latter is much more suspicious. Staying at a distance as the woman crouches in front of the girl.

Eleanor ignores her, turning towards the man as she pulls out a small gun. He pales, hand trying to reach for a weapon. He never finds one, the tranquiliser dart lodging in his throat a few seconds before he falls to the ground.

His wife runs to him, terror on her sweet face.

"Why are you doing this?" she begs.

So innocent.

"I got your names and address on a piece of paper. Keep the man alive, kill the woman," Eleanor tells her. "Bring in the son."

Now she truly starts to beg, but Eleanor walks closer, and with the flick of a wrist, embeds a dagger in her throat, leaning down to pull it out. She cuts a cross on her forehead, stepping away and turning towards the stairwell.

The boy is in his room, he doesn't realise what is happening until the dart hits his neck. As Eleanor walks out the front door, agents slip in the back, taking the two males away as she slides into a car.

"Good job, Kleiner Fuchs," her Vater grunts as the car pulls away.

"What will happen to the boy?" the girl asks, eyes turning to the man.

"Don't ask those questions," he replies. "You know the answer."

Eleanor shifts her weight slightly closer to the male, thumb flicking the safety on and off.

"How did Seb go?"

"Don't know," the man shrugs. "He's still in transit."

He opens his hand, the small pill waiting for her to pick up. She does, settling her head on his shoulder before placing the lolly on her tongue and letting it dissolve with her thoughts as she slips into blissful sleep.

~

Nikolas is crouching next to her as she regains awareness, hand on her arm. She wipes the stray tear, smiling slightly as he waits. A penny is pressed into her palm.

"Just a mission, as a child," Eleanor shrugs, letting her eyes flick towards the camera for a second.

'*Think what you want to say,*' he says, using the stray amounts of his Aspect he could.

'*You don't want to know,*' she sighs, head shaking just a little.

'*I do, Dulce Meum.*'

With an exasperated breath, Eleanor gives.

'*They would use children to capture Angeli, I think. Act scared, like people were after you, get let in. Knock out the target with a dart, kill the spouse. Find the children if there were any and knock them out as well. I only did a few, kept getting sick after, I was destined for better anyway,*' she says, holding his eyes as she does.

He nods carefully, hand squeezing hers as Eleanor leans against his shoulder. She presses the penny back into his hand.

'*You would have been getting sick because of your connection to me, Angeli's hurting Angeli's doesn't do well for the health. And don't in any way think I am blaming you for doing it, you had no choice and no idea.*'

Eleanor smiles in thanks, straightening out her back as the door unlocks and Kenichi walks in. He eyes them off for a second before dropping into the other chair, across the table, and rubbing his forehead.

"Tough day?" Eleanor asks, eyebrow raising in amusement.

"I get a ten minute break before I have to head back out, I was hoping you could identify what happened and check how your day went," the doctor replies, voice tense. He slides three pictures across the table to her.

The first; a man with a mask, just like Eleanor's. Barely readable on the side are enough letters for Eleanor to figure out it says Dunkler Bischof.

The second; a word spelled out with bodies. Lauf. Run.

The third; a legless fox.

The mother keeps her child's head pressed close to her, eyes glazing over the pictures.

"Where was this?"

"Virginia."

Eleanor shakes her head slightly.

"What type of building?"

"Courthouse. In the lobby, done overnight we think. Shortly after this was discovered, the nearest federal building was blown up. A lot dead. A lot injured. They were all brought here."

Eleanor looks away for a second, before releasing a stressed breath and looking at the man.

"It is a message. For me to run. Because if the wrong thing happens in my court case, I will take a lot of dead with me," she says. "You cannot publish any of these photos, or this part of the case, I doubt he was supposed to do it, and I'd hate for him to get hurt."

"Tell me exactly what the photos mean," Kenichi asks, needing the specifics.

Moving from left to right, she points at each as she speaks.

"Mein Vater, the 'dark bishop'. Lauf is run in German, you knew that. The bodies are just dramatics. The fox is for my restrained life. He is trying to tell me to run before I get so locked down that I can't escape anymore," she explains, glancing to Nikolas for support before turning back to Kenichi.

"Are you going to listen to him?" the man asks.

"If I was, I would have told you the fox was meant as a death threat. I've come to terms with the fact I am going to die and I just want to be able to see my daughter for as long as possible before I do."

"And the federal building?"

"Would have been his actual mission, I'd say there was someone important there," Eleanor shrugs. "Honestly, Mein Vater, he got in trouble way too many times because of me, he... I just hope he knew it would be in vain."

She desperately buries the pain that surfaces in her chest. Hiding away the overwhelming urge to do what he says, to recognise that she could live a full life. But she knows it would be a life of fear, a life constantly observed over a shoulder.

~

I find it odd they never used him to break her. Only ever Sebastian.

~

"How was school?" Kenichi asks, changing the subject.

"Good, the popular kids are twins, their father, I suspect is an agent, don't know about the mother," she grins. "It's fine though, I am an ACE for a reason."

Kenichi frowns at her in warning, "remember..."

"I know, I know."

Chapter 49

It shouldn't surprise you that Eleanor made it onto the Cheerleading Team. Or that she managed to secure her place with the 'popular' kids. Lana had ensured she had a place to sit in class, and would stick with her during breaks. At the same time, Skylar still hadn't fully warmed to the girl, but her brother had, and was trying to worm himself closer to her. To say Eleanor had absolutely no interest in him would be an understatement. The Scottish girl, Katalin was the most hostile towards her, clearly threatened she might lose her place to this new girl.

Where we pick up this story is a few weeks after she started, as she joins the rest of her 'friends' at a slumber party. Having gained permission from the Colonel and organised for Kaylee to watch Adelyn, Eleanor was catching a lift with Lana to the twin's house.

~

The sun is setting, the time reading eight o'clock.

"I'm surprised your guardian let you come," the girl muses as they drive, Eleanor tilting her head and looking at her in surprise.

"I had enough time to pass it with them, five day minimum for anything I want to do," she jokes, pulling the elastic out of her ponytail. "He's really not that bad, just understands I need to have an eye kept on me. I'm used to it by now."

"I don't think I'd survive having so many rules. As long as I don't end up in the hospital or jail, my parents don't care," Lana replies. "I hope you don't expect to get any sleep tonight, Skylar is always coming up with new things to do."

"I was not."

In fact, she was planning on forcing herself to stay up all night. She didn't trust anyone there nearly enough to sleep. And she didn't need to have a nightmare either.

"Oh, and try to ignore the boys, it's the deal Sky makes to have people over," Lana adds. "They mostly stay out of the way, but try not to end up in bed with one, it's the easiest way to fall out of favour with them all. And keep any secrets you spill in the realm of normal, they don't care that much."

"Will their parents be there?" Eleanor asks, forcing her face into curiosity.

"I think so, but they stay out of the way most of the time." The girl pauses, taking a breath. "Stay out of the way of their dad, he's a little... he gives me bad vibes."

As he should, Eleanor thinks to herself.

"I will."

The car pulls to a stop in front of a huge house, Lana pulling out her keys and exiting the vehicle. Eleanor follows, slinging her bag over her shoulder. She has to force herself to make a little noise with her feet, knowing she had to cover her constant silence around these people.

Skylar opens the door as they get there, bright smile on her face as she ushers them inside.

"Welcome, welcome," she grins. "We need to stay a little quiet, Dad has a business partner over. Once we're upstairs we should be fine."

Both girls smile and nod in agreement, following the blonde up the staircase. This house is smaller than Eleanor's, though still remarkably big. Unlike hers, this house is much more modern, all geometric shapes and white walls. Skylar's room is much the same, light grey bed and all the furniture was in the same greyscale, excusing a multitude of photos and a few cushions. The other girls are there already, and smile as the pair join them in the room.

"Now everyone is here... let's start!" the blonde grins. "I'm thinking, sunset swim in our pool?"

The seated girls squeal, Lana laughs along with them as they jump up. Everyone starts to grab their swimmers, so Eleanor shrugs, grabbing hers out. Each girl goes into the ensuite and changes quickly, coming back in wearing a variety of cuts and colours.

Eleanor's is the most modest, by far. A normal triangle cut green top, with black mesh making it a halter. The bottoms are green, and in no way a G-string. She puts her hair into a low bun, smiling tightly as she steps out to meet the others.

Her scars sit proud on her back, and she quells the raising confusion.

"Life as a diplomat's daughter isn't always peachy," she breathes. "It's purely marred skin."

Skylar, oddly, smiles in support, squeezing her arm before the tanned hand grabs her towel and so begins the trail of girls, moving through the house. When they arrive at the poolside, the towels form a pile on way over-priced pool chairs. With three even steps, Eleanor dives into the water, the picture of ethereal grace. When she pops up, a smile is on her face, daring the other girls into the water.

"Come on," she calls. "The water's beautiful."

Lana shrugs, gliding into water next to her. The others all follow.

An hour later, Eleanor glances inside, eyes catching on the figures of two men, standing in the kitchen. She does an excellent job of covering the shock, as she recognises both the men. One is the black-haired father, the head of the house. The other is apparently his leading ACE, and an expert on recognising her.

As if sensing her gaze, Nathan Myers looks over, raising a glass in acknowledgement. The teenager rolls her eyes and dives back under the water. Returning to ignoring them, Eleanor smiles to herself.

The girls get out of the pool shortly after, slinking up to Skylar's room to change and dry off their hair. Pizza is ordered, and a problem arises from the jocks across the hall.

"They steal our pizza, every time," Lana explains. "Even if one of us goes down early, they hear the bell and come steal it out of our hands."

Eleanor grins at this, folding her hands neatly in her lap as the girl's look at her.

"I hereby promise," she beams, "to deliver all the pizza, safe and sound."

"Don't worry if you can't, we've seriously tried everything," Vicky shrugs. "We usually just order another lot."

"Not today you won't…"

Deciding it was worth the try, Skylar gives her the money and wishes her luck.

And so Eleanor moves to the front door, perching on the arm of the leather couch in wait. Unsurprisingly, the two men turn up less than a minute later, her Vater hanging back as Eleanor smirks.

"Is there something I can do for you?" she asks, focus mainly on the other one.

"What are you doing in my house?" the man demands, stepping forward. Not a muscle in Eleanor's body shifts.

"Skylar invited me for a party. It would be rude to decline," she replies.

"Why have they released you on the world?" he continues.

"They haven't released me." She points out the band on her ankle. "Tracker. Taser. Microphone. I'd watch what you say."

Now, the Dunkler Bischof steps forward, turning only to the lesser agent for a second to tell him to leave. He does. Eleanor shifts slightly.

"I thought I told you to run," he grunts, speaking in Polish.

"I can't." She takes a breath. "My daughter, she deserves better."

"You're willing to die?"

"I deserve to. I… I've had most of the control, Ady and this boy, they make me come out more," Eleanor breathes. "I'm learning to deal better, and Ellsie… I am trying to keep her from biting everyone's head off."

"She's trying to protect you, you know that… Everything is different for her, she doesn't understand how to operate, without being so defensive. Remember, she's only ever lived in the Agency, she has to adapt."

The girl nods slowly, smiling gratefully at the man as her phone dings. One of the boys was on their way down. Quickly, Eleanor shows the man a picture of Adelyn, before straightening out.

"Someone's coming, you should go," she says. "And thank you."

Her Vater nods in appreciation, before disappearing just as Arthur rounds the corner.

As promised, she wins the pizza, and earns the rightful glory.

An hour or two later, Eleanor steps out, finding somewhere hidden to pump. She locks the door to the guest bedroom, knowing it to be her Vater's. Once she finishes, she unlocks the door but stays there, hidden from immediate sight.

Nikolas picks up the phone almost instantly, smiling at the girl as she says hello.

"What on Earth are you up to?" he replies, the scenery behind him moving until he sits down somewhere.

"I was just going to check if Ady is asleep yet," the mother breathes. "I've been stressing about it."

The boy laughs slightly, standing up from wherever he was and moving again. Across his room, she figures. For a few seconds, the camera shakes, before settling again with Nikolas holding the baby.

"She stopped fussing an hour ago, but we haven't been able to get her to sleep. The doctor said to just leave her, but she's been restless," he says, showing the baby the screen.

She gurgles happily, reaching for her mother. Eleanor coos at her, desperately wanting to have her in her arms. After a few seconds, Nikolas turns the camera away again.

"Go into my room, there should be a toy sitting on the end of my bed," Eleanor instructs, smiling slightly as the background moves. "It's a little white lamb, she was super calm this morning so I forgot to give it to someone. She usually sleeps with it."

In triumph, Nikolas waves the animal in front of the camera before giving it to the child.

"If she doesn't go to sleep with that, sing that lullaby to her, it usually works..."

"Great. How'd everything going?"

Eleanor relates what happened and who else is there, who's room she's in currently. She knew he wasn't going to tell.

~

It's one of the best things about their relationship, to me at least; he kept her secrets, kept her trust.

~

Eventually, the Dunkler Bischof walks in, staying absolutely silent as he shuts the door and turns his attention to her. She quickly signs for him to stay quiet, focus never leaving the conversation she was having.

Explaining that she should be getting back, Eleanor asks to say goodnight to her daughter, smile true as she says goodnight to first Adelyn, and then Nikolas, before ending the call. Like a good agent, she waits in silence for him to talk, staying perfectly still on the grey carpet. It struck her, that in all her years, she had only seen him so muted once before.

~

"I thought I taught you to be more careful, Nora," the man barks, pacing back and forth across the small living room of the safe house they occupy. "I told you to poison his food, not slip into his cell."

"There was a way out, and they had people testing the food," she explains. "And there were way more guards than I got told there were."

The man stops, looking at her in pain. Then he looks away and returns to giving her the silent treatment. She finishes the last of her food, shifting back into the couch as she watches her Vater.

"I didn't tell them anything."

"I know." A pause. "You would be dead by now if you had."

~

"Why did you save my life in that prison?" Eleanor asks, standing up and edging closer to the man.

He stills, not responding.

"I know that wasn't your mission..."

Silence.

"I never thanked you..."

"You never needed to," he says, voice gruff. "I meant what I said, last time we met..."

"Twice you've disobeyed orders to kill me."

"Are you asking me a question, Kleiner Fuchs?"

Eleanor swallows, walking the final steps up to the man and wrapping her arms around him, just as he turns to face her. He returns the hug, hand holding her head close.

"I don't know why, but I cannot hurt you Eleanor," he breathes. "You are a daughter to me, and I just want to keep you safe."

She nods slightly, pulling back to look up at his face. Blue meets grey, apology meets apology. So many things to say. So little time.

She looks away.

"I had to do it," Eleanor breathes.

"I know you did."

"I couldn't say goodbye..."

"I know you couldn't. I knew you were planning something. I knew something was wrong. That's why I allowed the box to go."

Those round eyes lift in surprise.

"I'd never seen you so quiet. You were off from the instant I walked you back to the apartment. It was Nora, I knew that much... but the next morning, when we asked you if you were okay, Ellsie came out stronger than I had seen in a long while. When you came back from Madrid, it was as if something had broken down inside you, because suddenly you were changing every few minutes. Sebastian didn't notice. I did."

"You didn't ask?"

Her head tilts. Lips purse in wait.

"I didn't. I had an inkling. I trusted you to make the right decision," he sighs. "And I think for you, it was. I saw your smile talking to your little girl... All this, so that she may breathe? I knew you were destined for other things, Kleiner Fuchs."

Eleanor smiles carefully, beginning to walk back towards the door. They both knew she needed to leave.

"What about him, should I watch my back?"

"I ordered him to get you sent back into containment, out of the field. They still want you alive. He will leak things to try to force retaliation."

Her head nods gently, smile thankful.

"Thank you for everything," she breathes. "And, goodbye."

Their eyes hold for a few seconds, before Eleanor slips away. By the time she makes it back to Skylar's room, the sobs she had been stifling have dissipated. She enters the room with a smile on her face.

"That took a while," Katalin sniffs, looking over Eleanor in suspicion. "Sure hope you didn't run into one of the boys..."

The assassin meets her gaze with perfect calm.

"If you must know, I got a call, from... a special friend."

Eleanor grins, flicking her eyebrows quickly. Lana giggles and pulls her down onto the bed.

"Tell us everything," she demands.

Chapter 50

One night, about a month later, the team and their delinquents are sitting eating dinner when Eleanor turns to start talking.

"I have a slight problem," she starts, gaining everyone's attention. "Since I've only been to one other person's house, Katalin is starting to prod at my home life. It doesn't help that Skylar keeps being given snippets of information on me from her father that she is using to turn others. They are getting a little suspicious, especially after queen bee decided to tell everyone that I was supposedly from Australia and had died when I was six¬—"

That had been a bit shocking, though having heard about the pressure Skylar had been getting from her parents (from Lana), it wasn't surprising. The assassin, who knew the accusation was completely true, had very easily blown it off, saying that she had received that name because that girl went missing, and since they had the same birthday, it was easy for the governments to forge a birth certificate out of it. Skylar had taken the excuse, though was constantly trying to dig up dirt.

And Katalin had grown even more jealous of the new girl, since Eleanor had become closer with Lana. Almost desperately, the girl had been trying to start fights with Eleanor, though it hadn't been working very well. It was no secret to Eleanor that Skylar had been influencing Katalin, telling her she would redeem herself if she got rid of their new nemesis.

Skylar was conflicted, though. Both her parents had been pressuring her to hurt Eleanor, but she really liked the girl. It was as if Eleanor understood her position, and she envied her strength. Eleanor knew this and was doing a brilliant job of maintaining her civility, especially as she became quite close friends with the kind Lana, who was ensuring the other two girls never went too far.

The boys had pretty much stopped trying to hit on her, luckily. Instead, they had adopted her as one of the group, when they weren't making up competitions, because Eleanor would not let herself lose to a bunch of high school jocks in any sort of physical challenge.

"What are you proposing?" Kenichi asks, watching his charge carefully.

"Can I have Lana over to study? That way, I can get closer to her, and she can vouch for my home life. I trust her enough for her not to cause any trouble if we stick to the story," Eleanor explains, eyes never staying on one member of the team for longer than a few seconds. "We have a Chem test on Friday, so that's the reason she would be coming. You guys are working tomorrow as well, so that means she won't be too overwhelmed by, this..." Eleanor gestures to their extreme bulk. "The Nanny will be here, as well as Nikolas to look after Ady, and there are always tonnes of guards anyway."

Kenichi looks between the members of his team for a few seconds, before looking back.

"Sure, we'll be back around eight," he says. "If she wants to stay, she can, the room next to Nikolas's is spare."

Sharing her thanks, Eleanor returns to her meal, eyes occasionally locking with Nikolas's across the table.

The two girls walk out of the school in sync, and it is almost surprising how opposite the girls are. One so brilliantly happy and free, and the other just trying to survive. As they make it to Eleanor's car, Lana laughs slightly upon seeing the driver.

"This seems very much like celebrity treatment," she says as they slide into the back seat.

"The house I live in is shared by a few people, but the owner is..." Eleanor giggles, "very rich. Fair warning, the house is huge."

"Noted," Lana replies.

She still stares in shock as they drive up to the manor, looking to her friend in surprise.

"You landed a good deal," she breathes as they drive into the carpark.

"That I did," Eleanor laughs, climbing out of the car to lead her friend into the actual building. "Do you want something to eat? Or should we just go straight through to the library?"

Grateful for the invitation, Lana replies, "I'm good for the moment, let's just go murder our brains."

For once an actual smile plants itself on Eleanor's face, the girl practically skipping over to her favourite room. Bronte meets them there, going immediately to the new person and sniffing her. Lana scratches the dog's side, instantly earning herself friendship with the hound. Eleanor sticks her head in the door, as expected, finding Nikolas sitting in his normal spot.

He looks up to find her there, smirking as she glares.

"Can we please have the library?" Eleanor begs, smiling as he starts to walk closer.

"And where am I supposed to go?" he chuckles, pulling the door slowly more open.

"Anywhere else?" Eleanor answers. "The nanny leaves soon so you could go watch Adelyn."

Agreeing, he finally pulls the door open all the way and steps out, nodding in acknowledgement to Lana, who blushes furiously. Eleanor slaps him as he smirks, slight jealousy in her eyes as he looks in her direction. Her Geminae laughs, pulling her into a side hug and ruffling her hair as she looks to her friend for help.

"Have fun studying," he grins, slipping away before either of them can respond.

Once the door is shut behind them, and they are settling into the couches they had pulled closer to the table, Lana turns to her.

"Who is that?" she asks, eyebrow raised.

"He's living here in a similar situation to me," Eleanor mutters.

"He's hot," Lana notes. "That the guy you were talking about?"

"Maybe, maybe not," Eleanor smirks. "Either way, not available."

Technically speaking, such was not the truth. But Eleanor still bore some of the protectiveness that he did, and while it was less in her case, she still didn't like it when other girls admired him. Which was part of the reason she hadn't shown anyone any photos of him.

"I can see why you want to keep him to yourself," Lana smiles. "He have a brother?"

To her own surprise, Eleanor starts laughing.

"He does, but he is seven years older than Nikolas, and ten years old than me," she grins. "That's one of the reasons why Nikolas and I aren't closer romantically... 'cause technically it's illegal for four more months."

With a supportive smile, Lana pulls out their chemistry textbook, dropping it on the table. And so they entered a special kind of hell, reserved for just their brains.

A few hours later, there is a short knock on the door just before Nikolas pokes his head in. Eleanor gets up, walking over with a frown as he smiles at her in apology.

"Sorry," he starts. "I couldn't get Adelyn to settle."

Eleanor nods in understanding, glancing back at her friend for a second before pushing Nikolas outside and shutting the door after them.

"I haven't flirted with anyone; I beg you to leave her alone," she breathes, eyes meeting his for a second.

"Of course, Dulce Meum," he smiles. "I have no interest in anyone, except you."

Eleanor blushes, turning away before he can see fully and opening the door again. She looks to Lana for a few seconds before starting.

"Sorry, Adelyn is Kaylee's daughter. Since she's out we've been looking after her, and she sometimes only settles for someone a little more... delicate¬¬¬" ¬—Nikolas huffs— "so, he's going to keep you company for a few minutes while I go get her to sleep. Sorry again."

"It's okay," Lana assures. "Have fun."

With a chuckle, Eleanor slips out of the room, leaving them behind. As she had guessed, Adelyn needed milk.

As she walks back down the stairs from her bedroom, she runs into Kenichi, who seemed to have just walked in, in front of the rest of the team. He hands over pizza boxes, three of them, catching her arm before she can slip away.

"Get your friend to call her parents; Nikolas can sleep on the couch in your room, if you would like him to," he says. "Give her some of the clothes from early on, they don't fit you now anyway."

"Come with me, her mum is a little iffy on me and might want a responsible adult to ensure she's safe," Eleanor replies, waiting for him to nod before walking back to the library. She pushes the door open with little ceremony, inwardly happy to see Nikolas sitting on the other side of the table to her friend. "It's getting a little late," she starts, addressing Lana, "if you want you can call your parents and ask to stay here, I have some clothes you can keep, and the guest room is spare. If your mum needs to talk to a responsible adult, let her talk to Kenichi."

With a bright smile on mulberry lips, the girl jumps up, sliding out the door and pulling it shut behind her. This leaves the two detainees alone. Eleanor moves to his couch, dropping next to him and letting her head fall back.

"What happens if you have a nightmare?" Nikolas asks, voice carrying an odd waver. Worry, Eleanor realised.

"Kenichi said you could stay in my room," she murmurs, "on the couch... if you'd like."

Her eyes flick up to meet his where they are looking down on her. Such kindness in the eyes of a murderer. Such care for one as well. He agrees, perfectly content with the couch. And somehow, in that moment, Eleanor Beck realised that he would be the end of her. Whether for good or for evil, Nikolas Mornblade would be the end of her.

Lana re-enters the room with a grin on her face, the act once again pulling onto Eleanor's face as she jumps up and smiles right back. The girls manage to convince Nikolas to stay to eat with them. And Eleanor does not let the smirks her friend sends her go unnoticed, already plotting a bloody (figuratively, not literally) revenge on the girl. To her disappointment, it wasn't going very well.

Payback; difficult when you can't hurt or maim.

Once they finish their pizza, the three decide it would be a good idea to go to bed, so Eleanor stands. She directs Lana towards the stairway; however the teenager's attention gets caught on the team. Only stopping for a few seconds, her wide eyes get stuck on Michael before Eleanor grabs her arm and starts to drag her up. Unfortunately, the damned Crown Prince catches them, calling them back down to the ground floor.

Leaving them to suffer, Nikolas slips up the stairs, laughing to himself.

"Why don't you introduce us to your friend, Eleanor?" Michael grins, knowing exactly what he was doing.

With a glare, she obliges, "Lana, this is Michael, Zach and Kaylee, you already met Kenichi. Michael is Nikolas's half-brother. Zach owns the house and Kaylee is the only one here that can help me keep the damn testosterone to a reasonable level."

Michael cracks his jaw and rolls his eyes at her, greeting Lana kindly. By now she has recovered herself and replies in the same manner. Eleanor notices the kind sparkle in her brown eyes, the untainted happiness. The purity. She is too good for this world.

It also occurred to her that every other person she can remember seeing has never shown the same happiness. There was always a stain. Death. Loss. Pain. Betrayal. In every pair of eyes she met.

Now released, the two girls jog up the stairs, Eleanor slipping into her room. She lets her door linger open, Lana leaning against the door frame and watching her as she pulls out a box from her wardrobe.

"Come in, what size are you?" Eleanor calls, barely turning around as the girl walks closer.

"I'm eight," she replies. "Sometimes ten…"

"Brilliant, grab something to wear tomorrow and some pyjamas. Sorry I don't have any new underpants, there is a shower if you'd like though," Eleanor smiles, waiting at the door for her friend to follow.

But as Lana stands, she catches a glance of the sketchbook, walking closer to it in surprise. Eleanor knew it was her sister waiting immortalised on the paper, and steps slightly into her room again as Lana picks it up.

"Who is this?" she asks quietly.

Eleanor steps slowly closer, staying silent as she reaches her friend's shoulder.

"Just… someone I used to know," she breathes.

"She's pretty."

To Eleanor's relief, Lana places the book back down turning and heading towards the door. She jogs in front of her friend, directing her to the room next to Nikolas's. They move in silence, Eleanor holding the door open as her friend slips in. She hangs awkwardly at the door, waiting for Lana to address her.

"You are a very good artist," Lana says, realising Eleanor had been thrown a little bit. "If it's alright with you, I am going to go to bed. What time do you wake up?"

"Too early," Eleanor forces herself to chuckle. "When do you usually get up?"

"Seven, generally."

With a quick calculation, Eleanor sighs easily.

"Message me when you're dressed, I'll probably be in the living room," she explains. "And if you hear anything in the night, just ignore it. It'll probably just be Adelyn wanting to be fed."

"Does she wake often?"

Needing to keep to her cover, Eleanor shakes her head. With quick goodnights, the girls part, Eleanor slipping quickly into her room. She pulls out the cot from her wardrobe and quickly changes into her pyjamas, before making her way to knock on the door across the corridor.

Nikolas walks out a few seconds later, handing her Adelyn (with her lamb in her fist) and following Eleanor back across the corridor. He gently shuts the door as he passes through, throwing the blanket and pillow he had brought onto the couch with ease.

"I forgot to put away the sketchbook…"

The girl places herself on her bed, knees tucked up and back against the headboard. With slow steps, Nikolas inches closer, hand eventually brushing her hair back over her shoulder.

"You could ask me anything about her on paper. Grades, hair colour, daily routine… but I, I couldn't even tell you if she had a nickname. Or what her favourite ice cream was…" Eleanor says. "I was supposed to be her big sister."

~

And instead I killed her…

~

The unspoken end to her sentence hangs between them as Nikolas sits gently next to her. His hand softly takes hers as she lets her head drop.

"Ellsie has been quiet recently," he says, obviously changing the topic.

Eleanor is glad for the distraction.

"She doesn't understand how to be friends with people," Eleanor shrugs. "All she knows is the Agency, which means she doesn't understand how to be civil, without a murderous plan. It's a slow process for her to learn to be kind. Really all she can be bothered with is us and Adelyn." Noticing Nikolas tensing slightly, she adds, "Don't worry, she's warming up to you."

The boy chuckles lightly, grin honest.

"It's like having an extremely protective older sister. Anything hurts you; she'll beat it up."

Now Eleanor laughs, light shining behind her eyes. It was weird for her, to talk so openly about her other self with someone. Make jokes.

It was nice.

~

It took a long time for me to find a connection like those two had. I spent a long time lying and concealing my past from my friends and the people I was in a relationship with. Eventually, I did, and I told him everything about my life. And he understood it all. He knew that getting married for me was hard, without Eleanor there. It felt wrong moving on without her. And he understood that I needed to keep a low profile, settling for a quiet life in the country.

He took our children to the safehouse without complaint and let me tell them why.

I had the life I imagined she would have wished for me.

Chapter 51

All in all, the sleepover had gone well. Having Nikolas in her room meant Eleanor didn't wake up screaming. She still woke up multiple times, and the pair gave up on sleep at four, going for a walk as the sun rose.

And it had done its job with her friends, so things had been quiet for the last few weeks. Luckily, Eleanor hadn't needed to think up an excuse for why she couldn't go to the Halloween party. Not when invitations for the entire team, including Eleanor and Nikolas, arrive for a wedding. Anastasia's wedding.

To say Nikolas wasn't happy would be an understatement. When Eleanor came home, his fist was, figuratively, already flying, and she put up with it for about five minutes. Then she grabbed her Geminae and dragged him up the stairs and shoved him into the gym.

"Wrap your knuckles, I'll be back in a minute," is all she said to him before changing into gym clothes and returning.

With Michael and Kenichi standing on the edge of the room, watching in worry, the pair started to spar. Nikolas was reluctant, of course, but after getting thrown to the ground a few times he gave up on protesting and started to fight back. It was quite amusing to the two observers, watching the Angeli Prince being knocked down over and over again. Eleanor was sounding more and more German the longer they fought, to the point where her accent was so thick that they were having trouble hearing what she was saying.

Eventually, Nikolas manages to pin her down, peeling backwards as the girl admits defeat. He doesn't offer her a hand, having fallen for that ploy too many times already. With an irritated huff, Eleanor picks herself up off the floor, grabbing a cord with weights on either end and flinging it towards his feet. It does its job, locking them together long enough for her to walk up and push him over with a grin.

"Must you always win?" Nikolas grunts.

With a dashing smile, Eleanor turns away, moving to walk out the door, where the two observers were still waiting, both looking surprised.

Speaking in fluent German, she only pauses for a second.

"And that is how I earned the name Kitten."

Dramatic much.

A week later they were headed for Angeli Terra. Adelyn was happily sleeping against her mother's chest, luckily having fallen asleep just before they took off. Eleanor was happy she had this time with Adelyn, knowing that the full-time nanny (a constantly armed agent who the Colonel trusted) would be looking after her most of the time.

As the plane touches down on the air strip, Eleanor notices her Geminae tensing, scowl setting onto his face. In a few steps she's next to him, Adelyn still in her arms as she elbows him.

"What is that for?" he grumbles, giving her a glare.

"The attitude. Your sister pulled a lot of strings to get you here, and I know you don't like that she's marrying Markus but would you prefer someone who was less courteous? You know she wouldn't have agreed if she hated him," Eleanor returns. "Be happy for her or I will not hesitate to embarrass you in front of the Angeli population."

Luckily for Nikolas, he manages to reign in his emotions by the time he makes it to the greeting party. As soon as the formalities (bowing and such) are over, Anastasia nearly squeals as she runs up to Eleanor, fingers wiggling at the baby.

"She's so cute!" she grins, smile widening as Adelyn grabs her finger. "Was she any trouble on the plane?"

"No, no," Eleanor smiles. "She was an angel. Ironically."

The Princess next turns to her brother, arms wrapping around Nikolas without thought. He returns the embrace, ignoring the glares the Captain and Crown Prince send him. The she remembers why they were there and returns to the front of the group, particularly to the newcomers. Even Eleanor lets her eyes drift in curiosity at the concealed runway and the beautiful forests. It smelled faintly like home.

Eleanor settles her daughter against her chest in a simple carrier. She walks immediately to Ferox, greeting the mare like an old friend.

Nikolas walks up behind her, happy to see his horse once more. But the mare quickly returns her attention to Adelyn, velvet nose reaching out and brushing against the baby.

"I see you've stolen my mare's heart," he chuckles lightly.

"I think she just likes babies; understands she need to be kind to them..."

With a pause, Nikolas smiles.

"She does. That's how I convinced Stasia to let you ride her," he says, watching Eleanor closely.

She frowns, head tilting slightly as she looks at him.

"I'm not allowed to ride her, you can, though. She'll keep you perfectly safe," he explains, guiding Eleanor to the saddle.

Easily, Nikolas lifts Eleanor into the saddle, hand staying lightly on the inside rein. He smiles up at Eleanor, winking lightly as she keeps one hand on Adelyn and takes the reins with the other.

"Don't think I'll ever let you do that again," she says, eyes rolling as Nikolas chuckles and moves to the horse next to them.

He swings up easily onto the supplied plodder, making sure Ferox is comfortable with his horse before moving closer. Following his Geminae's eyeline, they watch Michael talking to Kaylee. Eleanor, of course, had been picking up on the tension for a while, but Nikolas had no idea why she was smirking as Kaylee is thrown up into the saddle. Kenichi stays close to the pair as they moved off, far less comfortable in the saddle.

Keeping to a walk, the horses pick their way through the neat forests, Ferox doesn't place a foot wrong and other than Michael and Markus, barely anyone talks. It doesn't escape Anastasia's notice – as she rides silently next to Eleanor – that Nikolas has his hand resting just past the back of Eleanor's saddle. Nor that Eleanor occasionally drops her reins (which are carried in her left hand), to scratch his horse's neck.

Eventually, Anastasia trots up next to her fiancé, the rest of the group filing in behind them. People line the streets, all clapping as they process through. As they get closer to the castle, people start to throw flowers, and Eleanor freezes up. As she did last time, Ferox pauses to nudge her rider's leg, clearly not satisfied as Nikolas clicks her forward and reaches for Eleanor's hand. Her knuckles turn white as people start to release party poppers, before her head shakes as she relaxes. She grins across at the man, at their joined hands.

'*Please… try to hold your temper,*' Nikolas speaks into her head.

'*You didn't tell Nora that.*'

"I didn't need to."

Smoothly, Eleanor takes her hand back, just stopping her reins from slipping off Ferox's neck. As she does, they enter a channel, passing into the castle. Eleanor swings her leg forward over the mare's neck to dismount, Adelyn wriggling against her chest as the doors open. The same as last time, they walk up the carpet, to where the King sits in wait, but this time, the women curtsy, holding the position as the men drop to one knee. Finally, when they are allowed to rise, Eleanor links her arm with Nikolas's, cautious eyes watching the King.

Introductions happen, mostly the asshole ignores the pair. Until he notices their connected arms.

"Give me one good reason they shouldn't be in chains," he calls, taunting smirk meeting their indifferent stares.

Michael flashes the two remote controls as Nikolas tightens his grip on her arm. They both stick out their legs, bands sitting clear on their ankles. With the King satisfied, they are allowed to leave, Michael taking the three humans on a tour of the city, while Eleanor and Nikolas move up to his old room.

~

"Do you want to marry him?" Eleanor asks quietly, eyes meeting Anastasia's in the mirror.

The Princess lets out a breath before answering, "I think I do… I wish it wasn't now, I wish my mother was here, that Nik could be up the front. But I know I don't have a choice on those matters, so I am happy that it is Markus and not anyone else."

Eleanor nods slightly.

"And thank you for talking to Nikolas," Anastasia continues. "I know he wasn't very happy, and I know you helped him sort it out. You're good for him."

"I just know what bottled up emotions can turn into," she shrugs. "Plus... it gets harder and harder for me to hold my temper when I can't fight. A part of me needs it, has needed it ever since I became what I am. Forcing him to let go of his frustration meant I got to relinquish mine as well."

"Well, Michael said you have been doing a good job of keeping him out of trouble. It means a lot."

Eleanor just smiles, staying quiet as the Princess continues to do her hair.

"How have things been going between you two? You seem pretty close, and you are sharing a room," Anastasia prods, eyes carefully watching Eleanor.

"We are going fine, I... haven't really let myself get too close," Eleanor answers. "He has been completely fine with that, we go out riding sometimes, and read. And he helps with my nightmares. Looks after Adelyn when I'm at school and is perfectly happy to just be around, only ever sits close to me if I invite him. He knows things no-one else does... and I trust him."

Anastasia smiles, knowing Eleanor had started to fall in love. And that Nikolas had already.

"Are you going to let yourself get close to him?"

"I think I'm ready," Eleanor breathes. "I only have a few months left anyway, might as well make the most of it."

"Eleanor..." Anastasia softens. "I don't think they're going to kill you, not immediately anyway. The doctor wouldn't let them."

Her head tilts, confusion clear.

"Eleanor, Kenichi cares for you more than you realise. He knows you're a good person inside, he knows how much you love your daughter. I think he'll plead for a delayed sentence, give you time with her... And if you get one of the girls you go to school with to make testimony to your character..."

Appreciatively, Eleanor smiles, turning around as Anastasia steps back.

"I deserve everything coming for me," she says, "I know I do."

"And that, my dear, is why they will let you live. You have remorse."

Chapter 52

The cathedral they hold the wedding in is exquisite. The design much like that of the medieval period, the roof is high and stained-glass windows cast colourful patterns on the waiting assembly. Along the sides each window depicts a different angel, immortalised in glory. The glass towards the altar of the room is older, with faded colours and dulled metal in comparison to the Angels close to the entrance who appear to be more recent additions. Most brilliantly, six are arranged above the altar, around a bright gold ring. A wave of discomfort washes over Eleanor as she steps inside, the eyes in the windows following almost unnaturally.

At the front of the room, eight halos hang from golden hooks. Dull in colour, the gold hue has nearly faded away. They are the same ones that usually hung in the courtroom, however had been moved for the wedding. Both Eleanor and Nikolas try to avoid looking at the pieces of heavenly metal, taking their seats five rows back from the raised podium with the rest of the NAP team. Michael stands up next to his best friend, dressed in a black version of his normal outfit, the gold cape still brushing against the ground.

Both Zach and Kaylee had taken great pleasure in observing the outfit.

The organ starts to play, and everyone in the room rises, turning to look at the ornate doors at the far end of the room. As they swing open, the King steps out. And on his arm is Anastasia.

She looks ethereal. Her dress is an icy white, the skirt long and flowing. The bodice is strapless, with laced details moving past where the top finishes and to her shoulders. This lacing follows down her arms to her wrists, where one detail wraps around her middle finger. With her chestnut hair wound into a bun, the deep blue sapphire embedded in the gold tiara almost glows.

The smile on her painted lips is wide, and the sparkle in her eyes has returned. Nikolas can't help but smile back, proud to see his sister so happy. With a glance to her Geminae, Eleanor takes his hand and squeezes it, the smile on her own face bright.

As Markus takes Anastasia's hand, pure joy colours their faces, not an inch of regret shows. It humbles Nikolas a little bit, seeing them happy to be together.

Later that evening, once the ceremony is over and dinner has been finished, Eleanor is standing on the edge of the room with Nikolas. Her dress is her deep green, with spaghetti straps which cross over her back. It finishes at her waist and doesn't have a large slit, instead one hidden behind layers of tulle. The colour matches Nikolas's almost perfectly, the relation obvious as he stands in his old 'princely' uniform.

They stand with Kenichi and Zach, Eleanor standing with the same expression on her face as she carried when she was last there. No-one pulls her up on it though, perfectly happy to be left to themselves, as Michael was dancing with Kaylee. That doesn't escape anyone's notice, especially not Anastasia, who is eyeing them off as Markus spins her around as well. It's the Captain's sister who braves Eleanor's glare as she walks over to talk to them.

The look does not dissipate as the woman sends a smirk towards Nikolas, who only responds by rolling his eyes and gently brushing his hand against his Geminae's arm.

"Hello Rhiannon," he mutters, jaw clenched as she stops in front of them.

"Nikolas, I wasn't sure you were going to make it," she returns, glancing him up and down for a few seconds.

Now the touch on Eleanor's arm changes, Nikolas holding tight onto it to stop the girl from lunging forwards. On the other side of her, Kenichi does so as well, cautious of her temper.

"But it's good to see you anyway," she adds, turning towards Eleanor as the girl nearly snarls. "Eleanor, nice to see you again. Caused quite a stir, you did. Have to admire your guts though..."

Ellsie still holding the reins, Eleanor bites back, "be glad you still have yours."

The two males exhale in annoyance as Eleanor grins, Zach trying his hardest not to laugh behind Kenichi. With a glance between the two, Eleanor rolls her eyes, turning back to Rhiannon with an eyebrow still raised.

"Sorry, that was harsh. Nice to see you too," she sighs, offering an apologetic smile as Rhiannon laughs.

"It's good to find someone with actual bite in this do-good city," she chuckles, black hair flipping off her shoulder.

Still having not addressed the other two standing with them, she turns to Nikolas again. Her arched eyebrow rises, as if daring him. After a few seconds, he sighs, glancing down at Eleanor as she frowns again.

"Come on," he says, hand offered out to her. "We should dance."

With a light laugh, Eleanor tilts her head slightly, taking the hand but staying still.

"What about them," she says, kicking her head back to the two standing behind her.

"I'll keep them company," Rhiannon assures. "Now go."

They do, Kenichi still watching carefully from the sideline as Rhiannon starts to talk to them.

With a twirl, Nikolas finds a spot for them, hand fitting into her back with ease as she looks up in surprise. Just as her hand lands on his shoulder, they start to move. It would be easy to forget that both were trained in dancing, but it was obvious as they moved around the room, both keeping their eye's solely on each other.

It was one of the first times Nikolas had seen the unfinished cross on her back, much less felt it under his hand, and he does a good job of not reacting. Of course it makes him worried, and as Eleanor shifts slightly to place his hand off the scar, all he wants is to tell her that it was fine. Everything was fine. Nothing was wrong with the marred skin.

Eventually, Eleanor lets herself drift a little closer as the music slows, both hands moving to rest on his neck as his both move to her back. She doesn't move away this time, instead letting herself lean into his chest.

"She told you to do this didn't she?" Eleanor whispers lowly, head tilting up slightly to look at him.

"She did, but I wanted to anyway," he assures, lowly chuckling as he glances down. "I was too nervous to ask, admittedly."

With a quiet laugh, Eleanor lowers her chin again, eyes blinking shut.

"Well, I'm glad you did."

They retire not long after, saying goodnight to Anastasia and her new husband before slipping out for the quiet walk back through the palace. Their hands stay connected as they move up to his old room, Eleanor slipping in first, and moving to the balcony in silence. Having discarded her shoes, her arms lay perfectly on top of the banister. Nikolas balances on his forearms as he joins her.

Her hip bumps his lightly as she looks out over the city, at the stars sprinkled over the sky. With a slight laugh at her antics, Nikolas wraps an arm around her waist to pull her closer, embracing the warmth as she edges closer.

His thumb brushes gently against the ridge of her scar, looking down as she glances up quickly. All it takes is an assuring smile and she relaxes, turning in his arm to lean against the banister and look at his face. Slowly her hand raises, cupping first his cheek, then moving to run over the scar on his eye. She has to reign in the urge to grin as his face warms under her hand.

Eleanor steps away to change, leaving Nikolas on the balcony. He is still there when she comes back in, only pausing to put her dress away before spilling into the bed. Nikolas follows suit shortly after, slipping into the other side of the bed in silence. They don't curl together, staying on their individual sides. With only a low 'goodnight', they both drift into sleep.

Chapter 53

Christmas passes without incident, and Eleanor enters the new year. In January, they celebrate Adelyn's first birthday, and Eleanor spoils her rotten. The clock keeps ticking, the time running out before Eleanor becomes an adult, and goes on trial.

Two days after Adelyn's birthday, the first teenager at the school takes the drug. He manages to survive, and Eleanor goes on guard, now watching every person's movements. It isn't long until she spots a pair of students hiding something in their bags, and she doesn't hesitate to steal the two bags of powder, without a single person seeing her. Or so she thought.

Being a smart girl, Eleanor texted each member of the team when she took the drugs and put them in her bag. Skylar, the poor girl, didn't know this as she sends a photo to her father, who had told her to watch Eleanor closely and report anything unusual. These events lead us here, when Eleanor is sitting in History class.

~

Her eyes narrow as there is a knock on the door, head tilting ever so slightly as two policemen walk into the room. They find too easily then turn towards the front of the room again.

"We'd like to take Miss Beck for a locker search and questioning," one, with slicked black hair, tells the teacher.

With a nod, Eleanor rises and starts to walk towards the door, meeting Skylar's guilty eyes for only a second. As she does so, she pulls out her phone and speed-dials Michael, completely ignoring the two men as she walks outside.

"I need you to come here, regarding the message I sent this morning. I have company," she says, eyes watching the cops carefully. "Bring your badge."

"Do you think they're dirty?" he replies on the other end of the line.

"I do."

The two cops send her a grouchy look as she hangs up and stands still in the corridor, mouth staying firmly shut. They make a point of looking at nothing but her, entirely out of place in the warm and sunny hall. Begrudgingly, Eleanor lets herself be pushed towards the Principal's office.

"How's the Agency, boys?" she asks, face stoic.

The lighter haired one answers, "Strong and ready for deployment."

Obviously, his partner isn't happy with the answer, jaw tightening.

"They've finally gotten their hands on enough Sanctus for mass production?"

Once again, the light-haired man gloats, getting an elbow from his friend as he speaks of the ship full of it. They arrive at the office a few seconds after, Eleanor meets the eyes of the man with a grin. He scowls in return.

"Miss Beck, these two men have a warrant to search your belongings and take you to their station for questioning," he says. "Apparently, they got a tip off you were in possession of an illicit drug."

"Well the tip off was false, and either way, I'm not under their jurisdiction," Eleanor returns.

"Your parents are dead Miss Beck," Mr Cartellar warns. "You no longer have Diplomatic Immunity."

Finally, Michael walks into the room, looking quickly at the girl before turning to the adults.

"However, she is in possession of highly confidential information," he tells them. "So, until such time as Miss Beck is no longer in the care of my team and myself, as agents of the National Agency of Protection, she is under our jurisdiction and control. And, as such an agent, I prohibit the searching of her locker and questioning. We thank you for your cooperation."

Eleanor grins at Michael, who returns the look before returning to face the two fake cops.

"And thanks to the recording Miss Beck took on her way here, I hereby place you both under arrest for affiliation with a terrorist group and fraud. You have the right to remain silent, anything you say can and will be used against you in the court of law..."

Later that afternoon, as the cheerleaders start to head for their cars, Eleanor walks up to the blonde, their eyes meeting. Skylar looks away, trying to walk past but Eleanor grabs her arm.

"We need to talk, in private," Eleanor says, leading her towards an empty room.

When they are alone, the door shut behind them, Eleanor turns towards the scared girl.

"You called the cops on me," she starts, cracking her jaw.

"No, I didn't."

"Sorry, you called your father on me."

Blushing crimson, Skylar refuses to meet Eleanor's eyes.

"Why?"

With a gulp, Skylar speaks, "he told me you weren't who you said you were, he said you were dangerous. Made me swear to make you get in a fight with someone."

"Do you believe him?"

Silence hovers in the air before the girl weakly nods.

"You... the things he used to explain were true, and even my mother agreed with him."

With a long breath, Eleanor steps closer.

"Skylar, look at me," she orders, waiting for compliance before continuing, "If I was a danger to anyone except myself, I would not be here. For once, all I want to do is go to high school. Do you want to do the things your father is telling you to?"

Shakily Skylar shakes her head.

"You're one of the nicest people I've ever met," she swallows. "Everyone wants to be your friend, even Katalin, who honestly hated you to begin with. They just expect everything of me. Mum in particular, she wants me to be the best."

Eleanor once again steps closer, taking the girl's hand as she looks away in shame.

"That's nothing to ashamed of, Skylar," she says. "Your mother wants you to live the life she never got to. I understand what it is like, for your parents. I grew up in the same type of place as they did. It was oppressive, and violent. In particular, the women suffer for our ability to go under the radar, she just wants to make you the best she can. And they only want you to be perfect because they grew up knowing that if they weren't it could cost them everything."

With a few blinks, Skylar looks back up to her.

"How do you know how they grew up?"

"They grew up in a certain part of Germany, whether we've met before or not, most people can tell if they are from there. But you can't tell your parents what I've told you. Just remember that they cannot dictate what you do, and that they, in their own way, don't have a choice for what they are doing," Eleanor answers, words careful. "Don't ever take any drugs, they cause extreme damage and it's a miracle that boy survived. And don't dob me into your father again."

The blonde nods quickly, arms wrapping around Eleanor's middle for a few seconds before she steps back.

"Thank you," she says, starting to move towards the door. "And I'm sorry."

"It's okay," Eleanor assures, "if you ever need any help, just call me, yeah?"

Skylar nods, turning out the door and disappearing into the corridor.

~

It would be many years until Skylar called Eleanor. But true to her word, Eleanor would go to help and she would make herself a powerful ally.

Chapter 54

"**A**re you sure you just want me to come over today?" Lana asks, glancing at Eleanor as they put all their things back into their lockers. "It's your 18th, surely you want to have a party."

"No, I only want you to come," she replies, "I want to tell you something I don't want anyone else knowing."

The other girl raises an eyebrow, following Eleanor as they walk out of the school. They say goodbye to a few people as they walk, but once they clear the school gates, they find the black SUV waiting for them. Both slide into the back seat, Lana frowning slightly as she observes the earpiece in the driver's ear.

"Miss Beck, Miss Taylor," he greets, "Kaylee sends her apologies, something came up at her work."

"Who's home?" Eleanor replies, barely looking up.

"Just Mr Mornblade, ma'am."

"Brilliant," she smiles, before turning to her friend. "Can I trust you?"

"Of course you can," she assures. "If you don't want anyone else to know, I won't spill."

"Thank you."

Eleanor had built more trust in her friend than she thought was possible. It was becoming difficult for her to keep lying about Adelyn. She wanted to be able to talk to her friend about her little girl.

"What's your position on teen pregnancy?" she asks quietly.

"If it happens, it happens, but it's best to avoid it, why?" Lana replies carefully.

The car having arrived, they walk into the living room, Nikolas standing near the couches with Adelyn in his arms. He raises an eyebrow to Eleanor, smiling softly as she nods slightly in response (he knew of the plan, of course). She walks over, taking the child into her arms and cradling her happily.

"Adelyn is my daughter," she says. "I had her when I was about to turn 17."

Lana doesn't say anything for a few seconds, jaw dropping slightly.

"Is he, the father?" she then asks, suspicious eyes on the man standing to the side of the room.

"No," Eleanor laughs slightly. "The father is in jail for his crimes in the gang he was in and for raping me."

Blinking a few times, Lana looks over her, before speaking again. "That's why you were so tense when they were talking about that at school. Why you snapped at them..."

Nikolas is about to talk, not having heard about that particular incident, but Eleanor snaps her hand up to stop him before agreeing with her friend. (Kenichi had been the one to bring Eleanor home that day).

"The situation with her parentage is very complicated, which is why she has to stay a secret," she explains. "And my involvement in it is also quite complicated, and telling you about her isn't technically allowed. Luckily, he isn't going to tell on me."

"Is that why you have such strict rules?"

"It is, I'm in a form of witness protection. Same with him." Eleanor reveals, "but once again, you can't tell anyone, it will put me, and you, in danger."

"I won't, I promise."

Eleanor smiles in relief, hugging her best friend tightly. Quickly, she jogs up the stairs, placing her daughter in her cot and grabbing a coat before re-joining her friend. They go out on a horse ride, frigid February air biting at their smiling faces as they come back inside to find the team standing in the kitchen. Behind them stand the rest of Eleanor's friends, each grinning at Lana as she continues to push her friend forward.

"Come on," she laughs, "it's just for tonight, we're getting picked up at eleven. Skylar insisted on having a small party."

Getting a look from Kenichi, Eleanor sighs, then smiles, letting herself be dragged away.

Later that night, when only Skylar is waiting to be picked up, Eleanor sits down with her in the living room, where Kenichi waits as well. With a deep breath, and fidgeting hands, Eleanor turns towards her.

"Skylar, I have something to ask of you," she says, eyes wide open. "You know what your father said about me, well, I go on trial for some bad things I did, as a child. It starts in two days, since tomorrow I become an adult and can be charged to the full extent of the law for what I did..."

Skylar nods in understanding, taking Eleanor's hand kindly. Ever since the police issue, the Cheer Captain had been nothing but kind to Eleanor. And Eleanor knew she was suffering from it at home.

"I'm asking you to testify to my character, in front of an international assembly. You have a passport, and if you agree, it would be a summons, so your parents couldn't stop you. We would fly you over to The Hauge, in the Netherlands and you would be fully protected the entire time. My defence attorney seems to think this will be extremely beneficial to my case to have someone who sees me only in public settings and can attest to my control and kindness," Eleanor continues, eyes not turning away from her friend.

"Can you make sure my father doesn't know I knew about this before we get the summons?" Skylar asks carefully. "And will it be televised?"

Kenichi answers this time, "the summons will be completely out of the blue with no connection to this conversation, we are only asking as a courtesy. And the trial will not be televised nor let into the press unless the decision is made to put Eleanor immediately into prison. We also need your assurance that you will only speak what you believe to be true."

"I can do that, and I am perfectly happy to testify for her," Skylar agrees.

With many thanks, Kenichi drives Skylar back home while Eleanor, whose nerves were running high, slips to the piano.

Nikolas joins her shortly after, sitting carefully on the bench next to her as he places a medium sized lavender bear in her lap and pulls her slightly closer. Taking her fingers off the keys, Eleanor leans into his touch, lifting her present to her face. She puts it back down again as he gently kisses the side of her head.

"Happy Birthday, Dulce Meum," he murmurs, shifting to let her lean against his chest as she starts to tremble.

"Are you not scared we are going to die?" Is all she says in reply, fingers playing with his.

Carefully, he answers, "I am, but I am glad that we will be together when it happens. And I am glad you are scared; it means you care. When I first met you, you didn't."

With a weak nod, Eleanor rights herself and stands, hand caressing his face as she does. Silently, she slips out of the room and up to her bedroom, Nikolas going to his. But about half an hour later, Eleanor slips out of her bed, feet pacing back and forth on the soft carpet.

Then she gives up, door opening and closing silently as she stops in front of the door across the hall. Her fist hovers just off the wood, nearly trembling as scenarios play out in her head.

"It's unlocked," Nikolas calls, accent prominent.

Eleanor gently opens the door, slipping in and shutting it behind her. She then waits there, for a few seconds, until Nikolas rolls backwards to look at her. He smiles weakly, looking at her as she walks a little closer.

"What's up?" he asks gently, eyes still on only her.

"I'm too nervous," she replies, "can't sleep."

He nods slightly as she stops on the other side of the bed, hair falling out of her bun.

"What would you like?" Nikolas then asks, careful.

With a slight tilt of her head, her fingers tighten on her shirt hem.

"Could I stay here?" she whispers, eyes finding his in the dark.

"If you would like to, yes, you can."

With a soft smile, Eleanor lifts the blankets on his bed, green like hers, and slides underneath them. She shifts a little bit closer as she settles in, head resting on his arm as he runs his fingers through her hair. Her fist closes on his shirt, the other hugging her own stomach as she lets out a slow breath.

"Thank you," she says, nose burrowing closer.

"Anytime."

Both of them slip into easy sleep, shifting even closer as they slept.

Kenichi looks for the girl in the morning in all her normal places. Her room, gym, library, the piano. Checks for any missing horses. All are accounted for. Then, as a last attempt, he checks the tracker.

Michael spins around in surprise as the usually passive man swears. Watching from the corridor as Kenichi knocks on the door, pushing it open after he gets no response, he swears once again.

Eleanor buries herself deeper into the bed, Nikolas turning to face the door as she giggles. The doctor walks in, stopping at the end of the bed in annoyance. Flopping back into place in defeat, Nikolas slings an arm over Eleanor's waist and avoids making eye contact with the livid man.

"I swear to god, promise me you are both fully dressed under there," he growls, focus solely on Eleanor.

"Promise," she mutters. "Now, can you let me rest, please?"

"What about Adelyn?"

"Got up and fed her at three."

Kenichi huffs in annoyance, Eleanor finally looking up and meeting his eyes.

"I'm an adult now," she says, "it's perfectly legal."

Giving up on the venture, Kenichi sighs, throwing a pillow at her before leaving the room. Eleanor looks up at Nikolas smiling lightly as he brushes some of her hair off her shoulder. Softly she brushes his hair out of his face, twirling a few pieces in her fingers before dropping her hand again.

"You should stop gelling it," she mutters. "It looks bad."

Nikolas chuckles, rolling onto his back as Eleanor laughs.

Chapter 55

They left later that day for the Netherlands, Zach's private jet landing them without problem. From there, they went immediately to the hotel where they were staying. Extra security joined them, and both Eleanor and Nikolas were fitted with collars, to increase the effectiveness of the electric shocks. Safe to say, the Assembly of States Parties did not fancy two mass murderers with so few bindings hanging around their International Criminal Court.

It was odd, for most of the team, that Eleanor would stand trial as one human, in the place where countries would go to court. But in the same manner, they figured it was due to the high profile of her cases, in so many different countries. It was a political move, by the US, ensuring other countries get their chance at justice for their lost citizens.

And most oddly, the courtroom would be closed, no public, no one except those testifying, and those who already knew she had been caught. No press, none of the victims' families. Two members of the panel had to be replaced for this case, due to their proximity to the case. Eleanor was glad.

Strict instructions had come from her attorney on what to wear. No makeup was the first one, in an attempt to make her look as childish as possible. She was also told to put her hair half up and half down, to make her look civilian. She was to wear a tight-fitting long sleeve shirt tucked into black formal pants, with plain heels. Having no ear piercings, the only jewellery she wore was a locket Nikolas had given her, with a picture of Adelyn inside.

Kenichi was the one to ride with her to the courthouse, everybody else coming in different cars.

"You're worried..." Eleanor mutters, eyes glancing at Kenichi before returning to staring out the tinted window.

"I am," he replies. "Believe it or not, I care about the outcome."

She looks back again, head tilted slightly.

"In what way?" Eleanor asks.

Anastasia's words ring loud in her head.

"I think you deserve redemption. You're a good kid, Eleanor, you just had to adapt to horrible situations. I'm hoping they give you a delayed sentence, send you into hiding so you can see your daughter grow up," he explains, smiling as he looks forward. "Give you some time to be happy."

With a grateful smile, Eleanor returns to staring out the window, fingers twitching in her lap. The car pulls into the back of the courthouse, but even still, reporters are milling around the area, their interests piquing as each car in turn pulls up to a long, covered walkway. A way to get inside without anyone seeing.

When it's her turn, Eleanor slides into the artificially lit corridor, waiting for Kenichi before making her way to the double doors. The entire group is only in the hall for about a minute before they are ushered into a room. Nine officials sit behind a long table in front of them, a single table with two seats a few meters closer, with chairs behind. The walls are sandstone, with an all-purpose carpet that matches the chairs. A banner hangs from the long table which the officials sit at. International Criminal Court.

Eleanor moves to the table, joining the woman who was already there (her attorney, they had met a few times already), while everybody else stands in front of a chair.

"Thank you for joining us today, in which the trial of Eleanor Beck will commence. For the next few weeks we will discuss the guilt and punishment for her actions, and discuss justice for all those we have lost," the centre member of the table calls. "If you would please be seated, we will commence the proceedings."

Everybody sits, Eleanor keeping her eyes low and her breaths steady as a different official speaks.

"Miss Beck, would you please state your name, parentage, age, nationality and the charges against you," she says.

With a careful nod, Eleanor starts.

"My name is Eleanor Violet Beck, daughter of Luke Beck and Rosalie Beck nee Evans. I am 18, Australian, however I have not lived there since the age of six..."

"Where have you been in the meantime?"

"Germany until I was 16, America since then," Eleanor answers. "I am on trial for the murder of 627 people. Would you like me to be more in depth?"

"No, that is sufficient."

~

Over the next few weeks, they were there every second day, with different people testifying to her nature, her physical ability, her mental state. Eleanor did a lot of talking about herself, and had to undergo many different tests, much like if they were recruiting her. Skylar did her job well, Kenichi, Michael and the Colonel as well. They make a point of her remorse, the punishment she puts onto herself. How terribly the nightmares plague her.

On the second week, her attorney raises human rights. She raises not how Eleanor had broken them, but how her treatment had been in violation. Slavery was risen. Freedom. The reasons why Eleanor had to do what she did.

During these discussions she stays perfectly silent, content to let them spin the story but knowing that, at times, she did enjoy the fighting. The killing. She doesn't tell anyone, not more than enjoying the fight. She doesn't tell them of the bloodlust that slowly ate at her.

On the last day, they sit once again in the room, the officials not currently with them. Eleanor is silent, fingers playing Canon on the wooden table as the grandfather clock ticks away in the corner. She wants to curl into a ball. She wants to scream.

But she does neither, staying seated, eyes staring forward.

All rise as the officials walk in, taking their places behind their chairs. They look satisfied, almost happy with their decision.

~

"Today is the final day of the case of Eleanor Beck against humanity," one calls. "We will get straight to the point; I think we would all like to get home."

The centre official takes over, head lifting to look at the assembly.

"We, the International Criminal Court, hereby find Eleanor Beck guilty on all charges. This would normally incur life in prison, but this is not a normal situation. We are required to allow her to be tried under affected countries laws in conjunction with the ICC. This means she can and will be tried and delivered the death sentence with the support of our sentence of guilt. This will require a hearing of a size never seen before. Due to her treatment during her childhood years, going against the Universal Declaration of Human Rights, we are allowing for Miss Beck to delay the punishment until her 25th birthday, so she may have a chance to grow, live and atone for her actions. This should allow us to sort out a fair system for her future trial," he declares. "Or until Miss Beck breaks her contract, in which any contracted killing, or personal vengeance, is strictly prohibited. She is to stay in the field until the end of the school year, before being moved to a new country to start a new life."

Eleanor sags in relief, smile just on her lips as the man talks. As they call the court adjourned, Eleanor turns to her attorney, thanking her. The woman just smiles.

She hugs Kenichi next, the man somewhat surprised, before returning the gesture. She knows he was instrumental in the decision; she knows he cares. Nikolas is next, holding her to his chest. They have seven years to fix it all.

They return to America that same day. Eleanor goes to school the day after. She is a little more relaxed, happier. But otherwise life returns to normal.

She confiscates more of the drug, but she is just one girl, and the drug starts to become sought after, and people start getting increasingly annoyed as it disappears from their bags. To the rest of the world, she was just a girl, going to school. But she was not, she was a wolf, wrapped up tight in a sheep's skin.

Chapter 56

I wouldn't say Nikolas made a habit of picking up on Eleanor's emotions from afar, as other than a small instance of sickness in Adelyn which sent Eleanor over the edge, he only did it one other time. However, it was there, just waiting to be acknowledged.

Eleanor had created a little white lie, to get herself into a party hosted by the Demorae twins. She had told them it was just a slumber party with the girls, and had gotten dropped off super early.

She was a clever one, and Ellsie didn't hesitate at the opportunity to be let loose.

~

Providing herself with an alibi, Eleanor sets the first hour to finding the local dealer – why else would a businessman so easily allow his children to throw a party.

First, she found out the name of the boy who had received a package after arriving, found out who he sold it to (five very disappointed boys when they 'lost' their very expensive entertainment). Then, since her job is done, she takes the beer can offered to her and decides to have some fun.

About three hours later, Nikolas is hit by a pulse of drunkenness and adrenaline. He quickly pulls up a wall between them, and when Eleanor answers his call – the party loud in the background –, he hangs up and finds a guard with ease.

"We need to go and pick up Eleanor," he says simply. "I'd do it myself but I need an escort."

The man ignores him initially before calling over another guard. They converse for a few seconds, eventually, and without words, walking off towards the garage. Nikolas follows in triumph, sliding into the back seat as the car pulls out of the property.

As they pull into the Demorae mansion, they can feel the beat of the music through the ground. Nikolas is given half an hour, but it isn't hard to find the girl.

Not as she faces a jock, with a crowd forming around them. He moves in quickly, pulling her lead arm behind her back. She fights for half a second, before relaxing.

"Go away, Nikolas," she growls.

"Hm," he ponders. "No. We're going home."

Eleanor gets out of the grip, turning to face him before throwing a punch to his face. He catches it in one hand, repeating with the other as she swings it. Nikolas uses them to spin her around, arms pinned to her chest as he leans down to whisper in her ear.

"There are two guards in the car outside. We have 20 minutes until they activate our electric bands. And probably ten until the police arrive," he tells her, voice low, "and frankly I'm a little pissed off, so don't test me."

Eleanor remains glaring at the jock.

"He was forcing himself onto a girl," she returns, "and you know I can beat you."

"And if we could, I would beat his arse for you, but that will not go well," Nikolas hisses. "You're drunk, Incaendium, and if you were fully capable you would be out of my arms by now."

"Maybe I'm just comfortable..."

She was in fact, quite comfortable being pinned so close to him. Luckily, he thought she was being sarcastic.

"Now, I'm going to let you go. And you are going to walk away, grab your bag and we are going to leave," he says, carefully letting go of her arms.

With a smirk flashed at Nikolas, she rams her foot in between the jock's legs, spinning on her heel and walking away as he falls to the ground in pain. Nikolas follows her up the stairs and into a room. She only pauses momentarily as the two people on the bed scramble to find a blanket. With a slight shake of her head she moves fully into the room, grabbing a bag from Skylar's wardrobe and walking towards the door, glancing back for a second.

"Having sex with your sister's friend, in your sister's bed... tasteful," she says, Katalin paling considerably.

"Piss off," Arthur growls, and Eleanor obliges.

Their car pulls out just as the police arrive, Eleanor still glaring at Nikolas.

"You're an ass," she mutters.

He just rolls his eyes, continuing to watch her.

"Where's Dulce Meum? I'd think she would be more rational..."

Bitterly, Ellsie cracks her jaw.

"She is letting me have some fun and, at about the third drink, she got loose enough that I was able to take full control. Why, don't you like me?" she pouts.

"I like you fine," Nikolas replies, offering an arm which she moves into. "I just don't like it when you force her to lose control. When you act like she's weak."

Eleanor looks up, eyes locking onto his.

"You are both strong, just in different ways. I think you often forget she loves you more than anyone else, and will take the blame for anything you do."

Ellsie continues to look at him as she shakes her head slightly.

"I think she will love someone else more. I think we both will," she whispers, smile soft as she runs a hand through his hair.

For a second she starts to lean in to kiss him, but he places a hand over her mouth, head shaking in dismissal. Eleanor frowns, leaning back as he lowers his hand.

"Not while you're drunk," he says, smiling carefully as she nods slightly.

When they arrive back home, Eleanor half stumbles out of the car, the alcohol having caught up with her. She meets Nikolas at the front of the car, tripping and landing against his chest, cheeks flushed. With a sigh, Nikolas pushes her back slightly, eyebrow raising in question. With a nod, he places his hands on her ribs and lifts her up. Without prompt, Eleanor wraps her legs around his middle, head tipping towards his shoulder as he uses one arm to support her and the other rubbing her back as he carefully carries her up the staircase.

He places her on her feet in her room, about to go grab Adelyn when she runs to the bathroom. Her hair was already back, so he just rubs her back until she leans back, gratefully taking the hand he offers her and moving to brush her teeth. She takes a breath once she's finished, standing up straight.

"That tastes worse than normal," she groans as she moves towards her bed.

"That's because it has alcohol in it," Nikolas says, "you're going to regret it tomorrow."

Eleanor rolls her eyes, sitting on the bed. Nikolas goes to grab Adelyn, and Eleanor quickly changes. After passing the baby over, he also leaves to change.

Nikolas wakes considerably earlier than Eleanor, detangling himself from her and slipping downstairs to get a drink. Unluckily, Kenichi and Michael both sit down there as well, raising an eyebrow as he walks in.

"We heard about your little excursion last night..." Michael starts, blonde eyebrow high.

"Of course you did," Nikolas grunts.

"How drunk was she?" Kenichi follows, barely looking up.

"Quite. You'll be glad, I stopped her from getting into a fight," he answers, swallowing the cup in one gulp and getting another.

"What were you doing staying in her room?"

Nikolas can hear the steady anger in the doctor's voice. He looks up to meet his eyes as he speaks.

"She wasn't feeling well and asked me to stay with her. For once I fell asleep before she did," Nikolas says, "she did try to kiss me, but I stopped her."

Kenichi double takes, the immense surprise clear on his face.

"She tried to kiss you?"

"She did."

Oddly, Kenichi smiles at Nikolas, in thanks. But also in apprehension. It wasn't going to be long.

Nikolas slips back into her room, resting with a book open in one hand and the other around her. When she woke, she was very much hungover.

Chapter 57

Three girls are bustling around Eleanor's room. She's one, of course, but Skylar and Lana are also there, one in front of the mirror and the other pulling heels onto her feet. Eleanor is playing with Adelyn on her bed, fully dressed already and waiting for the other two to hurry up.

And why are they all together? Prom of course.

Eleanor was happy to have her friends getting ready with her, not having to hide the fact Adelyn was her daughter made it even better. The theme was The Stars, and of the three, Skylar was in silver silk, Lana was in mulberry, with jewelled stars over the chiffon skirt, and Eleanor was in navy. Strapless and laced up, her dress was exquisite, tiny flecks of silver and gold throughout. She had her hair up in a bun with an elaborate jewelled hair pin.

Finally, the other two finish, getting to sit for only a few seconds before the doorbell rings downstairs and there is a knock on the door. Eleanor had already slipped out and gotten photos with Adelyn (and with Nikolas as well), so she places her daughter in her crib and follows the two other girls.

Nikolas meets them as she steps out her door, offering his arm as Eleanor smiles up at him.

"You're looking very dapper," she compliments.

Michael had helped convince Nancy to let them go to prom together. To say they were happy would be an understatement.

Nikolas leans down to whisper in her ear, "I did used to be a Prince."

With a kind laugh, they reach the bottom of the stairs where Skylar's date, Ben and another boy, who was Lana's date, wait. Both of them were standing there with their mouths open, staying completely locked in place.

As Eleanor walks past, she pauses slightly.

"Compliment them, you idiots," she mutters, continuing forward to wait in the living room.

Her words spur them into action, stepping forward to take the girls' hands. Kenichi walks up to where Eleanor waits, hugging her lightly.

"You look brilliant," he smiles, kindness in his eyes.

Eleanor thanks him, hand linked with Nikolas's.

Lana is the one who offers to take photos of Nikolas and Eleanor as the night starts to finish. Her grin is wide as they stand together, the crown of Prom Queen resting in Eleanor's hair.

She is still wearing it when they get home, opting to take a short walk through the trees before going to sleep. Eleanor is half leaning on Nikolas as they follow the path blind, arm around his waist. They stop in a clearing, heads tilting up to look at the sky. Pulling out the hair bands and pins in her hair, Eleanor lets it cascade down her back, head just tucking under Nikolas's chin. Thank god for heels.

"You looked like you had fun..." he murmurs, fingers brushing hair off her neck.

"I did. Mostly because you were there..."

He glances down in surprise, finding her eyes still on the stars.

"You are a much kinder person than you try to make people think," she continues.

Nikolas breathes lightly. "Only for you," he whispers. Now she looks at him in surprise, eyes locking onto his. "You make me want to be happy. You give me hope."

She tilts her head slightly as he steps back and faces her fully.

"I had a dream, the other night," he says, hand resting in her hair. "I think it was what would have been, if our lives had gone well. You were in school, in Australia. I was sent there while Michael was sent here. You were laughing, and you had friends flocked around you at every angle. In the light, you looked like an angel...

"Our eyes met, and you just smiled, gave me a little wave. When I smiled back, you came right up to me, dismissing your friends. You said hello, asked my name. You never stopped smiling. And all I could think of was how beautiful you would look on Ferox, and sitting in the hall with me at dinner. Watching the sunset over the Flumine Magno. It was perfection.

"Then I woke up and, seeing you curled up like a puppy, it made me realise the things that happened to you and me, they happened for a reason. That I didn't want to wait for a false reality, I just wanted my life now. Because we are so much closer, as a result of our pain, and we can heal together."

Eleanor's lips parted slightly, hand tracing down his face before settling on the back of his neck. Slowly she pulls him closer, pushing herself higher onto her toes. But she stops just before their lips meet, smirking lightly.

"You going to let me kiss you this time?" she teases.

With a slight shake of his head, Nikolas places his lips on hers, only for a few seconds before pulling away. Eleanor pulls him back, pressing her lips to his with more passion.

When they break apart next, Eleanor drops back down off her tip toes. One hand stays on his chest, the other in his hair as he cups her face gently. Her cheeks are warm, eyes bright. Nikolas kisses her forehead lightly, pulling her to his side once again.

They stay there for a few more minutes, before returning to the house, Kaylee smirking at the pair as they disappear up the stairs. He kisses her goodnight, and they part ways.

~

It took many, many years for Anastasia to tell me part of what she saw when she got the photo from the prom. It haunted her, I think, because she saw Eleanor older.

She saw further into the future than she had ever before, past my life, past my children's. When exactly she wasn't sure, but the world was dark, there was unrest.

Like flashes, she saw Eleanor and Nikolas standing in front of the crowds of Angeli Terra, happy. Then she grew quiet, focus drifting. I didn't understand why she was so apprehensive. It was what we thought would likely happen. It is why they were put there.

It was on her deathbed Anastasia told me the rest.

Because she first saw them happy, and then she saw Eleanor screaming. On her knees and screaming for her Geminae. In the same place, from happy to screaming, over and over again. At Eleanor's side, she mentioned a Fallen Angel. Not one of the ones in the prison, the head guard had no idea who this man was, and he knew them all. But he trusted her, respected Eleanor and Nikolas so, preserved on white paper, the face hangs in his office. He would know when he saw the man, he will be the last remnant of the people here when they wake.

Chapter 58

Eleanor had noticed something odd at football practice the Monday after prom...

Other than a scout sitting on the sidelines, she had no explanation for why Arthur Demorae was playing way beyond his abilities. The next day, she hung around even though cheerleading practice wasn't on. The scout wasn't present today, planning on returning for the game on Friday.

Arthur was still working better than normal, though slightly less than the day before. The team were all working hard to keep up, and had started to go overtime when Kenichi appears to pick up Eleanor.

"What are you still doing here?" he asks, taking a seat next to her as she shows no signs of getting up.

"Something is off with Arthur, he's too fast, too strong. He has no drugs on him, and he cares too much about a scholarship to take any," she replies.

"You think his father is drugging him?"

Eleanor shakes her head softly, "I think the mother is. The man wouldn't get away with it, but she would easily be able to make a drink for her son and slip some of the drug in. There's more logistics but you get the gist of it."

With a silent nod, Kenichi settles back into his seat and watches the game.

As they finish up and start to walk towards them, Skylar walks up to where Eleanor is sitting, eyes still on the girl's brother. Just as she sits down, her brother collapses, starting to spasm wildly.

Eleanor and Kenichi are running over immediately, the former having grabbed a needle from her bag and handed it to the doctor. Like clockwork Eleanor drops her knee onto Arthur's shoulder, pinning him down as Kenichi empties the needle into his bloodstream.

"What the hell are you doing!" the coach yells, pushing through the crowd.

Calmly, Kenichi replies, "I work for the National Agency of Protection. Your student has gone into withdrawal of a new performance enhancing drug. My ward identified him as a possible victim, having been taught the symptoms and actions. The needle contains a counteractant which I administered, as a doctor, until we can get him into intensive care. If you don't mind, I need to call this in."

With a quick show of his badge, Kenichi walks slightly away while Eleanor stays at the boy's side watching him carefully. Skylar is there as well now, having been held back by her boyfriend. As Eleanor stands up, the blonde girl hugs her tight, shaking.

"What's happening?" she asks weakly, eyes still on her brother as Eleanor rubs her back (it was difficult, since Skylar was taller than her).

"There are two components to the drug, one making the user stronger and faster, the other making them more vicious. It is very addictive, and causes a very harsh side effects," Eleanor answers quietly. "The component we call Malum is attacking his blood cells currently, Kenichi injected him with some more of the other component, we call it Sanctus, to help fight off the Malum, but we need to get him into intensive care at the compound."

Skylar nods thankfully, breath still tight.

"My brother wouldn't take drugs," she whispers.

"I know, Sky," Eleanor comforts. "Did you notice him having a particular food or drink, that he didn't prepare yesterday morning, night and this morning?"

She thinks for a few seconds, before nodding slowly, face pale.

"Mum made him a power drink each time, he didn't finish it this morning," she shakes. "She has been disappearing a lot recently as well."

With a kind hand, Eleanor squeezes her shoulder, glancing up as the ambulance arrives. Her eyes roll in annoyance as two agents get out of the car following it, moving towards Eleanor. One is the NAP agent who gave her the oxygen mask way back when.

He grins at her as he gets close, looking to the body for a second before looking back.

"This one of yours?" he chuckles, stopping in front of them.

"No," she snips, "Why are you even here?"

With a roll of his eyes, the man answers, "we're here to find out how he ingested it, seize the remaining drugs."

"Oh, so I'm doing your job for you again?" Eleanor grins, before turning to Skylar. "Can you take us to the cup your brother used?"

The girl nods, leading the way to her car.

Later that night, Eleanor makes it back home, moving immediately to her room where she pulls out her uniform. Nikolas hangs in the doorway as Eleanor steps back and takes a stressed breath.

"What's going on?" he asks quietly, staying in the doorway.

"Skylar's mother was slipping Arthur some of the drug without his knowledge. He collapsed today," Eleanor tells him, turning around slowly. "I'm going to track their father to the source. He's not going to know his wife was doing it, so I believe he will go there to find out what other agents are in the field, he'll be clumsy because he's angry. I'll find the ship he goes to, get on myself, confirm the drugs are on it, get off and order the strike. Hopefully, I stumble upon the next shipment as well. It's an easy mission."

Now Nikolas steps closer, worry in his eyes.

"You're going now?"

Eleanor nods quickly, eyes meeting with his carefully.

"Skylar just told me he started to get dressed, she put a tracker on his car. I need to get ready," she says, a tight smile on her lips as he moves away.

When she steps out, he is waiting. Without words, he pulls her closer, hand brushing down her face gently. Their lips meet, Eleanor pulling away after a few seconds to look him in the eye. Her smile is weak, one hand on his neck, the other the hand he has against her face. She was staring up to his face, the crease in his forehead, the pull of his lips.

"Why are you worried?" she asks carefully, thumb moving idly.

With a slight shake of his head, Nikolas replies, "I am always worried for you. I never want to see you hurt, or scared. Doing this scares you, I know. You have no idea how much it scares me to see you heading out like this…" He takes a breath. "And you haven't let Ellsie take over."

Eleanor looks away for a few seconds, face being brought back with a finger on her chin.

"I will, once I'm clear of the house. Promise," she says, bringing her lips to his one last time. "And I will come home in one piece."

With a smile, Eleanor jogs off down the stairs to where Kaylee is waiting with weapons. Her swords, a handgun fitted with a suppressor, and a grappling hook loaded into a gun. Quickly, Eleanor attaches each to her suit, before pulling out her phone and taking a pair of keys.

She turns the motorbike on with ease, and without a final glance towards the house, speeds off.

The team watch the two trackers, one on Mr Demorae's car and the other Eleanor's, with avid attention. It doesn't take her long to catch up, but she keeps an equal distance until the car stops at the harbour. As she draws closer to the water, they listen too, to the audio coming through her ankle band.

Eleanor shuffles through the dockyard, eyes already adjusted to the darkness as she follows the slightly clumsy man. Not a single sound comes from her footfalls, her form melding with the darkness. When he arrives at a boat, he disappears into the hull, and Eleanor takes her chance, slipping on and hiding under a tarp.

She doesn't know much until the engine cuts off and there is some yelling. The boat shifts as the man climbs onto a ladder, and she looks out, grinning as they leave the apparatus attached and the door open. The idiots. She gives him a minute, before following him up.

Two guards wait inside the old cargo ship, both falling to the ground with two quiet pops. Ten more bullets. She slips through the mostly empty corridors, always alert. The people she meets along the way fall to her blades, not her gun (that would be for later) and it isn't long until she catches up to where her target is meeting with the captain.

"Your concern does not warrant revealing other agents in the field," the Captain is arguing.

Mr Demorae isn't happy.

"When it's risking exposing me it is! That damn disgrace has already turned my daughter against me, it won't be long until she leaves and runs to that damned team!" he yells. "I deserve to know."

"You do not, that is final!" the Captain growls. "You are no ACE. As dreadful as that girl is, she isn't your concern."

Bitterly, Mr Demorae gives up, instead demanding to know how much they had stored.

"This ship is still carrying 75% of its original capacity, according to the plan, we will be releasing most of that into circulation in three weeks. The 'Underworld' is still sitting two days off shore, holding everything else, as ordered. She is radio silent and outside of the coastguard's range, waiting for us to move her in."

Eleanor slips into proper darkness as her phone buzzes.

– That is all we need. Try and get coordinates for the other ship, make our search easier –

She shuts off the device, slipping out of the corner and using her sense to find her way to the Captain's quarters. As she arrives, an alarm sounds throughout the ship. She starts to move faster.

Like a good Daemone, the Captain wasn't very smart in hiding the location. Really, they were making it easy for her. Quickly she sends the photos to the team, moving then to finding herself another gun, replacing her one as she grabs the semi-automatic, blades on her back. Then she starts to make her way back to the boat. Logically, the agent wouldn't have left immediately, probably held up by the alarms.

But not for long enough she realises, as she makes it outside. She gets to the side of the boat before anyone can spot her, but as her eyes find him climbing into the boat, they do. Their guns are raised, ready to take her down as they start to pin her onto the railing. Eleanor switches the safety off as she looks back over the edge. Mr Demorae had just started the engine, and she wasn't too far from where the boat was.

They yell at her to put the gun down, surrender. She ignores them, eyeing up the distance to the water, not too far. They start to yell louder as she steps up to the edge, turning around for a second to grin at them before leaping off. Her feet stay pointed at the water, the semi-automatic pointing down (she was secretly glad she hadn't worn her normal mask, the soft-knit balaclava much less likely to break her jaw). After two seconds of falling, she starts to unload the gun downwards, breaking the water just before she hits. Five seconds later, she's above water again, grabbing her grappling hook and shooting it towards the retreating boat.

It just makes it, catching and pulling her along behind. The agent doesn't even notice he's pulling a girl along behind him.

To her, the trip is much longer this way than it was the other, arms starting to ache as they pull up. She stays in the water, just out of sight, until he disappears, swimming carefully to the dock and slipping onto dry land. Quickly she mutters...

"I'm clear, shoot away."

Eleanor leans back against a cargo container, letting her breath catch up with her. Not a minute later, a low hum starts to get louder, swooping low over her position and moving out to the ship in the harbour. The fighter jet drops it's payload exactly where it was supposed to, the ship incinerating in seconds. There isn't anything left, the bombs not meant to disable but eliminate entirely. She blocks her ears as the shockwave hits, shaking her head out once it passes.

About ten minutes after, there is another explosion much further off the coast, this shockwave barely a breeze as she stands up and starts to walk back towards the bike. Mr Demorae is gone, and she throws a leg over it quietly. Her phone rings in her pocket, so she just waits as she answers.

"Yes?" she answers, dabbing at her nose softly.

"What the hell happened there?" Is the only response. The Colonel.

"They found the bodies, sounded an alarm. I sent you the photos and found myself a bigger gun. I was pinned against the edge of the ship and my escape was about to leave, so instead of fighting my way off, I jumped, used the gun to break the water and the grapple hook to get pulled back to shore," Eleanor replies. "I'm coming home now."

"Do you plan on going to school tomorrow?" Nancy continues.

"I do. If there is any chance they don't think I did this, I need to go tomorrow. It'll be fine," she says. "Now, I really need to get home before I freeze to death, so I'm going to go."

"No pit stops…"

Eleanor did not freeze to death, but did take a nice long bath, in nice warm water as soon as she got back. She took some pain medications, and forced herself to eat. Once she had dressed in pyjamas and made sure Adelyn was asleep, she slipped downstairs where she knew Nikolas was in the library (it was only 9:30pm).

He raises an eyebrow as she walks in and face plants into the three person couch.

"Everything hurts," she moans, turning her head to look at him. "It's been too long since I've fallen into water."

He chuckles lightly, standing up and moving over to where she lies. When she flips over and sits up, he sits down, letting her lie back and rest her head in his lap.

"Don't ever do that again," he mutters, playing with a piece of her hair. "Nearly gave us all a heart attack."

Now Eleanor laughs.

"Would you have preferred I had to swim all the way back?" she grins.

"I would have preferred if you hadn't gone at all."

Their eyes meet carefully, apology in Eleanor, and worry still settled in Nikolas.

Chapter 59

The Berühmte Söldner were absolutely certain it was her who ruined their plan. Those two ships were carrying all of their supplies and who else would be able to sneak on and ruin everything than the infuriating runaway ACE.

Eleanor went to school the next day as if it was any other day. Except for the fact she was packing a handgun, suppressor and four magazines full of bullets. Over the top, maybe, but she was worried.

Rightly so.

~

Between third and fourth periods, while everyone was hanging in the corridors, a round of gunshots go off and everybody dives to the floor. Having more experience in this situation, Eleanor grabs Lana and Skylar, and instantly pulls them into the room next to them. She softly shuts the door. She takes off her watch, opening it and flipping the switch in one move.

The PA system turns on, a man's voice coming through.

"Hello Kitten," he sings, sending shivers through her spine. "You have been a very naughty girl, haven't you? Make this quick, the death toll won't be too steep. Give yourself over and we will leave your dear daughter alone. You are severely outnumbered, and we will get you. You have five minutes before we start to kill the hostages, you know we don't care. And quite frankly, we don't care all that much about getting you back. Your little boy-toy is awaiting your return, 828, see you soon."

Eleanor pales, breath coming quickly for a few second before it evens and she turns towards her friends.

"Don't let the red light go off until you hear help arrive," she whispers quickly, handing the watch to Lana before passing her phone to Skylar. "Call Kenichi immediately, just him. Use these exact words, 'bring my swords and my Geminae. I don't care if you don't like it, he will cause more harm at home, and I want him here.' Sprinkle in a few swear words if you'd like. Just only say that to Kenichi."

"Who was that?" Lana asks quietly. "And where are you going?"

"That was my handler. I haven't been completely honest with you but that's for later," she answers. "I am going to release the hostages and kill those assholes."

The two girls pale slightly as she pulls out the gun and screws on the suppressor. The magazines get tucked into her pants.

"You heard them, they want to kill you," Lana worries.

"People have wanted me dead for years. This is my job, and I will do anything but go back to that wretched place," Eleanor returns. "Do it before they get here, if they ask about me say I went out the window towards the back field."

She doesn't give them any more time to argue, throwing her bag out the window and following it noiselessly. Eleanor slips along the edge of the building, hidden by the bushes she can see the perimeter they had set up around the edge of the school. Quietly, she stays out of sight as she makes it to the Principal's window.

It sits open, making it easy for Eleanor to quickly check inside. Two targets. Her bullets find each, wincing as they hit the ground hard, but the door doesn't open and Eleanor jumps into the room, quickly telling the man sitting in his chair to be quiet as she tests the door. She does a good job of ignoring the horror as his eyes find the black blood.

"Get down," she whispers, gun turning to the door as the handle starts to turn.

Out of immediate sight, she takes out the first person with little trouble. Same with the second and third, but the fourth is more cautious, narrowly missing her with a bullet before she steps up close and kicks the gun away. She shoots two rounds blind around the corner, the Daemone falling to the ground. No one else comes into the room, so she carefully waves a hand out the door. The room remains silent, and she pokes her head out. As she does, someone comes around the corner to check on their teammates, he falls to the ground as she steps out and moves to the end of the next wall.

Two more men wait in the lobby, shifting nervously. One is just a Daemone, the other her handler.

The Daemone crumples to the ground, and her handler ducks, grabbing one of the hostages and pressing a gun to her head.

"This isn't a very nice way to thank me, Kitten," he calls, sick grin pulling onto his face as she steps out from around the corner.

"Such a huge welcoming party," Eleanor returns, smile just as sweet, accent heavy. "Blowing up those ships really must have hurt your egos."

The man growls.

"You better watch your tongue," he bites. "Boss already has things planned for you, wouldn't want to add to it."

Eleanor grins slightly, she was annoying him.

"Well, you wanted me, I'm here. How do you plan to get out of here?" she huffs, head still high.

The nurse, held still under the handler's gun, pales, face turning to shock.

"You're making this mighty easy, how do I know you're not bluffing?" he frowns.

"I would do anything to keep my baby girl safe," she shrugs. "That got us into this mess in the first place."

Slowly he nods, smirk returning.

"Prove it," he orders, stepping away from his hostage, "shoot her."

Eleanor lets the smile come onto her face easily, aiming at the terrified woman.

She swings the gun at the last second, the bullet going directly though the man's shoulder. He spins at the force, dropping his gun and landing on the floor. Without thought, Eleanor stalks over, kicking him onto his back and pinning him under her foot on his throat. He looks up to in terror.

"I made you," he chokes, a form of begging. For mercy.

He would get none.

"You ruined me," she growls, putting more pressure on his throat, "and I've sworn to myself, I will never lose myself again."

Two bullets lodge themselves in his forehead, and the assassin steps back.

"Get in the office, lock yourselves in," she says, turning to the group. "Help is already on its way."

Then she stalks to the PA, turning it on with ease.

"Your leader is dead," she calls. "Did you really think this plan would work? I am coming for you all, and I don't fail."

With one final glance towards the faculty, Eleanor heads towards the door to the corridor.

"Eleanor, you don't have to do this," the nurse calls, voice still shaking.

It doesn't help as the girl levels her with a gaze.

"I thank you very much for your kindness over the last few months. However, I have an obligation to ensure I do not end up back with them. And I just got my freedom, I don't want to die. So I will go out and fight until they are all dead," she says. "My friends are coming, but this is all my fault."

"Who says you have an obligation? You are just a child..."

She swallows tightly.

"The International Criminal Court," she answers. "That man was my handler, he made me kill many people. The terms of my delayed sentence mean that I have to help when innocent people are at risk because of me."

Eleanor leaves before she can get any more arguments. Moving through the corridors as quietly as possible. Since she had left her friends, it seemed that everyone had been moved onto the basketball courts, the corridors completely empty. As she gets closer, the Daemones become more frequent, each falling heavily before she passes. She takes out the two at the doors, slipping in closer to wait for the others to check their comrades.

These fall to her fists, heads knocked together hard enough to knock them out. She takes one of their guns as she presses herself to the bleachers and peers into the room. The students sit in a mob in the centre of the room, surrounded by ten Daemones, who walk aimlessly around the group.

One spots her, about to raise the alarm when a bullet enters his skull. The rest are looking now though, and she can only get five more of them down before they get too close for the rifle, and she has to duck into close range. She is left fighting the rest hand-to-hand, having all but two down when the door opens again.

Eleanor drops to the ground as she realises who it is, the two guards getting bullets to their heads and falling onto her. Nikolas offers a hand to pull her up, lips pressing to her forehead lightly as she catches her breath. She raises an eyebrow as she observes his outfit, the same one from his capture. Cape and all.

"Where's everyone else?" she asks quickly, worry in her eyes.

"I out ran them, there is a regiment moving in from the street, and the team will be here in a second," Nikolas replies, looking towards the students.

Eleanor nods slightly to his unasked question, stepping out and towards her schoolmates with confidence.

"Is there anyone hurt?" she calls, "a doctor will be here in a second, and we will need to move quickly. There will be a second wave soon."

A few raise their hands.

"If you can move to the side, or get some of your friends to help if you can't move, we need to get you lot hidden," Eleanor continues, smiling as they do. "Everyone else, please move to the locker rooms. I don't care if you're in the wrong one, just get in there and shut up."

They just stare at her.

"Who are you?" one of the cheerleaders calls, fear in her eyes.

It hurt Eleanor to see them scared of her.

"Someone who has done very bad things to a lot of people. But I defected and my employers want me either back with them, or dead," she answers. "Now, unless you would like to see more Daemones being killed, please move into the locker rooms."

They only shift in their spots, Eleanor losing her patience just as Michael, dressed in white and gold, steps through the door. He takes his place beside Eleanor as Kenichi and Kaylee jog over to the injured.

"Do as she says," he calls, Aspect floating through the words as they all stand and move silently into the locker rooms.

Just in time, Kenichi sends the last injured student to the rooms as the door breaks down. Having received them from Michael, Eleanor holds her twin blades in her hands while Kaylee and Zach start to fire on the Daemones spilling into the room. Most fall, but a few make it to where Eleanor stands between the two brothers, and they all start to fight.

It seemed that this wave wasn't armed with guns, only ugly pieces of sharpened steel. Steel that could still pack a punch. The military are doing their job as well, taking out the forces outside and slowly moving closer to the centre position.

The fight is bloody, mostly black blood making the floorboards slick as more come, and more fall to the blades. It was really a marvel to watch, as five people took on a force of death. As two Angeli, dressed in their uniforms, fight alongside humans for the first time in decades, and face off with the Daemones.

The fight is nearly over. Military forces inside the school, and the Daemones thinning out more and more with each kill. Eleanor is still fighting strong beside her friends, having moved apart more than when they began. They were no longer attempting to capture her, aiming only to kill. They aren't succeeding. Not until Eleanor's foot lands on a fallen arm and throws her off balance. The Daemone drops his bloodied sword and runs.

Nikolas screams as he spots her fall to the ground, swords discarded as she clutches at her throat. He is on his knees beside her in a few seconds, the Daemones either being gunned down by Zach and Kaylee to give Kenichi a chance to get to her from the side of the room, or running. Their mission was complete.

Blood bubbles through her fingers, terror in her eyes as Nikolas lifts her onto his lap, crying harsh tears. His head shaking in disbelief, words not making it past his lips. He looks up to his brother for just a second, their eyes meeting as Michael continues to fight them off. A nod. Assurance.

Nikolas pulls out a clean dagger, slicing his palm open before letting it drop to the ground. He doesn't realise Eleanor lets go by herself, knowing what he was doing. Their blood mixes as he places his hand on the cut, holding it tightly in place as she loses consciousness. He leans down and presses his lips to hers, praying to her to take another breath.

She does, a weak one. And then another. The pressure at his hand is lowering, to a point where blood is still trickling through his fingers, but it is no longer gushing.

The room is empty of anyone but the team now, Kenichi dropping on the other side of her as Michael runs over also.

"We need to get her to Angeli Terra," Michael says, eyes locking surely with Kenichi's. "The wards will help keep her alive, and the healers have magical abilities. They know about them and they can help her more than any human doctors. No offense."

The distraught man nods in agreement, eyes holding pain for the girl who had become like a daughter to him. Nikolas gently moves Eleanor so the arm that was pressing to her throat is under her head and uses the other arm to lift her up. He still hasn't said anything.

"How will you get her there?" Kenichi asks quietly, finger brushing down the unconscious girl's face.

"The helicopter, I can radio Angeli Terra from in there."

The doctor nods, watching hopelessly as the two men run from the room. Kaylee guides him over to the bleachers, making him sit down as the Colonel walks in, frowning as she only finds the three of them.

"Where is Eleanor? And the Angeli?" she asks cautiously, eyes heavily on Kenichi.

"Michael is taking them to Angeli Terra. Ellie..." Zach breathes carefully as he answers. "She is on the verge of death; Nikolas is keeping her alive. It's her only hope."

Nancy nods in acceptance, looking over to the door that opens across the court.

Lana and Skylar step out, the blonde holding tight to her friend, a small cut on her forehead.

"Is she going to live?" she asks weakly, fear in her eyes.

"We don't know," Kaylee tells her. "We just have to hope... Is there anything you need to tell us?"

Lana frowns, looking to the cheer captain in confusion.

"My father booked a business trip for an hour from now, last night. I think he wanted to take Eleanor back with him," Skylar whispers, tears starting to run down her face. "They will be at the airport, by now. They are going to Germany."

The Colonel nods in thanks turning on her heel and leaving.

Chapter 60

"This is Michael Mornblade radioing for Angeli Terra."

"We hear you, your Highness."

"I am an hour away from landing at this moment, I need two horses on the training flat. My normal horse and I need Ferox. Get Anastasia to bring her out."

"We were unaware of your arrival?"

"I will be landing in an hour, now you are aware. I need those two horses, at the training flat."

"Yes sir, anything else?"

"Make sure the Healers are ready, I am bringing in my brother and his Geminae. She is about to die and needs attention."

"A human?"

"A high-blooded Angeli's Geminae, whom is under mine and the Captain's protection. Ensure they are ready. And bring Ferox."

"Yes, your Highness. Would you like us to inform the King of this?"

"No."

~

The helicopter lands on short grass. Dry wind rips over the flat as they jump out. A storm is coming.

Nikolas holds his hand to Eleanor's seeping throat still, the girl having not woken up and still barely breathing. He runs faster than his brother to where a girl sits on her horse, a chestnut on one side and a black on the other. Nearly immediately, Ferox rears, ripping out of Anastasia's hand as she gallops up to meet her owner, and his Geminae.

Her wide nostrils tremble for a few seconds, as if assessing her charge. Nikolas releases her saddle, pushing it off as the mare turns side on and lies down in front of them. Nikolas steps onto her, resting Eleanor on Ferox's withers to take the reins in his hand, holding tight with his legs as the mare lurches up. Michael is close enough to grab his horse now, Anastasia nodding to her younger brother. Ferox barely requires a click to fly into a gallop, covering ground like a thoroughbred as she passes straight past the track to the city and instead cuts through a break in the fields. Anastasia is following behind, unable to keep up with the mare as she takes her riders directly into the city without a second's pause. Over the hard cobble she refuses to slow, taking them first to the castle, and then inside as she finally lets Nikolas guide her to the healers.

People stare as the black streak gallops through the halls, followed after a minute by the Prince and Princess on foot.

As he pulls her up, she lowers herself back onto the ground, understanding he couldn't let go of Eleanor as Healers run out of their corner of the castle and direct them through to the infirmary.

~

The King is furious. With Eleanor attached to many different machines and Nikolas at her side, it takes a lot of convincing to allow them to stay. It is harder for the fact it took three days for him to find out.

Eleanor stirs after a week. Bloodshot eyes landing on Nikolas, who is still sleeping at her side. She isn't able to do much, receiving some water from the Healers before falling back asleep. The next morning, she wakes up fully, nudging her Geminae awake as she pushes herself up.

He immediately calls for the Healers, who ran their checks and told her the rules.

1. No talking, her voice box was slightly injured and needed two more weeks to heal itself properly.
2. No solid foods for the next few days, but after that she could have whatever she liked.
3. Stay close to Nikolas, if not, all their work could be undone.

They give her a whiteboard to communicate with, leaving the pair alone as Nikolas turns to face her. He was sorry, she noticed. He felt like a liar. He was scared. She figured that whatever he had done to save her, it had strengthened their bond.

"Eleanor, I need to tell you something," he starts, hand holding her tightly. She nods for him to continue. "I lied about the connection we had, everyone did. We are, a thing we call Geminae Animarum, your world calls them soulmates and, do you understand what that means?"

She nods, writing on the board quickly.

"Read my mind."

He nods slowly, and she can almost hear him breathing in her head.

'I know, Nikolas. You don't have to explain yourself. Really, I'm not sure how you thought I wouldn't find out, I am smart, and I have read way too many books,' she tells him. 'Anastasia confirmed it when I first came here, suggested I wait and let you tell me when you were ready. As a sort of test. They were worried I would run straight to you. I know what it means, I know why I get the dreams, why I want to fall in love with you. I know how you saved my life.'

The man swallows deeply, eyes staying locked on Eleanor as she speaks. He smiles in relief as she finishes, squeezing her hand lightly.

"You aren't scared of it?" he asks gently, smile weakening as Eleanor looks away.

'Very. But that is because I am scared of loving someone. Of losing that love. Losing you. Why do you think I keep myself distant from Kenichi and Kaylee... I know that you would do anything to keep, to keep me safe. And I would understand why, because if there wasn't Adelyn, I would do it too,' there is a slight chuckle in Eleanor's tone as she thinks. 'Hell, it's what I plan to do to her. Die to keep her safe, live a life constantly monitored and under watch so she can live free. I couldn't say that, it would make me a hypocrite.'

Nikolas doesn't respond. Eyes holding disbelief as she gently tugs on his arm. He complies, lying next to her as she tucks herself close to his chest.

Now she uses the board to write, one word.

'Ady?'

"Safest child in America. Kenichi said he refuses to let her out of his sight," Nikolas assures. "From what Michael told me, he was very distraught when you..."

Eleanor nods slightly, lips pressing together as she presses herself close to him. They stay that way, relaxed into each other for the rest of the day.

Chapter 61

They returned home a week later; Kenichi having been provided strict instructions for her care. Staying inside, Adelyn was always within sight of her mother. A lot of the time, they could be found sitting side-by-side at the piano, sometimes with just one of them playing, sometimes they would all play. If you can call baby fists hitting the keys 'playing'.

Other than the occasional music, the house was silent. Kenichi was usually home, keeping an eye on Eleanor from a distance. She had made an effort to go up to him when she got back, to say he was happy about seeing her again would be an understatement.

Zach and Kaylee were working a lot more than they had previously, traveling to many different countries in search of somewhere they could place them in hiding. They had decided on Australia, a small village completely out of the way. It was four hours from Eleanor's childhood home, a safe distance, they figured.

But that was still being figured out, the specifics, having to go through the government lines as discretely as possible so the Berühmte Söldner couldn't find her. Her mental health had not improved after her brush with death and they were already lining up a therapist for her to see once she arrived at her new home.

She had grown muted in nature, but I can tell, more than others, that the weight of her handler's death had no effect on her. She was glad he was dead.

Lana and Skylar gave her a month to contact them, before they turned up at the gates. They hadn't discussed it however, so each turned up a day apart from each other. Their conversations differed greatly: Lana was first.

~

Kenichi lets the girl enter, having already warned her of Nikolas's protectiveness and shutting the door lightly behind her. Lana stops as soon as she is inside the door, waiting for the pair to notice her presence, which Nikolas does first.

"You have a visitor," he murmurs, causing Eleanor to turn and face her friend.

She smiles, brightly, grabbing her board and scribbling something onto it in perfectly neat script. Lana doesn't let herself look at the red ring around her throat.

'I was worried I wasn't going to be allowed to say goodbye,' it reads.

"You think I wasn't going to come see my best friend?" Lana laughs. "I would have broken in if I had to."

Eleanor frowns, shaking her head slightly at her friend.

"You wouldn't have made it very far, they have increased security ever since I got here," Nikolas fills. "Even I wouldn't be able to break in without leaving a messy trail."

Eleanor holds the board up again, pulling the attention back to their conversation.

'I really wanted to tell you.'

"I know, Eleanor. I understand why you couldn't."

'I still feel bad.'

"Well don't, because I don't care that you were undercover, that you haven't been the best person your entire life. You're still my best friend."

Lana had no idea how much that sentence meant to Eleanor, what she would remember in years to come.

'And you are mine,' Eleanor replies, playfully making sure the Angeli behind her can't see the board. He huffs in annoyance, but smiles anyway.

"You have my number, call me whenever, okay?"

'I'm not allowed...'

"Stuff them, you need a friend your age. Steal someone else's phone if you have to. Just know I'll pick up if you need to call."

'Thank you.'

"Really, thank you," Nikolas says, smiling down at his Geminae. "You are her first proper friend; it means a lot."

"Anytime."

~

As one may deduce, Lana was one of the kindest people you could find in this harsh world. She had accepted Eleanor without any hesitation, and that kindness wasn't forgotten lightly.

After her graduation, she went directly into social work, knowing she wanted to help people like her dear friend. It would be years until they met again.

Skylar came the next day. Her father was locked up, facing trial for the selling of illicit drugs to minors and involvement with a terrorist group. Her mother had gotten off free, of course, although Eleanor knew she was also guilty of the crime. Arthur had recovered fully, and Skylar was lost within herself.

~

This time, Eleanor is already waiting as Skylar enters her room, smile kind. Such a difference from the girl she had met 11 months ago.

"I'm so sorry," she starts immediately, perching on the end of Eleanor's bed and looking her in the eye.

'Whatever for?' Eleanor writes back, as Nikolas lay reading next to her.

"What my father did, I should have done something to stop him," the blonde frowns.

'No, you shouldn't have. You would have gotten hurt. That would have been worse,' Eleanor assures. 'You did nothing wrong, and you are at fault for nothing.'

Almost surprised, Skylar smiles in thanks, edging closer to her friend.

"You're going to disappear now, aren't you?" she asks, receiving a nod.

Eleanor then starts to scribble something down.

'You can still call me whenever, okay?' she writes. 'I am going to have a different number, but when I get my new one and I am settled, I will text you. Just, don't save me in your phone as Eleanor Beck. Anything else is fine.'

Skylar sags in relief, shuffling to hug her friend tight. A slight breathy laugh leaves Eleanor's lips, her head leaning on the taller girl's shoulder.

"Thank you, for everything," Skylar whispers. "You are a brilliant friend, and a brilliant mother. Adelyn is lucky to have you. And I hope you live the rest of your life well."

Eleanor blinks away the tear in her eye as she sits back. Silently she mouths thank you, giving her friend one more hug before she stands up.

'I hope you never have to call me, Skylar. You deserve the world,' she writes quickly, smile widening as Skylar thanks her, before leaving.

~

Skylar would become very successful. And one day she would pop up on the radar of the Berühmte Söldner. She would call Eleanor.

And Eleanor would go.

A very powerful ally.

Chapter 62

Oddly enough, it was harder to get clearance for Nikolas to fly than Eleanor. Though it could make sense since she did have citizenship in Australia already. By the time she was able to be apart from him, everything was sorted out. The choice was made to send her over a week early, while Nikolas's papers were going through.

The day she was due to leave, it felt off, somehow. Like many of the nights recently, she had slept with Nikolas (often in her bed, since his nightmares were worse at the moment than hers. Seeing your Geminae dying isn't something that passes easily), but in the morning he holds onto her for longer, snuggling tight into her neck. It was easy to assume it was because he wouldn't see her for a week.

Eleanor could feel his eyes lingering on her at breakfast, and when she tilted her head, he just smiled. Then came the time for her to leave and he wraps her in a hug, refusing to let go for a good minute. Once again, she was going to miss him as well, so was happy to stay there. Safe.

She says goodbye to Zach first, thanking him for letting her stay in his house, and ensuring he passed the message to his little sister as well. He was sad to see her go.

Kaylee is next, hugging Eleanor tightly with a smile wide on her face. She promises to stay in touch with her, and ensures that she can always call, if Eleanor wanted to.

Michael is a little different, taking her aside quietly.

"Thank you, Eleanor," he says. "You have managed to make my brother better. I truly thought he was a lost cause, but you showed me he wasn't. And, I'm sorry we grew apart, but I understand that we do not agree on many things, I hope I can say a proper goodbye when the time comes."

Eleanor returns the thanks and hugs him tightly before walking to where Nikolas is standing on the edge of the room.

They kiss long and slow, for once, not caring that there were people watching. As they pull apart, Eleanor's pale hands cup his face, holding him close to her. She could almost feel pain in his heart. His fingers traced down her face, pushing her hair out of her eyes with utmost care.

Without moving, he speaks into her head.

'I love you, Eleanor,' he says.

She lets out a breath of shock, smile appearing as she draws him closer, their lips meet again. Eleanor steps back, eyes soft as she doesn't say anything in return.

But Nikolas doesn't care, taking Adelyn out of her mother's arms kindly. He lets the baby play with his finger while he carefully kisses her hair covered head, arms bouncing the 18 month old slightly. Adelyn is given back to her mother and Eleanor tries to find his eyes.

"See you in a week?" she asks, voice on the verge of tears.

"In a week..."

His eyes don't meet hers, voice detached almost.

As she gets to the door, she turns back, finding his eyes. With a slight nod, she thinks.

'I love you, too.'

She turns away before he can respond, and before she can see his face.

The car ride is silent, only Kenichi accompanying her to the airport. He hugs her tighter than anyone else, saying a long goodbye to Adelyn – though the child doesn't quite understand.

"Please, keep in touch, Eleanor. If you need anything, just call and I will help as best I can," he says, holding her close. "Don't be a stranger."

"I won't, Kenichi," she promises. "I want Adelyn to know her Uncle Keni."

His smile is proud as he lets her go.

The majority of her stuff is already at her new home, only one suitcase accompanies them on this trip. Eleanor and Adelyn sit in first class, getting many dirty looks as Eleanor lets her daughter sleep, curled against her chest. Adelyn flies well, and her mother is prepared for every need Adelyn may encounter.

There is a car waiting for them when they land, now without guards. It was cold, the middle of winter. The drive is less quiet (Eleanor finally allowed to drive herself), music playing through the car as they left the city. Soon enough they are winding through the trees, following the road down into a valley. They stop only once, at a small shop next to the public school.

The waiter is kind, obviously surprised to see such a young girl with a baby in the middle of the week.

Eleanor is glad for her turtleneck, for it covered the scar that would sit forever on her throat.

"We don't get many visitors mid-week, where are you from?" she asks as she takes their order.

"America," Eleanor answers, making sure to cover her German accent, "but I was born in Australia. I'm moving into a house near here."

The woman smiles, slightly surprised.

"The two of you?" she questions.

"Yes, and we have someone else coming in a week to live with us," Eleanor assures, jiggling Adelyn lightly.

"That's nice, what's your name?"

"Diana, Diana Evans."

An alias. A necessary change.

"And your daughter?"

"Adelyn."

~

The next day, Eleanor starts to unpack. Again, she couldn't shake the feeling something was off.

A letter lays in the bottom of one of her bags, white paper. Neatly scripted was her name.

Nikolas's handwriting.

She tears the paper open, unfolds the letter that sits inside.

Hello, Dulce Meum,

Are you alone? If you aren't, don't continue reading until you are.

I am so sorry for what I am about to tell you. But at the same time it has to be done, because you need to be safe.
By the time you're reading this, I will be gone. I had to leave, I had to keep you safe. I realised as that knife slit your throat, that I couldn't let them touch you ever again. The only way to ensure they cannot find you is to make the target smaller. They would find me a hell of a lot quicker than they would you, and I can steer them away.
I have returned to work under them, to ensure they do not find you. To plant lies to keep you and your child safe.
Leave me behind, Eleanor. Don't make yourself wait; I won't come. I made sure I was never told where you were going; I don't want to know. Forget me, forget everything. It won't hurt you; I promise, nothing will ever hurt you. Hate me if you need to, I don't care.
Don't look for me, don't return to that manor. You will move past this, move past me. Raise your child, and let me keep you safe from afar.
I will be there at the end, I promise that much.

Yours only,
Nikolas

And Eleanor... you are worth the world. You are worth dying for. You are worth being the villain. You are worth helping them. You are worth it all. You are worthy of happiness and peace; I promise you that.
Don't punish yourself for your actions.
Don't you dare hurt yourself because of them.
Don't give up on yourself. You are worth it.

I'm sorry Dulce Meum, my Incaendium.
Take care of her Ellsie.

Her eyes grow wet, face pale as she reads it through.
Once.
Twice.
Three times.

Still the words don't make sense in her head. They don't register. Until they do, snapping into focus in her mind.

She runs, picking up the phone and dialling the number she had been told to memorise.

Kaylee picks up the other end of the line.

"Nikolas..." Eleanor starts, voice broken.

"Eleanor," Kaylee starts, voice soft. "He's gone. I'm sorry."

She hangs up, the phone clattering across the hardwood floor as Eleanor drops to her knees, then rolls back to sit on her tail, knees tucked up. Tears run down her face; heartbroken sobs break through her lips.

She loved him; she knew. And he loved her more. Loved her like Eleanor loved Adelyn.

She understood. She knew what she wished Adelyn would think of her when she was gone. It would take a while, but Eleanor had to give Nikolas's choice the same respect as she wished for, out of Adelyn. She understood.

Across the world, Nikolas collapses to the ground, clutching his chest as he groans. Punishment. Everything in his body burned, but most of all his heart. It was necessary, he promised himself. There was no other way to keep her safe.

He stayed in that room for a week before he was able to walk out, before he had learnt to tolerate the pain. At no point did he regret his decision, however. Her safety meant more to him than anything else.

There is a knock on Eleanor's door, about four hours later. A knock that wakes Adelyn, unfortunately. The mother picks herself off the floor, jogging to the nursery to pick up her now toddler. Then, as the person knocking does so again, she calls out for a second, juggling Adelyn onto her hip and going down the stairs onto the main floor of her house. When she makes it to the door and swings it open, she takes a few seconds to see if either of the two adults standing there are threats. Deducing they are not, she turns away, telling them to come in as she walks to the kitchen. The house is open-plan, so she has no troubles as they follow her in and stand on the other side of the bench.

"Sorry, Adelyn needs something to eat," she apologises, moving continuously as she tries to find a puree carton. "What are your names?"

"Amy, and this is my son Owen and husband James," the woman introduces, "Our daughter, Riley, would be Adelyn's age. She's sleeping in the car at the moment. We live on the next property over, back towards the main road."

Eleanor smiles kindly, keeping the pain in her heart from showing.

"Nice to meet you," she says, still juggling Adelyn on her hip. "I'm Diana, and this is my daughter Adelyn."

James looks around for a few seconds, listening for any other movement in the house.

"Is there anyone else here with you?" he asks, a slight frown on his face.

It takes Eleanor aback for a second, before she covers the pain on her face and shakes her head.

"No," she says, "there was someone who was supposed to come, but it was decided this would be... better."

The man takes her story without question, but the woman frowns, eyes watching Eleanor carefully as the girl starts to feed her child.

"Are you okay, dear?" she asks.

"Absolutely fine."

Acknowledgements

This book has been so long in the making that it is difficult to imagine how I got from there to here. It is not a journey I could have gone on alone, and I am so grateful for all the help that I have had. I would like to thank:

Firstly, my parents Sandy and Matt Thomas for their unfaltering support in this process. From numerous line edits and entire book reads to the very frequent requests for words that evaded me and mildly concerning questions on wound infliction, they have helped at every single step. Thanks Dad for your amazing cartography skills. Without Mum, this book wouldn't be anything like it is today, whether that be edits, or the entire typeset which she handled for me. I could not have published this book without your support.

To my beta readers, Karen Jones who was the first one to read So She May Breathe and has provided such unending support as I have written the subsequent books; Kerry Ann McKittrick who dedicated her time to give me feedback while she was moving house; and Ruth Goodwin who helped me get this book to a professional standard of editing and taught me so much about grammar. To Kelli Shaunessy for doing the final read: every one of you have been influential in the outcome of this book and to giving me the motivation to continue.

To my school friends who gave me the confidence to keep going with their constant support and frequent begging for copies. You guys are the best hype squad, so thanks heaps.

To everyone who follows me on Instagram and gave me the drive to finally put this book out there, I cannot thank you enough.

And to my readers, I hope you love this book, and thanks for giving it a piece of your time.